PRAISE FOR DANIELLE VALENTINE

"A knife-sharp thriller with a dash of horror set in the over-the-top world of professional cooking? Yes, please! Danielle Valentine's atmospheric chiller made my jaw drop and my mouth water."
—**Andrea Bartz**, bestselling author of *We Were Never Here*

"A simmering stew of secrets and suspense. Domestic bliss meets bloodshed. You'll want seconds!"
—**Joanna Wallace**, bestselling author of *You'd Look Better as a Ghost*

"Sizzling with a glamorously Gothic setting, tantalizing twists, and a premise that'll have you begging for seconds, *The Dead Husband's Cookbook* is the depravedly delicious foodie thriller you never knew you needed."
—**Leah Konen**, author of *The Last Room on the Left*

"*Knives Out* meets Evelyn Hugo with a pinch of Nora Ephron's *Heartburn*, *The Dead Husband Cookbook* takes a murder mystery, rolled in family drama, and roasts it in the heat of feminine fury. I devoured every page."
—**Stacie Grey**, author of *She Left*

"Delightfully twisted and utterly delicious. Danielle Valentine is a master of the horror thriller, and I can't wait to see what she does next!"
—**Sara Ochs**, author of *This Stays Between Us*

"A timely, terrifying, heartfelt thriller. I devoured it in one sitting."
—**Chris Whitaker**, *New York Times* bestselling author of *All the Colors of the Dark*

ALSO BY DANIELLE VALENTINE

Delicate Condition
How to Survive Your Murder
Two Sides to Every Murder

THE
DEAD
HUSBAND
COOKBOOK

THE
DEAD
HUSBAND
COOKBOOK

DANIELLE VALENTINE

RECIPES BY RON WILLIAMS

sourcebooks
landmark

Published by Sourcebooks Landmark, an imprint of Sourcebooks
1935 Brookdale RD, Naperville, IL 60563-2773
(630) 961-3900
sourcebooks.com

Library of Congress Cataloging-in-Publication Data

Names: Valentine, Danielle, author.
Title: The dead husband cookbook / Danielle Valentine.
Description: Naperville, Illinois : Sourcebooks Landmark, 2025.
Identifiers: LCCN 2025007306 | (hardcover) | (epub)
Subjects: LCGFT: Thrillers (Fiction). | Psychological fiction. | Novels.
Classification: LCC PS3622.A4334 D43 2025 | DDC 813/.6--dc23/eng/20250317
LC record available at https://lccn.loc.gov/2025007306

Printed and bound in the United States of America.
VP 10 9 8 7 6 5 4 3 2 1

For Ron, the love of my life. Consider this a warning. (Jk. Sort of.)

"I brined him in a deep salt bath, added thyme
and celery. Devoured him whole, in one big bite,
so he could see just how hungry a woman can be."

—*Kate Baer, "Like a Wife," in* What Kind of Woman

The Secret Ingredient

I've always said recipes are like family. Even the best ones are hiding something.

Take meatballs, for instance. Meatballs are a food built on secrets. People think they're Italian, but ground meat rolled into balls have been featured throughout Greece and Rome and the Middle East. In the Middle Ages, impoverished populations all over the world mixed their meat with breadcrumbs, onions, butter, and minced garlic to make it last.

Throughout the Ottoman Empire they were called köfte; in Sweden, köttbullar; in Belgium they were boulettes de viande and gehaktballen; in Finland, meatballs were called lihapullia, literally "meat buns"; in Ukraine, they were frykadel'ky.

And, in Italy, they were polpette. So that's what we called our restaurant. Polpette della Nonna. My grandmother's meatballs.

The grandmother in question was my late husband, Damien's. My beloved's nonna had died the year before we opened our restaurant, and we found a yellowed Tupperware of meatballs in the back of her freezer while cleaning out her house. The very last batch she would ever make.

"She made the most incredible meatballs," Damien told me, cradling that container as though it was precious. "But she never wrote down her recipe. I've been trying to re-create it my whole life."

It took Damien years to deconstruct his nonna's meatballs. Every week he would make them alongside his traditional Sunday gravy: tomato sauce and sausage and braciole. I still remember the rich aroma of ripe tomatoes, the freshly chopped basil, the sizzle of garlic and onions, sautéed to perfection in glistening olive oil.

While the sauce cooked, my love would toil over his own batch of meatballs, carefully measuring the breadcrumbs and soaking them in milk, rolling them together with veal and pork and beef. At the very last moment, he'd throw one of his nonna's frozen meatballs into the tomato sauce and we would test them side by side, his against hers.

Hers always won. They were better than anything else my talented husband put in that pot.

Until the day they weren't.

"How did you do it?" His family were the first to ask, and then the people who came to our restaurant. And then, after he was gone, the world.

What was his recipe? It made me smile when people would inevitably ask that question at every signing I ever did for one of my own cookbooks, at every event. It was a small, beautiful way of keeping him alive, of keeping him with me.

What was the secret ingredient? Do you know? What did he put in those meatballs that made them so good?

If my husband knew anything, it was how to keep a secret. But I was there the whole time. I shared his kitchen. I helped him stir and measure. I stood beside him as he perfected the recipe. I saw exactly how he did it.

And I've never been that good with secrets. I plan on telling you everything.

—MARIA CAPELLO, FEBRUARY 3, 2025

PART ONE
ANTIPASTO

1

THEA

SOMEONE WAS COOKING. I SMELLED IT THE SECOND I WALKED into our building, a rich and heady scent of meat and onions and garlic simmering together in a pot. My mouth filled with saliva, and for a moment, I forgot all about my wet shoes, the throbbing pain in my shoulder, my weighted-down tote bag and screaming toddler.

Maybe it's Jacob, I thought, hopeful. Maybe my husband had stepped away from work early for once, picked up one of my old cookbooks, and decided to make dinner. Stranger things have happened.

Ruthie's voice cut through my thoughts. "MOMMY, MOMMY, MOMMY, MOMMY!" She was always either screaming at the top of her lungs or speaking in a such a low mumble that I had to ask her several times to "please talk just a little louder, honey."

"Ruthie, Ruthie, Ruthie!" I said in my normal tone, hoping she'd take the hint. The entryway door slammed shut behind us, and I paused, taking a moment to adjust all the things I was carrying: the Hanes Press tote swollen with books; the still-open, drenched umbrella; the reusable grocery bag filled with overpriced bodega staples (toilet paper, milk, the carton of blueberries that currently composed 90 percent of Ruthie's diet); and, of course, Ruthie herself.

"Mommy, did you see the jamrock?" She was trying to say *shamrock*. It was a week or so before St. Patrick's Day, and our neighbor had one taped to her front door.

"I did see the shamrock. It's very pretty." I was starting to lose the feeling in my right arm. "Do you think you could try walking for a little while, sweetie?"

Ruthie responded by wrapping her arms tighter around my neck and wailing directly into my ear. She'd insisted on being carried halfway through our walk home. She hadn't liked the wet ground, and she'd wanted to be closer to the umbrella. I couldn't blame her. I also hated walking around Brooklyn in the rain. But we were inside now, facing four floors of stairs, and I was not an athletic person. My sole experience with working out consisted of a weight-lifting class I'd taken in my late twenties, the optimistically named "Couch to Barbell." It had promised to turn me into a weight lifter in just three sessions a week for twelve weeks. We hadn't even started with real weights. We'd started with a broom handle, which the instructor explained was for learning proper weight-lifting form and not building muscle.

I made it to the fourth session before pulling something in my shoulder. From lifting a *broom handle*. I'd been so embarrassed I never went back, which had meant forfeiting the $195 fee I'd paid in advance, a fortune back when I was on an assistant editor salary. I still felt a twinge of regret whenever I thought of it.

From somewhere within my tote, a sharp chime sounded. It was the specific tone I'd programmed for when my boss emailed—a short, clear, efficient-sounding chirp, like the sound of an old-fashioned metal call bell sitting on a hotel's reception desk. Whenever I heard it, I imagined Cassandra Hanes placing a single, elegantly manicured finger on a bell, eyebrows raised as she waited for me to give her my full attention. I used to hear that sound multiple times an hour as Cassandra emailed an inside joke or shot me a question about some high-profile project or checked to see if I wanted to grab lunch or a drink. Now, the sound shot a quick jolt of nerves up my spine. Lately, any email Cassandra had for me wasn't good.

The smell of food grew stronger as I hauled Ruthie up the stairs. It coated the insides of my nostrils so that each time I inhaled it was even more intoxicating. It was earthy mushrooms and rosemary, the sharp tang of mustard, all of it tempered with the honeyed sweetness of caramelized onions. Heavenly.

"Mommy, what's that smell?" Ruthie asked.

"Someone's cooking dinner. It smells like a roast."

Ruthie screwed up her face. "Eww. It's yucky."

"Yucky?" I laughed, amused that Ruthie's palate hadn't yet caught up to complex tastes and textures and scents.

But as I climbed further, I started to notice it, too. There was something beneath the heavy smell of the meat, something cloying. It reminded me of dying flowers, of fruit going soft in the basket we kept in the corner of our kitchen, and I found myself making the same face Ruthie had, even trying to breathe through my mouth.

Whoever was cooking had done a lot with the mushrooms and onions, but beneath that wonderful smell was something else, something too sweet. The meat they were cooking had gone bad.

It didn't smell like food anymore. It smelled like rot. Like the decay of dying things.

....

"*This* is why you couldn't come down and help us?" I asked Jacob when Ruthie and I had finally stumbled into our apartment. He was in workout clothes, his forehead red and shiny with sweat.

"I was in the middle of a set," he explained, breathless. He was panting, face flushed. "I just did ten reps. That's a personal best."

I could tell he wanted me to congratulate him, but I didn't have it in me. Our apartment was a fourth-floor walk-up. Standard, for a place in Brooklyn in our budget. Not a big deal when you're in your twenties; hell when you have a kid, groceries, and a tote bag filled with books to carry.

Oh, and an umbrella. I also had an umbrella.

DANIELLE VALENTINE

I glowered at Jacob as he refocused his attention on the pull-up bar hanging from the kitchen doorway. My husband was tall and slender with lean, ropy muscles, dark, wiry hair, and a long nose. The first time we met, he'd reminded me of a dog, a majestic Irish setter loping around some verdant green field, a hunting dog with a job to do, places to see, things to sniff out. It was an association that has only grown stronger the longer I've known him.

A podcast droned from the speaker in the kitchen. Something about World War II. Jacob was the only person I knew who worked out while listening to history podcasts.

"If you really needed help, you should have said." Jacob spoke loudly so I could hear him over the podcast hosts, who were now discussing something called Operation Pedestal. "I didn't realize you were carrying so much."

The text I'd sent had literally read, Please come help me I don't think I can carry all this up, but I was too distracted to point that out, trying to get Ruthie to take off her shoes and coat while she twirled in a lackadaisical circle in the middle of our entryway, singing three words of that song from *Frozen*, the only lyrics she knew: "I can't any-more!" They weren't the right words, but she didn't know that.

"Ruthie, c'mon," I said. "Let's get you out of your wet outside clothes."

"Mommy, I'm Elsa. I'm dancing." I finished pulling off her jacket and she darted into the apartment like a puppy finally released from her leash.

I collapsed against the wall. The effort of the climb and the jacket and all of the things clambering for my attention was too much. My bones were tired.

I looked up at Jacob without moving my head from the wall. "Something was going on at the office when I left. Final bids, I think."

"Bids for the top-secret…Beyoncé memoir?" Jacob grunted, hauling his chin up to the pull-up bar.

I considered it, then shook my head. "I don't think they would've been able to keep a celebrity that big under wraps. Someone would've

6

let something slip." Not to me, of course. Talking to me was still ver-boten. I hadn't heard a word about the submission that'd come in Monday, but I've been at Hanes long enough to note the signs: the closed-door meetings with the heads of every department, Cassandra hanging around more than usual, shades drawn over the glass walls of her office, assistants hovering at the printers, waiting for pages to spit out so they could secret them away before anyone's greedy eyes fell on the words. Most editors read on their computers, but Cassandra insisted on ink and paper. She said reading was as much a tactile expe-rience as a mental one. I used to wonder if she huffed printer ink when she was alone in her office. I really did.

And then there'd been the assistants in the bathroom who hadn't realized I was squatting in one of the stalls, their hushed whispers bouncing off the tiled walls, "Have you read *The Dead Husband Cookbook* yet?" and "No, have you?"

The Dead Husband Cookbook. It was a fake name, obviously, and didn't necessarily refer to an actual cookbook. Once upon a time, Cassandra and I would have come up with it together, making a joke of some throwaway line or image in the proposal, laughing until we were breathless. I felt an ache now, remembering. Had she called another editor in to her office to help her come up with this one? A new mentee to replace the one who'd failed her so miserably? The thought turned my stomach. I blinked, hard, to keep tears from forming.

Jacob looked like he was going to say something else, then decided against it and went back to the pull-up bar. "Ruthie's school called. Did you send in tuition this month?"

I went back to unpacking the bodega groceries. "Not yet."

"You want me to do it?"

"No," I said a bit too sharply. Then, adjusting my tone, "It's fine. I'll do it."

Watching him at the bar, I felt my teeth grit together. He'd gotten off before six for once, and instead of starting dinner or putting the dishes away, he'd used the time to work out. But it wasn't worth the fight, so I did my best to push the annoyance aside. I scanned my shelves of cookbooks, trying to come up with an idea for dinner. The smell of the hallway meat, though rotten, had inspired me to cook.

I pulled *The Italian Family Table* down from a shelf. My go-to cookbook since forever. It was hopelessly dated, a faded photograph of the famous chef Maria Capello standing in a Tuscan-style kitchen, all rustic wood and terra-cotta floors, Maria wielding a rolling pin like a weapon. It was by far the most tattered and worn of all my cookbooks. It had been my mother's originally, but I'd taken it with me when I moved away for college, reasoning that it was only fair. Maria had spent more time raising me than my mother had, after all. And I'd never even met her.

The book automatically fell open to a recipe near the middle, manicotti stuffed with braised meat and besciamella, my favorite since I was little. I could still remember making it on Sunday nights during a brief, disastrous year where I'd tried to get my mother to play-act like the two of us were a real family. Dragging a dining room chair across the kitchen so I could stir the meat on the back burner, watching cheese bubble and brown through the dirty glass of the oven. I owed my mother a call, actually. She'd tried to get me over lunch, but I'd let it go to voicemail. The longer I put her off, the worse the call was going to be.

I scanned the ingredients list, though I knew it by heart. I had pasta and pork, and I even had a jar of Capello besciamella sauce, Maria's brand, which was inevitably better than anything I made regardless of how closely I followed the recipe.

"How do you feel about manicotti?" I asked Jacob.

"You know that dish is the reason I married you," he said.

He meant it as a joke and I smiled dutifully. But it hit different today. Maybe it was just that I used to know I contributed more to the world than a meal I'd made following someone else's recipe. Now, I wasn't so sure.

....

It wasn't until much later in the evening, when the manicotti had been made and eaten, when Ruthie was in her favorite pajamas—the Hanna Anderson footie ones covered in lemons, so old we'd had to cut the feet off when she outgrew them—and I was brushing my teeth for bed, thinking about how I'd avoided calling my mother yet again and I really needed to just get it over with, that I remembered I'd gotten an email from Cassandra.

Something foul took root in my stomach as I fumbled for my phone, opened the email, and read. I'd known this email was coming, but the words were still like a punch to the gut. Tears pricked infuriatingly at my eyes. I felt like I needed to sit down.

The email read simply: *My office, first thing tomorrow morning.*

Which was, of course, the exact email you got before you were informed that you were being let go.

MANHATTAN TRIBUNE

Celebrity Chef Damien Capello Disappears Near Woodstock

By Benjamin Fields

JULY 20, 1996

WOODSTOCK, N.Y.—Celebrity chef Damien Capello has been reported missing. Capello was last seen on July 17 at his family farmhouse just outside Woodstock. His sudden disappearance has left both the local community and national followers in shock.

In the early hours of July 18, family members reported that Capello disappeared from his home. A subsequent search of the property revealed Capello's personal belongings—including his clothes, shoes, and watch—left by a riverbank. Given the proximity to the water, police are considering the possibility of an accidental drowning. However, with no body recovered from the creek yet, the investigation remains open.

Sgt. Mitchell Greene, who leads the investigation, commented, "While we are exploring the drowning theory due to the location of Capello's belongings, we are also pursuing other leads and treating this as an open investigation."

On the evening of his disappearance, the Capellos were hosting a party attended by immediate family, several close family friends, and the staff of their popular restaurant, Polpette della Nonna. Capello owns the restaurant with his wife and business partner, Maria Capello, who was also at the party. According to reports, the party ended early, around 10 p.m., with Maria Capello taking her and Damien's ten-year-old son, Enzo Capello, to the emergency room following an accident that resulted in the boy breaking his nose. Damien reportedly stayed behind to see off their guests.

Hank Casey, a longtime friend of the family, was reportedly the last to leave the house, at around 10:30 p.m. "Everything seemed fine when Damien said his goodbyes. I can't imagine what happened," Casey said.

Maria Capello stated, "I called home from the emergency room at eleven o'clock to update Damien on how Enzo was doing, but he didn't pick up. I assumed he was still talking to our guests. I had no reason to suspect that anything might have happened." According to Maria, the couple's children, Isabella and Enzo, were with her at the emergency room until approximately 1 a.m. Security footage from the hospital confirms this.

While Woodstock is a relatively quiet town, the sudden disappearance of such a high-profile figure has drawn significant media attention. The Capellos' restaurant, Polpette della Nonna, a fixture in the Woodstock dining scene, remains temporarily closed.

Police are urging anyone with information, no matter how insignificant it may seem, to step forward.

The investigation is ongoing. Further updates will be provided as more information becomes available.

2

THEA

HANES HOUSE PRESS WAS PRACTICALLY EMPTY WHEN I ARRIVED the next morning. An intern I didn't recognize was shelving books and Sean, our publicity director, was in his office. His low, steady voice boomed through the glass as the elevator doors closed, dinging softly behind me.

This had been a coveted office space, once. It took up the top two floors of the Bank Note building in the Bronx, a loftlike space with concrete floors and fifteen-foot-high windows, skylights, and exposed wooden beams soaring overhead. It also leaked year-round, had mold crawling up the walls of the bathroom, and moths had laid eggs in the expensive vintage rugs.

I swallowed, mouth dry. I felt like I had as a twenty-two-year-old college grad walking into this building for my interview with Hanes House's CEO and publisher. A six-foot-tall woman with arms like Michelle Obama's, Cassandra Hanes wore her silver hair in an elegant bob that hit just above her shoulders and dressed like she'd once had a fashionable person tell her exactly what colors and styles she needed to wear to complement every part of her figure.

"So," she'd said as soon as I was seated on the other side of an expansive glass desk that didn't seem to have a single smudge on it. "Who *are* you?"

I remembered wondering if she'd forgotten who she was supposed to be interviewing. I was the kind of person people tended to forget. Nothing about me was particularly exciting or dramatic. If you put every Caucasian twentysomething female face into an AI image generator and asked it to come up with a composite, you would probably end up with something like me. Average-sized nose and an average-shaped chin and two average brown eyes sitting an average distance apart. The only thing about me that tended to stick with people was my hair, which was a deep, vibrant auburn red.

I shuffled around inside my fake leather satchel for my résumé to help her out. "I'm…Thea Woods? I just graduated from NYU with a major in English lit, specializing in…"

"No," Cassandra had said, and I could tell she was disappointed, that this wasn't what she'd been after at all. "Who *are* you? How did you come to be sitting across from me?"

It had been a deeply annoying question, to be honest. Years later, after we'd become closer, I told her as much. *Who are you?* Had she wanted my life story? My opinion on organized religion? Should I have rattled off a bit of *The Faerie Queene*?

But at the interview, in the moment, I'd felt the chill of the air-conditioning raising the hair on my arms, and I'd been overcome with an almost physical need to impress her. I'd been applying for jobs for months by then, and editorial assistant positions were notoriously hard to get. But it was more than just that. I'd wanted *Cassandra* to think I was someone worthwhile. I'd always had an affinity for strong older women. Throughout high school, I would often spend lunch hours in the narrow office the algebra, geometry, and pre-calc teachers all shared, claiming I needed help with the homework when what I really needed was for three women in their sixties to look at my work and tell me I was smart, that they were proud of me. It was a little embarrassing to admit, to be honest.

Once I'd managed to gather my courage, I'd told her the truth, which wasn't exactly revolutionary but which I'd been afraid to share with anyone else I'd interviewed with. "I don't know who I am yet. The only time I've ever been brave was when I moved down to the city for school. I'm from upstate originally, near Utica. Girls like me usually end up as English teachers where I'm from, and that's if they even make it through college. But I've wanted to be an editor ever since I knew what they were, so I'd decided the risk was…worth it, I guess. That's why I'm here."

Cassandra had given me nothing, not even the slightest hint of a smile, but I'd always assumed that answer was what had gotten me the job. Many years later, after having one too many scotch and sodas at a holiday party, Cassandra had blurted, "It was because you said you knew Excel on your résumé. Ninety percent of an assistant's job is using Excel, and yet all these Ivy League grads come to my office talking about how much they love Salman Rushdie and Alice Munro."

Of course, that was seventeen years ago. In the years since, I'd been approached by other, bigger houses, but I'd never felt compelled to leave. I loved everything about Hanes House. I loved the moth-infested carpets and the concrete floors. I loved the old factory windows, even though they made the space drafty in the winter, sweltering in the summer. I loved the sound of rain tapping the skylights, even if it meant we'd had to pull buckets from the closet when the windows started to leak. And I'd loved Cassandra, the strong, confident woman who'd taken me under her wing, who'd mentored me. Up until a few years ago, I'd thought I would die an editor at Hanes House.

But so much had happened since then. I hadn't realized how much work came after you got the dream, how much you had to sacrifice to hold it together year after year. I felt like a completely different person from that meek, twenty-two-year-old who'd talked about how brave she'd had to be to leave her hometown. If that girl saw me now, I'm not sure she'd recognize me.

....

A lump formed in my throat as I settled into the leather ergonomic chair across from Cassandra's legendary glass desk. I could already feel the tears stinging my eyes, the muscles knotting in my shoulders and the back of my neck. I wanted to be anywhere else in the world. I wasn't ready for this. I wanted to beg Cassandra to reconsider. I wanted to turn the clock back, fix my big mistake, do everything differently.

"Thank you for coming in, Thea." Cassandra's voice was cool, professional. I would never get used to hearing her address me like this after years of inside jokes and gossip, her introducing me at parties as the daughter she never had, her second-in-command, her younger self. My throat closed and I had to push the memories aside.

She closed her office door and her heels clacked against the floor as she headed for the seat behind her desk.

"Of course." I knotted my hands in my lap, trying not to squirm. I took a deep, painful breath.

This was it. I just had to get through the next ten minutes without crying.

Cassandra leaned back in her chair, arching an eyebrow. Her silver hair lay in soft waves around her face. If she'd bothered to dye it, she wouldn't look a day over forty-five. As it was, she seemed alien and timeless.

She let the silence between us stretch for a moment, and then she said, "I think it's time we had a little chat."

I'd told myself I wouldn't beg for my job, that I'd accept my fate with some measure of dignity. But now, faced with the inevitable, I couldn't stop myself. "Cassandra," I choked out. "I—"

But Cassandra held up a hand, palm out, stopping me. "I want to talk to you about *The Dead Husband Cookbook*."

I closed my mouth, confused. She hadn't mentioned the submission to me, not once. As far as she was concerned, I didn't even know there *was* a submission. It seemed an odd way to open a conversation with someone you were about to fire. It took me a moment to recover enough to come up with an appropriate response, and still, all I had was a faltering "I… What?"

Cassandra considered me with a shrewd gaze, as if trying to decide whether I was faking my confusion. "I'm sure you've noticed there's been some excitement in the office over the past week," she said after a long moment. "On Monday, we received a submission for Maria Capello's new memoir. We found out late last night that she accepted our bid."

A small sound, like a sigh, escaped my lips. Just for a moment, like a fool, I let myself feel a lift of hope. *Maria Capello* was the secret author everyone had been talking about? Maria Capello, who I'd loved practically my whole life. I thought of all the hours I'd spent slowly turning the pages of her cookbook, running fingers over faded photographs of her in her kitchen, her hands wrinkled and soft-looking as they rolled out dough. I remembered watching her show, *Dinner at the Farm*, marveling over her infinite patience as she showed her children how to cut pasta or stir sauce, wondering what it would feel like to be in that kitchen with them, to be that well mothered.

The hope lingered for an instant and then it was gone, replaced with a sucking sick feeling as I remembered why I was here. What I'd done. A small pain slid into my chest like a sliver, deep and sharp.

"Rumor has it she's leaving her publisher because of some tiff with the publicity director, but I don't buy it. My niece is in the publicity department over there, and she told me they all adore her. Maria has luxury gift baskets sent over every holiday and release day. The last one had a bottle of Dom Pérignon in it. My niece wouldn't shut up about it, actually. Anyway, regardless of why, she *is* leaving, but she hasn't officially accepted our offer yet. She and her team are on their way here now, but she had a very specific request. That's why I wanted to meet with you this morning."

Maria and her team are on their way here? Now? I couldn't begin to fathom what this had to do with me.

Unless—and the thought was like a hard twist of that splinter— did Cassandra want me out of the office before they got here?

I somehow managed to choke out an "Oh?"

Cassandra stared at me. There wasn't a hint of a smile on her face.

Her voice grew several degrees colder as she said, "Maria said she'd only accept our bid if you were the one who edited her."

I blinked. I couldn't have heard that right. I opened my mouth, then closed it again. My brain felt slow. "I don't understand."

"Maria Capello told me that the only way she'd let Hanes publish her book was if Thea Woods was her editor."

Something began to hum inside my chest as I looked at Cassandra, the woman I used to trust more than my own mother. I could see instantly that she was telling me the truth.

But it didn't make sense. Maria Capello could've been edited by the same people who'd edited Obama and Prince Harry. I hadn't been that caliber of editor even before my big mistake. Now, I was a publishing cautionary tale.

Cassandra leaned forward, sliding her elbows onto her glass desk. She looked…irritated. Confused.

Curious.

"In fact," she said, "I was hoping you might enlighten me as to why Maria Capello is so keen to work with you."

I was at a loss. "I—I have no idea."

"You two have never met?"

"No."

"And you didn't talk to her at all? Get in touch when you found out about the book?" An annoyed twist to her lips when she said "found out about the book." She probably assumed one of my friends in the office had told me. I felt a brief, sharp pain that none of them had.

Still, she clearly thought I'd orchestrated this somehow. That I was trying to save my career with a last-ditch effort at landing a big celebrity memoir. Honestly, the idea was laughable.

"And say *what*?" I wanted to know. I supposed some other editor might have tried something like this, "accidentally" bumping into Maria at a restaurant or hotel lobby, pitching her a vision of the book in the hopes of wooing her away from a more successful editor at a bigger house. Cassandra, in fact, would be exactly the kind of person to do something like that. But I was not that person. I would've felt much too awkward. What would I have said to someone like Maria? The mechanics of it seemed impossible.

Cassandra stared, not blinking. I couldn't tell whether she believed me. After a moment, she said, "If you really didn't say anything to her, it's possible she wants you on this project for another reason. No one really knows why she decided to leave her publisher."

Her voice had defrosted the tiniest bit. It made my shoulders unclench. Sunlight reflected off her desk. Cassandra smelled like expensive soap, something with lavender. She pulled her lip between her teeth, eyes far away. She was holding something back, I could tell.

"What was in the proposal?" I wanted to know.

A shrug. "Bare-bones outline. One sample chapter."

"That's all?"

"They're being pretty cagey about the whole thing. Maria's agent said the book is going to be a memoir, possibly with recipes, maybe recounting her years with her late husband, Damien Capello." Cassandra's eyes slid back to mine. "Maybe something about the disappearance. Maybe."

The words *holy shit* slipped from my mouth, completely unplanned. The corner of Cassandra's lips twitched. It wasn't quite a smile, but it was the closest I'd gotten in months.

Maria had never spoken about the night her husband, world-famous chef Damien Capello, disappeared. Not once in three decades. In fact, she'd famously walked out on an interview with Barbara Walters because Walters had mentioned Damien's disappearance in passing. It was well known that the topic was off-limits.

"You really think she'll write about it?" I asked.

"It would explain the secrecy, the NDA." Cassandra ticked the points off on her fingers as she went. "That, frankly, insulting outline—"

"But why now? It's been thirty years."

Cassandra's eyebrow twitched upward. "Maybe she's finally going to admit that she killed him."

If we'd been on better terms I'd have laughed, certain she was joking. The rumor that Maria had killed her husband had been a part of her mythology since she first rose to fame, but believing it was like believing that Elvis was still alive or JFK killed Marilyn. Damien's suicide had seemed fishy at the time, yes, and people always assumed the wife was involved whenever there was a mysterious death. But the facts of the case were clear: multiple people had seen Maria Capello leave the party to take her son to the hospital, there was the camera footage showing her waiting in the emergency room lounge, and there was her signature on the visitor's log, her phone message on the answering machine.

The reasons people had for believing there'd been a cover-up—that the camera footage only showed the back of a woman's head, not Maria's face, that the signature hadn't looked exactly like hers, that Maria's cell phone call hadn't pinged the tower closest to the hospital—were interesting enough to keep the story alive for thirty years, but not enough for the police to get involved. Eventually, that night had become a dark anecdote in Maria's otherwise meteoric rise to fame, something that gave her an edge, like Martha Stewart's stint in jail.

I waited for Cassandra to laugh this idea off, tell me she was kidding. She didn't. She looked like she'd just caught the scent of blood in the water.

"Her publisher would never have passed on a memoir about the night Damien died," I pointed out.

Cassandra shrugged. "Maria might not have offered it to them. She might've thought a smaller publisher would be easier to deal with."

I tried to ignore my heartbeat, my breath running wild. Over the last three decades, remarkably few people had spoken publicly about what happened that night. A few members of Polpette's staff, some distant friends and relatives, a guy who was technically their neighbor even though he lived over a mile away. No one in the inner circle had ever said a word.

If Maria was really going to write about it, this would be the book of the season. The book of the year.

And if Cassandra let me edit it... It would be the shining highlight of my career. It would give me *back* my career. I felt breathless, light-headed. It was like winning the lottery.

Where was the catch?

"Why would she want *me* to edit it?" I asked.

Cassandra leaned over her desk, folding her hands in front of her. She looked like she was considering her words very carefully before she said, "You know how small this industry is, Thea. People talk. I can't imagine Maria doesn't know about what happened with the Kincaid Hughes book. She might've come away with the idea that you were someone who could be..." She hesitated before adding, "Handled."

I felt a sinking in my gut because this, unfortunately, made sense. "You mean manipulated?"

"I mean it's possible that she thinks she can write a version of the truth and you won't question it too closely because you need a win." Cassandra let her hands fall open. "She might want to get a specific story out there for reasons of her own."

I felt nauseous, actually sick to my stomach. I'd been an editor for nearly twenty years. How had *this* become my reputation? Was I going to spend the rest of my life being judged by the worst mistake I'd ever made?

"No, that doesn't make any sense," I said, after a moment. "If she's so worried about people questioning her story, why write the book at all? Especially now, after thirty years? Why not just let it be?"

"That is the question, isn't it?" Cassandra appeared to think about this for a moment. "Maybe she wants to set the record straight, put the rumors to rest once and for all. Or maybe she knows what really happened that night and she's tired of keeping silent. She could be protecting someone."

I was already shaking my head. "Damien died by suicide. He left a *note*." A note that was famously stolen from the Capello house and reprinted in tabloids nationwide. *By the time you find this I'll already be gone. I need it to be over.* "Multiple people said he was acting strange that night, that it felt like he was saying goodbye."

"I didn't realize you were such a fan."

To be honest, I didn't think the word *fan* really did justice to what I was. I was more than that. I was a devotee. But admitting that wouldn't win me any points here, so I kept quiet.

"I don't think it will surprise you to know that, before getting this very...*odd* ultimatum, I was planning on letting you go." Cassandra leveled her eyes on me, wiping the memory of the lip twitch that had almost been a smile from my mind. "The only reason I didn't fire you immediately is that I didn't want to add to the media scrutiny. But what happened with Hughes was completely unacceptable."

I nodded, my mouth suddenly dry. I was well aware of how bad it was.

"We're not a big publisher," Cassandra continued. "We can't afford to make mistakes like that." She hesitated before adding, "And I'm sure you know Maria's reputation."

Everyone knew Maria's reputation. She was notoriously difficult to work with, demanding, easily offended, manipulative. *Diva* was the word I'd heard used most often. It was difficult to know how much of that reputation was sexism and how much had been earned, but I had friends who'd worked with her, so I'd heard stories of an aloof, prickly woman who insisted on controlling the editorial schedule, rewriting press releases, even micromanaging the way her books were displayed in stores. She'd once had an editor reassigned because she didn't like his notes. His career never recovered afterward. I'd heard he'd left the industry, the *city*. And that wasn't the only story of someone who'd worked with Maria seeming to disappear.

But I'd heard other stories, too. Maria took care of people she liked. She helped a former assistant launch her own brand. Now, that woman had a line of cookbooks and Tupperware of her own. Maria could make your career, if she wanted to.

"This book is going to be a challenge," Cassandra continued. "But it could also be huge for us. And it would go a long way toward undoing some of the damage you did. So, what do you think? Are you up for it?"

Was I up for it? I felt awe, actual *awe*, like I was standing at the edge of the Grand Canyon, lost in that feeling of being at once very small and connected to everything. I was forty years old. I'd been an editor for nearly two decades. And I was good. I wanted *that* to be my legacy. Not Hughes.

And Maria… I'd seen every episode of her show; I'd cooked every recipe in her books. I didn't care if she was difficult. I could handle difficult. She was my idol. This was my dream job. I might not have concocted this plan on my own, but I wasn't stupid enough to walk away from it now that it had landed on my lap. It felt like an answered prayer.

But I also knew Cassandra. Once, while grabbing a drink at the divey Irish pub around the corner, she'd given me a quick tutorial on how to be a better negotiator. *Make the first offer. Ask for more than what you think you can get. Be clear about what you want.*

That Cassandra was different from the one staring back at me now. She'd wanted me to succeed. This Cassandra regarded me like a shark. It took every last ounce of bravery I had to say, "I would want to reopen our discussion about my promotion." Sarah Stewart, one of Hanes's two editorial directors, had just announced she was stepping down. I hadn't been in any position to ask Cassandra to consider me to replace her. Until about two minutes ago.

"Of course," Cassandra said. There was no hesitation in her voice. She'd expected this.

"I want Sarah's job," I added, so there wouldn't be any confusion later.

Cassandra didn't blink. "Done."

"And," I added, thinking fast, "I'll need a raise. Childcare costs are insane right now."

I had no right to ask for that, but I thought I saw something glint in Cassandra's eye. Was I fooling myself to think it could have been pride?

Cassandra leaned across the desk and said, her voice low, "Get Maria Capello to write us a memoir about what happened the night her husband disappeared and you'll get your promotion and your raise. But, Thea... I hope you understand how rare this opportunity is. I don't offer second chances. You would not be sitting here if Maria hadn't insisted."

I nodded. "Yes. I realize that."

"Good," Cassandra said, voice clipped. "Then you should also realize that one misstep, one complaint from Maria, one *hint* of a problem and that's it. You're done here."

....

I hurried out of Cassandra's office and into the bathroom, barely breathing. The air felt stagnant, hot.

I stopped at the row of sinks and the faucets groaned, then creaked as I turned them on, icy water thundering into the basin.

My reflection winced as I met my eyes, blinking rapidly. There was a tingling in my chest that could have been excitement or anxiety or dread, a tightening of my heart, my breath gone short and shallow. What was happening? What the *hell* had just happened?

I'm not fired, I told myself, testing the thought. *I'm not getting fired.* Not today, at least.

Maria Capello asked me to edit her book. *Me.*

A smile tugged at the corners of my lips. Slow at first, then unraveling like a flag in the wind. Holy shit. *Holy shit.*

Everything had gotten so messed up but this, *finally*, was a way to get things back on track.

I used to have plans. Not long ago, I knew exactly where my life would be in one year, five, ten. The last time one of the bigger houses had tried to poach me, I'd gone to Casandra with my shiny new offer and a list of demands: I wouldn't leave, and, in exchange, I expected to make executive editor in two years. Editorial director in four.

Who knows, maybe that's exactly what would have happened if things had gone differently. But then I got pregnant with Ruthie, and I'd had to go on bed rest when I was only six months along, which had meant taking maternity leave early. I'd gotten a pelvis fracture while giving birth that had left me unable to stand without leaning heavily on a walker, requiring months of intensive physical therapy as I basically relearned how to move my legs. I was only supposed to be gone for four months. I'd ended up staying out for the better part of a year.

And when I finally did get back to work, I was...different. There was no other way to put it. Motherhood had shifted something fundamental inside of me. I was like that paradox, the Ship of Theseus: If all parts of a ship were replaced gradually over time, was it still the same ship? I felt different on a cellular basis, even though I looked the same. It was as though someone had switched out my blood, my bones, my brain.

The project that ruined everything was a memoir by a politician out of Iowa named Kincaid Hughes. At the time I'd acquired the book Hughes had an unimpeachable reputation. There'd even been rumors that he was planning a presidential bid in the next decade or so. It was the first book I worked on after coming back from maternity leave, but Hughes had made it all so easy. He'd hired a ghostwriter, an outside editor, and by the time the book got to me it was nearly perfect. I barely managed to fill a page with notes.

Hughes though. I'd known from our very first meeting that there was something about Hughes I didn't like. His eyes lingered a beat too long and in inappropriate places. Some of the jokes he told could've been considered tasteless, if he'd meant them a certain way, or could've been completely innocent if he hadn't. Once, I thought he'd touched my lower back, but when I turned around, I couldn't be entirely sure that it wasn't the edge of his bag.

Early motherhood compounded all these anxieties: I was exhausted, barely sleeping through the night. I obsessed about Hughes. Sometimes I gaslit myself into thinking I'd imagined everything; other times I'd convince myself that I had a duty to out him—that I owed it to the next generation. Eventually, the whole situation unnerved me enough that I'd started asking around. Just a few conversations over drinks or in the quieter corners of parties. *Did Hughes ever say... Did you ever feel...* The responses weren't too scandalous, but it was enough to put together a sketchy picture of a guy who made women uncomfortable. A guy who maybe enjoyed making women uncomfortable.

Then this woman, a publicity director at another house who I'd always been friendly with, mentioned in passing that I should talk to her assistant, Riley. Riley didn't just have a story, my friend told me. She had receipts. She'd interned with Hughes's PR firm back when she was in college. And, according to her, he wasn't just kind of creepy. He was a full-on predator.

Riley seemed happy to talk to me. She showed me dozens of DMs from Hughes. They started friendly, flirty, then quickly became crude. Hughes—who, by the way, had been *married* and was about thirty years older than Riley at the time—had sent sexually explicit photos, written disgusting things, and even insinuated that if Riley were to give him sex, he'd make sure the PR firm hired her on full time. *"You take care of me and I'll take care of you,"* he'd written.

The whole thing had infuriated me. I took screenshots of the DMs and showed them to Cassandra the very next day. I told her we had to drop Hughes's book, which, by the way, was impossible. Every bookstore in the country already had their copies. The book was coming out in weeks, and it was supposed to be our biggest book of the season. If we pulled it, Hanes House would be out hundreds of thousands of dollars. Cassandra was apologetic. She told me she felt the same way about Hughes, that we'd never publish him again. But this book was going to come out.

The next part was where I fucked up. There's no other way to look at it. And I truly hate to put any of the blame for this mistake on hormones, but in this case, it was accurate. I was only a few months out from giving birth to a daughter and more sensitive than usual about the idea of anyone out there preying on girls. When I looked at Riley, I didn't see a twentysomething woman. I saw a child, someone's daughter, a little girl who it was my job to protect. It deeply bothered me that Hughes was going to get away with what he'd done, that there was nothing I could do about it.

And so drunk on half a glass of wine (which was all it took to get me tipsy back when I was still breastfeeding) and bored at some media party Jacob had dragged me to, I'd told a stranger everything I'd heard about Hughes. In fairness, she'd asked me about him. She'd just gotten hired to do some social media work with his campaign for reelection and wanted to know about my experience working with him. Still, I shouldn't have said anything. I didn't even know this person. It was just that she'd looked so impossibly young. I couldn't stop thinking about how Riley's hand had trembled when she'd shown me those disgusting DMs, or about my daughter's perfect, innocent face. I'd only wanted to warn her.

Later that night, an anonymous TikTok account called HushHush released a video: a series of still shots of Hughes, over which they'd added audio of me warning the young social media manager about what a predator he was, that he preyed on young women, how I desperately wished we could pull his book. Someone had recorded our entire conversation without my knowledge.

It would have been bad enough on its own. But whoever was behind the HushHush account also ended up with the screenshots I took of Riley's DMs, screenshots Riley had warned me to keep secret because she'd signed an NDA. The screenshots were included in the video with the pics, which made it look like I'd provided them, and HushHush had credited me with a hat tip in the caption.

The post immediately went viral. The story got picked up by every major news publication. And while the media circus tended to focus on Hughes, publishing TikTok had plenty to say about me. There were people who thought I was a hero and slammed Hanes Press as cowardly, and others who said I was an example of "woke liberalism" run amok. I didn't agree with either take. I wasn't a hero. I wasn't a symbol of anything. I was just a mother and a woman and I'd wanted Hughes to go down.

Unfortunately, that's not exactly what happened. No one could agree over whether Hughes's DMs proved he was a predatory monster. Riley wouldn't come forward—too afraid of violating her NDA—but she texted me to let me know she would never forgive me for releasing her name and private DMs, and that she never wanted to hear from me again. That's what upset me most of all, that my actions had hurt more than they'd helped her. I felt like a monster.

We never officially pulled Hughes's book, but most of the bookstores returned their orders, so we may as well have. Hughes wasn't canceled, not even close, but his people still sued Hanes. I wasn't privy to much on the financial side of things, since Cassandra tended to keep that information strictly need to know. But I knew we were still in the red. Because of me.

I took a deep breath and splashed the cold water onto my face, my neck, firmly pushing those memories away. Cassandra had publicly backed me when all this went down, but that was just to save face. She'd built Hanes House herself, and she couldn't afford to have its name dragged through the mud. Behind closed doors, she'd been incandescent with anger. She hadn't fired me then, but it was clear that it was only a matter of time. A promotion was laughable. And it's not like I could go anywhere else. Publishing was a small industry and everyone knew what I'd done. Even the people who thought I was a hero for revealing Hughes wouldn't ignore the fact that I'd violated Riley's NDA by sharing her screenshots and trashed Hanes for not pulling his book. I wasn't getting another offer, and I couldn't move up at Hanes. I was stuck, just waiting for Cassandra to put me out of my misery.

But now. Now there was hope.

My phone buzzed in my pocket. I pulled it out and saw a text from my mother: Can we talk? A familiar mix of emotions bubbled up inside of me: guilt and annoyance and anger and more guilt.

Then, a soft rap on the door, the sound so sudden it made me jump. "Thea?" came Cassandra's voice. "Maria and her team are here. We'll be in the big conference room."

I stuffed the phone back into my pocket. I absolutely could not deal with my mother's drama right now. I switched the faucet off. The fluorescent lights flickered more erratically, casting long shadows over the ceiling and floor.

For a moment it looked as if it were reaching for me.

CHRONICLE MAGAZINE

How She Did It: Maria Capello on Her Unlikely Transformation from Celebrity Chef's Widow to the Woman Behind the Stove

By Lila Wentworth

NOVEMBER 19, 2001

Maria Capello is draining the pasta for her baked ziti, a dish her husband, the late Damien Capello, famously claimed was "much too prosaic" for his restaurant, Polpette della Nonna, in a 1995 interview for the *New York Times*. Maria insists she doesn't feel the same way. This ziti, she tells me, is special, a family recipe passed down through generations, from her great-grandmother to her grandmother to her mother to her. I've been in the kitchen with her for every single step she took to create this masterpiece, and I'm still not entirely sure how she made it so good. The intoxicating aroma of sausages and butter has filled the room. I have to admit, I'm already salivating.

It's mid-April, and much too early for baked ziti at just after ten o'clock in the morning, but Capello needs to complete the all-day shoot for her *Dinner at the Farm* television series. Later tonight, she leaves on a seven-city tour for her new cookbook, *The Italian Family Table*, out March 28. At Maria's insistence, we're meeting in the spacious upstate kitchen where she films. Modeled after a traditional Tuscan villa, with its rustic wooden beams and terracotta floors, the room is so homey you could almost forget it's also the set of a television show. Cameras and crew move swiftly, capturing the golden hues of the afternoon light pouring through all the windows.

Pots and pans clutter the stovetop behind her. The counter is crowded with fresh vegetables, loaves of bread, cheese wrapped in butcher paper, and a smattering of unlabeled jars containing spices and herbs. It's chaotic. There are at least three different cooking projects in rotation at all times, but Maria is unfazed. Chopping a handful of fresh basil, she muses aloud to the cameras, "The best ingredients are simple and fresh. Basil, tomatoes, mozzarella. You don't need fancy or expensive foods to be an *exquisite* home cook."

Such missives are, perhaps, what makes her show so popular among American home chefs. The 2001 "Christmas Special" of *Dinner at the Farm* was among the most viewed programs in America the day it aired. Watching the program feels like joining Maria for an intimate family meal, one where you won't be chided for burning the rolls or letting the sauce simmer for a few minutes too long. Capello feels like the Italian mother you wish you had—the one who tells you you're too skinny, who calmly explains that you can tell the oil is ready by watching the smoke spiral from the surface, who shrugs and pours you a glass of aged Sangiovese when things don't turn out as expected.

Capello certainly knows a thing or two about things not turning out as expected. In the summer of 1996, her husband, the famous chef Damien Capello, committed suicide in the creek behind their family farmhouse. At the time, the media painted Maria Capello as a grief-stricken widow desperately trying not to fall apart in the wake of a horrible tragedy. A widely circulated photograph showed her clutching her two children, Isabella Capello, then 12, and Enzo Capello, 10, on the church steps just after her husband's funeral, grief evident on her face.

That photograph is still the image many associate with Maria Capello. If you find yourself wondering how she not only survived that loss but somehow came out stronger on the other side, you wouldn't be the only one. Recently, Capello's name and reputation have been subjected to endless attacks in the news and in late-night hosts' jokey monologues. The kinder outlets have remarked that it seems crass for the widow to pursue a career in food so soon after her husband's death, while the crueler ones have gone so far as to call the official story of her husband's suicide into question. *Saturday Night Live* even aired a skit that depicted Maria killing her husband and gleefully chopping up his body to add to those famous meatballs. Though NBC later issued a statement making it clear that the skit was written in jest and was by no means intended to be an accurate account of what happened, the rumor had already taken hold, fueled by the supposed inconsistencies in her story of that night. Conspiracy theorists worldwide have since adopted the theory.

For her part, Capello has never responded to any of these rumors. This is the woman who showed up to film a segment on the *Today* show just hours after the same network aired the infamous skit. During the segment, an anchor doggedly questioned Capello about the conspiracy, as well as the resulting slogan, *Maria's Meatballs Are People*, which can be found on T-shirts, posters, and bumper stickers. Capello steadily refused to answer, repeating that she was just there to make pasta.

As she speaks to me now, all Capello will say on the topic is, "Damien and I had planned a very specific life together when we first got married. I was going to take care of our home and our family so that he could become the culinary genius we all knew he could be. After he died, I wasn't just grieving him but this dream that the two of us had shared. In the end, I realized I had two choices. I could let our dream disappear, or I could find a way to keep it going without him. That's all that I've been trying to do."

Today, she's adamant about rewriting her narrative. "People will always talk," she remarks as she plates her ziti, "but my focus now is on sharing the recipes that helped me through the hardest times of my life. I'll let the food speak for itself."

As a final touch to the dish, she sprinkles a little something extra from that famous blue tin that she pulls out at the end of every episode of *Dinner at the Farm*.

"Every family has a secret ingredient," she tells me when I ask her about the blue tin, just like she says at the end of every one of her shows. "Even if it's just the love you have for one another. We all put a little something extra into our food."

Her new cookbook is set to release next month, and if the

scents wafting from her kitchen are anything to go by, it promises to be a culinary revelation. Her past may have been marred by controversy, but Maria Capello's future, much like her ziti, seems rich and promising.

Must be the secret ingredient she keeps in that little blue tin. I wasn't able to pry it out of her this time. But don't worry, I'll keep trying.

Maria's "Prosaic" Baked Ziti with Sausage

This recipe is comfort food, pure and simple. It's certainly not for every day, but I like to think that makes it even more special. For years, I would make this dish when a neighbor had a new baby, or when there was a sudden death or illness in the family, or anytime someone was in need of little extra nurturing. It got to the point that I began keeping a frozen ziti in my freezer at all times, just in case. When you need something decadent, there's simply nothing better than baked pasta.

INGREDIENTS

2 tablespoons olive oil, and more as needed
1½ pounds sweet Italian sausage links
5 cloves garlic
2 (28-ounce) cans of crushed tomatoes
1 small bunch basil, leaves only
1 pound ziti
¾ cup ricotta cheese
¼ cup heavy cream (optional)
½ pound hard mozzarella cheese
½ cup grated Parmesan Reggiano cheese
3 tablespoons butter, plus more to grease baking pan

STEPS

Serves 8 to 10

1. Heat 1 tablespoon olive oil in a large pot over medium heat. Prick the sausages all over with a pin (or, failing that, a fork) and sear on all sides in the hot oil, about 10 minutes.
2. Pour the fat out of the pot and replace with 1 tablespoon fresh olive oil. Lightly crush the garlic cloves and add to the hot oil, stirring until lightly browned, then pour in the crushed tomatoes.

3. Bring to a boil, then reduce to a low simmer, scraping the bottom of the pot with a wooden spoon to release any brown bits stuck to the bottom of the pot. Partially cover with a lid and braise the sausages for 45 minutes, stirring from time to time. Remove the pot from the heat and then add in the basil, tearing it into small pieces and dropping them into the sauce. Remove the garlic cloves and discard. If the sauce is too thick, loosen with a bit of water, then season to taste with salt and set aside.

4. While the sauce cooks, preheat your oven to 325°F and prepare the pasta. Bring a large pot of water to a rolling boil and salt aggressively. Drop in the pasta and cook 4 minutes less than the package directions. You want the pasta to be not quite al dente. (It will finish cooking in the oven.) Drain and set aside.

5. Remove the sausages from the sauce and cut into bite-sized pieces. Mix the sausages in with the pasta, and pour in 3 cups of the tomato sauce.

6. Smear a 9" x 13" baking dish with butter, spread 1 cup of the tomato sauce evenly over the bottom, and then pour the pasta mix into the dish, distributing evenly with a spoon. Pour an additional 1 to 2 cups of the tomato sauce over the top.

7. If using the heavy cream, mix with the ricotta in a large bowl. Plop large spoonfuls of the ricotta into the ziti, nestling them down into the pasta. Sprinkle the mozzarella evenly over the top, then sprinkle the grated Parmesan cheese over. Cut the butter into small cubes and distribute over the cheese.

8. Cover the dish tightly with aluminum foil and pop into the oven to bake for 35 minutes. Remove the foil and continue baking an additional 10 to 15 minutes, until the cheese is browning on top and the sauce bubbles lightly around the edges of the dish.

9. Remove from the oven and let rest for 10 minutes. Serve hot.

3

THEA

I SAW THE BACK OF MARIA'S HEAD THROUGH THE CONFERENCE room's glass walls as soon as I stepped out of the bathroom. There was her thick, black hair, familiarly streaked with gray and piled on top of her head in loose curls, and when she turned, there were the sharp corners of her black-framed glasses.

Publishing wasn't nearly as glamorous as it was portrayed on television or in the movies, but we still met our fair share of famous people wanting to write a memoir or inspirational self-help guide, even the occasional novel. I was fairly accustomed to interacting with celebrities. But this was *Maria Capello*. Her television show had kept me company every day after school, during the long, lonely hours when my own mother was out. *Dinner at the Farm* aired during the day, but I'd record the episodes, and when I got home, I'd unplug our 13-inch TV-VCR combo and carry it into our kitchen so I could work my way through the recipes alongside Maria. Saltimbocca di pollo alla romana, spaghetti alla carbonara, bucatini all'amatriciana. It was easy to pretend Maria was standing beside me at the narrow, crowded counter, showing me how to layer my seasoning and mix pasta water with my sauce to help it coat the noodles. This woman taught me more about cooking than my own mother did.

Cassandra was seated at the table across from her, listening intently as Maria said something to the man beside her—her literary agent, Henry Perse. I couldn't make out the words, just the low mumble of their voices through the thick glass. A moment later, they all erupted into laughter.

I stopped by the kitchen to pour myself some coffee, trying to remember absolutely everything I knew about Maria Capello in the thirty seconds it took to reach the conference room door. Normally, I'd have spent days prepping. But I was going into this meeting cold. The thought made me feel like I was walking across the room in too-high heels. The floor beneath me swayed.

Luckily there wasn't much about Maria's life I didn't already know. She and Damien had met in their early twenties, while working at an Italian restaurant called La Villetta that had since closed. They had a small wedding, only close family and a few friends, choosing to pour all their money into their own restaurant. Polpette della Nonna opened in Woodstock, New York, in the 1980s, and it was incredibly successful until Damien's sudden, unexpected disappearance in 1996.

That was the part of the story everyone knew: the disappearance, the scandal, and what came after. Lurid rumors of murder and theft and cannibalism. Even the people who understood that this was baseless gossip still loved to spread the stories.

Maria scored the Food Network series *Dinner at the Farm* in the late '90s or early 2000s and shortly after released *The Italian Family Table*, which became an instant bestseller. Not long after that came the line of pasta sauces and frozen foods, all of them almost impossibly good, better than any other prepared-food brand I'd ever tried. Despite the controversies, people loved her. Or maybe it was because of the controversies. They certainly added a dimension to her character that other home chefs didn't have. Maria was complicated and mysterious and just a little dangerous. And she made a to-die-for lasagna. Pun very much intended.

Whatever it was, it'd worked for her. In the last twenty-five years,

Maria Capello had transformed from mere celebrity to icon to GOAT. Everyone owned at least one of her cookbooks, everyone knew at least one of her recipes by heart, brought it to every dinner party, beamed as they accepted the compliments. Drag queens dressed up as her. Hip-hop artists and starlets came to her show to make gnocchi. (Yes, her show was still running.) And, decades after that infamous *SNL* skit, people still donned blousy shirt-dresses and funky glasses every Halloween, frequently pairing their "Maria Capello" costumes with bloody butcher knives and a tray of her famous meatballs. Often with a rubber finger or toe sticking out of them. Classy.

And now she was sitting in the Hanes House conference room. Waiting for me.

I took a deep breath and nudged the door open.

Maria and Henry were seated at the head of the long, reclaimed-wood conference table. Its warm honey tone contrasted with the surrounding exposed brick walls, aged steel beams, and polished floor. I took a moment to thank early-in-the-morning Thea for choosing an appropriate outfit: my favorite cream-colored turtleneck and houndstooth blazer and a pair of black loafers. I looked smart and a little nerdy. Exactly what people wanted in an editor.

Maria turned in her seat as I pushed the door open. She was smaller in person than she looked on TV, couldn't have been taller than five two or three and bird-boned, with a sharp, angular face, deep wrinkles surrounding full lips and hooded eyes. Her skin looked very soft and very clear, just the slightest pink tint to her cheeks and lips. I knew she was in her mid-seventies, but I'm not sure I would've guessed that by looking at her. She gave the impression that she would never grow older than she was in this moment, that she would never do something so prosaic as die.

She was dressed more professionally than I'd ever seen her before, in black slacks and a white silk shirt, her glasses thick and black and minimal, no ornate jewelry, dangling earrings, or clanking bracelets. She wore only a slim, gold Cartier watch, her basic black pumps screaming *expensive*.

"Hello," Maria said. God, that voice. It was unmistakable. Warm and crinkly, the voice of the mother everyone wished they had. It was somehow richer and deeper in person than it was on television and so warm. It filled my body like soup. "It's so good to meet you. I'm Maria."

She rose halfway from her seat. I don't know how I'd expected her to greet me. Her reputation was so unnerving. I'd imagined her refusing to look me in the eye, like Elton John was rumored to do. But she surprised me by immediately clasping my hand in both of hers and squeezing.

"H-hi," I faltered, caught off guard. "I'm Thea Woods." I hoped my name would elicit an explanation for why she'd wanted to work with me. When she said nothing, I nervously added, "It's so nice to meet you. I'm such a fan."

For a beat, her expression didn't change. Her dark, shrewd eyes moved over my face, and I had the strangest feeling that I was being scanned, every detail noted and filed away for later. My chest tightened. Once again, I thought of my interview with Cassandra seventeen years ago. The last time I'd been this desperate to make a good first impression.

Then, Maria broke into a wide smile. Her teeth were perfect in the way that only very rich women's teeth could be perfect, all of them straight and white and as unchipped as a strand of pearls. "Is that so? How lovely."

It was a perfectly normal, perfectly polite exchange. And yet I exhaled as Maria lowered herself back to her seat. I had the strangest feeling of having passed a test.

"Thea, good to see you again," Henry said, standing to shake my hand as well. He was tall and thin and nondescript, with small, wire-frame glasses and thinning blond hair. We rarely worked together. Henry was a Big Deal agent, capital B, capital D. Think celebrity clients, TV personalities, movie stars who thought they could write novels, a few notable politicians. Even before the Hughes nightmare, he'd considered me beneath him.

"Nice to see you too, Henry," I said.

"We were just discussing the schedule," Cassandra explained as I took a seat. "I told Henry and Maria that I want to crash this, get it out to stores in time for the holidays. But that means we'll need a full manuscript as soon as possible." She turned to Maria and Henry. "*Is* there a manuscript yet?"

Henry looked at Maria, who folded her hands on the table in front of her. Small though she was, she seemed to fill the conference room. It was impossible to look away from her. "I have a full manuscript ready to read as soon as I accept your offer," she said. "But I have a few conditions we'll need to discuss before we get that far."

A fist tightened in my stomach. This was it. The real reason Maria wanted me to edit her book, the catch. I flushed. I felt as though everyone was looking at me, like they all knew *I* was the reason for any precautions Maria would want to take. I braced myself and said, trying to keep my voice even, "Conditions?"

Maria turned to me and there was the faintest shift in her demeanor. The corner of a smile and she leaned in almost conspiratorially, as though the two of us were close friends sharing a secret. I felt a rush of pleasure. Embarrassing as it was to admit, it thrilled me to think that she might confide in me.

"I had problems with my last publisher," Maria explained, a confessional drop in her voice. "Early pages of my books seemed to find their way online well ahead of publication. No one could tell me how it was happening, but when we did some digging, it turned out an editorial assistant was bringing the manuscript home, leaving it lying around where her roommate could take photos of the pages."

I waited for her to call out my slip with Hughes, that awful video. She said nothing. I wondered, with a rush of relief, if she'd even seen it.

"Wow," I murmured. Out of the corner of my eye, I saw Cassandra shift in her seat, murmuring "Unacceptable" under her breath. She seemed to be intentionally avoiding my eye.

"It *was* unacceptable," Maria said. Then, with a slight shrug, she added, "Though I suppose the silver lining was that the books that leaked were all cookbooks. *This* book, my memoir, is a lot closer to my heart. It's why I couldn't let my former publisher have it. And the subject matter is so much more sensitive. In the interest of avoiding any future leaks, there's currently only one copy of the manuscript." She lifted a single finger, *one*. "And I'm afraid I won't be able to permit you to email it or make any copies."

I blinked a few times. It was a neat trick. That voice, so warm it seemed impossible that she would use it to ask for anything unreasonable. For a moment I was so soothed by it that I didn't hear what she'd actually said.

"I... I'm sorry, you won't *email* it?" I asked. My brain went blank, thoughts skidding past without catching. I glanced at Cassandra, wondering if she'd known. Her expression made it clear she hadn't. "Then... sorry, but I don't understand. How do you expect that to work?"

Maria continued, unfazed. "I will provide you with the draft, but you will be expected to read it in my presence and provide me with any notes you have then. Once we have a final draft that we both agree is acceptable, I'll permit you to email and copy as necessary." Her eyes flicked to Cassandra. "All pages will be watermarked with your name, of course, but I'm sure that can be managed."

She made it all sound so normal, impossible to argue with. I was stunned. I'd never heard of an editor working like this before. And I could feel Cassandra's eyes on me, waiting to see how I would respond. But what was I going to say? Those precautions are unnecessary? You can *trust* me?

Laughable. If there was one person in publishing who couldn't argue with those terms, it was me. It was starting to feel increasingly likely that it was why I was sitting here.

I wet my lips. It was going to take more than that to rattle me. "That won't be a problem," I told Maria. "What else?"

Henry said, "You will need to sign an NDA, Thea, the same one Cassandra signed to see the sample chapters, and it will remain in effect throughout the duration of this project. That means you will not be permitted to announce the sale until we give the go-ahead. And you won't discuss the book—or Maria—with anyone outside of this room. That point is firm."

I was at a loss for words for the second time in the space of about thirty seconds. No one outside of this room? There were things that had to be done before a book could be published, people I would need to talk to. I had to start coordinating the cover design process and production schedule, not to mention discussing marketing and PR plans. And this book was on a tight schedule. We couldn't waste a second.

I pretended to take a sip of my coffee to cover a quick glance at Cassandra, wondering how she was taking all this. She appeared poised enough, but she was blinking very fast, clearly shocked.

After a moment, she said, "We'll need to discuss the book internally with a few other departments. Sales and marketing—"

Henry waved her concerns away. "You and I can hammer out the particulars once we have a deal, Cassandra. The last thing any of us want is to hurt the sell-in. But we'd like this project to be strictly need to know. That's the most important thing to keep in mind here."

Henry looked at me. Pointedly, I thought. My mouth went dry.

"I won't discuss the project with anyone outside of this room," I agreed. "You have my word. Henry and Cassandra can come up with a list of internal departments who need to know, but other than that, my lips are sealed."

Cassandra cleared her throat. "Need to know. Of course. We can work with that."

"Great," Henry said, looking pleased. "Then that's—"

Before he could finish, Maria lifted a hand, cutting him off. "Just one last thing." Turning to me, she said, "Thea, I'd like to work on the first draft at the Farm."

It took a moment for me to realize she meant she wanted me to come to *the* Farm, as in the farm from *Dinner at the Farm*.

Maria kept talking. "You're welcome to look at your schedule and let me know what timing works for you, but it sounds like you'll need the final manuscript sooner rather than later." She glanced at Cassandra, who nodded.

"As soon as possible, yes," she confirmed.

"In that case, let's get you up sometime in the next week," Maria said. Just the right amount of steel undercutting that warm smile, the "we're all friends here" voice.

I barely noticed. In an instant, images of the Farm filled my head: tall golden grass swaying in the wind, fog obscuring the tops of the Catskill Mountains, the cozy kitchen I'd seen on television so many times I practically had it memorized. A place where I'd dreamed of going ever since I was a child. My mouth went dry.

It was hitting me, really hitting me, just how big this was. My brain was moving too fast, ideas pinging around inside my skull, impossible to sort through them all.

The terms were ridiculous. The timeline might be impossible. And I had no idea how I was going to convince Jacob to let me leave him and Ruthie for however long it would take to edit a book I couldn't tell him anything about.

And yet, the whole thing felt like a dream.

"Yes, of course," I told Maria, when I could find my voice again. "That would be lovely."

Inside, I was thinking that this book wouldn't just keep me from getting fired. It wouldn't just get me a promotion. It could alter the rest of my career.

It could make me a legend.

METRO CITY NEWS

Chef Damien Capello's Suicide Note Surfaces, Puts Tragic End to Speculation Around His Disappearance

By Evie Harper

JANUARY 8, 1999

A suicide note left by Damien Capello has recently surfaced, casting a new light on the mysterious disappearance of the renowned chef. Capello, famous for his culinary prowess and his beloved restaurant, Polpette della Nonna, in Woodstock, N.Y., vanished from his family home late on the evening of July 17, 1996.

In the aftermath of his disappearance, Capello's wife, Maria, was extensively questioned by authorities. Despite the scrutiny, no charges were ever brought against her. The investigation into Capello's sudden departure remained open but stagnant, leaving family, friends, and fans of his culinary talents in a state of prolonged uncertainty.

Damien Capello was last seen by his family before vanishing without a trace from their upstate New York farm. The following day, his clothes were found on the bank of a nearby creek, prompting a frantic search and numerous speculations about his fate.

The recent discovery of Capello's suicide note has led authorities to reconsider the circumstances surrounding his disappearance. The note, written in Capello's distinctive handwriting, was sent anonymously to several well-known publications. The contents have led investigators to believe that Capello took his own life on that fateful night in 1996—this despite persistent rumors of his wife's involvement in his disappearance as well as more sensational conspiracies involving murder and grotesque ideas about how involved parties may have disposed of a body.

The note is reprinted in its entirety below.

Dear Maria,

By the time you find this, I'll already be gone. I know this will come as a shock, but please understand that I wouldn't be doing this if I saw any other way. For a long time now, it's felt like I've been walking down a dark tunnel. And, no matter how hard I try, I just can't seem to find the light at the end.

I can't do it anymore. I want out. I need it all to be over.

My love to you and the kids,
Damien

4

THEA

"I DON'T GET IT," JACOB WAS SAYING. HE STOOD IN FRONT OF our open refrigerator door, blinking and confused. I think he'd forgotten why he'd opened the fridge, actually. "Is it another politician? Is that why all the secrecy?"

It was later that night. I'd waited until I got back home to tell Jacob what happened. As much as I *could* tell. He was a writer at large with the *Tribune*, which meant he was usually the one with the shocking stories—the marine with PTSD who'd insisted on meeting him at the Gump Shrimp in Times Square, or the editor who'd emailed out of the blue to see if he had any interest in tackling a story about a group of skiers who'd nearly been killed in an avalanche. I so rarely got to be the surprising one. It was intoxicating.

"It's not a politician," I said. "Nothing like that. This author… They're just a little…prickly, is all. They've had problems with the press in the past so they're being extra cautious."

"That's really cautious," Jacob muttered. Ruthie was bouncing back and forth between the two of us, begging for a piece of pasta. Jacob had been staring off into space, fridge still open, brows knit in confusion. He blinked, suddenly seemed to come back to the kitchen for long enough to murmur, "Ask your mom, sweetie."

We were both standing about a foot away from the strainer of pasta. I wanted to point out that he could've reached it just as easily as I could've, but that seemed petty, so I plucked a piece out and handed it to her.

"Thank you," Ruthie said. Her little voice made the words sound like *tank-oo.*

Jacob's phone rang. He glanced at it, hit Ignore before turning to me. "It's not Elon Musk, is it? You have to tell me if it is."

"God no." I bustled around the kitchen, sloshing oil in a frying pan, setting the back burner to medium. The air was already thick with the smell of tomatoes and pork. "No one like that, I promise."

"I don't see why you can't just tell me. It's not like anyone would know."

I shook my head. I was dying to tell him, obviously. Maria was the reason Jacob and I had met, ironically. It'd been at one of my favorite bookstores in Brooklyn, Greenlight, this tiny independent place in Fort Greene with overstuffed shelves and huge windows, branded tote bags hanging from the walls. I hadn't even been looking for a cook- book, but the store's sections all sort of overlapped, so I could see the cookbook section from where I was standing.

Jacob had been frowning over the spines on the shelves, adorably lost. I'd been watching him for a minute, trying to decide whether I could risk the potential humiliation of actually starting a conversa- tion, when he'd pulled one of Maria Capello's books off the shelf. It'd felt like a sign.

"That's my favorite cookbook," I'd told him. It was the one and only time in my life that I'd made the first move with a guy, and I'd immediately blushed. I expected him to blow me off. Instead, he'd turned and smiled. I remember thinking it was the best smile I'd ever seen, wide and open and uninhibited, the way little kids smiled. My stomach had flipped.

"Yeah?" He turned the book over, studying Maria's photo on the back. "I've heard she's kind of..." He'd made the universal sign for *crazy*—finger looping his ear, eyes wide. "Didn't she turn her husband into spaghetti?"

If it hadn't been for that great smile, I might've rolled my eyes and walked away, thinking *sexist asshole*. Instead, I'd berated him for listening to over-the-top conspiracy theories. We'd spent the next twenty minutes laughing and arguing before Jacob, somewhat bashfully, suggested we continue the discussion at the bar next door. There, we'd talked about his job and mine. We'd learned that we'd grown up just an hour and a half from each other, him in Albany, me in Utica. He even told me that his mom, Gloria, had worked at the hospital that had served as Maria's alibi, that she'd seen Maria bring her son in the night Damien went missing. To this day, it remains the coolest celebrity sighting I've ever heard.

Now, Jacob turned to me and said, "I don't know, Thea. You're sure you want to do this?"

I looked over my shoulder, studying his face. "You're not serious."

"It's just…you're not allowed to tell anyone you're working on this book, you don't know why this author—whoever they are—even wanted you, and you can't read the thing without them looking over your shoulder. You don't think that's a little weird?"

He leveled his gaze at me. It took me aback. Jacob was not a serious person, not usually. That's what I'd always loved about him. On our third date, some drunk chick had spilled an entire pint of beer over his head, and instead of getting angry, he'd laughed, licked the side of his mouth, and said, "Hey, free beer."

"I guess it's a little odd, but celebrities are like that." I took the sauce off the back burner and turned the heat down. "Remember that TikTok influencer who refused to turn in a draft if Mercury was in retrograde?"

"This isn't just sending a draft in a few days late." Jacob was studying me, concern etched across his normally smiling face.

"You're acting like it's going to be dangerous." I forced myself to laugh, to cut the tension. "I'm not Clarice going to some hospital for the criminally insane to talk to Hannibal Lecter. This is just a famous person." Despite what the tabloids had been saying for years.

Jacob gave me a look. "Every celebrity has a few skeletons in their closet. You really aren't weirded out?"

"I don't know." I swallowed. I could feel my heart beating in my throat, and my shoulders hadn't unclenched since I first saw Maria in the conference room. I'd been trying to ignore my nerves, but of course Jacob knew me better than that. "Maybe a little?"

"Then don't do it." He made it sound easy, like skipping a workout because you were too tired. I stared at him. Did he really not understand how badly I needed this?

"Nerves aren't enough reason to walk away from this. It's an incredible opportunity." I grabbed a towel off the hook beside the sink and wiped a streak of tomato sauce from the counter. "This morning, I thought Cassandra was going to fire me—"

"She wasn't going to fire you," Jacob said, talking over me.

A flare of annoyance shot through me. "Yes, she was. She *told* me she was."

"She actually said, 'Take this project or I'm going to fire you?'"

I hesitated. "Not in those exact words, but yes."

Jacob still looked unconvinced. "Fine, if that's the way it's gotta be, then I support you." Then, smile widening, he added, "Is it Martha Stewart?"

Too close for comfort. "*Stop* guessing," I said, swatting him with the towel. He laughed, ducking away a second before it could catch him on the hip.

"Hey, before I forget, Ruthie's day care called again," he said. "Did you send the tuition?"

"I sent it this afternoon," I lied. "I'll call to make sure they got it." My phone beeped and I glanced at the screen. My mother. Again. *Shit.*

"I should take this," I told Jacob, snatching the phone off the counter. Ruthie was at my leg again, standing on tiptoes, begging for another piece of pasta. "Ask Daddy," I told her and took my phone into the hall outside our apartment, where I wouldn't be overheard.

"You picked up," Mom said when I answered, her surprise obvious. She cleared her throat. "I figured you were screening my calls."

"I just haven't had time to talk." My voice was hard, flat. I closed my eyes for a moment, hesitating, but I already knew I wouldn't be able to stop myself from asking. "Is he there?"

An exasperated sigh reached across the two thousand miles between us, blew into my ear so loudly I flinched and pulled the phone away. Typical. Mom didn't like having to explain herself.

"I was calling to ask about my granddaughter," she said, once I'd brought the phone back to my ear. "If I'd known you were going to be nasty, I wouldn't have bothered."

I exhaled and leaned against the wall, waiting to see whether she'd hang up on me. I could just make out the sound of her breathing on the other end of the line.

"How *is* Ruthie?" my mom asked, after deciding she'd punished me with her silence for long enough. "It's been so long since I've seen her, I've forgotten what she looks like."

"I've never kept you from FaceTiming Ruthie, Mom. You just need to tell me a time that works for you and we'll schedule it."

She made a *hmm* noise in the back of her throat, as though she wanted to disagree with me but thought better of it.

We talked for a few minutes longer, setting up a day for her call with Ruthie, exchanging banal pleasantries. By the time we finally said goodbye, the pressure of keeping things nice, of trying so hard not to be bated by her passive-aggressive comments, was making blood pump hard and hot in my ears.

After we hung up, I closed my eyes and pinched the bridge of my nose, closing in on myself.

Every time I spoke to my mother, some small part of me thought that maybe *this* time she'd be different. Maybe she'd ask about Jacob or my job or what I'd done over the weekend. Maybe she'd tell me a story, something funny she'd heard, something that made her think about me. It wasn't an intentional thought; it was ancient and mysterious, an undertow dragging me into the depths of hope whether I wanted to go or not. Always, I started our conversations thinking *maybe,* and always, I ended them like this: drained and depressed, reminded that our relationship would never be any different from what it had always been.

My dad left us when I was still little and started a whole new life unencumbered by the wife and six-year-old daughter he'd never been particularly fond of. I could still remember the way Mom cried when the divorce papers showed up, great, gasping sobs that reverberated through the walls of our small apartment. Like she couldn't catch her breath. Like she was drowning on dry land. I fell asleep to that sound more nights than I can remember. Even now, when I hear someone crying, it plucks at some nerve deep inside me and causes me to freeze like a deer alerted to a predator.

If only he'd just stayed gone. Plenty of people grew up without their dads. I could have done it. But he showed up again ten years after he first left, rang our apartment doorbell completely out of the blue. "Is this Thea?" he'd said, when I answered. "It's your dad."

He had a soft southern accent, just enough to make his words nice and lazy. I hadn't known that about him. A moment of silence passed between us. And when I said nothing, too shocked to form words, he'd added, "Wild, huh?"

Mom let him come up, and he stayed with us for a few months. He wasn't a bad guy. He was nice to me, and Mom was so much more present the months that he was there. She'd be home for dinner most nights and the three of us would cook and eat together. It was good. I was almost used to having him around when he left again.

It happened again a few years later, and again a few years after that, until it became a pattern. Dear old Dad would suddenly drop back into our lives, act like he'd been there all along, buy me candy and playing cards, get Mom to dust off the old bottle of Jim Beam that no one else touched, eat dinner around our tiny kitchen table for a few weeks, and then disappear just as quickly, leaving Mom to cry herself to sleep in her room.

It was so hard not to compare her to Maria. Maria's husband disappeared, too, but she didn't completely fall apart. She did what she had to do. She took care of her kids. She showed up. I don't think I could ever forgive my mother for not doing the same for me.

I didn't figure out why my dad kept coming back until I was a sophomore in college. Money, of course. Every time Dad swooped into our lives, he swooped back out with a couple grand.

I begged Mom to stop letting him in, stop giving him money. And, when begging didn't work, I threatened. Didn't matter. Her allegiance was to him, always. She'd give him whatever he wanted if it meant he'd pretend he loved her for a few more days.

About five years ago, I realized I would need to take over her finances if she was ever going to have a chance of retiring. I hired someone to consolidate her retirement accounts, put her on a budget, a savings plan, and Jacob and I scrimped to make sure she had a little cushion in case of an emergency. For a little while, at least, it looked like things might be okay.

And then Dad came back and gave her some bullshit about medical bills from what I could tell, trying to cobble the story together after the fact. It might have even been true—how the hell would I know? I'd been in the middle of my own shit, taking care of a brand-new baby and my own health problems, struggling through work. When I finally logged onto her bank account again, I saw that the motherfucker had taken every last cent we'd spent the last five years saving.

I didn't tell Jacob. I knew what he'd say. It was the same thing I'd said myself, again and again, every time Mom gave Dad more of what she'd earned. Just stop giving him money! Cut him off! Enough is enough.

I saw this quote online once. *When you no longer need your parents, you treat them the way they treated you when you were little.* I think it was supposed to help millennials justify cutting their parents off, but I didn't think it was true. Because I could have let my mom waste away in the same awful apartment where I was raised. I could have left her alone with nothing. I could've done the same thing to her that she'd done to me. But when it came time to do it, I just couldn't. It hurt too much. She was my mother.

Jacob always let me handle our finances. He wasn't good at keeping track of things, was even worse with numbers. He could go months without checking our joint bank account, always trusting me to tell him when we had money to spend and how much.

Which was lucky, I guess. Because if he'd bothered to check that account in the last few weeks, he'd have seen that I'd drained it. We were once again living paycheck to paycheck, which meant we wouldn't have enough to pay Ruthie's tuition until Friday, when my check hit my account. I'd screwed myself and my family over to make sure my mom was okay, just like she'd screwed me over to make sure my dad was okay.

A wave of shame rose inside of me. Jacob didn't know it yet, but he and I were completely broke. It was a little poetic if you thought about it. Like mother, like daughter.

r/AskForum

What Celebrity Conspiracy Theory Do You Fully Believe In?

SmokeyJoe98

>

[NebulaNarwhal] That Maria Capello killed her husband.

>

[Digital_Dynamo42] Oh, this is a good one...

>

[PixiePixiePixie] I've always suspected this too even though it's not true. Probably.

>

[NebulaNarwhal] What do you think happened, then?

>

[PixiePixiePixie] Dude just killed himself.

>

[NebulaNarwhal] Right and then Maria magically became famous overnight.

>

[Digitial_Dynamo42] Nah man. Damien's not really dead. Maria's keeping him locked up in her basement and making him come up with recipes for her whenever she needs to sell a new book.

>

[NebulaNarwhal] Facts. That's exactly what's happening.

>

[PixiePixiePixie] Y'all are twisted.

>

[NebulaNarwhal] Do you really think she'd be as famous and successful now if he was still around?

>

[maryoirish] Who cares about any of that. What's her secret ingredient?

>

[NebulaNarwhal] The blood of her enemies.

>

[Digitial_Dynamo42] The blood of her husband.

PART TWO
MEAT

5

THEA

I GOT IN TOUCH WITH MARIA'S PERSONAL ASSISTANT TO SET UP
my visit to the Farm. The next morning I was booking a car with
my newly reinstated corporate credit card, a Kia Soul, lipstick-red
and garish. I spent the remainder of the week moving things around
on my calendar, rescheduling meetings and making sure I didn't owe
anyone notes or a phone call, and then it was Friday afternoon and I
was on the highway, the city disappearing in my rearview mirror. It
came together that quickly.

I saw Maria's house miles before I reached it. I'd been climbing up
a steep peak, my little Kia Soul clinging to the highway as it cork-
screwed up and up and up. And then, just when I thought I couldn't
possibly drive further toward the sky, the rock wall fell away, revealing
a wide, low green valley and bubbling creek surrounded on all sides by
mountains, trees, and low-hanging clouds.

A bridge spanned the distance between the mountain my little car
had been crawling up and an even taller peak opposite. Another highway zigzagged up the side of that mountain, the gray road visible here
and there through thick trees. I allowed my gaze to travel to the near
top of the mountain, where trees gave way to a wide expanse of manicured lawn.

Standing in the middle of that lawn was the Capello farmhouse. It was alien, foreboding, all glass and steel, a series of interconnected cubes, their sharp lines and angles juxtaposed against the organic, free-flowing shapes of the surrounding trees. It looked nothing like other Catskills houses I'd seen: friendly, hundred-year-old Victorians with creaking floors and windows that never stayed closed. I'd once read an interview where Maria explained that she'd lived in the farmhouse since the 1980s but had it renovated in the 2010s. Now, it was modern, fortress-like. Beautiful—of course it was beautiful. But there was something. Staring at it, I was reminded of AI-rendered images, how they always felt vaguely otherworldly, even if they were perfect. Maybe *because* they were perfect. Maria's house didn't seem like a place you could step inside. It was a trick of the eyes. A glitch in the Matrix. It didn't belong.

The road wound through trees, switching back on itself and then winding around again, on and on until finally the trees opened and a circular driveway appeared like a mirage.

A man appeared and I slowed the car to a stop. He was tall, thin, and had the kind of face where you could easily picture the skull beneath his skin. Sharp cheekbones and firm jaw, sunken eyes.

"Thea Woods," he said when I rolled down my window. "May I take your keys?"

I handed him my keys and climbed out of the car, ancient canvas overnight bag in tow. As he drove my car off, I turned to face the farmhouse.

I had never before had the experience of feeling so completely out of place, but I felt it now, acutely. Everything about me, from my worn Converse sneakers to my ill-fitting skinny jeans and army jacket, felt too cheap for this house, these woods, this driveway, these oversized wooden doors.

The house was perfect. The doors were easily nine feet tall, made of heavy wood and painted a color that was definitely black but also something else. Purple or blue or gray. The walkway was brick, but the bricks all looked artfully tumbled and whitewashed. Not old, but intentionally and expensively weathered, and they'd been set in a complicated mosaic pattern that must've taken the bricklayer ages to complete. Massive, artfully trimmed hedges lined the drive, shaped into undulating curves that seemed to suggest some animal's body without actually looking like any animal that I'd ever seen.

I swallowed and shifted my grip on my overnight bag. Stalling. It was as though these details were pointing accusing fingers at me, sneering haughtily. *Why me?*

The question beat in my head like a drum, *why, why, why?*

I wasn't stupid; the obvious reason she had for choosing me was that she could smell my desperation like a pheromone and planned to use it to her benefit. And yet I couldn't help the feeling that it couldn't *just* be that. There had to be something else, something I hadn't considered.

I took a step forward and knocked on Maria's door.

Footsteps echoed inside, high heels from the sound of it, sharp on a hardwood floor. I hadn't expected Maria Capello to answer herself, but I still felt some disappointment when the door swung open to reveal a young woman dressed all in black.

"Thea Woods?" she said in an efficient clip.

"Um, yes, that's me," I said.

The woman moved aside, waving me in. "Come in, come in," she said with a quick smile. "I'm Maria's assistant. She's expecting you."

I stepped into the house, feeling as though I were entering a chapel. The interior was all sleek lines and soaring ceilings and wide, echoing hallways, shadows creeping along the edges and around corners. Expansive windows stretched from floor to ceiling, flooding the space with an eerie, dim light.

The effect was unsettling. I turned in place, ignoring the nerves dancing in my belly. It wasn't anything like where I'd expected Maria to live. On her show, she came off as loving and warm, a little chaotic. But this space was minimalist, disquieting. A cold finger touched the base of my spine, and I had to steel my shoulders to hold back a shiver. It struck me, for the first time, that I might know the character Maria played on her show, but I didn't know the real woman at all.

"It's...bigger than I thought it would be," I said.

"Hmm? Oh, yeah, that's what everyone says." The woman's voice echoed in the vast space. "Come on; I'll take you to Maria."

I followed her down one hall and then another. The anxious feeling I'd gotten when I first stepped through the doors only intensified as I moved deeper into the space. This place was weird; there was no other way to put it. There was no homeyness to it, no warmth. It felt like a movie set, like all the walls were false. I half expected to see scaffolding and prop tables every time I turned a corner.

Then, a sound like a soft squeak and the assistant's head snapped up fast. I looked, too: it was just a door moving on its hinges.

"Sorry," she muttered, shaking out her shoulders. "The way sound travels in this place can be freaky. I keep thinking I'll get used to it."

"Is it haunted?" I joked.

She released an unamused laugh and left it, which wasn't exactly reassuring.

The house was minimally furnished, everything designer, bespoke. Chairs with too-tall backs, tables balanced on three long, skinny legs, looking like they'd topple under the weight of a single coffee mug. It didn't look like furniture. It looked like art, like modern sculpture.

At one point, I caught sight of a tiny, pale face peering out at me from around a corner at the end of the hall. A little girl, Ruthie's age, maybe a year older. She had such pale skin that I could easily see the blue of her veins around her dark eyes, and her hair was long and dark and curled like a doll's. She stared, unblinking, as we walked toward her.

"Hi there?" I said. At the sound of my voice, the girl's eyes widened and she disappeared back around the corner.

"Did you say something?" the assistant—she still hadn't told me her name—asked.

"I was just saying hi to that little girl." I gestured down the now empty hall. "But she's gone now."

"Maria's granddaughter. She probably heard the doorbell." The assistant led me into a wide, open kitchen. I'd expected the kitchen from *Dinner at the Farm*: heavy wooden cabinets and open shelves crowded with pottery, a wood-burning fireplace and colorful, hand-made tiles. But they clearly didn't film here. Maria's actual kitchen was elegant and tasteful, like the rest of her house. Black soapstone counters and open shelving showed off modern ceramic dishes and smoke-colored wineglasses with remarkably long stems, all the appliances cleverly blending with the rest of the cabinetry. A massive island took up the center of the room, flanked by tall, narrow doors that probably led to powder rooms or closets, and a hall twisted off to one side. A butler's pantry, maybe?

There was that soft squeak again, right behind us. I jerked around fast, sure I'd find someone standing there—that little girl, maybe, creeping up on us, all bare feet and tiptoes. There was nothing, not even a door swaying on its hinges this time. A shadow moved outside the windows, flickering through tree branches, and I had the precise, nerve-deep feeling of being watched.

"See what I mean about the sounds?" The assistant spoke quietly, like she didn't want to be overheard. I felt a pluck of nerve as soon as the thought entered my head. *Overheard by what?*

I swallowed. I felt the size of the house around us, the stillness, and for a moment it didn't feel like a house at all. It felt like a living thing that had swallowed us whole.

"Yeah," I murmured. My gaze lingered on a narrow wooden door with a thick padlock hanging from the latch. *Every celebrity has skeletons in their closet,* I thought.

"Can I get you coffee? A glass of water?" the assistant asked, pulling my attention away from the lock.

"Oh, uh, no," I said quickly. It felt much too late to ask her name now. "Thank you; I'm fine."

She nodded curtly, eyes flicking down to my bag. "Great. Then all that's left is for me to take your phone."

I blinked, certain I'd misheard. "Excuse me?"

The woman looked confused. "My apologies. I assumed Maria already told you. We'll need to hold on to your phone while you look at the manuscript. Just a precaution."

My throat tightened. This felt like a message, an intentional warning from Maria. *I know what you did*, I imagined her saying. *You won't pull the same crap with me.*

I was like a child who'd proven I couldn't be trusted with phone privileges. Humiliating.

I caught a quick glance at my screen as I removed my phone—two missed texts from Jacob—and felt suddenly uneasy. I didn't like being cut off from contact with my family. Ever since Ruthie was born, I'd been instantly reachable, within arm's distance of my phone at all times. I had a split second of thinking I should read Jacob's texts now, while I had the chance, but then my phone was disappearing into Maria's assistant's pocket and she was spinning on her heel, calling over one shoulder that she'd let Maria know I was here.

My shoulders drew together as I waited, nerves dancing down my spine. And then I heard footsteps behind me and turned to see Maria Capello crossing the kitchen.

She was dressed differently than she'd been in the conference room at Hanes House, in the kind of eclectic, homey outfit she always wore on *Dinner at the Farm*: brightly colored sundress, mismatched bracelets, dangly earrings.

"Thea, hello." Maria smiled with such genuine affection that it took me aback. "I just got back from the set," she explained, gesturing toward her outfit. "We shoot most weekday mornings."

"For some reason I always assumed you filmed the show here," I said.

"Oh no, not since the early aughts. After we renovated, it made sense to move the set into town. I like to have a little space between my work and home life," Maria swept me into the hall. "Come. I'll give you the tour before we get started."

The nerves I'd felt since stepping into this house changed instantly. Now, it wasn't anxiety but excitement prickling over my skin. *Maria Capello* was giving me a tour. Of her *house*. Any moment now, someone was going to snap their fingers and I would wake up.

"This is our living room." Maria gestured to a room the size of a

60

banquet hall. "You're welcome to sit here and read or work if you like, though not many people do, strangely."

"It's lovely," I said, taking note of specific details so I could relay them to Jacob later: the coffee table made from a single slice of petrified wood, the windows that took up three entire walls, making it feel as though the living room were floating in a sea of mountains and trees.

Maria pointed out music rooms and studies, a library. Countless nooks and crannies, so many hiding spots and alcoves. My footsteps echoed off the walls, the sound hollow.

"Why do you call this place a farm?" I wanted to know. "Do you keep animals here?"

"We do!" Maria seemed delighted that I'd asked, and for a moment—just a fraction of a moment, really—I forgot who she was. She seemed like any sweet older lady excited to show me around her home, much more like my mother-in-law, Gloria, than the demanding business tycoon I'd been expecting. It was disorienting, like seeing her reflection in a fun-house mirror.

"Would you like to see the animals?" Maria wanted to know, and before I could answer, she was ushering me out a side door onto a back patio.

Tufts of golden wild grass brushed against my ankles as I followed her onto the overgrown lawn. The setting sun cast long shadows across the grounds and turned the sky a deep shade of orange. Wind whispered through the trees around us, making them sway and creak as though they were alive. Listening.

"The original farmhouse was over two hundred years old when we moved in," Maria explained as we walked. "I was so sad to tear it down. My kids grew up there, after all. But we had a bad mold problem and our contractors said it would be better to build something new." She nodded to a tall stone-and-raw-wood building made up entirely of straight lines and oversized windows on the opposite side of the grounds. "That barn is the only structure that's still standing from when Damien and I lived here together. He had it built in the 1990s—had this idea that we'd see our meat through from birth to slaughter, that we'd know exactly where every cut we served at Polpette came from. The slaughterhouse attached to the barn is up to code and everything."

"And you keep animals in the barn?"

Maria nodded. "Chickens and goats, horses, a few pigs. They're all very sweet."

The barn was hazy, dark, its floors brick, unfinished wooden beams crisscrossing the ceiling. There wasn't enough light to fill the space. The corners of the room were so entirely in shadow that it seemed possible they weren't actually there. It made me think of a photograph with the corners ripped away, a freaky thought that I immediately pushed to the back of my mind.

Two oversized metal fans hung from the highest point, whirring at a shocking speed. I flinched when I stepped beneath them, unnerved by the strength of the breeze. They were like airplane propellers. But they did their job. Only the faintest scent of animal and sweat and manure lingered.

Pens lined either side of the space. I saw black-and-white cows and russet-colored horses, a tangle of fat pigs grunting and rustling. Maria and I walked down the center aisle, our shadows strolling ahead of us, the propellers of those massive metal fans slicing into them every few seconds, giving me the sense that I was being cut in half again and again. Animals trudged right up to their gates to peer out at us. Snorting. Wanting food.

I heard another strange creak, just like back in the house. But this time, when I stopped and squinted into the shadows, something dark loomed up. I stopped short and released a surprised, "Oh!"

Unfazed, Maria said, "Ava, darling? Is that you?"

A figure separated from the shadows at the end of the aisle—the little girl I'd seen back in the house. She'd been lying on her side on the brick floor, wearing only a thin Little Mermaid nightgown and fuzzy Ugg slippers, even though it couldn't be warmer than fifty degrees outside. At the sound of Maria's voice, she lifted her head.

"I'm just feeding the piggies, Grandma." Her voice was very high and sweet, like a little girl from a Disney movie.

"Thea, this is my granddaughter, Ava," Maria said. "She likes to sneak out of her bed and come out here to sleep by the animals." To Ava, she added, faux-stern, "No matter how many times we tell her not to."

"It's very nice to meet you," Ava told me.

"It's very nice to meet you, too," I said, shaking off my unease. Now that I could see her more clearly, I was sure Ava couldn't be more than a few months older than Ruthie. But, where Ruthie hid behind my leg when she met new people and spoke in halting half sentences, Ava was polite and friendly.

I cleared my throat. "Who are your friends?" I asked. Inside the pen lay a large mama pig, her teats exposed while a dozen or so tiny baby pigs scrambled over themselves to get to her. Pink pigs and black-and-white pigs and little brown pigs. The mama pig's teats were raw and bloody from so many mouths, her eyes clouded with exhaustion and pain. She didn't move but simply lay there, present-ing her body for feeding.

Now that I was closer, I could smell her, could smell all of them, industrial-sized fans be damned. It was an earthy, musky odor, cut through with the tang of manure. The unmistakable scent of farm. My nose wrinkled.

"That's Dumpling. She's the mama pig, and these are all her babies," Ava explained.

"Do you want to hold one?" Maria unlatched the door to the pen and scooped up a tiny, wriggling black-and-white piglet.

"That one's Oreo," Ava said, scrambling to her feet as Maria placed the piglet into my arms. "She's the friendliest."

I released a little gasp of breath, instantly delighted. Oreo was downy soft with liquid black eyes expressive as a toddler's. I laughed out loud as she snorted into my face and neck.

The mama pig began to moan in the pen below. It was a low keen-ing, more cry than grunt. I caught a whiff of sweat and something else, something metallic, and my arms stiffened around the little pig. I was suddenly overcome with the specific unsettled feeling I always got when I was a guest in someone else's house: that I was in the way, at risk of knocking over something expensive or accidentally leaving dirt smudges on a white rug. It made me want to make my body as small as possible to lessen the chances that I might ruin something.

But the longer I sat with the feeling, the more I realized it wasn't the only thing bothering me. It was this space, these people. There was something off.

Maybe it was Ava. The little girl stared up at me, looking like a doll come to life. It was unnerving me.

"I think she likes you," Ava said. I smiled, the unsettled feeling spreading. Children weren't supposed to be so articulate. Children were shy, hiding behind their mothers. I looked around. Where *was* this child's mother?

"Ava would know—she keeps tabs on all the animals in our farm," Maria explained. She leaned over to scratch the pig behind her ears. I stopped looking for Ava's mother and shook out my shoulders, trying to calm myself.

This is nice, I told myself. *You're with Maria Capello, getting a tour of her home. It's a dream come true. Calm down.*

The pep talk helped, some. The setting sun had painted Maria's skin gold, blurring her wrinkles, softening the gray in her hair. She looked just like the woman on the cover of the cookbook I'd held on to since the nineties. Like she hadn't aged a day.

The mama pig was still making that moaning sound, though. I glanced back at her lying on the ground, baby pigs crawling over themselves to gnaw at her. The smell, too, was growing. It turned my stomach. The unsettled, anxious feeling grew stronger.

It's because I don't know what I'm doing here, I thought, doing my best to block the moaning out. I knew, instantly, that I was right. A woman like Maria didn't make decisions lightly. All it took was one glance at her house, at every perfect detail, to see that she was not someone who overlooked anything. Which meant that I was chosen for a very specific purpose. It didn't matter that this project was a dream come true, that a million other editors would kill to stand where I was currently standing. This uneasy feeling wasn't going to go away until I knew for sure why I'd been brought here.

I licked my lips, trying out versions of the question in my head before saying, "Cassandra mentioned that you'd specifically asked for me to be your editor on this project."

Maria didn't look at me but kept her attention on the pig. She let the silence stretch for a beat, just long enough that I started to feel nervous, wondering if it'd been inappropriate of me to bring that up. And then she said, almost casually, "Did she?"

"May I ask why? Out of all the editors—"

Maria made a soft noise under her breath, *hmm*, and lifted Oreo out of my arms. "I didn't go to any other editors, dear. Hanes House was the only publisher I submitted the book to. *You* were the only editor I considered working with."

My mouth went dry. For a moment, I forgot all about being careful with my wording. "Why would you do that?"

Maria was quiet for a long moment. I stared at the top of her head as she knelt toward her granddaughter, feeling a bit like I was having an out-of-body experience, like I was watching the three of us from above.

Finally, she said, "*Blue Body.*"

I blinked. *Blue Body* had been the last book I'd worked on before taking maternity leave. It was a memoir about cancer, death, and love, written by a relatively unknown young author. It hadn't become a huge commercial success, but it was still the book I was most proud of, quiet and moving and real. She could've found my name in the acknowledgments.

"*Blue Body?*" I repeated, frowning. "I'm sorry, I still don't understand. You read it?"

"I did." Maria turned back to me, the corner of her mouth twitching upward. The mama pig was moaning louder now; it was all I could hear. Maria seemed not to notice. The overhead fan's propellers flashed above us, casting her face in shadow and light, shadow and light. I was reminded of the iconic dramatic masks: smiling Thalia, the muse of comedy, and sobbing Melpomene, the muse of tragedy. Even though I knew, logically, that Maria's expression wasn't changing, the shadows made it seem as though it were going from dark and sad to bright and smiling over and over again.

"My dear, you mentioned you were a fan of mine," Maria said. Light and dark, light and dark. "Did it ever occur to you that I might be a fan of yours as well?"

....

"And this is your room," Maria told me a few minutes later, sweeping open a door.

The room was lit only by the light from the hall behind me. The shadowy outline of a king-sized four-poster bed dominated the space, heaped with linens and pillows, the top beams only emphasizing how high the ceiling soared above it. Blackout shades covered the windows, leaving the rest of the room in an almost suffocating darkness.

For a moment, I remained rooted in the doorway, attempting to take in the room's sheer size and opulence.

And then something moved in the far corner, shadows stirring like water.

"Oh!" I blurted, one hand coming up over my mouth. There was someone else here.

"Issie?" Maria frowned, moving past me. "Is that you?"

Issie. It was short for Isabella Capello, I knew. Like anyone who'd watched *Dinner at the Farm*, I remembered Issie as a chestnut-haired preteen in floor-skimming farm dresses running around the kitchen in bare feet, braids unraveling over her shoulders. I'd grown up with her, remembered her transformation from gangly limbs and adolescent acne to the beautiful young woman who shied away from the camera.

"Sorry, Mom." Issie spoke in a low, scratchy voice, like she'd just woken up from a nap. "I didn't realize you were going to use this room."

I didn't register the dull droning sound until it switched off, leaving my ears ringing in the sudden silence. I searched the shadows for the source of the noise, caught the outline of what looked like a breast pump on the table next to Issie's chair.

"Oh!" I said. Issie had been pumping when we'd interrupted her. "I'm so sorry. I didn't—"

"Don't worry about it." Issie laughed, but the sound was grating, fingernails on sandpaper. She removed her breast from the pump. In the dim light, I saw cracked, reddened nipples and instantly thought of the mama pig we'd just left in the barn. I looked away, out of respect.

"Why aren't you doing that in your own room, dear?" Maria asked.

"Ava's sleeping," Issie said. "I was looking for someplace where she wouldn't hear the motor."

"Ava was out in the barn visiting the pigs again," Maria said.

Issie groaned. "I keep telling her not to go outside without me. Sorry again. I really didn't think anyone would come in here." She put her breast back into her shirt and finished packing up her pump. Then, smiling apologetically, she slipped past us.

I caught a brief glimpse of her face before she turned down the hall. This Issie was much different from the version I'd remembered. She'd…aged, was the nicest way to put it. The golden-brown hair she'd had as a teenager had darkened in the years since she'd last appeared on the show. It was dirt brown now, straight and thin. She'd lost the childish fullness she'd had in her face. Now, I could see the hollows beneath her cheekbones, the sockets around her eyes. She looked like she'd stopped taking care of herself a while ago, like she hadn't slept in days, which I suppose made sense for a breastfeeding mom. When she smiled, I saw that her teeth were perfect, like her mother's. A gleaming row of white.

They had to be fake. No one's teeth looked like that naturally.

"See you at dinner," she called as she walked down the hall. She didn't bother turning back around but only lifted a hand to wave over one shoulder.

"How old is her baby?" I asked Maria.

Maria was still watching the place where Issie had disappeared, even though Issie was no longer there. "Ava is four."

I had to bite my lip to keep from reacting. *Ava?* Issie was still breast-feeding that adorable, precocious preschooler I'd seen in the barn? I had friends who'd breastfed until their children were two. But Ava would be able to walk up to her mother and ask for it, using a full sentence and proper grammar.

I must've done a poor job keeping the shock from my face because Maria turned to me, registered it. "Issie can be particular about nutri-tion," she explained. "There are some substances that can only be found in a mother's body." She blinked, seeming to come back to her-self. "I'll leave you to freshen up, take a nap, whatever you like. Will you join us for dinner in two hours?"

"Of course," I said. And then, because I couldn't let her leave with-out asking about it, "About your book… I'd like to start reading as soon as possible. When do you think you could get me the copy of the manuscript?"

This morning before I'd left, Cassandra had again reminded me how important it was to get the draft in as soon as possible. I was worried Maria would take this moment to tell me she didn't actually have a full manuscript ready, that I would have to make do with a few chapters until she found the time to write the rest. Nerves pulled the muscles along my spine together. That would mess up our entire timeline. I'd have to call Cassandra and tell her I'd failed before I even got started.

But Maria said, "I'll have it brought over now," and left me to my room with a small wave.

After she'd gone, I pulled out my computer, planning to FaceTime Jacob and Ruthie and touch base with Cassandra, but the grayed-out Wi-Fi icon in the corner of the screen instantly altered my plans. I hadn't thought to ask Maria for the password. I felt another pang at the knowledge that my family would be unable to reach me.

I opened my email inbox and quickly scanned the messages that had come in before I lost service. Cassandra had gotten approval to share the news about Maria's book internally with a few departments that needed to get started ahead of manuscript delivery. I had emails from the art department, wanting to know what I was thinking in terms of covers and asking me for comps, as well as some messages from marketing and publicity asking about potential plans. *(Do you think Maria will be willing to do events? Would* People *be a good option for the cover reveal?)* The production team wanted my thoughts on a schedule. *(Is Friday too early for a draft of the manuscript?)*

Before I'd started working in publishing, I'd imagined authors as geniuses scribbling away in their offices, handing in polished masterpieces to eagerly awaiting editors. The reality was that books were the products of dozens of people's hard work. They came together over hundreds of emails and thousands of seemingly tiny decisions, each pivotal to the final product. By the end, it could be hard to see the magic through the tracked changes on a Word document, the comment bubbles pointing out an unnecessary comma or the wrong use of the word *fewer*. The process was so much more collaborative than people realized.

As I scanned the messages in my inbox, I saw an unread message from Cassandra. I clicked: *We really need a draft by Friday to make this schedule work. Let me know if that sounds doable as soon as you see the manuscript.*

A lump formed in my throat. Friday was less than a week away. In order to make that tight of a deadline, I was going to have to work nonstop all weekend, then trust Maria to spend every minute of next week editing. I had no idea whether that was possible.

I stood, shaking the tension from my shoulders. I didn't have time to waste. I needed to find someone with the Wi-Fi password—Maria's assistant, perhaps. But before I could even cross the room, there was the sound of footsteps in the hall, and then something shot out from below my door: a thin stack of paper. I crouched and picked it up.

Maria's book. *The Secret Ingredient.*

"Shit," I said out loud, flipping through the pages. There wasn't a lot here. A chapter, at most. Was she portioning the book out? Only giving me one chapter at a time? Why would she do that?

This was going to take forever.

I opened my bedroom door, hoping to catch whoever had delivered the pages before they slipped away. But the hall outside my room was already empty.

I stared down the empty hall for a moment longer, my pulse beating in my temple. *Had they dropped the pages and run? Why?*

Shaking my head, I closed the door, thinking I'd take the pages to the little sitting area. I scanned Maria's words as I walked.

The air around me seemed to shimmer as I caught bits and phrases: *forget everything you think you know* and *no one knows the whole story*. I could feel my heartbeat fluttering in the base of my throat. This time it wasn't nerves; it was excitement.

Practically holding my breath, I began to read.

THE SECRET INGREDIENT

CHAPTER ONE

Before you begin this book, I must ask you to forget everything you've already read about me and my husband.

Believe me, I know what a large request that is, how difficult it might seem to wipe away the stories that have circulated for the last thirty years. It's difficult for me, too. Every so often I'll find myself ruminating on some fiction I'd heard or read, doubting my own memories, wondering if I'd gotten some detail wrong along the way. But you must trust me on this. The only way for this to work is for you to forget everything. *This* account is the whole story, the only story. The truth, finally.

Conventional wisdom says we must begin at the beginning. This story could only begin with my Damien, our restaurant, our life together, our children. I've heard it said that all stories are love stories and that is certainly true here. Damien's and my story is, above all else, a love story.

I first met my beloved husband at La Villetta, a mediocre Italian restaurant in Midtown that catered to theatergoers and tourists. Damien was the sous-chef there. There have been so many stories over the years, so many people questioning where I learned to cook, but I've always loved food. The sous-chef position was the job I'd originally applied and been rejected for. I supposed I couldn't blame the owner for giving it to Damien rather than me. Damien had been trained at the Culinary Institute of America. He knew the proper ways to make a sauce and skim fat, and he knew a load of impressive vocabulary.

I, meanwhile, was entirely home-taught. My mother spent my childhood showing me how to make golden custard tarts dusted in snowy powdered sugar, octopus and potatoes in pools of olive oil, succulent, fatty cuts of black pork slow-cooked to perfection. I was never ambitious in my life, except in cooking. I never wanted to go to college or become famous. I wanted to roll the flakiest pie crust, perfect the braise on my pork shank, come up with new and different ways to fry a mushroom. When my mother got sick and could no longer work, it seemed only right that I would support us both by finding work in a restaurant. My one talent.

Alas, it was much harder than I'd imagined. Several months after I failed to get the sous-chef position, La Villetta called and offered me a different job—as a hostess. It was somewhat insulting, but I'd been searching for work as a cook for months by then with no luck. This was a job and we needed the money badly. And so I took it.

I tell you all this so you understand that I was destined to hate Damien when we first met. He'd gotten the job I'd wanted, yes, but there was more to it than that. I'd heard stories about Damien Capello before I ever saw his face. They started during my orientation, the training hostess giggling as she told me how Damien ruthlessly hit on the female staff, how he would certainly try to get me to go out with him, that a night with the attractive young sous-chef was quickly becoming a rite of passage at La Villetta. Perhaps it was because of these stories, but I was determined to be the woman who would not succumb to this man's charms. I promised myself I would loathe him, that I would be the one he couldn't get. And then I saw him.

I had always thought myself far too sensible to believe in something as silly as love at first sight. I'm embarrassed now by how wrong I was. What else could I call what I felt for Damien in those moments, if not love?

I first laid eyes on him at a restaurant-wide staff meeting. I was seated near the front of the room because the manager was planning to introduce me to the rest of the staff after going over the new additions to the menu. Damien showed up late. I still remember hearing a door open and close near the back of the restaurant while the manager droned on about Alfredo and how the sound distracted him, making him stumble over his explanation of the dish. I'd turned in my chair, squinting to see all the way to the back of the house. And there he was.

Damien was disheveled, his white chef's coat unbuttoned, hair mussed and unruly, dark-blond curls hanging over his forehead. He had a sharp jaw and chin, and even in the darkness of the restaurant, I could see that his eyes were clear and blue as pool water. He had stooped down to whisper something to a woman seated near the back, but almost as though he could feel me looking at him, his eyes flicked up. And met mine.

The feeling I got when Damien first looked into my eyes was like the sizzle of two wires touching. In that moment, every other person in the room faded away, and it was just the two of us. He stared at me, unblinking, and the corner of his mouth curled into a little smile, like a question mark. *Who are you?* Even now, I remember how my face blazed with heat, how I was certain I'd turned bright red. I couldn't breathe. I couldn't look away. I had never felt like that before. In those brief moments of looking at Damien, I could see my entire future. I saw us dancing and making love, I saw him kneeling with a ring, children with his blue eyes and my dark hair cooking side by side in a kitchen full of pots and pans, him lifting a wooden spoon to my mouth so I could taste the sauce that he'd made, his wrinkled hand holding mine. A whole lifetime.

And then the moment passed. Damien looked away, and the world rushed back in. The meeting continued. The manager introduced me and I stood at the front of the room, shy and blushing, trying not to stare at the man I'd sworn to myself I'd hate on sight, the man I was already in love with.

I remember waiting impatiently for the meeting to be over, sure that Damien would find me after. Whatever I'd felt, I knew he felt it, too. I was like a little kid waiting for Christmas morning, except that this was so much bigger than that. I wasn't just waiting for a gift. I was waiting for the love of my life; I was waiting for the rest of my life to begin. I was so anxious I could hardly think.

But Damien didn't speak to me that night. Not that night, or the night after, or the one after that. Despite everyone's warnings about what a flirt he was, how he was certain to hit on me, Damien did not say one word to me for three months.

Of course, *I* could have spoken to *him*. I'm not such a wilting violet that I wouldn't approach a man first. But I can be stubborn when I want to be. And I knew I hadn't imagined what had passed between us. If Damien wasn't going to introduce himself, there was no way I would give him the satisfaction of speaking first. And so, when he ignored me, I ignored him right back. It became something of a game, the two of us pretending the other didn't exist, talking around each other, never speaking to the other directly, never making eye contact.

Then, one night, the restaurant was extremely busy. There was a line out the door, angry patrons yelling at me, demanding to be seated immediately. I knew Damien wasn't faring any better. There were always two chefs in back at the same time, but I'd heard one of the waitresses mention that he was alone that night, covering for the second chef, who'd gone home with some stomach bug. Despite myself, I'd felt a little bad for him.

I remember exactly how he looked when he stormed out from the back of the kitchen. He was incredibly sexy: his face red, blond curls messy, sweaty. I'd stared at him, imagining how it might feel to run my hands through those curls, taste the sweat on his lips.

He scanned the dining room, clearly looking for someone, and I felt a jolt of surprise and delight when his eyes landed on me.

"You," he'd called, pointing. "It's Maria?"

He'd never asked me my name, but I wasn't surprised that he knew it. "Yes," I'd said.

"You cook, right?"

I nodded, and it was nearly impossible to hide my delight. I'd never told Damien I could cook, but several members of the waitstaff knew. It could only mean that he'd been asking about me.

I don't remember who I found to cover my post, but I'll never forget the excitement that rose in my chest as I followed Damien back into the kitchen. I acted as his sous-chef for the rest of the night, chopping and sautéing and stirring. It was the most erotic night of my life, cooking next to Damien. We hardly spoke a word to each other. I made the occasional suggestion—the oil's going to burn, or the sauce needs more oregano—and whatever it was, Damien would nod in agreement and fix it without comment. But the whole time, the air between us was charged. Once, our hands brushed while I reached for a pot holder and he jerked away, almost like he'd been burned.

After the restaurant closed for the night, I handed Damien my apron, assuming we'd go back to our little game of pretending the other didn't exist. Instead, he touched my waist, the first time he'd ever intentionally touched me.

"There's an Italian spot downtown that I've been wanting to try," he'd said, his hand moving to my lower back, drawing me close. I felt his touch like a trail of fire down my spine. "Come with me."

Of course, I said yes.

The name of the restaurant where we had our first date is lost to me now. It was tucked away in the back alleys of the city, an unremarkable-looking spot serving the best agnolotti I'd ever tasted. I remember that the lights were low, and it was loud enough that we'd had to lean in close in order to dissect every element of each dish, talking about what had worked and what hadn't, arguing passionately whenever we disagreed.

I'd loved arguing with Damien. I loved so much about him. The stubble on his cheeks, the fullness of his lips, the way he closed his eyes and moaned in the back of his throat when he liked the way something tasted. I remembered wondering what it might be like to touch those lips. To feel the coarseness of his cheeks against mine. To make him moan.

"So, Damien," I said, as we shared a rich, flourless chocolate cake with raspberry compote. I held eye contact with him, hoping to make him nervous as I lifted another bite of chocolate and raspberry to my mouth. "What took you so long? I've been waiting for you to ask me out for three months."

Damien held my gaze, and he didn't so much as blink as he said, "I wasn't ready for you."

I'd lifted an eyebrow. It had sounded like a line, but it didn't matter. I was already so in love with him. I'd wanted so badly to believe it was true. "Is that right?"

Damien put his own fork down and leaned across the table, placing his hand over mine. Electric shocks burned through me the moment his palm touched my knuckles. It was almost like I was on fire. Damien's voice was deep and gravelly as he said, "The moment I saw you, I knew you were going to be the last woman I would ever be with. I wasn't ready for that yet."

I'd swallowed, somehow managing to say, "And now?"

"And now I am."

It was a line. I wasn't so foolish back then that I didn't know that. But I have to admit, it was a very, very good one.

LOVE AT FIRST SIGHT AGNOLOTTI

INGREDIENTS

2 honeynut squash, or half of a small butternut squash
1 egg
1 small bunch thyme sprigs
Olive oil
½ cup finely grated Parmesan Reggiano, plus 1 tablespoon
    shaved Parmesan Reggiano, for garnish
⅓ cup mascarpone cream
Salt and black pepper to taste
Nutmeg (optional)
¾ pounds yellow pasta dough (see note)
1 stick butter
1 tablespoon balsamic glaze

STEPS

Serves 8 to 10

1. Preheat your oven to 325°F. Cut the squash in half and scoop out the seeds and pulp with a spoon. Beat the egg and set aside. Rinse and dry the thyme sprigs.

2. Rub the cut sides of the squash lightly with olive oil, and then spread the thyme sprigs on a 9" x 13" sheet pan. Place the squash cut side down on the thyme sprigs and slide into the upper third of your preheated oven. Roast for 35 minutes or more, depending on the thickness of your squash, until the flesh offers no resistance when pierced with a paring knife. Remove from the oven and let cool.

3. Discard the thyme and pick off any leaves stuck to the squash. Remove the squash from its skin using a large spoon and transfer to a mixing bowl. You should have about 1 cup. If there is more or less, scale the other ingredients to match. Stir in the Parmesan Reggiano, mascarpone cream, and egg. Season with salt, pepper, and optional nutmeg. Mix very well until

homogeneous and free of lumps, then transfer into a piping bag.

4. Cut off one-eighth of the pasta dough at a time, leaving the rest tightly covered while you work. Roll the piece of dough into a long strip, using a pasta machine. Place the sheet on your work surface and carefully pipe a half-inch line of filling lengthwise down the strip close to one edge. Roll the sheet over the filling to form a tube on one side of the sheet, leaving a border of an inch or more on the other side. Run your fingers along the length of the tube, pushing out any air pockets to prevent bursting during cooking. Press to seal the dough all around the tube of filling, and then pinch into three-quarter-inch lengths to form individual pillows. Trim the border of the sheet lengthwise so that the edge extends a half-inch away from the pillows.

5. Using the same cutter, separate the agnolotti from each other, cutting along the seams that have been pinched shut, toward the half-inch border to form the characteristic pocket of the agnolotti. Transfer to a floured sheet pan and store in the freezer until ready to cook. Repeat with the remaining dough and filling until all the filling is used up.

6. Gently brown the butter in a frying pan for about 8 to 12 minutes, then turn off the heat.

7. Bring a large pot of salted water to a boil and drop in the agnolotti. Work in batches of no more than 12 at a time to avoid them sticking together, stirring gently with a wooden spoon. Simmer until the agnolotti float to the surface, about 3 to 5 minutes. Remove with a spider or a slotted spoon, transferring directly into the brown butter with a splash of the pasta cooking water. Repeat with the remaining agnolotti until they are all cooked.

8. Turn the heat on low to reheat the agnolotti and butter, tossing gently to coat, then transfer onto warmed plates, drizzling with the balsamic glaze. Garnish with thyme sprigs and shaved Parmesan Reggiano.

- It is best to flash freeze your agnolotti. Doing so will allow you to do the time-consuming part ahead, and what you don't use can be stored in air-tight bags for up to two months.
- Yellow pasta dough has a higher ratio of yolks to whole eggs and includes some olive oil. This will make your dough more pliable and reduce the likelihood that the agnolotti will crack in the freezer. To prepare enough dough for this recipe, use 1 cup all-purpose flour, 5 egg yolks, 1 tablespoon olive oil, and a tablespoon of water if the dough is too dry.

6

THEA

THAT WAS ALL THERE WAS.

I never made it back to the sofa on the other side of the room but had instead sunk to the floor cross-legged, unable to stop reading for a moment. I leaned back against the bedroom wall once I'd finished, pages falling onto my lap as I tried to gather my thoughts.

The drive up here had given me plenty of time to worry about this book. I'd worried that Maria wouldn't be able to write, that we'd need to hire a ghostwriter to smooth out her prose. I'd worried she'd want to focus on the kind of banal anecdotes that usually preceded her recipes, that I'd have to find some manipulative way to coax a real story out of her.

But her prose was beautiful. It didn't sound anything like the Maria Capello I'd grown up with. The woman in this chapter was raw, young, *sexy*. It was strange to read about her and Damien being drawn to each other that way, like discovering condoms in your parents' bedroom. Maria wasn't supposed to be sexual. She was supposed to make agnolotti.

And yet there was something about her story, something that made me desperate to keep reading.

Anticipation buzzed in my belly. If the rest of her pages were this polished, having a draft of the manuscript to share by the end of next week might not be impossible.

I brought the pages to my bed and read through them again, more slowly this time, making notes in my laptop as I went. She was too vague about her past. She'd mentioned growing up in Queens with her mother, but there was no mention of whether she had other family nearby, or what had happened to her father. I dug a half-dried-out red pen from the bottom of my tote bag and circled the section, scrawled a question mark beside it. People were going to want to know more about her family, her history. Her.

And then there was the section where she met Damien. I tapped my pen against my lip as I read it again. This had been my main concern since accepting this project. Damien's disappearance, his suicide, what happened to him: *that* was the hook. The book would sell no matter what; Maria's name was big enough that we could count on that. Damien's story would make the difference between a bestseller and the kind of runaway hit that might actually salvage my mangled career.

But in thirty years, Maria had never *once* spoken—or written—a word about that night. What if she planned to write about her entire history with Damien and just leave that part out?

I needed to convince her to tell that story. But how?

I turned this problem over in my head for a few minutes. Finally, I wrote: *You're making a promise to the reader by opening the book with this story. If you begin your memoir with how Damien came into your life, your reader will expect you to end it with how he left.*

It wasn't a good enough argument to convince her to do anything she wasn't already planning to do, but I had to be careful here. If I pushed too hard too soon, I could piss her off. I thought of the editor she'd had reassigned, the one who'd basically disappeared after his project with her fell apart. Nerves danced down my back.

I glanced at the time at the corner of my screen. I was going to be late for dinner. I'd have to come back to this again after.

I stowed the manuscript and pen on my dresser and changed into my never-fail New York uniform: black jeans and a black shirt, paired with the one fashionable purchase I'd made this year, a pair of chunky black loafers that, I reasoned, made the rest of my outfit seem on trend, even if the jeans were too tight.

I immediately forgot everything Maria had told me about the layout of the house. Hallways seemed to twist around and dump back onto each other, stairways skipped certain floors and let out onto others that I felt certain I wasn't supposed to be wandering around. I would follow the sound of voices, only to reach a dead end. My skin crept. It was as though the house itself were keeping me from everyone else inside of it.

I was just retracing my steps, trying to make my way back to my room and start over completely, when I walked past a doorway almost by accident and found a dining room and inside of it—thank God—people.

I stepped into the room. "Hello?"

Four heads turned toward me. It was as though they had intention-ally seated themselves in a tableau of domestic perfection: Issie was beside Ava, carefully tucking a bib into the collar of her nightgown. Across from them, an attractive man in his early forties was lean-ing back in his chair, smiling like he was mid-joke. He was a young Damien Capello brought back to life, with the same clear blue eyes and firm jaw, the same smile. The only difference I noticed was that he was clean-shaven, his dark-blond hair slicked away from his face and neatly combed, like he was a politician.

As I approached the table, the man rose halfway from his seat and offered me his hand. "Enzo," he said, smiling wide. "Capello. I'm Maria's son."

My eyes lingered on his canines. They were a touch too long and sharp, utterly at odds with the rest of his perfect teeth.

His smile widened and he added, "It's okay. Despite the rumors, we don't actually bite."

I blushed. "Sorry," I murmured, stepping forward to shake his hand. "I'm Thea Woods. It's nice to meet you." I remembered Enzo from the show, just as I remembered Issie. He'd been a golden-haired child with large, dimpled cheeks and a mischievous grin.

It was surreal to be eating dinner with them both, like meeting characters from a favorite storybook. I'd envied them and I'd imagined myself as one of them, in equal measure. Once, around second grade, I'd told another little girl that I had a brother and sister. I'd even named them Enzo and Issie, apparently unworried that she might recognize the names. Of course, I immediately realized that I would never be able to keep up the lie, and the next time she mentioned them, I gaslit the crap out of her, insisting she had me confused with someone else. But I always remembered them. My imaginary siblings.

Now, they were seated in front of me. I didn't realize I was still staring until Enzo broke out in a nervous laugh.

"Oh God," I said, pulling my eyes away. "I'm so sorry. You just look so much like your dad."

"I get that a lot," he said. "Issie tells me you two have already met. And this is Amy Ryan," Enzo added as he affectionately wrapped an arm around the young woman sitting beside him. "My girlfriend."

The word *girlfriend* surprised me, but I tried not to show it. I'd have assumed Enzo would go for a Caroline Bessette-Kennedy type, the kind of flawlessly elegant woman who made the rest of us feel like slobs because of our frizzy hair and wrinkled shirts. But Amy looked normal, familiar even. She was young—late twenties, maybe—and she wore a rumpled men's oxford, hair swept up in a messy ponytail. Her lipstick was bright red, a little smudged, and she had thick, black glasses pushed up the bridge of her nose. A tiny diamond stud winked from her left nostril.

"You're an editor, right?" Enzo cast an adoring look at Amy. "Amy works in media, too."

"Is that right?" I asked, turning to her. That was likely why she looked familiar. I'd probably run into her at a party at some point. "Are you in publishing?"

Amy flashed a polite smile. "No, I'm a freelance digital marketing consultant. I work with the occasional author, but mostly it's small businesses and influencers."

I froze in the process of pulling my chair from the table, a sudden connection forming in my brain, the spark of two wires touching, so real I could swear the smell of burned metal filled my nose.

Oh God.

I knew why I recognized this woman.

I remembered the party that nearly ruined my career, the glass of wine I didn't even finish before the room started dipping and swaying, how I'd told a young social media manager every horrible thing I'd heard about Kincaid Hughes. *I have screenshots of the DMs and explicit photos he sent some young girl on my phone,* I'd said. *I can't show them to you but they're disgusting.*

I remembered the next moment as clearly as if it'd just happened: the alarm I'd set to remind myself to pump had gone off. I'd unlocked my phone to switch the alarm off, but I'd been holding too much—my wine, my phone, the oversized tote I'd used to cart my breast pump with me to the event. I was flustered, a little tipsy, mad at myself for drinking the half a glass of wine, which meant I was going to have to dump whatever I'd pumped anyway. And then my breasts had started leaking, two humiliating wet spots appearing on my shirt.

The young woman had been so helpful, taking my phone and wine from me, quickly ushering me into the bathroom to clean myself up.

That woman was Amy Ryan. She was the social media manager I'd warned about Hughes, the only person I'd told about Hughes, in fact. She'd known about the screenshots on my phone, and she'd even had access to them while I was in the bathroom. Hell, I'd *unlocked* the damn thing before handing it to her.

It wasn't until the video went up that I realized what had happened: Amy must've been curious about these alleged DMs. Who wouldn't have been? She'd looked through my phone while I was in the bathroom, and when she'd seen just how bad they were, I'm guessing she experienced some version of the same moral dilemma that I did: *How was she supposed to work with such a monster? Wasn't it her duty to warn other women about him?*

I think she forwarded herself the screenshots and then sent them to HushHush, along with an audio recording she'd taken of me spilling the whole story. As outraged as I was—and believe me, I was pretty outraged—I couldn't exactly blame her. Was it really so different from what I'd done?

I forced myself to murmur, "Nice to meet you," as I glanced around the table. All of a sudden, I felt paranoid, jumpy. How was this woman *here*? How was she Enzo's girlfriend? It was just too random and weird to be a coincidence. Did she remember me? Did she realize that she'd nearly destroyed my career?

Before I could work out what to say next, Maria swept through the door at the far end of the room, holding a tray of food. "Thea! I'm so glad to have you joining us. Please, please, take a seat."

She'd changed for dinner, too. Her hair had been pulled into an elegant chignon, and she wore a sleek black shift dress, a white silk scarf knotted around her neck.

"Thank you," I murmured, my eyes moving to the tray. The food smelled incredible. Tomato sauce and garlic and something else, something meaty. My mouth filled with saliva.

Maria placed the tray on the table. It was braciole, the steaks pounded thin, rolled with breadcrumbs and herbs, slow-cooked in tomato sauce until the meat was falling apart. I'd attempted to make the recipe before, but mine always turned out dry, the meat too tough, too thick. The braciole sitting on the tray looked perfect, tender and juicy, the breadcrumbs flecked with tiny pieces of parsley and garlic, the smell so thick in the air that I could practically see it.

Almost without realizing what I was doing, I slid into a seat at the table. I was about to eat a meal prepared by Maria Capello. *The* Maria Capello. How many people in the world got to say that?

"So, Thea," Enzo said. His entire body shifted to face mine, as though I were the most interesting person in the room, as though he couldn't wait to hear all about how fascinating my life was. The corner of his eye crinkled mischievously as he said, "You're the one Mom's spilling all our family secrets to?"

"I… What?" I nearly choked on the words.

"I thought we weren't allowed to talk about the book," Issie said. Her voice was pleasant, but there was an edge to her words, as though she was still bitter about whatever conversation they'd had about me before I'd arrived. She leaned over to cut Ava's food into smaller pieces. The four-year-old, meanwhile, stared at me from beneath her mother's arm. In the dim light of the dining room, she looked even paler than she had before, and her skin had an almost yellowish tint to it, though that might have been the dim overhead lighting. The blue veins around her eyes made them look bruised.

Enzo's smile tightened at the corners. He rubbed his jaw and the smile relaxed again. "I'm just asking Thea about her job."

Issie said, "Her job editing Mom's *book*. Which none of us want her to write."

"Issie," Maria said, her voice sharp.

Issie flinched and dropped her eyes to her plate, chastened. I felt heat rise up the back of my neck, like I was the one who'd just been scolded.

For her part, Amy looked bewildered and ever so slightly shocked by the turn the dinner conversation was taking. "You're writing a book?" she asked, looking at Maria. My shoulders clenched.

But Maria seemed unconcerned. "I am, yes," she said, smiling. "But it hasn't been announced yet, dear, so I'd appreciate—"

Amy mimed zipping her lips shut. "I won't say a word," she promised. Then, glancing at me, she added, "Congratulations to you both."

"Thank you," I murmured. But I was thrown. Maria had made such a big deal about keeping the book secret. Would she make Amy sign an NDA, too?

A horrible thought occurred to me. Amy could send HushHush an anonymous tip about the book. If she did, there was no way to prove it hadn't come from me.

Someone stopped beside me (A waiter? I wondered. In a private residence?) and offered to fill my glass with wine, which I gratefully accepted. Enzo began talking animatedly about a book that had been popular back in 2009, asking if I'd read it. (I had.) Meanwhile, more food was brought to the table: heaping plates of pasta, thick fettuccine noodles and oversized shells, all of it clearly handmade, bowls of Sunday gravy surrounding roasting meat like a thick red moat, carrots and celery, broccoli rabe with its sharp, bitter flavor, a loaf of focaccia glistening with olive oil. Ava didn't cry or sing or climb around on her chair, like Ruthie did whenever we ate dinner with her, but politely ate her pasta and sipped her water like a tiny adult. The smell of garlic and meat hung heavy in the air.

I lifted a forkful of pasta to my mouth and bit into the long, thick slabs of al dente noodles, tasted creamy béchamel, sausage seasoned with the sharp bite of anise. I closed my eyes, holding back a moan. The flavors were a time machine. For a moment I forgot my concerns, instantly transported to a Christmas dinner years ago, when I'd attempted this exact recipe. Mom had never made a big deal about holidays, but *Dinner at the Farm* had aired a Christmas special that year, and I'd been completely enamored with the decorations and the food, with Maria herself and the way the family all seemed to pitch in, everyone happy to help create this one perfect meal. I'd wanted to climb into the television set and join them at the table. I could vividly remember hunching in front of our tiny oven, ingredients exploded across the kitchen, heat wafting around me as I pulled the door open and took my creation out. It had been so good, one of the best things I'd ever cooked. And yet it was nothing—*nothing*—like this. This was transcendent. It tasted like family, like the best Christmas you'd ever had, like love.

"What do you think?" Maria asked, watching me expectantly. She actually seemed like she wanted to know, like she cared what I thought.

"It's unbelievable," I said. I took another bite, unable to stop myself. "I follow the exact same recipes but I can never get my food to taste this good," I admitted. I was thinking about the little blue tin she kept in her set kitchen, the "secret ingredient" she sprinkled over every one of her dishes, I added, "Must be your secret ingredient."

Maria smiled. "Every family has a secret ingredient," she said with a wink. Despite myself, I felt a little thrill of excitement and disbelief. It was *exactly* what she always said on her show. How many times had I imagined she might say the same words to me? My heart was so full that it hurt.

"I don't know how you all eat like this all the time," Amy said. She'd filled her plate with vegetables, covered them with tomato sauce, and now she was pushing them around with her fork. "It's so heavy."

On the other side of the table, Issie had stopped in the middle of refilling Ava's water and said, "Enzo? Be a doll and pass the bread?"

Enzo turned to grab her the basket, and I used the opportunity to shift my attention back to Amy. I would be uneasy until I figured out what she was doing here. But did I pretend I didn't recognize her? Did I mention the party?

"Digital marketing is an interesting job, Amy," I said eventually, opting for ignorance. "What kind of clients do you work with?" My face felt hot as I said the words. I studied her, trying to figure out if she remembered me.

But Amy seemed clueless as she put a piece of bread into her mouth, sipped her wine. "It's boring, really. I mostly consult with small-business owners who don't know how to leverage their social media accounts. Recently I've had a few calls with women trying to break into the TikTok tradwife scene, which is a little depressing."

From the corner of my eye, I noticed Issie turn toward us, still holding a fork with a bit of Ava's meat speared on the end. She said, "Why depressing?"

Amy wrinkled her nose. "I don't know. These poor women have been duped into giving up their own lives so they can cosplay as these 'traditional' mothers. You don't think that's depressing?"

Issie's voice was steel. "What's depressing about motherhood?"

I looked at my plate and said nothing. Let them argue. It was my secret shame that I followed a few of the more well-known tradwives online. I'd always been in awe of the kind of women who could transform motherhood into something beautiful and romantic. Flowy dresses fluttering in the wind while you hung laundry out to dry and canning peaches and making bread from scratch while a toddler in a white dress and unbrushed hair watched in delight. The way I always imagined motherhood should be.

After dinner, Maria served us all thimble-sized servings of an Italian digestif that I didn't catch the name of, something so bitter it burned going down my throat.

But even after the drink, I could still taste that meal. Salt and acid. The tiniest hint of sweetness from the tomato sauce. And something else, some indescribable, incredible taste that I couldn't quite pinpoint.

Her secret ingredient, maybe. Whatever it was.

....

I got the Wi-Fi password from Issie before leaving the dinner table and messaged Jacob from my laptop, letting him know I'd gotten in okay and that I'd be without my phone for a few days, so he should email if he needed to get a hold of me. He didn't respond, but that didn't surprise me. It was already past eleven, and Jacob was an early riser. He usually fell asleep on the couch while I tried to get him to watch just one more episode of *The Sopranos*, which we'd decided to make our way through for the first time this year. Without me there to keep him up, he'd probably gone to bed at nine thirty. I felt a little disappointed that I hadn't been able to wish Ruthie goodnight.

Cassandra had messaged and emailed several versions of *Do you have an update???* She would be annoyed that I'd kept her waiting. I felt a hit of nerves as I opened a new email and stared at the cursor flashing in the blank white box for a moment, trying to think of what to say, whether I should mention that Amy Ryan was here or that Maria told me she'd found me because of *Blue Bodies*, if I should say anything about the single chapter I'd managed to read so far.

But when I'd finally gathered my thoughts and started typing, the Wi-Fi icon in the corner of my laptop screen blinked out again.

I frowned and clicked on it, then retyped the password Issie had given me after dinner. It was easy enough to remember: *P0lp3tt3*, the *o* replaced with a zero, the *e*'s with two 3's. I was sure I had it right. But it didn't work. I tried to connect two more times before I accepted that someone had changed it.

I listened for a moment, trying to hear footsteps or voices, any sign that someone else was still awake in this house. There was only the thin, high rattle of wind at the window. The sound unnerved me, and I couldn't figure out why.

Then, I realized: it reminded me of crying.

....

I awoke hours later. It was pitch-black in my room, the middle of the night. I knew without looking at a clock that it was between two and three in the morning. I'd had terrible insomnia since Ruthie was born and always woke up at least once, between two and three.

I clenched my eyes shut and tried to get myself to fall back to sleep through sheer force of will.

Didn't work. It never did.

Finally, I rolled over and switched on my bedside lamp. The dim lights painted the dark room dusty gold and made it even more apparent how big it was, shadows gathering in the corners and the darkness above my bed. It was as though the room had grown while I'd slept, gotten taller, wider, expanded, like it was in the middle of taking a deep breath.

I pulled my tote bag off my bedside table and fished out the water bottle and Ziploc baggie of Benadryl that I'd packed for this very reason. Once I'd swallowed the pill, I closed my eyes, again, collapsing back against my pillow.

I'd just started to drift when a voice spoke right outside my door. "Terrified of Maria..."

The voice was muffled. I couldn't tell who it was. A woman, I thought, but I wasn't sure. Whoever it was, she was trying to keep her voice low, probably didn't want to draw anyone's attention. It had the opposite effect on me. I was instantly awake, aware of the cold pillow against my cheek, the late-night air tickling the back of my neck. I shifted positions, turning to face the door.

"I need something more damning," the voice said. "Something that will make her talk." Then, a second later, a deep sigh, "I'm not the one who used the word 'blackmail' but…"

The voice drifted close and then away again, like someone moving quickly down the hall outside my door. Even with the Benadryl starting to kick in, my mind wouldn't shut up. What was someone doing out in the hall at two o'clock in the morning? Were they on the phone? The thought sent an instant shot of shame through me. Apparently, I was the only one who couldn't be trusted to keep my phone.

Who were they blackmailing? What was going *on*?

I climbed out of bed, floorboards cold beneath my feet. I didn't realize what I was doing until I'd pushed my door open and stepped out into the hall.

All the lights were out. The house was silent, not even the creak of floorboards or the moan of a heater kicking on.

I stayed in my doorway for several more moments. Motionless and alert. Listening.

Eventually, I heard footsteps, another door opening and closing, and silence.

....

Maria was already in the kitchen by the time I made my way upstairs the next morning. I smelled coffee brewing and there was something sizzling on the stovetop. *Sausages.*

"Thea, good morning," Maria said. She had her back to me, turning the sausages so each side browned evenly, but she looked over her shoulder and smiled as I walked in. Her hair looked freshly washed and dried, and she was already dressed for the day in loose-fitting khakis and a bright-green sweater. She must've been awake for hours. "Did you sleep well?"

"I did, thank you."

Maria nodded at the coffee carafe. "Would you like some coffee, dear?"

A flush rose in my cheeks at the word *dear*. Such a familiar term, like I was already part of the family. I told her I would, and Maria got a mug down from the cupboard. It was misshapen and painted in bright primary colors, handmade. As I took it from her, I thought of the little pinch pot Ruthie had made at school just a few weeks ago, a hunk of clay painted in swirls of bright blue, barely recognizable as a pot but more precious to me than any of the expensive ceramics Jacob and I had collected from farmers' markets and specialty shops over the years. For a moment, I missed my daughter so much I couldn't breathe.

"Would it be possible to get my phone back so I can call my family?" I asked, sliding into a seat at the table. "I tried using the Wi-Fi last night, but I think someone might've changed the password. I couldn't get my computer to connect."

"I'm sorry, dear. I should've warned you. We turned the Wi-Fi off overnight." Maria said this as if it were a perfectly normal thing to do. It took me a moment to process.

"You turned the Wi-Fi off?" I repeated. "Why?"

"Just a precaution. We have so many new people in the house this weekend."

She spoke kindly enough, but I still felt a sinking in my gut. She didn't want another slip, like what had happened with Hughes.

I thought of the voice I'd heard in the middle of the night. Someone had been talking on a phone, creeping around the halls, talking about blackmail.

I glanced at Maria, wondering if I should tell her. But I didn't know who I'd overheard or what they'd been talking about. They'd called her by her first name, which made me think it must've been Amy. But there had been other people in this house yesterday. Did Maria's assistant stay overnight? Did Issie sometimes refer to her mother by her first name?

"Of course, I understand," I said instead, offering a smile. "I'd like to call my family to let them know I got in safely, though. And Cassandra wants an update, just to make sure we'll be able to keep everything on schedule."

"There's a landline right there. You're welcome to use it anytime you like."

Maria sat at the kitchen table, watching me with those shrewd eyes. It took me a second to understand that she wanted me to use the phone now. In front of her. Where she could overhear absolutely everything I said.

Nerves danced between my shoulder blades, pulling them together. *Prickly*, I thought. Just one of the words people used to describe Maria. I'd been imagining someone who shouted and threatened when they didn't get their way. This was different. She was being so perfectly pleasant that I couldn't quite make myself tell her she was being unreasonable.

I smiled nervously and walked over to the phone. It wasn't like I had another choice. I had to call Jacob and let him know I was okay.

I removed the phone from its wall mount, took a second to recall my husband's number. It had been so long since I'd had to actually dial it.

"Hello?" he answered. He sounded exhausted, like he hadn't slept for a week.

I frowned and turned to face the wall. "Hey, it's me."

"Thea? Finally...didn't you see all my texts?"

"Sorry, I haven't had service." I heard Ruthie saying something in the background on Jacob's end of the line, just one word over and over, though her little-kid voice was high-pitched, making it hard for me to understand what it was. "Kitty," maybe? "What's wrong? Is everything okay?"

"She's sick."

My chest clenched. I heard Ruthie's voice again. She wasn't saying *kitty* anymore, but *mommy*. It sounded like she was crying.

I was suddenly desperate to see her, wished I could reach through the phone to grab her, hug her, smell her sweaty hair, tell her I hoped she'd feel better soon.

"How sick?" I asked.

"Fever," Jacob explained. "It broke last night, thank God, but she really doesn't feel good. She won't sleep but somehow has all this energy. It's... God, I'm just so fucking exhausted. I didn't sleep at all last night. When are you coming back?"

"I was planning on staying through tomorrow." *At least*, I thought, thinking of the one chapter I'd managed to read so far. I had no idea how long it would take Maria to dole out an entire book.

There was a pause, and then Jacob said, "I don't think that's going to work, Thea. She never wants me when she's sick. She keeps asking for you."

I tensed, feeling a slow surge of anger. *When was the last time I went out of town?* I wanted to ask. But I could feel Maria sitting at the table behind me, listening to every word, so I swallowed it down. "This is important," I said instead. "Maybe you could take her up to your mom's?" Jacob's mom and stepdad lived upstate, too, just a few hours north of the city. It would be an annoyingly long trip with a sick toddler. But it was doable if he was desperate.

"Yeah..." Jacob sighed. "I mean, I definitely need the help. It's been a really hard couple of days."

I could feel something in the back of my throat, guilt bubbling up like acid. But it hadn't been a couple of days. It had been *one* day. Not even a full day. Ever since Ruthie was born, I'd given every weekend to my family, even as Jacob flew off to cover stories, to attend bachelor parties, to have a life of his own. I'd lain awake with her at night when she felt sick and didn't want to sleep, and I'd been with her the next day, even when I was so tired I could barely open my eyes, managing to stay upright only because I'd made my way through an entire pot of coffee. This was the only time in her entire life that I hadn't been there. And he expected me to drop everything and come back.

I felt suddenly claustrophobic, as though *I* had been the one in that small apartment back in Brooklyn, overtired, with a sick child to entertain for the next twelve hours. I looked down and saw that my hands were clenched.

I loved my daughter more than anything. I adored our family. But I didn't know how to be *everything* to them all the time.

I cleared my throat. Maria was waiting. I couldn't have this argument right now. "I have to go."

Jacob made a frustrated noise in the back of his throat. "Hey, there's something else. My debit card was declined yesterday. Do you know anything about that?"

Shit. "No, I don't," I lied. "Listen, I don't know when I'll have cell service again, so just...call this number if she gets any worse?"

"Thea, wait, don't—"

"Bye. I'll try to get in touch again soon." And I hung up the phone before he could say another word, my heart beating in my throat.

"Everything all right?" Maria asked from behind me.

I turned and offered up a faint smile. "My daughter's sick."

Maria's face fell. "Oh, no. I'm so sorry."

"She'll be okay—her fever already broke—but it sounds like my husband had a tricky night with her."

"I completely understand," Maria said. "It's so hard when they're little."

I felt a fresh hit of guilt, remembering how I'd watched Issie standing next to her mother at the stove on *Dinner at the Farm*, long, brown braids dangling down her back like two thick ropes. Maria hadn't left her kids behind for her job. She'd taken them with her, made them part of her life.

I cleared my throat. "I have no idea how you did it on your own. Issie and Enzo used to film with you, didn't they?"

Maria nodded. "They did. But they hated it, would have rather been out with their friends."

This surprised me. I used to be so jealous of Issie, so desperate to trade places with her. "Really?"

"Oh, yes," Maria said. "We didn't have much choice about it, though. I didn't have a lot of family around after Damien died. I had to decide between doing what they wanted and what I knew was best for all of us."

I frowned. That didn't quite match the image I'd always had of Maria as the perfect mother. But here, at least, was a way to transition our conversation into talking about the book. I thought of the thin stack of pages I had in my tote bag, the notes I'd already taken on my laptop. *If you begin your memoir with how Damien came into your life, your reader will expect you to end it with how he left.*

But the last time someone had pushed Maria to talk about her husband's disappearance, she'd gotten up in the middle of a live interview and walked away. I had to be careful here.

I swallowed and slid into a seat at the table. "I've already finished what you've given me so far, the story of how you and Damien met. The writing is beautiful, truly."

Maria pulled the coffeepot off its burner and filled my cup. "Thank you."

"I read pretty quickly. If you give me the rest of the book now, I could probably finish before dinner tonight."

"I'm sure you could." Maria leaned forward and placed a hand over mine, smiling softly. "But you have to understand, this is a difficult story for me to tell."

"Right, of course." I swallowed, considering how to put this. "That's why I think it would be better for me to read it all at once. If I'm going to help you shape the narrative, it's important for me to know how you intend to end it."

I was being so careful and yet I could see, instantly, that it had been the wrong thing to say. Maria's expression, which had until that moment been open and kind, shifted. A muscle in her jaw clenched and her lips pressed firmly together.

"I'm not interested in *shaping* anything," she said in a voice that was different from the one she'd used only seconds ago. She pulled her hand away from mine. "I just want to tell what happened. There are details in these pages that I've never spoken about publicly."

I felt my heart beating in my throat, every pulse whispering *shit, shit, shit.*

But, at the same time, what she'd just said seemed to echo in my skull. *There are details in these pages that I've never spoken about publicly.*

She is going to do it, I thought. She was really going to write about the night Damien disappeared. What else could she be referring to?

"I—I apologize," I said quickly. I had to fix this. "I shouldn't have used those words. That was insensitive of me."

Maria didn't say anything, but the muscle in her jaw relaxed. She blinked a few times.

"I can work with whatever schedule is best for you," I tried again. "Really. We'll do this however you want."

"It's just that I would feel more comfortable if we were able to touch base regularly as you read," Maria explained. Sunlight filtered through the curtains, casting a glow over the kitchen and her warm, weathered face. "Damien's and my story might be the most important one I ever tell. I was no one before I met him."

I frowned. "I'm sure that's not true."

"I'm not trying to be self-deprecating. I'm just saying that if I hadn't met Damien, I doubt I would have made much of myself." Then, as if catching herself, she added, "I was just another first-generation daughter of an immigrant, living in Queens. I doubt I would have become a household name."

I swallowed. It was a small opening, a way to steer this conversation back to the pages and away from my embarrassing gaff. "What about your parents? You don't write much about them. You mention your mother a little, but your father…"

"Left before I was born," Maria finished for me.

I swallowed. "Mine too. Or, he didn't leave before I was born, but he left."

Maria seemed interested in this. "How old were you?"

"Six."

She shook her head. "A whole person."

Something clenched inside of me, the same muscle that always clenched whenever anyone brought up my father. I'd managed to go most of my life without thinking about him, but things changed after I had Ruthie. Getting to know her, seeing her little personality emerge… I just didn't get it. My father had six whole years with me. How could anyone spend six years with a child and just leave them behind? It was unfathomable.

And then to come back, again and again. To take and take and take…

I felt something form in my throat, some emotion, and I worked hard to choke it back down, to appear calm and collected.

Maria was studying me. I wondered if she saw it.

"It's so strange to me how men can do that," she said after a moment. "How they can leave children behind like it's nothing."

"Women do it, too," I pointed out, half-heartedly.

Maria shrugged. "I suppose. But not on the same level, not in the same numbers. If a mother leaves her children, it's a tragedy. If a man does it…" Her shoulder jerked up and down again. "It's no big deal. Sometimes, it's expected. Are you in contact with your father at all?"

"No," I said quickly. But I wanted her to trust me, didn't I? At least enough to tell me all these "details she'd never spoken about publicly," whatever they were. And what better way to get her to trust me than to show that I was willing to trust her?

And there was something else, too. An echo of the feeling I had whenever I spoke with my mother, an almost primal desire to connect. I cleared my throat and added, "I mean, not regularly. He pops in and out of my mom's life occasionally."

Maria made a nose in her throat, a kind of *hmm* sound. "That poor woman," she murmured.

I looked up, surprised. "You mean my mother?"

"It must be hard for her, having him come and go," Maria said. "There's so much sacrifice in motherhood. She probably felt so alone."

I rolled my bottom lip between my teeth, nodding. But the thing was, my mother had never actually sacrificed anything for me. That was our problem.

Maria was studying me, her eyes moving across my face, seeming to take all this in. After a moment, she stood, as if making a sudden decision. She slid a narrow, red folder from behind a fruit bowl on the kitchen counter, and turning back to me, she asked, "Do you have the pages you've already finished with you?"

"Oh, yes." I took the pages out of my tote and handed them to her. Maria removed another slim stack of pages, which she placed on the table between us.

THE SECRET INGREDIENT, Chapter Two, I read from beneath her hands, half the letters blocked by heavily ringed fingers. I lifted my eyes to hers and found her watching me. She didn't seem motherly just now. Her eyes were hungry and unblinking, seeing everything. Seeing far more than I'd meant to share, I worried.

A prickle of unease went through the air. I felt vaguely tricked. It was almost like this conversation had been a test, like she'd been trying to get something from me before trusting me with more of her story.

A pound of flesh. My painful past in exchange for hers.

THE SECRET INGREDIENT

....

CHAPTER TWO

I can't tell you whether Damien and I started talking about getting married or becoming business partners first. We fell in love with each other at the same time that we fell in love with each other's food. Damien wanted a restaurant where he could do the kind of cooking he loved, the kind of cooking he'd grown up with. And by that point, all of his dreams were my dreams as well. I wanted to help him in any way that I could.

Our wedding was small, just his family and mine, a little church, a tasteful reception in the yard out back. We didn't even go on a honeymoon. I happily traded a weekend at some cloying bed-and-breakfast upstate for a few days holed up with my new husband in his apartment, enjoying each other, repeating the words *husband* and *wife* until they lost all meaning. Besides, we were saving all our money for our restaurant.

We would never be able to afford a place in the city. But I'd heard of a few restaurants that had luck setting up shop in the Catskills. Woodstock appealed to us because of the community. I even had a close cousin who lived locally: Hank Casey, a butcher, like my mother. There was a small farm stand selling fresh fruits and vegetables on the same street as his shop, as well as a fishmonger and a bakery. I remember how giddy Damien was as we first walked down the block.

"We'll source everything locally," he told me. "Everything fresh."

But money was an issue. Of all the places we'd visited, Woodstock was by far the most expensive. And the little spot we'd been hoping to lease hadn't been used as a restaurant previously, which meant extensive renovations. There were other up-front costs we would need to come up with as well: money to hire staff and buy food and furnish the place.

"How will we afford it?" I wanted to know. Neither of us had family money. And though we'd manage to stow away some savings, that felt meager in light of all we would need.

And yet, whenever I broached the subject with Damien, he would wrap his arms around me and kiss me on the back of the neck, in that spot that always made me swoon.

"I'm talking to some people," he would tell me. "I've got everything under control. There's no need for you to worry."

I wasn't used to being left out of important financial decisions. I'd been in charge of the finances back home, spending hours every week hunched over my mother's checkbook, making sure our meager funds were always balanced. But Damien was so good at taking care of me. He always knew a guy; no matter the problem, he had the number of someone who could help out. It made me feel so safe knowing that whatever the problem was, he would handle it.

When the oven I'd had my eye on was exorbitantly expensive, far outside our budget, he told me not to worry, that he had someone who could help. And then, not even a week later, I'd find that same oven in our kitchen, still wrapped in plastic. If I stressed that we'd never find a cheese supplier that fit our exacting standards, Damien would call someone up, and the next morning we'd have a delivery of the freshest mozzarella I'd ever seen. There was always money when we needed it, just enough to cover whatever we had to buy, never a penny to spare. I was so in awe of him, my husband, who was going to make our dreams happen through sheer force of will, even when they felt impossible.

I wonder now if I wasn't just a little naive, if I'd been so blinded by love that I'd willfully ignored signs that, in hindsight, seem so obvious. As far as I know, Damien's immediate family never had ties to organized crime, but there were always people on the periphery. An uncle with a pager no one had the number to and a Rolex that looked real, a second cousin who'd spent time in prison, friends who didn't like to talk about their jobs, who subtly changed the subject if you asked. Damien liked to use cash whenever possible, liked to do things under the table, tried to avoid any kind of paper trail.

But he was so confident, so sure. It had been easy to ignore those things, to trust him. And, to be fair, I had other things on my mind. There were vendors to find, furniture and kitchenware to source, the entire business of opening a restaurant. In some ways, that time was the happiest of my life. Damien and I would spend our days building our dream and our nights wrapped in each other's arms, falling asleep after making love in the dilapidated farmhouse we bought a few miles from town, the one we were going to fix up someday after the restaurant had become a monumental success.

In other ways, that time was difficult, one stressor after another. Meat, in particular, was a problem. Damien wanted to raise livestock and butcher it himself. It was part of his vision for Polpette, a true farm-to-table restaurant in every sense. But I'd grown up with people who understood meat, and my family were all strong believers in eating every part of any animal that had been killed. It was already going to be incredibly difficult to live by this creed while running a restaurant—and the challenge of raising the meat ourselves would have made the undertaking nearly impossible. And so I introduced Damien to my cousin, Hank.

Hank's mother was my mother's sister, though Hank's family had elected to Americanize their name. (Hank's real name was Humberto Castiglione, so you can understand why Hank Casey was preferable, considering the way things still were back then.) He was a bear of a man. He wore a white apron that was nearly always splattered with blood, and he often seemed to forget he was holding a cleaver when he went from butchering an animal to speaking with his customers.

He and his wife owned a farm nearby, and they sourced all their meat from there. Hank shared our family's deep respect for the animals he butchered. Nothing went to waste: bones were used for soup stock and marrow, fat was rendered into lard and made into soap, hides were skinned and tanned. Hank believed that every part of an animal has earned the right to be used. He was the only butcher I considered working with. His shop was an old-world, traditional place that reminded me of where my mom used to work when I was a child back in Astoria. I was certain it would be perfect for us as a source of meat.

Damien, on the other hand, was not so easily swayed. He made a big show of kneeling down to look over Hank's selection: tomahawk steaks as thick as my arm, slabs of bacon, pastrami, and smoked, bone-in ham.

Hank, meanwhile, glowered at Damien, holding that bloody cleaver like an extension of his hand.

"I don't know," Damien had said in an offhand way. He rapped his fingers on the top of the glass counter, wrinkling his nose in distaste. "I worry you won't have the quality we were hoping for."

Hank grunted again. "What are you looking for?" he wanted to know.

Damien chose a cut at random. "Pork shoulder."

Without another word, Hank disappeared into the back room.

When he returned, he held a slab of raw pork lying in a pool of blood. Its pale-pink flesh was mottled with streaks of white fat and veined with bluish tendrils of cartilage and sinew. It looked fresh.

"What do you think of this quality?" Hank asked. Damien shrugged, but I could tell he was impressed.

I had just turned back to Hank and was preparing to open the conversation on sourcing his meat for our restaurant, when a voice called out from the back room. "Hank? Do we still need this chicken quartered?"

A woman walked into the main shop—a young, strikingly beautiful woman with long, brown hair framing high cheekbones and expressive green eyes. She wore bangles on her wrists that jingled when she grabbed one of her husband's knives from the back wall, her movements precise and graceful.

"Oh," she'd said, starting when she saw us. "I'm so sorry. I didn't realize my husband was with a customer. I'm Nina."

I hadn't met Nina before, though I'd known Hank was married. She held out a hand to me, bracelets dangling. I started to reach for it, but Damien got there first.

"Damien Capello," he said, smiling at her. "I'm the owner and chef of the new Italian place opening down the street."

"Oh, how lovely!" Nina had said, grinning at us. "I've walked past that space before. It'll be incredible to have a new restaurant in town."

I waited for Damien to introduce me, but he seemed to have forgotten I was there. The man I loved was looking at Nina, studying this beautiful woman with the same intensity that he'd studied the pork shoulder. And he looked…

Hungry.

Roast Pork Shoulder (for when you catch your husband looking at another woman)

This is the simplest meat recipe I know. There are only two ingredients, including salt. Why even write this recipe down? This one is about technique, but beyond that you'll be shocked at how amazing this tastes with nothing but salt. The quality of the meat you use will have a big impact, which is why it's important to get friendly with your butcher.

INGREDIENTS

1 pork shoulder roast, about 2 to 3 pounds
Kosher salt, as needed

STEPS

Serves 4 to 9

1. Remove the pork from its packaging, rinse, and pat dry. Score the pork with a very sharp knife and sprinkle the salt all over in a very generous coating. You want as much salt on the outside as you would a dry rub. This is your dry brine.

2. Place the pork on a wire rack over a tray to catch any juices and pop in the fridge for at least 8 hours, preferably overnight. If you don't have 8 hours, this step can be done to achieve a notable improvement in your roast with as little as 2 hours. Remove from the fridge and rinse to remove excess salt, then pat dry with kitchen towels.

3. Preheat your oven to 325°F on bake/roast mode.

4. Insert a meat thermometer into the pork, place in a medium roasting dish fat side up, then insert into the lower third of the oven. Roast approximately 3 hours, or more if you have a larger cut, and remove when the temperature reaches between 155° and 160°F.

5. Tent with foil and leave the thermometer in. Let rest for at least 15 minutes. You will see the temperature rise by approximately 10°F. Remove from the roasting dish, slice, and serve hot.

NOTES FOR THE HOME COOK

This recipe is intentionally vague and can be extended in a number of ways. Try the following ideas:

- After roasting, cut thick slices and sear on both sides in a cast-iron skillet with fresh herbs such as rosemary, thyme and sage. Serve with mashed potatoes or polenta.
- Cut thin slices and serve over sushi rice with soy sauce and sriracha.
- Use the leftovers to make ragout by dicing and simmering with white wine, tomato paste, and sautéed vegetables.

7

THEA

MARIA DIDN'T ASK ME TO READ THE CHAPTER IN FRONT OF HER, so I took it back to my room and devoured it in the space of about five minutes.

It ended with Maria noticing Damien noticing Nina. Reading those words, I felt the tiniest bit let down. I thought of that old Mark Twain quote "There's no such thing as a new idea." This was true. I think editors all accepted, to some degree, that every story had already been told, that all we had left were bits and pieces of old stories we could throw in a kaleidoscope, twist around, and hope something new came out the other side.

But I couldn't help it—while signing the NDAs and agreeing to Maria's over-the-top terms, I'd had a feeling like a vibration through my spine. The secrecy had me expecting something special, something rare. Not just another celebrity scandal, but something much more precious than that: a truly original story.

This was good. And, even better than good, this would *sell*. But it was also the same as a hundred celebrity memoirs I'd read before. Sex and lies and betrayal.

I shouldn't have been surprised. There'd been rumors about this kind of thing forever. Mob ties. Affairs. Vicious fights that customers overheard from the dining room of Polpette. But the anecdotes Maria included in all of her cookbooks made her life with Damien seem idyllic. People assumed something was going on behind the scenes, but if anyone ever even brought up some of the more salacious rumors in an interview, Maria would roll her eyes and say something in Italian under her breath. Even without interpreting, her meaning was clear: *These silly rumors again? How disappointing.*

I reread the pages, making notes on my laptop. I already felt like a broken record as I typed "More details!" and "Can you dig deeper here?" over and over again. But, with only five pages to work with, there wasn't much left for me to comment on.

After a few minutes, I started a new document and typed the word *THEME* at the top in all caps. Below, I wrote *Family secrets?* and *The difference between a public persona and a private one?* But after staring at the blinking cursor for a few minutes, I gave up. I needed the rest of the book. Without it, I felt like I was trying to edit with one hand tied behind my back.

I glanced at the Wi-Fi icon in the corner of my computer screen. It was grayed out again. I went to my settings to look for Maria's network, but it wasn't there. Someone had turned it off. I was without access to the outside world. Again.

I couldn't work like this. I needed to give Cassandra an update. I'm sure she was already furious with me. And if I didn't have more pages to read, I wanted to do some research online, go over the most salacious Capello family conspiracies one last time, make sure I had all my facts straight. If we were going to have a polished manuscript by Friday, I couldn't waste a moment. And I wanted to text Jacob, to see how Ruthie was feeling, if they'd decided to go to his mother's.

I slapped my laptop shut. On top of everything else, I wanted to get away from this house for a while, go to town, find somewhere to grab coffee and a pastry, stretch my legs. I slid my computer into my tote bag and made my way back up to the kitchen. No sign of Maria, but it looked like someone had started a cooking project. The stove was on and something was boiling, and Tupperware covered in home-made labels and bottles of ingredients crowded around the sink.

Ava was perched on a barstool at the counter, coloring. She wore the same Little Mermaid nightgown I'd seen her in yesterday. It was threadbare, a few of the seams ripped through, loose threads dangling around her ankles. She had her bare feet hooked on a rung of her barstool, the remnants of some glittery nail polish on her toenails.

She looked up when I walked in and smiled. "Good morning, Thea."

God, this was a polite child. "Good morning, Ava," I said. In the bright morning light, it was much more obvious that there was some sort of yellow tint to her skin. Was she jaundiced?

I looked around for Issie but didn't see her. "Is your mommy here?"

Ava nodded, head bouncing up and down like it was on a string. "She went to the bathroom. She's making skull soup."

"Skull soup?"

"We're allergic to soy, like soy in soup mixes and soups they make at restaurants, so we make all our soups ourself I'm helping." She said this like it was all one sentence, not even stopping to take a breath.

Skull soup, I thought, ever so slightly creeped out. She'd probably just messed up the name of some other soup, but still. Lucky the cannibal conspiracists weren't here for that one.

"I bet you're a big help," I said. "What are you coloring?"

If I knew anything, it was that no child could resist showing off their artwork. Ava dropped her crayon and held up her picture, grinning proudly.

I tried to keep my expression blank as I studied it. The drawing was…shocking. It was a crude scribble, similar to the pictures Ruthie brought home in her backpack every day. But where Ruthie favored blues and pinks and purples, Ava had used only red. She'd sketched a simple figure: circles for the torso and head, lines to indicate arms and legs, a frowning face.

But that wasn't the shocking part. The shocking part was the red scribbles—was that *blood?*—pooled all around the figure.

Something thick formed in my throat. Had Ava drawn a picture of someone lying on the ground bleeding?

I didn't know what to say. I blinked fast, trying not to let my horror show on my face. "Can you tell me about that, Ava?" I asked. I'd read in some parenting book that this was how you were supposed to ask kids about their artwork, that you should never assume you knew what you were looking at.

Ava nodded and pointed to the figure in the middle of the page. "This is Dumpling, the mommy pig, and this is her milk, and she's sad because the baby pigs are too rough with her when they're hungry."

Oh God. It was a drawing of the pig we'd seen, nursing her piglets. The red was *milk*, not blood. And, now that I looked closer, I could see a little scribble on top of the "pig's" head that was probably supposed to be her ears. I exhaled, relieved.

"That's beautiful, Ava," I said when I managed to find my voice again.

Ava looked up at me and beamed.

In the dim morning light, I could see every vein beneath her skin. Tiny blue lines crisscrossing the area around her eyes and down her neck. Blood pumping through her, keeping her alive.

....

It took me another two missed turns, and then I was outside.

The air was crisp and foggy. The weather had started to turn, getting that "spring" feeling. I stopped just outside the house and inhaled deeply, wanting to feel it all through my body, in my lungs.

It wasn't until I opened my eyes again that I remembered I had no idea where my car was. I'd given it to that guy when I'd gotten here, and he'd driven it off somewhere. I turned in a slow circle, scanning the area, trying to figure out where he might've taken it, half expecting the man himself to pop out of the house, drawn by my confusion.

There was no one around, no obvious place to go looking for my car. I shuffled inside my tote bag for a moment, looking for my phone before I remembered that I didn't have my phone.

"Shit," I muttered. A slow, creeping dread began to wrap around my bones, making me hug my arms close to my chest. There was no way for me to leave.

A bird arced over me, singing. Wind rustled the trees. My mind flashed to Ruthie, all those texts I'd missed letting me know she was sick. It was bad enough that I didn't have my phone, worse that I didn't even have Wi-Fi access so I could check my email, but now I was stranded at this house. What if Ruthie had gotten worse? What if Jacob had been trying to get in touch with me?

There was a sound right above me, soft, like someone sighing. I looked up quickly, but there was nothing. Even the trees were still.

I stayed looking, watching for movement. Nerves pricked along the back of my neck. I hated the feeling of being trapped. Being watched.

I was just starting to turn when a red sports car appeared at the end of the driveway. I shielded my eyes, watching the car approach. It was a little two-person convertible, red and possibly vintage, definitely expensive. It entered the circular drive too fast, gravel spitting up behind the tires, and skidded to a stop right in front of me as though that had been the plan all along. It took me a second squinting into the sunshine to recognize Enzo at the wheel.

"Thea Woods, editor. Good afternoon." He flashed a bright, white smile.

"Enzo, hi." I had no idea what to say to him. I cleared my throat. "Where's Amy?"

"Took a walk. I've been sent to town for snacks. What are you doing out here?"

"I was actually looking for my car."

"Gavin probably locked it in the garage overnight." He squinted in the sunlight. "You need a ride?" He leaned across the passenger seat and unlatched the door before I could answer.

I made no move to reach for the door. Gavin must've been the man who'd taken my keys.

"He won't be here for another hour or two," Enzo said apologetically. "C'mon, I can take you wherever you want to go." Another smile, wider than the last one. I stared at his canines for a long moment. I didn't know this guy at all. But I needed a ride to someplace with Wi-Fi and strong coffee.

"You know where I can find a coffee shop?"

"I'll drop you in Woodstock. Get in."

....

Woodstock was a twenty-minute drive. I stared out over the passenger-side door, wind in my face, in my ears.

"Do you and Issie live up here, too?" I had to shout a little.

"Issie does, but I'm down in the city. Finance," Enzo explained, raising his voice to match mine. "I come up most weekends, though. Gotta catch up with my bud, Ava."

Finance. I should have guessed. He had the vibe, the cocky confidence, the preppy haircut.

"What about Ava's dad?" I asked. Issie had mentioned solo parenting last night. "He and Issie aren't together anymore?"

"Charles died about three years back. Car accident."

"Oh, I'm so sorry."

A shadow slid over Enzo's face, gone a second later. Clearing his throat, he said, "How's Ma's book going?"

It took a moment to switch the topic in my head. "It's good. I've only read a few chapters, but so far, it's really interesting. Different from anything she's done before."

"Great. Yeah, that's really great." Enzo sounded distracted. His shoulders shifted, and he added, "You figure out why she wanted to work with you yet?"

The question caught me off guard. "What?"

"She's had editors crawling up her ass for years, begging her to write a memoir about what happened that night to Dad. She's always turned them down. Now, out of nowhere, she decides to just give the story to you. It's weird." He glanced at me, studying my reaction. "We're all pretty curious what her angle is."

I thought of what Issie had said at dinner last night, the way she'd blurted, *Which none of us want her to write.* My stomach clenched. Was it that they genuinely didn't want the story to get out? Or that they just didn't want their mom to give the story to *me*? The thought caused a blaze of heat to move through my face, a sudden rush of embarrassment. I wondered if they'd seen the Hughes video. If they knew what I did.

"I have no idea why she wants to work with me." My voice came out sounding meek, a concession.

"Shame." Enzo squinted into the sun. "Mom never lets us in on any of her plans. It's like she still thinks we're teenagers. I bet Issie fifty bucks I could figure it out before she did."

Which meant Issie would be questioning me about my résumé as well. Excellent.

Enzo slowed when we entered the town, drove us down idyllic streets past adorable storefronts and antique shops, finally pulling over next to a coffee shop called Perk Up!, which took up the bottom floor of a sprawling house with a wide, open porch.

"Meet me back here in an hour?" he asked, climbing out of the car.

"Sounds good."

As Enzo rounded a corner, I went into the bakery, considered ordering an oat milk latte, then decided on a small black coffee when I saw the prices. The café's Wi-Fi password was scrawled on a chalkboard behind the register. I found a place to sit and typed in the password, exhaling in relief when the icon on my computer screen blinked to life. I was connected to the outside world again. *Thank God.* It had only been a few hours, but it felt like longer.

I sent Jacob a quick email asking about Ruthie, letting him know that over the next few days email would be the fastest way to reach me, and then I scanned the unread messages that had been piling up in my inbox. Two more were from Cassandra (subject line for the first: *Are you dead?* Subject line for the second: *If you aren't dead, you better have an incredible reason for ignoring my emails*). I hit Respond to the latest and wrote back: *Can we hop on Zoom?*

"Woods, for fuck's sake," Cassandra greeted me a few minutes later. She looked like she was just out of the shower, no makeup, her hair damp and combed away from her face to dry.

I opened my mouth, then closed it and glanced around the coffee shop, instantly paranoid. I was the only customer, but what if the baristas knew Maria? Enzo had driven me right here. Maybe the family came into this shop all the time. Maybe they were friends with the people who owned it. I had to be careful.

"Hold on," I told Cassandra. I dug a pair of old, wired headphones out of my tote and plugged them in, then held the mic to my mouth, lowering my voice so it was barely above a whisper. "Okay, I'm back."

Cassandra was squinting into the camera, clearly confused. "Where *are* you?"

"Coffee shop. I'm really sorry I didn't call earlier. She, uh, took my phone and turned off the Wi-Fi at the house."

"You're kidding," Cassandra said. I could hear someone talking in the background of her apartment. The television. A voice that sounded remarkably like Paul Hollywood when he said, "Stodgy."

"She's incredibly paranoid."

"I suppose she has a reason to be."

I couldn't tell whether that was meant as a slight or a remark about Maria's scandal-filled past, but it was as good a segue as any. "That reminds me, uh... There's someone else here. I don't know if you remember, but I told you I spoke to a woman right before all that stuff with Kincaid Hughes went down. Her name was Amy Ryan? I was pretty sure she was the one who took the screenshots off my phone."

Cassandra blinked twice, fast, which was how I knew she remembered. "Wait, she's there?" In the background, I heard someone say something about apple tarts.

"She's dating Enzo. That's Maria's son."

Cassandra was quiet for a long time, and she must've turned *The Great British Baking Show* off, because I could no longer hear the contestants mumbling in the background. After a while, I said, "Cassandra?"

"Yeah, I'm still here," she murmured. She pinched the bridge of her nose between her fingers. "I'm just thinking. It's a weird coincidence, isn't it?"

I made a noise of agreement. "I know. But it doesn't have to change anything."

"If this Amy person sent HushHush the tip about Hughes, she might send them something about Maria," Cassandra pointed out. "She could be one of these people who get off on knowing all the dirt on celebrities." She seemed to think a moment, then added, "Or maybe they're paying her for tips."

That hadn't occurred to me, but now that Cassandra said it, I had to admit it made sense. "Whatever it is, she won't get anything from me. I'm going to let my guard down around her again."

Cassandra lifted an eyebrow: *You're sure?*

I ignored it. "And these pages… Cassandra, they're *good*. I haven't read a ton, yet, but Maria's being incredibly candid. In just ten pages, she's already opened up about the rumors that Damien was involved with organized crime, the affairs—"

"Has she agreed to write about the disappearance?"

I hesitated. "She… I don't actually know yet. She's being open, like I said, but she's still a little cagey. She won't give me the whole manuscript at once. She's sort of dispensing the chapters one at a time."

Cassandra exhaled, a sharp puff of air. She moved off-screen, and a moment later, I heard something that sounded like a door opening, the clink of glass. I pictured her standing before the bar in her Manhattan apartment, tipping a bottle of Macallan over a rocks glass. I knew better than to point out that it wasn't quite five yet.

"Okay," Cassandra said, coming back onto the screen. "I want to hear immediately if Amy says or does anything strange. Got it?"

"Do you think I should say something to Maria?"

"No." Cassandra lifted the rocks glass to her lips and took a slow drink. "Maria's already high-strung, so better not to stress her out unnecessarily. But you keep me updated. Got it? None of this bullshit about the house not having internet access. Something happens, you hitchhike into town, use the landline, send me a fucking smoke signal, okay?"

I hesitated, wondering if I should mention the phone call I overheard last night. But I still didn't know whether that had been Amy, so I just nodded. "Understood."

"And, Thea, the disappearance *is* the book. Without it..." Cassandra's voice trailed off, and she took another swallow of scotch. "You have to get her to write about it. Whatever it takes."

"Whatever it takes," I echoed.

Cassandra stared right into the camera, seemed to stare right into me. "I don't have to tell you how much is riding on this," she said. And she hung up the call without another word.

....

Now that I'd checked in with the outside world, all I wanted was to get back to the house and find another chapter from Maria waiting in my room. But I still had a few minutes before I was supposed to meet Enzo.

I should've been savoring this rare moment of freedom. I couldn't remember the last time I drank an entire cup of coffee while it was still hot. But my mind was racing.

The disappearance is the book. You have to get her to write about it.

I did a search for news articles containing Maria's name and spent the next twenty minutes scrolling. I'd seen most of it before. CNN did a look at her life in pictures. There was a shot of her and Damien standing in front of their old farmhouse in the 1980s, before it had been renovated. They both wore duck boots and field jackets, like they'd just stopped working in the garden to take the picture. Damien was smiling wide, one hand wrapped around Maria's shoulders, and she was looking up at him with such adoration on her face that, for a moment, I couldn't breathe.

The next photograph was iconic. It was the day of Damien's funeral. Maria was dressed all in black, standing on the steps of what looked like a church. Her children were pressed in to either side of her, twelve-year-old Issie and ten-year-old Enzo, nose still bandaged from his trip to the ER the night his father died, both of them looking completely shell-shocked. But Maria... Maria's face was devastating. She had her eyes closed, her mouth slack, so much pain and grief in her expression that it was hard to look at her, harder still to look away. It was as though the photographer had snapped the shot during the one moment she'd allowed herself to fall apart on the worst day of her life.

I swallowed. I couldn't imagine how painful that would be—to lose your husband, the father of your children. My eyes flicked to the comments below. A user named ChiliPop had written: Bitch obviously killed him why is she crying?

Below, someone else had added: he musta gave her indigestion.

I tasted something bitter on my tongue. People were assholes. Back in Google, I changed my search to *Maria Capello scandals*.

Thousands of results popped up. Millions. I was pretty familiar with the things people had said about Maria back in the '90s, and my eyes glazed as I scanned article after article claiming that she'd killed her husband, faked his suicide, that she'd chopped him up into tiny pieces and fed him to their children.

I went back to Google, this time doing a search for "Nina Casey." I was curious about this woman Damien might've cheated on Maria with. I wanted to see a photograph, to know what she'd looked like. But none of the pictures that came up seemed like the right Nina. They were all much too young. I tried again, this time adding Damien Capello's name in quote marks, hoping to narrow down the search. No hits.

I frowned. Wouldn't Nina have been mentioned in the articles about Damien's disappearance? I was sure I'd read that she and Hank were at the party that night. Unless she hadn't gone, for some reason.

I felt the first zip of something more, something deeper than all the other conspiracies. I tried a couple of other versions of the search, but I didn't find a single mention of anyone named Nina Casey ever having been connected with Damien and Maria Capello. I tried a few searches using Hank Casey's name, but that didn't turn up anything, either.

Maybe I just had her name wrong. Maybe she'd never been a Casey. I pulled Maria's pages out of my bag and reread how she'd introduced Nina. She was definitely Hank's wife, not his girlfriend, but I suppose it was possible that she hadn't taken his last name. However, searching "Nina and Hank Casey" still should've pulled up any article mentioning Hank Casey and someone named Nina, regardless of her last name, so that didn't explain it, either. I tried "Hank Casey wife" but that didn't turn up anything. It was almost like this person Maria had written about had never existed.

I looked up "Hank Casey" next. That got me a few hits, though not as many as I was expecting. The first was the website for Hank Casey Meats. I clicked, finding a bare-bones website, little more than a list of the store's hours and contact information and a map. There wasn't even an "about" page showing a photograph of the owner. It was almost intentionally vague, like he didn't want to put information about the store online. Maybe this was why my search for Nina hadn't turned anything up. Hank definitely seemed private.

I studied the map for a second. His store was just a block away. And I still had fifteen minutes before it was time to meet up with Enzo. I packed my things and took the rest of my coffee to go.

I doubt I'd have found Hank's if I hadn't seen the location on that map first. The sign hanging above the door was nearly impossible to read. The words were faded, like they'd been there for generations: HANK CASEY MEATS.

A bell jingled above me, announcing my arrival. Sawdust crunched beneath my shoes. Hank Casey Meats wasn't adorable and bougie in the way of the Brooklyn butcher shops Jacob and I went to, with their subway-tile walls and gleaming marble counters. It was old school. Cow legs and pig heads dangled above a stainless steel counter, eye sockets stretched out, leaving their heads strange and vacant, like masks. My stomach turned over as I looked around. I wasn't used to seeing dead animals displayed like this, the line between food and living thing so thin. My gaze landed on the rows of violent-looking machines along the back wall. Grinders and slicers. Cleavers the size of small axes, blades sharp.

I'd just wanted to get a glimpse of the place so I had a picture of it in my head while I was reading. Peek inside and then step back out onto the sidewalk and be on my way. I had no intention of talking to anyone. But the bell that announced my arrival had alerted someone in the back of the shop to my presence.

"Hold on!" called a gruff voice. There was a shuffling sound, and, seconds later a man appeared.

I thought of how Maria had described Hank in her pages. *A bear of a man.* She'd hardly done his size justice. He was massive, a mountain, much too large for this small shop. I couldn't believe he still worked here. He had to be in his seventies, with shockingly white hair and a face made of old leather. His mouth arced downward, a perpetual frown, and a mustache twitched above, hiding his top lip. He had a dead rabbit tossed over one shoulder, like a scarf.

"Afternoon," he said, with a single nod. "What can I do for you?"

For a moment, I couldn't find my voice. I was too distracted by the rabbit. The animal was shockingly limp. It was impossible to believe it had ever been alive. I had the strange sensation that it wasn't a real animal at all, but a stuffed rabbit, a toy. My eyes moved over its greasy fur, its dangling legs, then landed on the blood leaking onto Hank's apron, staining it a deep, brownish red. All at once the scent of it filled my nose, so strong that I started to cough. My stomach turned.

"Sorry," I choked, embarrassed by my reaction. I wasn't sure what to say. Hank clearly expected me to order something, and maybe I would've if it hadn't been for the rabbit, the cold reminder of what, exactly, I would be ordering.

Hypocrite, I thought, cheeks warming. I ate meat all the time. I wasn't above ordering the rabbit at a bougie restaurant back in the city. It's not like I hadn't known where the meat came from. But it was such a different experience, seeing it in animal form, something that had so recently been alive.

"I was just…" I started, my throat dry. "I mean, I…"

"Thea?"

I flinched and jerked toward the entrance. I hadn't heard the bell on the butcher shop door ring, but Enzo was standing in the doorway now, eyebrows pulled together in confusion. "I thought we were meeting back at the coffee shop?"

"You two know each other?" Hank asked before I could respond.

"Yeah… This is Thea Woods," Enzo explained. "Friend of Mom's. She's staying at the Farm for the weekend."

He left out the part about the book, I noted. I wondered if Maria had told him to keep it quiet, like she'd told me. I wondered if she had her own kids sign the same NDAs she'd sent to everyone at Hanes House.

Hank made a kind of grunt in the back of his throat. His expression didn't change as he pulled the rabbit from his shoulder and slammed it onto the cutting board in front of him. The animal's head bounced, its neck snapping once, then going still. I flinched. There was no compassion in the way he treated the dead animal. It was as though it were a thing, an object. Something that had never been alive. I was either going to be sick or burst into tears. I couldn't figure out which.

Hank must've sensed my discomfort. "This is when I butcher the animals," he explained, his voice low and cold.

"Right, of course." My cheeks flushed. What was wrong with me? I'd never been so weird around meat before.

Hank pulled a knife from the wall behind him, not the axe-like cleaver, but something with a short, sharp blade. With one deft motion, he made an incision at the base of the rabbit's neck and began to peel the fur back.

That was all I could take. I murmured, "Excuse me," under my breath and turned to face the wall.

"What can I do for you, Enzo?" I heard Hank ask behind me. Maybe it was my imagination, but his voice sounded amused.

"Mom wanted me to see if you were still planning on stopping by the house later," Enzo said.

I tuned them out. The whole back wall of the butcher shop was covered in old photographs. A worn, sepia-toned print showed a man with a stern expression, white apron tied tight around his waist. Next to that was a photo of a teenage Hank standing arm in arm with a woman, presumably his mother, her smile wide and infectious.

I kept studying the photos to keep my mind off the steady sound of the knife hitting the cutting board behind me. Enzo and Hank continued to talk, but I didn't pay attention to what they were saying.

The photos changed, showing the passing of the years, images growing crisper, colors more saturated. I scanned them until the hairstyles and clothes indicated that we'd made it to the 1980s, and there it was: a single photo of an adult Hank with his arm looped around the shoulder of a striking woman with dark hair and green eyes. *Nina.*

I leaned in close to the photo, studying it. *Was* it Nina? When Maria had described her in her memoir, she'd said she was pretty, but she hadn't mentioned how similar the two of them had looked. The woman in this photograph's hair was a bit longer than I'd ever seen Maria's and her smile was softer, a little less sure of herself. But, otherwise, they could be sisters. I waited until I no longer heard the sound of a knife hitting the cutting board before I turned back around. "Is this your wife?"

I couldn't tell if Hank heard me. His movements stilled, but he didn't answer. Enzo had been standing near the door, looking at something on his phone, but now he glanced up, frowning. "Ex-wife," he explained, when he saw the photo I was pointing to. "Hank and Nina divorced when Issie and I were kids."

Hank sniffed. "Nina and me never got divorced."

"Really?" Enzo seemed confused. "But she hasn't lived in Woodstock since I was little."

Hank continued wiping the blood from his knife, his movements slow and even. There was nothing left of the rabbit on the cutting board, I noticed. Even the blood had been stowed away somewhere.

He really did use every part of the animal, I thought.

"She took off," Hank said. "Haven't heard from her in thirty years."

Enzo released a short, surprised laugh and said, "Hank, man, that's wild. Mom never told me that." His tone was conversational, casual, but I felt something inside of me prick, suddenly curious. Here was another person who vanished into thin air after pissing Maria off.

I looked up to see Hank watching me. When I met his eyes, he scratched his jaw and looked away. He left a streak of rabbit's blood across his skin, the red practically neon under the shop's flickering fluorescent lights.

....

There was another chapter waiting just inside the door of my room when I got back to the Farm. It wasn't much, just seven or eight pages. The corner of the door caught the stack when I pushed it open, sending the pages skimming over the hardwood. The sight of them made my heart start beating faster.

I dropped to my knees and gathered the pages with trembling hands, quickly double-checking the page numbers to make sure they were in the right order.

And then, unable to wait another moment, I collapsed against the door and began to read.

THE SECRET INGREDIENT

CHAPTER THREE

Most restaurants fail, but we were one of the lucky ones. Our modest little eatery was an instant success. The *New York Times* gave us a particularly lovely review. We bought every copy in town, had one framed and hung on the wall behind Polpette's bar. There were glowing reviews, write-ups in national publications, people driving up from the city to try our food. Jack Nicholson and Dyan Cannon were photographed chatting at Polpette's bar in 1988. Barbra Streisand came to dinner once and took up three whole tables in the back with her entourage. Paul Newman frequented the place so often that he and Damien grew to be friends.

Damien became something of a celebrity himself. A year after Polpette opened, he was named in *Cook's Magazine's* "1982 Who's Who Top 50," a huge honor. An editor got in touch to see whether he was interested in writing a cookbook, and shortly after, Damien signed with a talent agency and began taking meetings. Investors reached out to ask about franchising. There was even talk of a television show.

Yet, despite all this, we were making next to nothing. We were prepared for this; most restaurants took three, five, even *ten* years to see profits. It was enough for me to be able to work doing the thing I was most passionate about with the man I loved. But it was still a difficult time in our lives. I sometimes found Damien in his little office at the back of the restaurant, poring over bills, muttering to himself. He never wanted to talk about the books, would insist he could figure out the finances himself, but I always made sure to stop and comfort him with a squeeze on the shoulder.

"The first few years of a business are always hard," I would tell him. "And that goes double for a successful business."

I was stressed about money too, of course, but handling the finances was Damien's role. My role was to support him, no matter what. I took care of everything he didn't have the time or energy to think about so he could focus on running the parts of the business only he could do. He was the face of Polpette all through the '80s, the only person newspapers and magazines wanted to talk to. Our restaurant—and family's—beating heart.

Around this time, Damien got it into his head that we had to have a whole suckling pig on our menu. And not only that, but he became convinced that if he was to cook a pig, he ought to understand the entire process, from the living animal through to the stunning, killing, and butchering. Damien had never butchered an animal before, but it seemed important to him to learn. He even insisted on building a slaughterhouse behind our barn.

Hank agreed to teach Damien everything he knew about butchering pigs. I still remember the day Hank arrived in Damien's brand-new slaughterhouse, leading a fully grown sow behind him. Hank had clearly performed this chore many times before, and he carried out the procedure with swift precision: stunning the pig instantly with a shot to her forehead, then hanging it from a hook over a bit of dirt floor, slitting its throat to bleed it, making sure to collect as much blood as possible to use for later. This all took him minutes. Less. The pig only let out a few screams before it was all over, but they were terrible to hear. The sound was almost human.

Once he'd finished, Hank handed Damien the tools and a second pig was led out.

Damien's first attempt at stunning was anything but smooth. His hands shook as he fumbled with the heavy stunning gun, which alerted the pig to what he was doing a moment before he was ready. The pig squealed and tried to get away. I can still remember the look of fear in its eyes, how it seemed to know exactly what Damien was preparing to do.

Damien should have given up, placed the gun aside, and waited to try again once the pig had calmed, but he was embarrassed, and I think he wanted to show Hank that he could do the job as well as he could. But his hands were trembling, and he couldn't hold the gun steady. It slipped when he went to shoot, and he wound up grazing the pig's temple rather than making the solid, decisive shot in between its eyes, as Hank had done. Because of this, the pig didn't immediately fall unconscious but collapsed to the ground, kicking and screaming, miserable and afraid.

Of course, Damien got better with each pig thereafter. The slaughterhouse became the place on the farm where he spent the most time, and with each pig, his process became more streamlined, less shaky. But I know he always remembered that first pig, and the discomfort he had with taking a life never disappeared—nor should it have.

Before he met me, Damien was the type of chef who would casually toss a cut of meat in the trash bin and start over if he'd accidentally overcooked it. And he was by no means the only cook who did that. I can tell you, having worked in restaurants for most of my adult life, that I've seen far too many professional chefs do the same. But my family taught me that you're responsible for the life that provides your food. You can't let it go to waste. I couldn't let the animals we'd killed be used in vain, their meat discarded carelessly because of a culinary misstep. I was so grateful to Damien for taking on this belief, for working to make sure Polpette respected the lives we took to provide our dinners.

Meanwhile, I became quite a force behind the scenes, if I do say so myself. I wasn't featured in magazines, but I managed the front-of-house staff, and I oversaw the menu and the kitchen. Damien might have been the one who cooked the restaurant's most famous dishes, but there wasn't a recipe on the menu that I didn't write and test myself. I made sure that each detail of Polpette ran with precision.

It was right in the middle of all this that I found out I was pregnant.

Even now, I cannot imagine a worse time for us to have a baby, but you know what they say: there's never a good time. And I couldn't help it; I was elated. I couldn't stop thinking about the life growing inside me, the baby who would be half me and half Damien. I began to smile at every child who came into the restaurant and make faces at them behind their parents' backs to try to get them to laugh. During staff meetings, I would awkwardly steer our conversations toward family. Who had children? What were their names? How old? I still remember the looks I got from the cooks and busboys, confused, cautious. You'd think I was losing my mind! I stopped tasting dishes, just in case there was something in them that could hurt the baby, and I found myself stealing away, just for a moment or two, just to relish in the miracle that was occurring inside my body. I'd press a hand to my belly and close my eyes, imagining I could feel her in there. I couldn't have been more than eight weeks along; it was far too early for me to know she was a "she" or to feel anything at all, but those things didn't seem to matter. I *knew* I was having a daughter.

But as much as I'd wanted our baby, I was terrified to tell Damien about her. We'd never discussed whether or not we wanted children. The only future we saw was the future of our restaurant. I worried Damien wouldn't see my pregnancy as a blessing, not then. At that time, he was so focused on the restaurant, on his food, on how in debt we were.

"Sometimes I think we made a huge mistake," he used to tell me in those early days. He'd talk about how he'd had no idea that he'd signed up for this, that he hadn't realized how much work the place would be. It wasn't like a normal job; there was no signing off for the day, no weekends. Damien would get up at four in the morning so he could get to the fishmonger and the farmers' markets to source ingredients first thing, and he wouldn't stop working until the restaurant closed, often well after midnight. On the weekends, he was in the slaughter-house with the pigs. It was exhausting.

"Sometimes I think we should just burn it all down, collect the insurance money, and run," he used to say. "We could go down to South America, live in some hut on the beach, just you and me."

It was a joke, of course. But it was also just like Damien to think it would be easier to throw it all away and start over, start fresh, just like he'd throw away an overcooked cut of meat. I knew it was just the stress talking. Damien wasn't used to being in the spotlight. I honestly don't think he particularly liked it.

Whenever he started talking like that, I'd rub his shoulders and tell him it was all going to get easier. That the most important part was that we were together, a team. And I knew it couldn't be long before we started making money. Polpette was doing so well.

Of course, pregnancy would change all of that. Babies never made anything easier. It worried me to think of adding this to the already heavy burden he was carrying. But what choice did I have?

It's long been a tradition in my family to reveal good news along-side a good meal. And so I decided to tell Damien he was going to be a father by surprising him with his favorite dish: veal and onions, a twist on liver and onions I came up with because Damien wasn't a fan of liver. Tender veal is a nice stand-in, and it's easy to cook.

The most important part of this meal is the veal itself. Veal is more flavorful when it's allowed to walk around, which is why it's so important to get a quality cut from the butcher instead of relying on what you might find in the supermarket. Nina and Hank's veal was pastured, organic, and came from calves who were milk-fed and raised alongside their mothers.

I wanted the meal to be perfect so I'd ducked out of the restaurant early to Nina and Hank's before they closed for the day. Damien had been at the restaurant until close the night before, and he was spending the afternoon sleeping the late night off at home. I wanted him to wake up to the smell of meat and onions.

The bell on Hank's door jingled as I stepped inside, announcing my arrival in the shop, but no one hurried out of the back room to greet me. This was very strange. Either Nina or Hank was always manning the shop, and they didn't like to keep customers waiting. I remembered starting to worry that something was wrong as I waited for one minute, then two. No one came.

I called out for Hank. There was no answer, but I thought I heard someone in the back, the sound of voices. Hank once told me that it could be difficult to hear customers up front on account of the thick walls in the back freezer, so I took it upon myself to make my way behind the counter and into the little room where they stored the meat.

It was the first time I'd been back there, and I remembered being surprised by how dark it was, how cold. I also realized that Hank was right; the walls were quite thick. No wonder he hadn't heard me call out for him. I started looking for a light switch, my hand grasping at the wall, when I saw the movement.

Someone was back there in the dark. I was so shocked I didn't even think to call out again. I just stood there, staring. Whoever was back there was writhing. Moaning.

Nina, I realized as my eyes adjusted. But not just Nina. She was in the back room with someone; she was screwing someone. Even in the dark I could see that he was much too small to be her husband.

I would've left right then, backed out into the main room and slipped out the door, pretending I'd never been there at all. But then the man moaned. It was a low, familiar moan. A sound I knew down to my bones, as familiar to me as my own voice.

Damien. My husband, the love of my life, was having sex with another woman.

The moment I heard that moan, I was transported back to the tiny, crowded restaurant where we spent our first date. I felt Damien's hand on mine, heard his low, husky voice whisper the words, "I wasn't ready for you yet" into my ear, and I broke in ways I didn't realize it was possible to break.

TELL YOUR CHEATING HUSBAND YOU'RE PREGNANT VEAL

The success of this recipe relies on the ingredients: fresh, thinly sliced veal and a good extra-virgin olive oil.

INGREDIENTS

1 large Vidalia onion
1 cup all-purpose flour
Salt and black pepper to taste
1 pound thinly sliced veal cutlets
4 tablespoons olive oil, divided, plus more as needed
3 tablespoons butter, divided, plus more as needed
6 sage leaves
¼ cup veal or chicken demi-glace

STEPS

Serves 4

1. Slice your onion as thinly as possible, ideally using a mandoline. Spread the flour on a plate. If the veal slices are more than ⅛-inch thick, cover in a double layer of plastic wrap and gently pound flat using a meat mallet. Season on both sides with salt and black pepper, and store in the fridge until needed.

2. Place the onion slices in a medium-sized sauté pan with 3 tablespoons of olive oil (don't be shy with the oil) and a big pinch of salt, then set over low heat. Cook, stirring occasionally, for 30 minutes. Take care not to brown the onions; they should become soft, almost melted. Remove from the heat and set aside.

3. Wipe out the pan and add the remaining 1 tablespoon olive oil and 1 tablespoon butter. Heat over medium high until the butter foams and subsides.

4. Working in batches, dredge the veal in the flour and shake to remove the excess. Lay in the hot oil, adding more oil or butter as needed. Cook 2 minutes per side, until barely browning. Take

care not to overcook, or the tender veal will dry out and become chewy. The cutlets should maintain a slight pink tint.

5. After all the veal has been removed from the pan, add the sage leaves and reduce the heat to low. Cook 30 seconds until fragrant, then add demi-glace and reserved onions with their juices, scraping up the browned bits from the pan. Heat until bubbling, then remove from the heat. Season the sauce with salt and pepper, and stir in the remaining 2 tablespoons butter.

6. Serve immediately on shallow plates, spooning the onions and sauce around the veal.

8

THEA

"Asshole," I breathed, dropping the pages onto my lap. In over thirty years, Maria had never let on. Even when there'd been rumors of affairs and cheating, she'd always refuted them. She'd painted Damien as the perfect husband, the perfect partner and father. Until now.

I began to rethink my earlier belief that this was just another cheating-husband story. The strength of Maria's writing elevated it into something else. It didn't feel cliché so much as classic. A Shakespearean tragedy. And we all already knew the end.

I was somewhere between my second and my third reread when I heard something out in the hall. A murmured voice, floorboards creaking.

Someone said, "Hold on; I'm going outside."

My ears pricked. It was just like what had happened last night, the 2:00 a.m. phone call. I doubt I'd have heard anything if I hadn't been sitting on the floor with my head leaning against the door, but now that I had, I couldn't think of anything else. *Who was it? Were they really going to blackmail someone?* I had to know.

I waited until I heard the footsteps move past my door and down the hall, and only then did I ease it open. The hall was empty. But I heard that murmured voice one more time and then the sound of a door opening and closing. Just like they had last night, they'd taken the phone call outside.

I slipped Maria's pages into my tote bag and quietly pushed myself to my feet. When I reached the end of the hall, I peered around the corner. There was the glass door that led to the back patio. Through it, I could see a figure quickly cutting through the tall grass, heading for the distant tree line. I instantly recognized Amy's messy ponytail.

Now I was desperate to hear the phone call, to know who Amy was "blackmailing." But, by the time I made it to the tree line, she was too far away. I turned in place, eyes peeled for any sign of where she'd gone. Tree branches reached over my head like big, protective arms. Sunlight filtered through the leaves, casting patterns of light and shadow on the ground. The air carried the scent of damp earth and decaying leaves. But Amy was gone.

I walked for a while, disappointed, keeping my ears alert for the sound of Amy's voice amid the soft crunch of fallen leaves and the occasional snap of a twig. But there was nothing.

The foliage began to thin, and a narrow creek appeared. Seeing it, I stopped short. According to the news reports from the time, Damien was supposed to have drowned in the creek behind the farmhouse.

This creek.

I felt my breathing change as I took a careful step closer. The water was so bright that it hurt to look at it directly. I peered over the side, easily glimpsing the rocky riverbed below. It was strange to me that anyone would think someone could drown here. Wouldn't a human body have washed up onto the land or gotten caught on the rocks?

Patches of sun pierced the dense canopy overhead, casting flickering light onto the water's surface, pulsing as it rippled over rocks. The creek twisted on through the trees. I walked alongside it for a while, looking for Amy, trying to figure out where the creek got deep enough for a man to drown.

It took nearly a mile for it to fill out. Here, the grass grew past my knees, almost to my hips. Trees loomed here and there, casting deep shadows over the water, shielding it from the sun. There was an eeriness to the air, a stillness. This whole place felt tainted.

The water was still shallow, even here. I took a step back, examining the creek. Even at its highest tide, the creek would only be a few feet higher than it was right now. A dilapidated barn loomed on the opposite shore.

I was about to head back when I caught a flicker of something from the corner of my eye. A moment later, I heard movement. Leaves rustled. A twig snapped. I froze like a deer, nerves itching along the back of my arms. I caught sight of something red—a coat—and took a step closer.

Amy. I could see the back of her head through the trees, that dark ponytail bobbing as she made her way along the opposite side of the creek bank. She must've crossed over a mile ago, where the creek was shallow and narrow. I wouldn't be able to follow her from here, not where the creek was so much wider. But I watched her trudge through the tall grass, up toward the barn.

She didn't seem to be on the phone anymore. Still, I gingerly made my way closer to the side of the water, carefully picking over rocks, through weeds, trying not to make a noise that might draw her attention.

Amy wasn't the only person up by the old barn. There was a car, too. As I watched, Amy leaned down toward the driver-side window and said something to whoever was inside. I craned my neck, trying to see, but it was impossible. They were too far away. Amy hurried over to the passenger side, opened the car door, and slipped inside. A moment later, the car pulled away from the barn and disappeared into the trees. And I was left alone in the woods, wondering what the hell I'd just seen.

....

I woke in bed much later that night. The ceiling blinked in and out of focus, and I knew without bothering to check my phone that it would be sometime between two and three in the morning, like always.

I tried to force myself back to sleep for a few minutes, but it was immediately clear that wasn't going to work. Groaning, I switched on my bedside light, grabbed my Ziploc bag of sleeping pills, saw that my water glass was empty.

I considered swallowing the pill dry, but I was like a kid when it came to swallowing pills. They always managed to get stuck, that bitter taste trailing over my tongue and down my throat. After a minute of arguing silently with myself, I grabbed my glass and stumbled out of my room and up to the kitchen.

Moonlight drifted in through the big windows. Everything was awash in dusty purples and silvers. I filled the water glass at the faucet, a slick of sweat clinging to my forehead like plastic wrap. I closed my eyes, leaning against the wall.

"Thea? Is everything okay?"

I jerked toward the voice, shocked enough that I released a choked scream.

Maria stood in the kitchen doorway. She wore pajamas, her dark hair knotted on top of her head, a single skunk's stripe of gray visible. She tilted her head, studying me.

"You don't look well, dear," she said. "Can't you sleep?"

She sounded worried, the way a mother would sound worried. It was so touching that for a moment, I thought I might cry. She crossed the kitchen, pressed a hand to my forehead. Her skin was soft, cool. I smelled soap, a fresh, maternal smell. My throat closed up.

"I—I'm fine," I said, exhaling. An obvious lie. Maria tilted her head, mouth pressed in a thin line, so I went on, explaining, "I've had terrible insomnia ever since my daughter was born. This happens every night."

Maria smiled knowingly. "You know, I think I have something that should help. Hold on."

"Oh no, you don't have to—"

But she was already crossing the kitchen, her bare feet soundless in the night. I expected her to vanish back into the hall, but instead she crossed to the padlocked door, pulled a small, silver key out of her pocket, unlocked the padlock, and slipped inside.

I was instantly curious. Whatever was on the other side of that door couldn't just be a closet. It must be a basement. It felt like ages before I heard the creak of footsteps on what sounded like stairs. And when Maria reappeared, she was holding a small glass filled with something murky and green.

"Try this," she said, offering it to me.

I hesitated, my eyes flicking between the glass and Maria's face. "What is it?"

"A few herbs. Nothing too strong, but I swear it works. Go on, try it."

Maybe I should have asked for more details. Usually, I was better about that. But there was something about the moonlight drifting in through the windows and Maria's soft voice, the expression on her face—eyebrows pulled together with concern, lips a thin, pained line—that touched at a core wound as easily as a finger pressing on a button. I would have done anything she asked in that moment. I lifted the cup to my lips.

The taste was bitter, earthy, like incredibly strong, undiluted tea, not a hit of sweetness. I choked as I swallowed, felt the liquid slide down my throat, burning slightly as it hit my stomach. For a moment, I worried I was about to be sick.

The burning feeling spread, and just afterward there was…

Exhaustion.

It was shocking how suddenly the feeling hit, how it spread through me like blood in water. My eyelids grew heavy. I could barely keep them open.

I blinked up at Maria, shocked. "What was that?"

"Did it work?" she asked.

"I think so," I admitted. I leaned against the sink, rubbing a hand over my forehead. I'd never before taken anything that made me feel so immediately tired. That couldn't have been over the counter. But it hadn't looked like it was prescription, either.

My mind wandered back to the old-world remedies I'd learned about when studying early modern literature in school, strange concoctions that some people thought worked better than modern medicines.

"Seriously," I said to Maria. "What was that?"

Maria shrugged. "Old family recipe."

I didn't have the energy to keep questioning her. I felt strange, shaky.

"Would you like me to help you back to your room, dear?" Her voice was gentle, and once again, it made me want to cry. It had been so long since someone had taken care of me, since someone had asked if *I* was okay. Years. Longer.

I blinked. Tears welled up in my eyes. *What the hell was happening to me?* I looked away from Maria's sympathetic face, blinked hard. "Sorry, I didn't realize I was—" I shook my head, adding on an exhale, "You're a really good mom."

Maria laughed and patted my hand. "I'm not sure my kids would agree with you. They think this sort of thing is too controlling. They would tell me to stop treating them like children. But I've found that it's impossible to get the balance right. You're always either neglectful or overbearing."

I blinked the remnants of the tears from my eyes. This wasn't exactly professional. I needed to pull myself together.

"I finished the last stack of pages you gave me," I said. "What you wrote... It was so different from how I imagined your life was. I always thought you had the perfect family."

Maria nodded once. "I'm not surprised."

Whatever she'd given me had loosened my tongue. I said, before I could question whether it was wise, "Why would you spend so many years pretending Damien was this great guy if he treated you so badly?"

The corner of Maria's eye narrowed slightly. A barely perceptible flinch. I felt my cheeks warm. I shouldn't have been so blunt. I opened my mouth to apologize, but before I could, Maria said, "We had children, dear. The idea of them growing up thinking their father was a monster... I couldn't bear it. Not then."

I closed my mouth, an exhale slipping out of me. I thought about Ruthie, who, at three years old, thought her daddy was perfect. If Jacob ever died, wouldn't I do everything in my power to preserve that image of him? A little gift for a girl who'd lost her father, something that didn't hurt anyone. Didn't I *still* do the same thing with her grandmother?

Of course. It was what good mothers did, a magic trick. We swept the bad things under the rug and pretended everything was beautiful, that it took no effort whatsoever to make it that way.

There was nothing I wouldn't do to make the world perfect for my daughter.

....

I woke the next morning feeling groggy and slow. Hungover from whatever Maria had given me. I felt like I'd slept for twelve hours. It took all my willpower to haul myself out of bed.

Maria was in the hall outside the kitchen when I wandered out of my room. "Thea," she said, brightly, "I was just coming to find you."

"Good morning," I murmured. "Sorry I'm late. That stuff you gave me to help me sleep left me a little—"

A scream cut me off. It was a high, shrilling sound that rose and fell like an alarm. It sounded human.

I felt like I was tipped back in a chair, that sudden dip in your gut when the balance slips and you tilt sharply backward. My fingers groped for the wall, even though I wasn't falling. I was standing still.

"What was that?" I choked out, once the scream had faded.

Maria offered me an apologetic look. "I'm so sorry, dear. I should have warned you. I promised Hank he could come by to use our slaughterhouse. Pigs make the most unpleasant sound when they're shot, but trust me, after a while you won't even hear them. I hardly notice anymore."

I'd read about this in Maria's memoir. But I was so out of it that the first thing I thought of was the picture Ava had drawn, the pig surrounded by red scribbles that looked like blood. She'd said it was the mama pig milking its young, but it hadn't looked like that. It had looked like an animal dying in a pool of blood.

I dropped my hand from the wall, shrugged out the rest of my nerves. I needed to wake up.

"I finished the new chapter," I reminded Maria. "I couldn't stop reading. I feel like I'm getting a much clearer idea of the story you're trying to tell."

I was hoping this might prompt her to give me more pages, but instead Maria motioned for me to follow her into the kitchen. "Let's discuss. I'd love to hear your notes."

Her voice was kind enough, yet my whole body clenched. I thought of the story of the editor whose career ended because of the notes he'd given Maria. I hadn't had the chance to go over my thoughts, make sure I was being kind and constructive with any criticism.

"Okay," I said, taking a seat at the kitchen table. "Right now, my only real note is that I want more. I like that you start with your history. People know so much about your life after Damien died, but they want to know you, who you were before you met him, how you grew up, what your family was like." I pulled my laptop out of my tote bag and fired it up so I could read the other notes I'd jotted down as I read. "Not just how you met Damien, although that part is great, but your life with your mother before you started working in the city. You said she was a butcher?"

"A meat cutter," Maria clarified. "At a butcher shop, yes."

"That's fascinating," I said. "You could go into more detail there. And you don't say much about your early years with Damien, dating and falling in love, the beginning of your marriage. Personally, I'd love to read more about that. You touched on that already, but you could go so much deeper." I hesitated for a moment, not entirely sure how to address the next part. "And then there's the possibility that Damien was involved in organized crime."

Maria nodded, a single dip of her chin. "Yes."

"It's a deeply interesting story. It'll obviously be a huge hook for readers." I narrowed my eyes, scanning the pages until I found a note I'd made. "I found myself wanting more examples of Damien getting his hands on things without explanation, like the cheese and the oven. Do you have more stories like that?"

"I have dozens," Maria murmured. "And there are things I haven't even touched on. We were investigated by the FBI for a while, near the end. And then there was the gambling."

Amy came around the corner. "Good morning," she said, smiling at us. Her cheeks were still pink from the cold outside.

I stared at her for a moment, distracted. Had she been out meeting up with whoever had been in that car again? I studied her face, expecting her to look guilty, ashamed, something. But she just crossed the kitchen to pour herself a cup of coffee.

I wanted to wait until Amy left the room to say anything else. But Maria kept talking, seemingly unconcerned by her presence. "You know, Damien's gambling got so bad that I stopped keeping our money in the bank, where he could get to it. I had a couple of spots around the farm where I used to bury it, if you can believe that."

Amy was hesitating at the coffeepot, I noticed, fumbling unnecessarily with a spoon. I tensed. Was she listening?

"Funny, I haven't thought about all that in years." Maria was frowning now, deep in thought. "I know I didn't dig up all the money I hid. I'm sure I buried something in the slaughterhouse. I remember because I made a mark on the wall right above it, so I'd know where to go to dig it back up. But I don't remember ever going back to look for it." She laughed and shook her head. "You know, I bet it's still out there."

Amy was sipping her coffee, a frown line between her eyes. I cleared my throat and said, "I had a few questions about structure. The current chapters are all in chronological order. Do you intend to continue like that?"

The boring structure talk seemed to do the trick. Amy headed for the door, calmly sipping her coffee. A few seconds later, I heard the sound of her footsteps making their way down the hall. I exhaled, relieved.

I couldn't tell if it was coincidence or not, but Maria seemed to have waited for Amy to leave the room before saying, "Last night you mentioned my husband's affair. Did you have any more thoughts about it?"

I nodded. "It's odd. I tried to look Nina Casey up online, but I couldn't find any mention of her."

"That doesn't surprise me. From what I remember of her, she doesn't strike me as the type who'd have gotten into social media. She was more of a bohemian, off-the-grid sort."

"Hank mentioned she ran out on him."

Maria looked surprised. "You met Hank?"

"Enzo gave me a ride into town earlier," I explained. "I had to peek into Hank's shop after reading about it in your pages. You know he still has a photo of Nina on the wall?"

But Maria was suddenly serious. She had her hands folded in front of her, her gaze sharp. "Thea, I would prefer that you didn't do your own research outside of the reading."

Her tone of voice had shifted. It was the confident steel of a boardroom executive, completely different from the maternal quality it usually had when she spoke with me.

I stiffened. I had no idea how to respond to this. I had some sense that I should apologize. But I hadn't done anything wrong. Research was part of my job. "What do you mean?"

"I don't want you talking to people in town, looking names up online. There have been a lot of things said about me and my family over the years. This memoir needs to stand on its own."

"Oh," I said slowly. Her words left no room for argument, but I was having trouble seeing this from her point of view. Honestly, the request felt like a red flag. Didn't she understand what a risk this was for me, with her reputation? With my past mistakes? *Of course* I'd have to look things up online.

And it wasn't just me. We'd have copy editors poring over all her facts, making absolutely certain that every detail in the story was correct. Once this was published, the entire world was going to go through her words with a fine-tooth comb, checking and double-checking and triple-checking that everything she said was accurate. She had to know that. Didn't she?

I thought of the line she'd opened the memoir with. *Before you begin this book, I must ask you to forget everything you've already read about me and my husband.* It was a lovely line, but she couldn't actually believe that was possible. People were going to bring everything they knew about Maria into their reading experience. She couldn't change that. She couldn't take every other reader's phone and cut off their access to the internet. She might be able to control me now, but she couldn't control everything.

Maria slid a fresh stack of pages across the table to me, and then she slipped the pages I'd already read into that same red folder where she'd put the others and folded her hands on top of them. It was a final, definitive gesture, and I understood that there would be no more discussion about this. We were done talking through my thoughts. Now, I was to read.

"Right," I said, gathering the new pages. *I knew Maria was like this*, I reminded myself as I stood. And I needed this. As risky as it was to trust Maria, it was so much riskier to walk away.

But as I stared at her folded hands, I thought I felt something, an electric jolt through my skin, and I thought, *Is she messing with me?*

For the first time, I wondered if I was ever going to see those pages again. If she had any intention of actually publishing them.

THE SECRET INGREDIENT

CHAPTER FOUR

I went straight home after finding Damien with Nina, and I took a bottle of chardonnay down from the cupboard. Then, remembering I was pregnant, I put the chardonnay back and instead got a spiced pear galette I'd made the day before from the counter.

I took the galette into our bedroom, got under our duvet, and ate the whole thing myself, like the utter cliché that I was.

My husband was cheating on me. My Damien was cheating on me. And I was pregnant.

I wouldn't get an abortion. I couldn't. It wasn't the done thing back then, but even if it had been, I'd already bought a stack of shiny childbirth books and a copy of *Goodnight Moon* in all its iconic, brightly colored glory. I hadn't wanted Damien to find them, so I'd hidden them in an old Adidas shoebox in the closet, still wrapped in the bag from the bookstore. When I thought of those books, so new there was still a receipt tucked between the pages, their spines not yet broken, it made me so emotional I started to cry into my galette.

No, I wasn't going to get an abortion. And I wasn't going to give Damien a divorce, either. He was my husband. And, more than that, he was the only man I'd ever loved. The baby inside of me was half his. We were going to have a family. I couldn't let go of that. And so I'd scooped the last bite of galette and told myself the story that every woman who has ever been cheated on has told herself at least once: that it was a onetime thing, that it would end, that he would come back to me once he'd gotten bored or once he realized how much he loved me. In my case, this lie even had a deadline. Or, rather, a due date. Damien would come back to me once our baby was born. He had to.

The next day, I told him about the baby exactly as I'd originally planned. I'd gone back to Hank's and ordered a pound of veal chops, and I served them with broccoli rabe drizzled in olive oil and sea salt and a fresh loaf of focaccia. I lit candles and squeezed into Damien's favorite dress of mine, a red velvet thing with a plunging neckline and a slight flare at my hips that somewhat hid my growing belly. I even put on heels, black ones that pinched my swollen feet. I'd wanted everything to be perfect. I wanted him to see what we had together, all the things he stood to lose.

He was ecstatic about the baby. He leaped out of his chair so quickly he knocked it to the floor, and then he held me and he cried and he told me he was so, so happy. He kissed my belly through my velvet dress. He insisted I take off those stupid heels. It was enough to push whatever fear I'd had about Nina completely out of my head. Yes, he'd strayed. But he came back to me. Nina had been a momentary thing. I was forever.

Over the months that followed, Damien truly seemed content. He rubbed my feet and helped me pick baby names and a color for her room: Rose Blush, chosen from a book of paint samples we'd picked up at the hardware store. We painted the room together one Saturday afternoon, laughing as we got paint on our faces and in our hair, ordering pizza with anchovies and mushrooms because that was all I wanted to eat at the time, pretending we didn't notice the spots of pink paint we'd gotten onto the ceiling and one corner of the floor.

After a while, it was easy to believe that whatever had been going on with Nina had run its course. Damien was my husband; he was going to be a father. We were a family.

Isabella was born at the end of September 1984, this tiny, scream-ing, miraculous thing. They placed her on my chest and she looked up at me with these liquid black eyes, so trusting, so perfect. Damien had started crying, a steady stream of silent tears that he wiped away with the back of his hand. He was looking at me like I was a goddess, like I was made of magic. All the nurses told us she was the most beautiful newborn they'd ever seen. Our Isabella.

Other mothers said their newborns slept all the time; they told me stories of having to come up with clever ways to keep them awake for long enough to eat. I listened to them talk about draping cold washcloths on their babies' necks, blaring loud music, or turning on all the lights.

Isabella wasn't like that. She wouldn't sleep for longer than forty-five minutes at a time, and she always woke up screaming, enraged. She refused to let Damien feed her or hold her, would cry until her face turned red, only settling when I rescued her from his arms. And so it fell to me to take care of her. Damien would get up with me in the beginning, for moral support, but eventually we decided that one of us needed to be well rested. He was the one needed at the restaurant, the one our entire financial future relied on. So he stopped.

Those nights were among the loneliest I'd ever experienced. I missed Damien dreadfully. Shameful though it is to admit, I missed the life we had together, just the two of us. And I was so tired. The only time Isabella stayed asleep was when she was in her car seat, and so I started taking long late-night drives. One night, when I got back from one of those long drives with Isabella, I found our house empty. Damien was gone.

I experienced something like true terror then. I'd thought that was it, that he'd disappeared for good, like my father had done. I pictured him halfway to South America, to his dream of a little hut on the beach with no responsibilities. I figured he was tired of being a dad, tired of holding the restaurant together through sheer force of will, tired of *me*. He'd thrown us away and started over.

But he came back the next morning at dawn, slipping through the front door and into our bed without a word of explanation. I was so relieved he came back that I pretended to believe whatever lie he'd told me. But of course I knew where he'd really gone. He'd been with her, with Nina.

I didn't know what to do. I wanted to tell someone. But who? I couldn't tell Hank. My dear cousin would have been destroyed by the knowledge that his wife was cheating. I would never do that to him. I was friendly with a few other mothers in town, and I'd stayed in touch with some former coworkers from La Villetta, but no one I could confide in about *this*. I knew what they'd say if they knew, how they'd tell me I deserved better, that I should leave him before he could leave me. I couldn't do that. Despite everything, I still loved Damien. His future was my future, his dreams my dreams. Leaving him was unimaginable. And so I kept it to myself. Even as he slipped away night after night after night.

Not even two full years after I had Isabella, I got pregnant with

Enzo. The experience was night and day from my first pregnancy. No more foot rubs or baby names, no weekends painting the nursery. Damien was busy with the restaurant and—though he never told me as much—I suspected with Nina, and I was busy with two-year-old Isabella, with my new domestic life, with pregnancy. We felt more like roommates than husband and wife in those days.

And yet I still remembered the Damien who'd made me cavatelli from scratch on our third date, the one who'd handpicked the best pieces of pasta for my plate so that it would be perfect. I remembered watching him work and knowing that, some day, he would teach our children to roll pasta and cook sauce. In that moment, I'd thought I was so lucky, that the two of us were going to be happy forever. I imagined Sunday mornings cooking and dancing around our kitchen, the air filled with the sound of our laughter. I wanted that man back. I knew he was still out there somewhere.

Eventually, desperate, I told my mother about the affair. "You know what they say about a man who cheats," she said to me.

"What?" I asked her, though I was certain I didn't want to know. I imagined her spouting some hollow phrase she'd heard on a sitcom. *Once a cheater, always a cheater.*

But she'd only shrugged and said, "Eventually, they leave."

Leave. Of course, it had already occurred to me that he might do that. It was my deepest fear, the thing that woke me in the middle of the night and made it so I couldn't drift back to sleep but only stare at the cracks running across my ceiling, frozen with dread.

Damien couldn't leave me. I couldn't live without him. I couldn't.

I realized, right then, that I had to do something to stop him.

Eat Away Your Pain Spiced Pear Galette

INGREDIENTS

½ pound pie dough
2 under-ripe Bosc pears
¼ cup granulated sugar
2 teaspoons ground cinnamon
1 teaspoon ground ginger
½ teaspoon ground cardamom
5 whole cloves, or ¼ tablespoon ground
1 egg
2 tablespoons turbinado sugar

STEPS

Serves 8

1. Form the dough into a thick disk before rolling it out. Wrap in plastic wrap and place in the freezer to chill for 20 to 30 minutes. The dough will be easier to work with if chilled.

2. Cut the pears in half, de-stem, and scoop out the cores with a spoon. Lay the pears cut side down on your cutting board and slice thinly, keeping the cut pears together. Mix the sugar and spices together and set aside. In a separate bowl, beat the egg with 1 tablespoon water and set aside.

3. Roll out your dough into a circle. If the dough cracks, it can be patched with spare bits of dough or pieces cut from the other side. The dough should be ⅛ inch thick and larger than a pie plate. Lightly grease and flour your baking sheet, and then transfer the dough to the sheet.

4. Sprinkle 1 tablespoon of the sugar mixture over the center of the dough and transfer the cut pears directly on top of the sugar, keeping the slices together. Fan the pear slices out to create a decorative pattern. There should be a 2- to 3-inch border of dough all around the edges of the pears. Sprinkle the spiced sugar mixture over the pears, using your fingers to lift up the slices and

get the sugar down in between the pears. Fold the edges of the dough over the pears, starting on one side and working all the way around, creating folds in the same direction.

5. Transfer the entire galette on the baking sheet into the freezer for 30 minutes to firm up. This will help it keep its shape. Preheat the oven to 400°F. When the galette is chilled, remove from the freezer and brush the dough with the egg wash. Sprinkle the turbinado sugar all over the dough, then place in the center of the hot oven and bake for 30 to 35 minutes, until golden brown.

6. Let rest for 10 minutes, then carve into 8 slices and serve warm, placing dollops of vanilla ice cream over the top.

9

THEA

I READ THE NEW PAGES ON THE WALK BACK TO MY ROOM, HEAD down, shuffling along the hall without paying any attention to where I was going.

Eventually they leave. The line lingered in my brain. *It was my deepest fear*, she'd written.

I knew just how she felt. I often worried Jacob would meet someone else, that he'd get tired of being a husband and father, that he'd disappear in the night and Ruthie and I would be all alone, just like my mother and I had been. Not a family, not really, just two people who lived together, wondering why they weren't worth staying for. I imagined howling myself to sleep like my mother used to, my pain keeping Ruthie awake. Making her feel just as scared and alone as I'd felt.

That was my deepest fear. That I was capable of inflicting that kind of pain on the person I loved most. That I'd leave my daughter the same way my mother left me.

Back in my room, I collapsed into bed. My brain still felt muddy, sluggish. Whatever had been in that draft Maria had given me just wouldn't wear off. I could barely keep my eyes open.

I wasn't a napper but I let myself sink deeper into the bed. Dark pressed down on my eyelids. I don't know how long I drifted before the dream started playing in my head.

In it, I was standing in a barn with Damien. We watched a fully grown pig be led out before us. I looked down, noticing the gun in Damien's hands.

I thought I knew what he was about to do. But Damien didn't walk toward the pig. Instead, he turned to me and stunned me with a sharp shot to my head. I felt dazed, dizzy. The room around me spun.

When I came to, I was upside down, swinging from a hook over a bit of floor that was angled toward a drain. Damien was before me, knife in his hand. He made a quick cut at my throat, slitting it. *Motherhood is about sacrifice*, he whispered.

I kicked and screamed, but the sound that came out of my mouth wasn't mine. It was a pig's squeal. The chain I hung from swayed wildly, but I couldn't get myself free. Blood poured from my neck, dripping over my chin, soaking into the ground.

The next time I opened my mouth, the blood spilled over my lips and onto my tongue as I screamed and screamed—

I bolted upright in bed, drenched with sweat, panting. I was awake now, but I still heard screaming. I sat in the dark for a long time, listening, my chest rising and falling, my own breath roaring in my ears.

I took a few deep inhales, trying to shake off the feeling of horror that lingered from the dream. As the scream faded, I realized it was just Hank again. Hank, slaughtering those pigs.

I looked toward the window and saw that it had gotten dark outside, the oppressive, smothering dark of night in the woods. What time was it?

"Shit," I murmured, rubbing my eyes with my hands. I felt shaky, unsteady on my feet. I'd wasted an entire afternoon of work. Maria would be looking for me. She might even have another chapter ready. I crept out of my room to go find her, floorboards groaning beneath my feet.

I followed the hall past darkened bedrooms. It was strange how there weren't a lot of lights in the farmhouse, just a few lamps in the corners, sconces I couldn't figure out how to turn on. I didn't want to try all the switches on the walls to find the right ones, so I wandered in the dark. The air grew colder as I walked, darkness seeming to press in on all sides.

I made my way back to the kitchen where I'd given Maria notes a few hours ago, but there was no one here now. The room was dark, empty.

A feeling of dread crept through my shoulders as I turned in place. There was something off about the space, something I couldn't quite put my finger on. The air felt strange. Like it was holding its breath.

I was about to go back to my room when my eyes landed on the small door set into the wall, the one with the thick padlock hanging from the latch.

The padlock dangled from the shackle, open.

A zip of curiosity went through me. When would I ever get a chance to look inside Maria's locked closet again? I stared at the padlock, fingers twitching. I felt drawn like a magnet.

I swallowed, trying to ignore the feeling. I couldn't just go snooping around Maria's private spaces. I was too awkward. I would get caught.

But it *was* strange that Maria had a padlock on a door in her kitchen. What could she possibly be keeping back there that needed to be locked up? That secret ingredient that no one had ever managed to pry out of her? The thought was so enticing that I actually started salivating. I looked around. No one else was here. No sound indicated anyone was coming.

I could claim I was looking for the bathroom, for Maria.

I crossed the room and removed the padlock before I could talk myself out of it, then slowly turned the knob. It opened with a creak, revealing a narrow staircase descending into darkness.

For a moment I hesitated, but the promise of discovering Maria's mysterious secret was simply too strong to ignore. My legs seemed to move on their own, carrying me step by step.

I couldn't see much. Rough stone walls and a ceiling made of wooden beams. No lights, not even a naked bulb dangling from a chain. And the stone was so thick, it muted everything outside the stairwell. All I could hear was my own breath. It sounded loud and close.

I kept walking down. The air grew colder, damper, the scent of mildew thick in my nostrils. I couldn't shake the feeling that I was intruding on some forbidden space, that I was about to uncover something terrible. But I couldn't make myself turn around, either.

At one point, I thought I heard something behind me, a creak on the stairs that sounded like a footstep, and I flinched and whirled around, certain I was about to see Maria or one of her children framed in the doorway, demanding to know what the hell I was doing. But there was no one. I was alone.

I paused for a moment to let my breath steady.

There was an open space at the bottom of the stairs. In the dim light from the kitchen, I could see a long, wooden prep table. It looked vintage, expensive. Maria had clearly been using it as a desk. It was covered in stacks of books and papers, mason jars where she'd stowed old pens and wooden spoons, a shiny new laptop that looked out of place in the middle of all of it. Above, cluttered and chaotic shelves were filled with dozens of different-shaped jars of powders and liquids. I leaned forward, squinting at the labels. They were all handwritten in tiny script, impossible to read. One of the labels looked like it said *usnea*. I stared at the word for a long moment, recognizing it. *Sweetness and wit, they'are but mummy, possess'd*, I thought, a line from an old poem. A larger bottle beside it held a liquid that seemed to be of a similar consistency to blood.

On the opposite wall was a large metal door. I only hesitated a moment before I crossed the room and pulled the door open with a grunt. A shock of cold air hit me, surprising me so much that I took a quick step back, nearly losing my grip on the handle.

It was an industrial-sized freezer. Large cuts of meat hung from the ceiling, swaying slightly on creaking hooks. Shelves and drawers lined the walls.

I stepped inside. The icy air pierced my skin, drawing goose bumps along my arms and the back of my neck. I ran my hands up and down my arms fast for warmth. Most of the slabs bore neat labels, telling me exactly what type of animal they'd once been. *Venison, beef, lamb.* I moved cautiously, my footsteps echoing in the eerily still room as I scanned the inventory, reading the labels.

A few of the larger cuts were unlabeled. They hung from chains attached to the ceiling, flesh stripped away, only the curve of a leg or a torso to hint at the animal they had once been.

I paused, studying the unlabeled meat. Could this be Maria's secret ingredient? Some exotic meat? She kept her ingredient in a little blue tin, but she could have this dried and powdered, only ever sprinkling a little over the top for flavor.

Or maybe it was something illegal. Was that why this room was kept locked? I knew you weren't allowed to eat horse or shark fin meat in the United States, but Maria was wealthy enough that she could probably source it from somewhere, if she'd really wanted to. And I suppose it made sense that a chef would want to try everything. The scent of blood hung heavy in the air, turning my stomach. My gaze fell upon several neatly packaged bags, the familiar size and shape making it clear that the white liquid inside was human breast milk.

I made my way to the far end of the room, and my breath caught in my throat, the air so cold it seemed to freeze my lungs. There were whole animals back here, frozen before they'd been butchered. Pigs.

No, not pigs. *Piglets.*

I lifted a hand to my mouth, disgust gripping my chest as my eyes moved over the animals lined up at the back of the room. Tiny, baby pigs stacked on top of each other like firewood. Just yesterday those pigs had been alive, crawling all over each other to get to their mother, grunting happily. And now they were *here.* Dead. I released an involuntary moan when I saw Oreo, the black-and-white piglet that I'd held. I could still remember how he'd pushed his soft snout against my chin, how he'd blinked up at me with those deep, liquid black eyes that had seemed so intelligent, almost like he was a little person.

Now, he was lying on the freezer floor with his brothers and sisters, curled in a fetal position and so wrinkled I knew his blood had been drained. Ice crawled up around his nose and over his eyes, a dark, purple bruise in the middle of his forehead from where he'd been stunned and killed.

Despite the chill of the freezer, it suddenly felt stifling in this room. I didn't want to be in here anymore. Maybe it was better if Maria's secret ingredient stayed a secret.

But when I stepped out of the freezer, my eyes caught on the papers scattered across Maria's desk. I shouldn't snoop. But I couldn't help feeling curious. Was this where Maria wrote her memoir? Were those new pages?

I could just take a peek, just to see how she'd planned on ending it…

I moved the corner of her laptop aside, shifting a few smaller sheets of paper below. I could see, instantly, that it wasn't her memoir. These papers were older, the corners dog-eared, a deep fold line through the center. They'd been torn out of one of those pads that waiters used to write down orders at a restaurant. Whatever was on them was hand-written. A letter, maybe? I scanned the first line.

Dear Maria,

By the time you find this, I'll already be gone.

I jerked my hand back, like I'd been burned. This wasn't just a letter. It was Damien's suicide note. Years ago, some horrible tabloid had reprinted the whole thing. I'd read it, of course, along with every-one else who'd followed the case. That letter was what had convinced most of the world that Damien had, in fact, died by suicide.

I swallowed. Even though I'd already read it, it was different to see it here among Maria's private things. To read the *actual* letter instead of a badly photocopied version reprinted in some tabloid. I moved to shift it back below the laptop—then stopped.

This letter was three pages long. The one printed in the tabloid had been much shorter.

My heart was beating hard in my ears. Did that mean... Had it been only part of the real letter?

I couldn't stop myself; my curiosity was too strong. I pulled the letter all the way out and read.

Dear Maria,

By the time you find this, I'll already be gone. I know this will come as a shock, but please understand that I wouldn't be doing this if I saw any other way. For a long time now, it's felt like I've been walking down a dark tunnel. And, no matter how hard I try, I just can't seem to find the light at the end.

I can't do it anymore. I want out. I need it all to be over.

That was where the suicide note that I remembered ended. But it was only the first page. Holding my breath, I turned to the second page.

I think I deserve to find a bit of happiness while I'm still alive. We both do. I know now that we won't find it here, with each other. Please don't look for me. Just let me go. It'll be easier for us both. This is the only way.

You keep my secrets and I'll keep yours.

That's where the second page ended. The third page read only,

My love to you and the kids,
Damien

10

THEA

I STUDIED THE PAGES, DUMBFOUNDED. I COULD HARDLY BREATHE.

This wasn't a suicide note. It was a *goodbye* note.

That line: *I think I deserve to find a bit of happiness while I'm still alive...* It was clear from that line alone that Damien had no intention of taking his own life. He wouldn't write a goodbye letter, tell Maria he wanted to start over and find happiness somewhere else, and then drown himself in a creek. He hadn't been planning to die. He'd been planning to leave.

And yet. His clothes had been found by the creek bank. And someone had leaked this note to the press, intentionally omitting the second page so it read like a suicide note. Someone had wanted it to seem like Damien had committed suicide.

I dug my palms into my eyes. The air around me felt suddenly hot and shimmering, soupy. It was that damn sleeping draft. It was still hanging on, making me feel hungover. The colors down here were all wrong. Too bright, like a Technicolor remastering of an old movie.

Maybe that was why I couldn't make this make sense. My brain felt slow. Why go through the trouble of staging a suicide if Damien was already going to leave? Why not just let him leave? Why convince the world he was dead?

I could feel my heartbeat in the base of my throat, fluttering like a moth. Something else was bothering me. The letter was *still here*. It hadn't been sent anonymously to the media, stolen by someone Maria had thought was her friend and sold to the highest bidder. Maria had it. Which meant that someone in this house had sent it.

Issie and Enzo would have been in their early teens, plenty old enough to steal a letter and send it to a tabloid. And Hank seemed to be in and out of the house regularly, so it could have been him, too. But the most obvious culprit was Maria. I mean, the letter was *here*, on her desk.

Why would Maria try to make it seem like Damien had died by suicide?

My throat closed as the cleanest explanation occurred to me: to cover up the fact that she'd killed him.

I lowered my hands and stared at the note, at the last two lines on the second page: *You keep my secrets and I'll keep yours*. A buzzing noise started in the back of my head, like the distant drone of bees. I thought, unwillingly, of the old *Saturday Night Live* sketch, a comedian whose name I couldn't remember wearing one of the brightly colored house dresses that had always been Maria's uniform, arty glasses perched on her nose as she delightedly chopped up a fake, rubber arm. "Every family has a secret ingredient," she'd said, voice manic, edging on hysteria. My stomach clenched.

Then: a sound behind me, a creak. I whirled around, breathing hard, sure I was about to be caught. No one there. I was still alone in the strange basement room, right outside the walk-in freezer.

I looked at the freezer, thought of the big cuts of meat hanging from the ceiling, all of it unlabeled. I stood very still, breathing hard. I thought of all of the people who'd gone missing after pissing Maria off, and a sudden intrusive thought elbowed its way into my brain. *They could lock me in that freezer and no one would ever find me*. No one even knew I was here.

I was properly scared now. I didn't want to be alone down here. I shoved the letter back where I'd found it, and then I turned and fled up the stairs.

Halfway up, I heard footsteps in the kitchen.

"Please sit still," someone was saying. *Issie*, I thought. I stopped climbing and shrank back against the wall.

"Can we play unicorns?" said a little girl's voice. Ava.

"We can play when you're finished with your food. I'll set a timer, okay? You have five minutes."

A fumbling sound. I pictured Issie taking her phone out of her pocket, setting a timer just as I'd done so many times with Ruthie.

I swallowed, staring hard at the rectangle of light at the top of the stairs. A shadow passed, momentarily casting the stairway in perfect darkness.

I had a suddenly horrible thought: What if Issie closed the door? What if she snapped the padlock shut? I could be locked down here.

My throat closed. I felt suddenly claustrophobic, the walls around me inching closer.

Up in the kitchen, Ava said, "My unicorn needs a urinalysis. Where's Lila?"

Despite my fear, the word snagged. What kind of four-year-old knew the word *urinalysis*?

"Lila's in the other room right now," Issie was saying.

Ava started to whine. "I want *Lila*."

"Let's leave her in the other room while you eat, okay? That way we won't get her messy."

This, at least, sounded normal. So similar to arguments I'd had with Ruthie, her always wanting some toy with her at the dinner table, me trying to distract her. I kept my eyes on that rectangle of light and thought, *Please go get the toy please.*

Ava's whine became a full-on cry, the kind of desperate, gulping cry that children seem to be able to instantly produce.

Below the sound, I heard Issie groan. "Okay, okay, I'll go find her."

Footsteps told me she'd left the room. I exhaled. *Thank God.*

I hurried the rest of the way up the stairs and back into the kitchen, holding my breath, willing my footsteps to be silent.

Ava sat at the kitchen counter, clutching a plastic cup. I couldn't see what was in it because the sides were opaque, covered in the cartoon dog characters from *Bluey*. But then Ava turned to look at me. And I saw her face.

I felt a cold zip down my back, like someone had dragged an ice cube over my spine. Something strange happened to my breath.

It looked like Ava had been drinking straight chocolate syrup. Whatever was smeared across her lips and chin had that same thick, viscous consistency. But it wasn't brown. It was red. A deep red that was nearly black.

Blood, I thought, a fresh shudder moving through me. Ava's face was covered in blood. It created a mustache above her top lip and dribbled down her chin. It was smeared across her neck, her T-shirt.

My mouth dropped open in a silent gasp. My first thought was that she must've gotten hurt. I pictured her accidentally smacking her face against the counter, knocking out a tooth, blood pouring from her gums. I needed to help her. I took a step toward her, eyes roaming her body for the injury.

But Ava calmly took another drink from her little cup, swallowed. When she smiled at me, I saw that all her teeth were red.

The feeling changed. Not concern, not anymore. Now it was disgust, confusion, fear. I felt lightheaded, my eyes not quite focusing. For a moment, I was dizzied by the impulse to run far away from this strange little girl.

Was she drinking blood?

I didn't hear the footsteps behind me, didn't even realize Issie had come back into the room until she said, "Thea, I didn't know you were here."

I whirled around. "Issie..." I choked out, pointing, "I—I just saw—"

Issie's eyes moved past me and landed on her daughter. I expected shock, surprise, but she just blinked and said in a very calm voice, "Oh no, honey. Did you get another bloody nose?" She grabbed a towel off the counter and swooped in, pressing it to her daughter's face. To me, she added easily, "She gets them all the time. The air up here is so dry."

"Oh," I said, blinking. Of course. Ruthie got bloody noses too, sometimes. In the winter. Here was a logical explanation. One that I—a mother—should have come to before I jumped to *drinking blood*. My face flushed. Yet the uneasy feeling lingered.

"Come on, baby. Let's get you cleaned up." Issie helped Ava down from the stool and ushered her out of the kitchen, still pressing that towel to her face.

I crossed my arms over my chest, smiling awkwardly as I watched them leave. I felt groggy and keyed up at the same time, as though I'd gotten drunk last night and overcorrected with too much coffee. After the dark of the basement, it seemed much, much too bright in this room. Light glinted off the stainless steel sink, shining right into my eyes. The beginnings of a headache tapped at my temples.

Calm down, I imagined Jacob telling me. *This isn't* Jane Eyre. *They aren't keeping Damien Capello locked in their secret freezer.*

The *SNL* sketch had been a horrible, sexist joke. Ava was a normal little girl who'd gotten a bloody nose. And that note…

A muscle in my chest tightened. I still couldn't explain the note.

....

Back in my room, I couldn't stop thinking about it. The suicide note that wasn't actually a suicide note. Definitive proof that someone in this house was a liar.

Maria had promised me the truth. *This account is the whole story, the only story,* she'd written. *The truth, finally.* Even if she hadn't been the one to send the note to the press, she'd still read it. She knew Damien had run off, and she'd lied to me about it. Lied by omission, but still. She'd known this whole time that Damien hadn't died by suicide. And she'd never said.

I felt the betrayal as a twist in my gut. It was a moment before I recognized the emotion. *Humiliation.* I'd trusted Maria. I knew this story would be hard for her and I'd wanted to make it easier, and so I'd told her things about my past, about my father, things I didn't usually talk about.

I thought of the weight of Maria's hand on my own in the middle of the night. The gentle way she'd called me "dear." Suddenly, I was blinking too hard, tears gathering behind my eyelids. I perched on the edge of my bed and dropped my head in my hands.

Maria must be planning to tell me the truth at the end of this project, I told myself. It was the only explanation that made sense. She'd already admitted to lying to her kids so they wouldn't grow up thinking their dad was a monster. Wasn't this just more of the same? Wouldn't it be easier for them to believe their dad had died than that he'd left them? I bet this book was her way of finally coming clean, that she was planning to end it with the revelation that Damien was still alive, that he was living it up somewhere with Nina.

I took a breath, feeling a little better. That would explain why she was being so weird about the chapters. She'd loved Damien more than anything, and he'd left her. And she'd maintained this lie for years. She would certainly want people to understand why before she admitted to it.

I stared at the space below my door, willing another chapter to slide into my room and explain everything. Nothing came. I chewed on my lip. I was antsy, unsettled. And so tired of waiting. This was starting to feel like what had happened with Hughes all over again, but it was a million times worse because it was *Maria.* A woman I'd trusted, a woman I'd loved.

I wanted answers. And I wanted them now, not whenever Maria felt like handing out a new chapter.

I thought for a second, chewing my lip. It was a long shot, but there might be someone else in this house who could give them to me.

....

I could just make out a face in the shadows behind the cracked-open door, the lines of a chin and jaw, the faintest reflective glow of light glinting off glasses.

"Amy?" I asked.

"Thea?" She pulled the door open wider. Hair fell from her bun and red lipstick smudged across her cheek, like she'd forgotten she was wearing it and had wiped a hand over her mouth. "What are you doing here?"

"Is Enzo with you?"

Amy shook her head. "Maria has us in separate rooms. Wouldn't have expected her to be so puritanical, but I guess you never know."

"Right." I took a breath. "Actually, I wanted to talk to you."

Amy lifted her eyebrows. "Yeah?"

"Do you remember me?" I asked. Amy looked politely bewildered, so I added, "We've met before. At a party?"

She started to shake her head. "I'm sorry—"

"We talked about Kincaid Hughes," I said, interrupting her. Then, gathering courage I didn't entirely feel, I blurted, "You had my phone while I was in the bathroom. In fact, you were the only person other than me who had access to my phone that night, which is why I thought it was weird when the screenshots I told you about in private found their way online the next day."

Amy's expression didn't change, but there was a slight chill to her voice as she said, "Why don't you come in?"

I stepped into her room, and she closed the door behind me. She still hadn't turned the light on, but a bit of sunlight made its way through the trees outside her window. I could just see the edges of overstuffed leather chairs and bookshelves crowded with dustcover-less books, a heavy wooden bed. She hadn't unpacked so much as she'd exploded into the room. There were things—clothes, toiletries, shoes, electronic equipment—strewn everywhere.

Amy nudged a window open. Cool air blew in all around us. "I don't know what you—" she started, but I wasn't in the mood. Whether she meant to or not, this woman had nearly destroyed my career. I wasn't about to let her push me around.

"I overheard you on the phone the other night," I interrupted. "You said something about Maria and blackmail. And then I saw you meeting up with someone in the woods." I made myself look at her directly. "I know you have some ulterior motive for being here. I wasn't planning to tell Maria, but if you keep lying to me, I might change my mind."

For a moment, Amy's expression stayed carefully blank. Then, a smile tugged at the corner of her lips. "Wow, okay." With her free hand, she removed a carton of cigarettes from her pocket. "I really didn't think you had it in you to play hardball."

"So you do remember me?"

Amy nodded. "You were pretty shit-faced at that party, I didn't think you remembered me." She pulled a canary-yellow cigarette out of the carton with her teeth. I stared for a moment. I'd never seen cigarettes like that before.

"They're CBD," she explained when she saw me looking. "Been trying to quit the real ones." She leaned out the window to light the cigarette, careful to blow the smoke outside. "So, you gathered up your courage and burst into my room, chest out, all brave, threatening to blow up my spot. Why?" She wrinkled her nose. "Something got you spooked?"

Her entire demeanor was different than it had been moments ago. Her back was straighter, her voice deeper. It was like the other Amy had been a character she was playing.

"I guess you could say that," I said carefully. "I found something just now. It has me a little confused."

"Let me guess. You don't think Maria's being entirely honest with you. You realized that something about this place doesn't quite add up?" Amy motioned to the room with her cigarette, smoke lazily drifting around her. The earthy, herbal-scented smoke was burning the back of my throat.

I shrugged my shoulders. Something was bothering me. Amy didn't seem like a girl embarrassed to be caught snooping around her boyfriend's family. She didn't seem embarrassed to be found out at all, actually. "Is that why you've been poking around? Because you found something that doesn't add up?"

Amy raised an eyebrow, amused. "You first. What'd you find?"

I shook my head. I wasn't going to tell her about the letter. For all I knew, she'd sneak down to the basement and snap a picture of it, send it straight to HushHush. If they really were paying her for tips like Cassandra thought, they'd probably cough up a lot of cash for that.

Instead, I said, "I only came here because I wanted to ask..." I hesitated, thinking how to phrase this. "I wanted to know if you've found anything that led you to believe that Damien might still be alive? That he and Nina Casey maybe...ran away together?"

Amy blew smoke out from between her teeth, watching me. After a long moment, she started to laugh. "That's all you could come up with? C'mon, Woods, I know you've heard what people say about this family." She dropped her voice, making it sound faux-spooky as she said, "Murder, cannibalism, meatballs made of people."

I thought of the *SNL* sketch. Rubber hands in a pot. Ava's mouth smeared with blood. I felt suddenly queasy.

"You don't really think I went all undercover because Damien Capello ran away with his girlfriend, do you?" Amy added.

"You can't think any of that cannibal stuff is true."

Amy shrugged. "Maybe I do, maybe I don't. Before we get into it, I want to hear more about this memoir Maria's writing."

All at once, I realized what was bothering me. The shift in Amy's demeanor, the comment she let slip about how she was "undercover." No one would go through all this trouble to send a tip to some anonymous social media account, not even if they were getting paid.

"It's your account, isn't it?" I said. I knew I was right. "You run HushHush?"

Amy smiled wide. "Surprised?"

Surprised was an understatement. I was stunned, shocked. The shock felt like a fist to my chest; it winded me. I swallowed, an involuntary gulp for air.

This woman had destroyed me. Or she'd tried to. I wanted to slap her. I curled my hand into a fist.

"Forget I came here," I said and turned toward the door.

"Wait," Amy said. "Anything you tell me can be off the record this time, I promise." But she was already shuffling around in a tote bag.

After a moment she produced a small, black leather notebook and folded it open.

I glanced at the notebook. "Doesn't seem very off the record to me."

"You're worried about this?" Amy looked surprised. "Don't be. No one sees it but me. It's basically my brain." She pointed her yellow cigarette at me. "I can tell you whatever you want to know about Damien. But I want some more information about this book Maria's writing."

I hesitated at the door. Despite everything, I couldn't help being curious about what she knew. "I really can't talk about the book," I told her. "I signed an NDA."

"That's not how this works. You have to give me something if you want something from me." She watched me, expectant.

"Seems like I've already given you something," I pointed out. "You stole screenshots from my phone. You nearly destroyed my career, and I never got anything in exchange. The way I see it, it's your turn."

Amy studied me for a moment and then took another drag on her cigarette. "Fair enough," she said. "I'm here because Enzo went to Exeter with my older brother. Back when they were in school together there were all these stories about Enzo. His junior year, he started hanging out with this other kid, skipping classes, smoking pot, that sort of thing. It got so bad they were both suspended for a few weeks. Enzo came back, but the other kid never did."

Amy kept her eyes on me for one beat too long, then shivered and added, "No one ever found out what happened to him. And that's not the only time I've heard about someone the Capellos don't like disappearing into thin air. There was another butcher who tried to open a place in Woodstock. His name was Todd Sheridan. Look him up. Two months after his shop opened, it closed without warning and no one ever saw poor Todd again."

I thought of the story I'd heard, about the editor who'd worked with Maria, who'd wound up leaving his job, the city. I tried not to shiver.

With her free hand, Amy slapped her notebook closed. "Now it's your turn. Tell me what Maria wrote about the night Damien died." When she said the word *died*, she did air quotes with her free hand.

"We haven't gotten to that part yet."

Amy groaned and stubbed the cigarette out on the windowsill. "You're killing me here, Woods."

"I can't tell you something I don't know."

She shook her head, annoyed now. "Fine, have it your way. I have to head into town to see a source. If you change your mind about talking, I'll be at that coffee shop, Perk Up!, for the next hour." The corner of her mouth quirked. "Unless you're planning on following me around in the woods again tonight?"

My throat closed. "You saw me?"

"Yeah, spying is maybe not your strong suit." Amy walked over to the bed and lifted a corner of the mattress, producing a small, black flip phone. A burner. "What's your number?"

I hesitated. Amy rolled her eyes. "It's not violating your NDA to give me your phone number."

"Fine." I gave in and told her, watching as she tapped it in.

"I know Maria took your phone—she took mine, too—but I'm texting you my number anyway," Amy said, tucking the burner back under the mattress. She straightened and led me back into the hall. "Once you get back to the city, I think you're going to realize you'd rather read what I know about the Capellos before it's published."

Something inside of me went cold. "Read?"

In response, Amy smiled wide. It was a gotcha smile. The smile of a cartoon cat zeroing in on its prey. "I'm not just doing some dumb video about the Capellos," she told me. "I'm writing a book about them."

....

A book. It was all I could think about as I walked back to my room. Amy was writing a book.

About *what*?

I thought about the story she'd told about Enzo leaving school. Another person who'd disappeared after upsetting Maria.

I closed my eyes, pushing the thought out of my head. Who knows if the story was even true? Amy could just be trying to goad me into giving her something. The cannibalism rumors had been around for the last thirty years, but there had *never* been a shred of truth to them. They'd started because of a comedy sketch, for crying out loud. And, even if the story was true, lots of kids transferred schools. There was probably a perfectly rational explanation. The story only seemed creepy because Amy was making it sound mysterious.

Go to town, I told myself. *Ask her yourself.* But that would mean making the same mistake I'd made with Hughes. Doing the one thing Maria had told me not to do. Potentially ruining my last chance to save my career.

I wanted to call Cassandra, see what she thought about all this. But, of course, I didn't have my phone. I could check the Wi-Fi, try to set up another Zoom. Or I could go upstairs and use the landline. Hell, maybe I'd get lucky and find the kitchen empty.

Neither option appealed. I understood why Amy kept taking phone calls outside in the middle of the night. I felt strangely exposed in this house, even alone in my room. It would be incredibly easy to listen in on someone's conversation here. There were so many shadowy, unlit corners and odd nooks and crannies where anyone could hide.

I was still turning my options over in my head when I opened the door to my room and saw the fresh stack of pages sitting on the floor, waiting for me. My whole body tensed.

The next chapter was here.

THE SECRET INGREDIENT

CHAPTER FIVE

There are reasons fairy tales always end right after the wedding. Before babies and a house in the suburbs, before the bills and the chores, kids complaining that they don't want to eat their breakfast or wear socks, a husband who snores and a wife who stops shaving her legs. Parents with health problems. Before *life*.

Believe me, staying home with two kids under the age of five was not the thing of fairy tales, and it was certainly not the future I'd dreamed of when Damien and I first fell in love. Every day was painfully monotonous. Isabella would wake first, around five in the morning, long before a single ray of sunlight had a chance to pierce the sky. I'd hear her sweet, high voice in her bedroom, singing "Row, Row, Row Your Boat," or her ABCs, and I'd stumble into the hall, eyes crusted with sleep, and sweep her out of her room and into my bed before she had a chance to wake the baby. For the next hour or so I would try to snooze while she played tea party on my back, until Enzo finally began to scream and I realized I'd gotten all the sleep I was going to get for the day.

Then it was down to the kitchen, balancing Enzo in one arm as Issie grabbed my leg, begging for pizza and cupcakes for breakfast, settling for scrambled eggs as long as I didn't put any butter or cheese or salt or pepper in them, and if I shook the blue and purple sprinkles left over from her last birthday over the top.

Occasionally, I'd reminisce while I stirred those eggs. I used to be a cook. A *real* cook. When Damien and I first married, I'd made a study of eggs. I'd spent weeks experimenting with heat and time, with whether to stir the eggs constantly or not at all, whether to add cheese or let the insides remain creamy, whether to fold or scramble, how much to season. I used to make *phenomenal* scrambled eggs. Damien once told me they were the best he'd ever eaten.

But, in those early days, with just the kids to cook for, my eggs were bland and weirdly sweet, from the sprinkles. The only other cooking I did was slicing fruit and scattering Cheerios onto the table, occasionally slapping peanut butter and jelly on soft, tasteless bread.

The kids and I spent afternoons taking meandering walks around the neighborhood, no matter the weather. I'd bundle us all up when it got chilly, wear waterproof shoes when it rained. I didn't care that it was uncomfortable, that I was miserable and cold, that the kids complained. I was so desperate to see something other than the four walls of our playroom, to speak to another adult. I made awkward conversation with everyone I came across, asking the grocery check-out boy his plans for the weekend, smiling too enthusiastically at the strangers I passed on the street.

When dinner rolled around, I made pasta. Issie didn't like tomato sauce or meat or cheese. She wanted everything to be bland mush, easy to digest, always the same. When she wasn't looking, I'd mix in the smallest amount of butter I could manage without her calling me out on it. I couldn't help myself.

Perhaps you're wondering where Damien was those days. To be perfectly honest, I didn't always know. He was around, sometimes, usually out in the slaughterhouse with the pigs. But more often than not he wasn't there, always tied up with the reality of owning a restaurant. There were staff meetings to attend, fish markets that opened at five in the morning that he had to arrive at early if he was going to nab the freshest cuts. There were meetings with investors, and of course, there was the restaurant itself, open every day from five until ten.

Damien could've come home right at ten—he had staff to handle closing the restaurant. But more often than not, he wouldn't stroll through our front door until well after midnight, would head straight to the shower to wash the smell of garlic and tomato sauce from his skin. Among other things.

The realist in me, of course, wondered if he was still screwing Nina. I'd never asked him about it. I wouldn't have been able to stand listening to him tell me that it didn't mean anything. Or, unthinkably, that it did. Instead, I'd lie awake in bed, listening to the drone of water hitting tile, and wonder if he'd been with her while I made dinner for his children, if he'd whispered sweet nothings into her ear while I wiped snotty noses and ran warm baths and kissed scraped knees and missed him.

And then there were the interviews. As the restaurant's popularity grew, more and more publications got in touch, wanting to talk to the brilliant mind behind the food. Mind. Never minds. *I* had written

Polpette's menu, *I'd* been the one who'd painstakingly tested each and every dish. But of course the papers only ever wanted to talk to Damien. He was the genius chef, the person inevitably photographed with the celebrities who would sometimes drive up from the city to try the food. He was the star. I was just his wife.

He would leave the publications out for me, magazines and newspapers spread across our sticky kitchen tables, already turned to the page of his interview. So proud. I read what my husband had to say about our lives while mixing formula, Enzo wailing on my hip.

I hear you're a family man as well as a restaurateur. Do you find it hard to balance?
It's definitely tricky at times. Of course, I'm lucky that Polpette is primarily dinner service so I'm able to be home in the morning to help with breakfast. And I have the most amazing wife, Maria.

You opened Polpette with your wife, right?
I did, yes. Maria is a truly incredible partner, both in business and in life. In the early days we ran the business together, but lately she's been spending her time with the children and leaving the restaurant world to me. Sometimes I think she got the better end of the deal! But she honestly makes it all look easy. Maria was born to be a mother.

I can't tell you how many times I reread the things he said about me. He always said the nicest things, things he hadn't said *to* me in months. *Maria is the most incredible partner. I have the most amazing wife. She makes it look easy.*

I had to believe he meant it. It was something I held on to. He loved me, even if he did go directly to the butcher shop after he finished speaking to these reporters, to fuck Nina against the counter while, back in his house, I swayed and bounced and sang, desperately trying to rock his children to sleep. I was his "incredible partner," his "amazing wife." He *loved* me; he only had sex with her.

I told myself this was just a bump in a long marriage. It wasn't surprising that Damien had needs I couldn't fulfill just then. The kids drained me of all desire to touch, to be touched. I'd spend long days with both of their small, hot bodies pressed against mine, their sticky hands on my face, in my hair. They'd give me kisses until my skin felt raw, hold me so tight I'd find it hard to breathe, and when I finally unwound them from me and put them to bed, I wanted nothing more than to be by myself, to be untouched. To have a moment where my body belonged only to me.

I missed my husband. But I missed myself more. I missed the woman I'd been before I'd become a mother. And I missed cooking, *really* cooking. I missed my restaurant and my staff, missed the challenge of making sure everyone who came through our doors left well fed.

I started writing while the kids napped. Nothing too exciting, just jotting down recipes I wanted to try once I had some free time. A perfect braciole and stuffed chicken legs wrapped in prosciutto, duck with sage and onion confit and Broccolini smothered with schmaltz and pistachio.

Once, I woke in the night, the sound of our front door opening and closing cutting through my dreams like an alarm. When I came into the living room, Damien was there, smelling of the slaughterhouse and wide awake even though, to me, it was the middle of the night. I must've left the pages I'd written that afternoon on the counter, because he was reading them.

He looked up when he heard me in the hall, a little V creasing the skin between his eyebrows. He seemed disappointed that I was awake.

"These are good," he'd told me, flipping to the next recipe. Then, under his breath, "Really good."

I'd stayed in the hall, not sure how to respond. Perhaps I should've been flattered. But there was something about the way he'd said that. *Really good.* It hadn't sounded like a compliment.

For the last three decades, that moment has stuck in my mind. The expression on Damien's face when he looked up at me after reading my recipes, it had been almost like jealousy. But why should he be jeal-ous? Our love of cooking was always something we'd shared. Wasn't it enough that I'd mothered his children, that I'd stood beside him, helped him build his dream from the ground up?

Even after all that, he seemed to want more. The way he'd looked at me, it was like he wanted to crack my head like a nut and scrape out whatever talent I had left. Keep it for himself.

A Perfect Wife and Mother's Braciole

These braciole use flavors that are traditional to my family. Other variants will add pine nuts and currants, or prosciutto with cheese, omitting the breadcrumbs. Some recipes will instruct you to use a tomato basil sauce or deglaze with red wine. Another common variant will use thinly sliced tough cuts like top round instead of flank steak. All are fine options in my opinion, but to me this basic preparation evokes memories of my grandmother's kitchen, and sometimes the basics are the best. The only nonnegotiable is the breadcrumbs, which must not be prepackaged but real, fresh breadcrumbs, which are easy to make and last indefinitely in your freezer.

INGREDIENTS

7 medium garlic cloves
1 handful parsley
1 cup breadcrumbs
Salt and black pepper to taste
2 tablespoons olive oil
½ cup Pecorino Romano
1 whole flank steak, about 1½ to 2 pounds
½ of a large onion
1 small carrot
1 celery stalk
1 small handful thyme sprigs
1 (28-ounce) can crushed tomatoes
3 bay leaves
2 tablespoons tomato paste

STEPS

Serves 4 to 6

1. First make the filling. Very finely mince 4 of the garlic cloves and parsley. Mix with the breadcrumbs, a few gratings of black

pepper, a big pinch of salt, a drizzle of olive oil, and the cheese. Set aside.

2. Butterfly the flank steak and then place on a flat working surface under a double layer of plastic wrap. Pound to a quarter-inch thick using a meat mallet. The meat should be an irregular square shape. Typically braciola will be smaller, about the length of sausages, but in this case we will make 2 long braciole.

3. Season the meat on both sides with salt and pepper, then lay flat. Cover with the breadcrumb mixture, leaving a little border so it doesn't spill out, then roll up, jelly-roll style, pressing and tucking to form a tight, even braciole. Cut 2 long lengths of kitchen twine and truss securely, then set aside.

4. To make the sauce, cut the onion, carrot, and celery into small dice, tie the thyme sprigs with some kitchen twine into a small bouquet, and lightly crush the remaining 3 garlic cloves. In a large pot, sweat the vegetables in 2 tablespoons olive oil with a big pinch of salt over medium low until caramelizing, about 10 to 15 minutes. Add in the tomato paste and stir for a few minutes, until lightly browning, then pour in the crushed tomatoes, swirling 1 cup of water in the can to get the last of the tomatoes and adding that. Scrape up any brown bits from the bottom of the pot, then add the thyme bouquet, bay leaves, and crushed garlic. Bring to a boil, then reduce to a simmer, cooking for about 30 minutes. Remove the thyme before proceeding with the recipe.

5. For the braciole, heat a drizzle of olive oil in a fry pan over medium heat and sear on all sides. This should take between 8 and 15 minutes. Remove from the pan and deglaze with a splash of water, scraping up the brown bits. Pour the deglazed liquid into the tomato sauce, then add in the braciole.

6. Adjust the heat to a low simmer and set the lid ajar. Simmer for 1½ hours, stirring frequently to avoid any burning on the bottom of the pot.

7. Remove the braciole from the pot and check for doneness with a meat thermometer. The internal temperature should be at least 180°F, preferably closer to 190°F to 200°F. Set the braciole on a cutting board and tent with foil. Remove the bay leaves and crushed garlic, and season to taste with salt.

8. Snip the strings on the braciole and discard, then cut crosswise into half-inch medallions, handling with tongs to avoid burning your hands. Serve hot over Parmesan polenta, spooning some of the sauce over the top and garnishing with lemon and pine nut gremolata and a drizzle of high-quality olive oil.

11

THEA

I FINISHED THE NEW PAGES IN MINUTES, AND THEN I DROPPED
my head into my hands, groaning.

Maria's story was so similar to mine. It wasn't the same thing my
dad had done to me and my mom, but I couldn't stop my mind from
going there. It hurt to read.

I remembered how I'd come home after school the day my dad left
us for the second time, excited because I'd stopped by a Walgreens
on the way home and picked up a new deck of cards, ones with Ren
and Stimpy characters on them because he thought that show was so
funny and I knew he'd like them. But he was just…gone. No note or
anything. He'd simply thrown me and my mom away. Like we were
trash. Like we were nothing.

My throat felt suddenly tight. I'd wanted these pages to give me
answers, but all they'd done was open up old wounds. Had Damien
left his family for the same reasons my dad had left his? Because things
had gotten too hard, too real, because he hadn't wanted the responsibility anymore? Had he left Maria alone with two small kids and a
business that was hemorrhaging money? Disappeared the way so many
men disappeared—because family life wasn't what they'd expected,

because it was so much easier for them to leave than it was for women? Because they *could*?

The thought left me feeling ill. If that's what happened, it would explain why Maria had lied about the note, not just to me but to the world. It would explain why she'd spent her whole life becoming the perfect housewife, the perfect mother. I'd always feared I wasn't someone worth staying for. A therapist might say it was why I was so reluctant to ask Jacob for help with Ruthie, why I was so much more likely to keep my complaints to myself, even when it felt like I was drowning. I thought of all those sad, quiet meals after my dad had gone, just me and my mom in our shitty little apartment, water stains on the ceiling, a toilet that never stopped gurgling. Even when I was a kid, it had been clear to me why he'd wanted to leave. *I'd* wanted to leave.

I pinched the bridge of my nose, right below the place where my glasses rested. I started to wish I hadn't gone to see Amy. I could almost convince myself of all of this, that the note meant nothing, that Maria hadn't lied so much as she'd withheld the whole truth. But Amy's taunt echoed in my head.

You really think I went all undercover and came out here because Damien Capello ran away with his girlfriend?

Murder, cannibalism, meatballs made of people.

She couldn't be telling the truth. It was too outlandish. She could've just said all that to get me to tell her what I'd learned from Maria's memoir, to trick me.

I reread everything Maria had written, all my own notes. There wasn't anything there that I hadn't already pored over dozens of times. I tried to connect to the internet, but it was off again. Calling Cassandra was out. So was doing my own research. All I had were Maria's words, Maria's story, and this growing suspicion that something wasn't right.

Anger and frustration bubbled up inside of me. I couldn't work like this. I needed internet access. I needed to check my email and get in touch with Cassandra. I needed answers.

If you change your mind about talking, I'll be at that coffee shop, Perk Up!, for the next hour, Amy had said. *It can be off the record.*

I started gathering my things before I'd fully made the decision. I didn't have to talk to Amy. I could just go to the coffee shop to get some work done. I knew they had internet access. And I wanted to call Jacob and Ruthie again, anyway.

But I knew I was fooling myself. By the time I'd left my room, hurrying down the hall in search of my car, I'd basically already decided.

I *needed* to know whether the woman I'd loved practically my entire life was a monster. If that meant giving up a few details about the book, I could stomach that. No one would have to know.

....

This morning, Enzo said Gavin probably stuck my car in the garage for safekeeping. I had no idea where the garage was, and it took me longer than I expected to find it. I wandered along the hallway for fifteen minutes, twenty, knocking softly on closed doors before easing them open to peer into dark bedrooms and bathrooms.

Finally, I opened a door into a wide-open space that looked like a showroom. Marble floors and white walls and a high wooden-beam ceiling, two rows of shiny cars lined up along the walls, like jewels.

My footsteps echoed hollowly. I wasn't a car person, I didn't know the names of any of the vehicles lined up in here, but even I could tell they were expensive. Hood ornaments flashed at the corners of my eyes. I recognized the blue and white of BMWs, a horse that I was pretty sure meant Ferrari, but there was also a blocky B with wings, a woman with a flowing dress, and yet more wings. I resisted the urge to run my fingers along the spotless paint. To touch the ornaments. Find out what obscene levels of wealth felt like.

My Kia was parked beside a floor-to-ceiling window, the world on the other side a perfect pitch-black.

I stopped walking. Okay, so I found my car. Now how the hell was I supposed to get it out of here?

"Do you need some help?"

The voice made me jump. I spun around.

A figure stood in the door that led back to the hallway, face all in shadow. Could've been anyone. But there was something about the build and the set of his shoulders that made me think of that photograph of Damien and Maria standing in front of the farmhouse back in the '80s.

Nerves crawled up my spine. I took an automatic step backward.

But then the figure moved forward and the garage lights caught the sharp lines of his face, a swoop of blond hair. Not Damien, Enzo.

He looked more casual than I'd seen him so far, in a raggedy Princeton T-shirt, basketball shorts, and running shoes. With him dressed like this, I could almost picture him on one of the neighborhood basketball courts with Jacob, trying to get a game going.

"Need to get your car out?" he asked.

Before I could answer, he produced a remote, seemingly out of nowhere, and pointed it at the back of the room. A second later, there was a grinding noise, and the floor-to-ceiling windows that took up the entire back wall began to roll upward.

Relief moved through me. I didn't realize how trapped I'd felt until that exact moment.

I turned back to Enzo. "You don't happen to know where the keys…"

Enzo was already popping open a shiny silver case near the door and scanning a row of keys until he found the ones for the Kia. He plucked them off a hook, tossed them to me.

I caught them in one hand, my one and only moment of athletic grace in a highly uncoordinated life. "Thanks."

"No problem." He flashed me a smile that seemed to glow in the dark.

I turned back to the Kia, fumbling with the key. But when I reached the driver's-side door, I stopped short.

The front left wheel sat directly on the marble floor, the deflated tire pooled around it.

Nestled deep in the rubber was a shiny silver nail.

12

THEA

THE BACK OF MY NECK FELT SUDDENLY COLD. MY THROAT CON-
stricted. I couldn't hear anything over the sound of blood thumping
in my temples, a steady hammering that blurred my vision, making it
impossible to focus on anything outside of the tire, the nail.

"Damn," Enzo said under his breath. He was right behind me all of
a sudden, too close. I was aware of the heat coming off his body, the
smell of his sweat.

I jerked away. My heart was still going too fast, and there was a
strange, bitter taste in the back of my throat.

The car hadn't had a flat when I drove it up to this house. I was sure
of it. I was a nervy driver, I hated changing tires, and I was more aware
than most of that specific off-balance feeling a vehicle gets when the
tire is deflating, the uneven thud of the wheel hitting pavement. I was
sure I'd have noticed.

Which could only mean that someone had *put* that nail in my tire.
That someone wanted to keep me here.

The walls around me seemed to press in, the air becoming heavy,
oppressive. I felt trapped. I felt like an animal locked in a cage.

Enzo frowned at me and he must've seen something in my face

that made him nervous because he shifted his weight, putting a little more space between the two of us. The soles of his shoes squeaked on marble. "Hey, that's really bad luck. But don't worry; this sort of thing happens all the time. The roads out here are terrible. We'll get it fixed."

I nodded, but I couldn't bring myself to speak. The roads out here *were* terrible. Was I being paranoid? Maybe the tire had picked up a nail on the way from the front drive to the garage. That was certainly possible, wasn't it?

But something tugged at my brain as I stared at the tire. It was the nail head: shiny, new, like it had just been plucked out of a plastic carton purchased from the hardware store. I knelt next to the tire, tried to slide the edge of my fingernail beneath the nail head, to pull it out. Impossible. It was driven in too deep. Like someone had taken a hammer to it.

Enzo was already pulling a phone out of his pocket, dialing. After a moment, said, "Gavin? Enzo. Listen, we have a flat in the garage. Can you get the mechanic to take a look?" A few more grunts and, "Sounds good," and Enzo hung up. To me, he said, "You want to borrow something while you're waiting?"

I hesitated, my mind immediately going to all those trashy thrillers I'd read where killers cut brake lines, where the hero's car swerved off the road into the woods.

"I think I'll just call an Uber," I said. An Uber was safer.

But Enzo gave me a look. "Yeah, not really possible to get an Uber out here."

I closed my eyes thinking, *Of course*. And, anyway, I still didn't have my phone.

"You can take the Beemer," Enzo said, nodding to a sleek, silver sedan. Then, perhaps seeing the look of apprehension on my face, he added, "Don't worry, Thea. Gavin will have this fixed up in no time."

I nodded. But I wasn't sure I believed him.

....

I was hoping Enzo would let me take the car and leave, but he took his time. It was fifteen minutes before Gavin arrived, and then he wanted me to explain exactly where I'd driven and when I'd first noticed the nail. He studied the tire, noted the brand, disappeared for a few minutes to see if they had a similar one they could part with. Only then did Enzo hand me the keys.

Perk Up! was already closed for the day by the time I got to town, nearly forty-five minutes after Amy had told me she'd be there. The door was locked, lights off, chairs neatly stacked on tables. I parked out front, then walked all the way around the building, hoping Amy might still be hanging around one of the outdoor café tables or leaning against the brick wall in the parking lot, smoking. But there was no one. I'd missed her.

A flare of disproportionate, almost irrational anger shot through me. It was one thing to miss meeting Amy. But now I had no way to read my email or call my family. I hadn't spoken to Ruthie and Jacob all day.

Why the *hell* had I let these people take my phone? I felt manipulated, controlled. Even here in town, with the BMW parked at the curb, I felt completely cut off from the outside world.

I pressed my thumb into the space between my eyes. A migraine was building in my skull, the pain a dull, spreading fog. I needed water, food, another nap.

Think, I told myself. Coffee shops would all be closed for the day, but they weren't the only places where you could access the internet. Where else could I go? A restaurant or bar? A library? I started walking down the street, found a bar that was already open. The tattooed bartender told me they didn't have Wi-Fi but directed me to the Woodstock Public Library.

"It's only open until six," she warned, jerking her head to indicate the clock hanging on the wall behind her. It was five, the minute hand slowly inching past the three. I had forty-five minutes.

I went back to the BMW and drove a block past town, even though the library was only a ten-minute walk.

I noticed, detachedly, that my fingers were trembling. I pulled to a stop at a red light, forced myself to take my hands off the wheel and shake them out, to take a breath. When I closed my eyes, I saw that nail in the tire of my rental car. So shiny and new.

Had someone done that on purpose? Put the nail in my car intentionally to keep me from leaving the farm?

And, if so, *why*?

Any member of Maria's family could've had their reasons. Issie didn't want her mom working on this book. She'd made that clear. And she didn't seem to like Amy. I'd assumed the animosity she'd shown toward her at dinner my first night here was about that awkward tradwife comment, but maybe it was deeper than that. Maybe Issie knew about Amy's channel and that she was working on a story about her family. She could've overheard us talking in Amy's room. I pictured Issie wandering down the hall, looking for a place to pump, the sound of our voices stopping her. I imagined her pressing her ear to the door to listen, and for a moment, the image was so clear that I was sure it was true. Issie could've driven that nail into my tire to keep me from talking to Amy, easy.

And then there was Enzo, who seemed so oblivious, who trusted Amy despite her obvious ulterior motives. Could all that be a lie? Could he know more than he let on, have some plan I hadn't figured out yet? Amy didn't look like his normal type. Maybe I'd gotten it all wrong. Maybe she wasn't using him. Maybe he was using her.

A possibility occurred to me, so suddenly that I was annoyed with myself for not considering it before. Damien was Enzo's dad. If Amy knew Damien was alive, wouldn't Enzo want to help find him?

I chewed my lip, turning that theory over in my head. He could have gotten back from working out early, overheard me and Amy talking, and Amy's offer to meet me in town. Maybe he knew Amy had something on his family and he was trying to keep it from getting out. He'd lent me the BMW without a second thought, but he'd also delayed me just long enough to miss meeting Amy. That felt a little convenient.

There was one other person it could've been, the person I was most desperate to believe wouldn't do this, even as I had to admit she was a likely culprit.

Maria.

Maria had controlled everything I'd done since I stepped foot inside her house. She'd taken my phone, cut off my internet access, had me waiting by the door for another scrap of her manuscript like Pavlov's dog.

Something deep inside me gave a horrible sick lurch. She'd also told me she hadn't wanted me to do any outside research. That I wasn't supposed to talk to anyone else about what I'd read. She could've overheard us and decided to do something to save me from myself. I thought of stories I'd heard from friends with overbearing mothers, how they used to lock their bedroom doors at night, take their phones, search the kids' bedrooms for cigarettes and drugs. Things my own mother never would've bothered with.

I tightened my fingers around the steering wheel, watched the light turn green, and stepped on the gas.

....

There was no one else at the Woodstock Public Library except for the librarian, a man in his seventies hunched behind the front desk, reading a paperback copy of *Needful Things* by Stephen King. I asked him for the Wi-Fi password, then made my way to an area at the back of the building where beat-up wooden desks had been arranged with older-model black monitors and keyboards and various assorted computer equipment. I cleared a space between two monitors, pulled out my laptop, and emailed Cassandra: We need to talk ASAP. Let me know when you can hop on Zoom.

I stared at my inbox, willing a new message from Cassandra to appear. The clock in the corner of my computer screen changed from 5:27 to 5:28 to 5:29. Nothing came.

I googled "Damien Capello fake death." There were a few Reddit threads, a link to Quora, a YouTube video. Halfway down the page of results was a story from *Delish*: "Is Damien Capello Alive? Here Are Seven Reasons People Believe It."

I had some vague memory of hearing about this conspiracy before, but it had never grabbed my attention. It wasn't like the rumors that Maria had been involved in Damien's disappearance, or even the more grotesque conspiracies about cannibalism. It was more fringe, the kind of thing nobody really believed. Honestly, I was surprised to find a real article about it at all.

I scanned the *Delish* article. Most of the "proof" was bogus: blurry photos that sort of looked like Damien Capello if you squinted, a few eyewitness accounts from people claiming to have seen him in Canada and Mexico and Argentina.

Then, at the bottom of the article, a single clear photograph that made me pause.

It was a man who appeared to be in his seventies, with white hair and deep lines around his eyes and mouth, looking over his shoulder, an expression of utter disbelief on his face, like he hadn't expected to see someone with a camera.

I stared at the photo for a long moment, forgetting to breathe. Damien Capello had shockingly light-blue eyes. My mom always called eyes like that wolf eyes. They weren't uncommon—Jacob and Ruthie both had them. But they were distinct, beautiful.

The man in the photo had wolf eyes. And he had Damien's slightly wild hair, gray now, instead of blond, and his strong jaw and straight nose, his thick eyebrows. It looked just like him. Identical.

I stared at the photograph for a long time, going over all the reasons I was so sure Damien had committed suicide. The clothes left by the side of the creek. The note, which I knew now was proof of nothing. Everything else could've been faked or planted.

You really think I went all undercover and came out here because Damien Capello ran away with his girlfriend? Amy had said.

I chewed my lip. Reluctantly, I typed "Maria Capello, Murder" into the search engine. Hit Enter.

There was a lot more here than there had been for Damien faking his death. I scanned article after article, my migraine continuing to build behind my eyelids. The most compelling evidence was the cell phone stuff. Maria had a cell phone—rare but not unheard of back in 1996—and she'd used it to call home at around 11:00 p.m., only a few minutes after the security footage showed her sitting in the hospital waiting room. But the phone hadn't pinged the cell tower near the hospital; it had pinged one only a mile from the farmhouse. People thought it was strange, but cell phone towers were notoriously unreliable, and anyway, I knew Maria had been at the hospital that night because Jacob's mother had been there, too. In fact, that was the thing I'd held on to for all these years, the reason I'd always been so certain of Maria's story: Gloria had *seen* Maria at the hospital that night.

The thought made me exhale, feeling a little better. If Gloria had seen Maria, then she couldn't have been back at the farm murdering her husband. Which meant that whatever Amy knew—or thought she knew—was bullshit.

Ruthie, Jacob, and I FaceTimed Gloria all the time, and we usually used my computer because the screen was bigger. I dug my headphones out of my tote bag, casting a glance around the library to make sure there was no one else here, that the librarian was still lost in Stephen King. Then I clicked on the little camera icon.

Gloria answered surprisingly fast. The screen shifted, my image disappearing as a new, blurrier picture took its place. Gloria was in her kitchen, and it looked like she was cooking something. Produce crowded the counter around her: cilantro and limes and cabbage.

"Thea!" she said, the corners of her eyes crinkling as she looked into the camera. Over the years, Gloria had grown plump and round, and she'd cut her graying hair into a short, pixie style, but I still remembered her like she was when we'd first met, with her long, dark hair streaked through with gray, a pair of oversized glasses perched on her nose. "It's so good to see you. Jacob and Ruthie just got in. I was going to teach Ruthie how to make tacos. You want me to grab her so you can say hi?"

I felt a momentary pang of jealousy at the thought of them all crowded in Gloria's friendly kitchen. I loved Jacob's mom, had fallen in love with her the first time Jacob introduced us. She'd reminded me of Maria a little. Both women had been small and dark-haired, had loved food and their families.

She doesn't live far from here, I thought, out of nowhere. I could leave now, be in her kitchen making tacos with them in an hour. But if I left, I'd never get my hands on another page from Maria's memoir.

"Actually, I was calling to talk to you," I said. "I have a question."

Gloria looked surprised. "Oh! Isn't that nice. What's on your mind, hon?"

"I..." I hesitated. There was no way to ask her this without mentioning Maria. And Jacob wasn't stupid. If Gloria mentioned this conversation, he'd figure out who my big mystery author was for sure. Was I okay with that?

I swallowed. Up until this moment, I'd held up my end of the NDA to the letter. And I wasn't really talking about the book, I was double-checking a story my husband had told me.

"I had a question about Maria Capello," I said. "Jacob once told me you were working at Woodstock Hospital the night Damien Capello died, when she brought her son in? He said you saw her there."

"Hold on a moment... Jacob told you that?" Gloria wiped a hand across her mouth and folded her arms. She stared blankly at the camera, looking taken aback. "Huh. That's odd."

I felt a shifting, sinking feeling, the sensation of standing on unsteady ground. I went back over the memory in my head. Jacob and I at the bar next to the bookstore, him grinning as he told me how his mother had been there the night Maria brought her kid into the hospital. I'd never mentioned the story to Gloria because Jacob had insisted she didn't like to talk about it.

Now, for the first time, I realized that might not be why he didn't want me to ask her. "Isn't it true?"

Gloria kept staring for another long moment. She licked her lips.

"Well…I worked at that hospital, sure. But I never saw Maria there. I wasn't even working the night she brought her son in."

I blinked, fast. The memory rewrote itself in my head, and now, for the first time, I saw it as it really was: Jacob was talking me up, wanting to hold my interest, so he'd told me a story that he knew I'd like, only he'd changed some of the details to make it more impressive. His mother hadn't just worked at the hospital that had famously served as Maria Capello's alibi; she'd been there that night, she'd *seen* her. Almost, but not quite true. I groaned inwardly. He had no idea how much damage he'd done.

I asked to talk to Ruthie after that, and I spent a few minutes trying to decipher a meandering story about a kid at her school who'd taken her toy pony at recess. After a while, Jacob popped on to say hi. He told me Ruthie was feeling a lot better and that his mom was so happy they'd come up to visit that she'd offered to get up with Ruthie in the morning, let him sleep in. I bit back questions about the lie he'd told when we first met, even though I was dying to bring it up. But if Gloria didn't mention I was asking about Maria Capello, I didn't want to blow up my spot.

"You're coming back tomorrow, right?" Jacob wanted to know. "Ruthie and I were planning to drive back to Brooklyn after lunch."

"Uh…" I hesitated. "I don't think I can, actually. This project is trickier than I thought it would be."

Jacob looked annoyed. "Come on, Thea; you've already been gone all weekend."

I didn't have the energy to have this argument with him now, not on top of anything else. "I'm doing this as quickly as I can."

He must've heard the annoyance in my voice because he frowned and added, "Are you okay? You don't sound great."

"I'm…a little stressed." I said. Could there be a bigger understatement?

Cassandra still hadn't gotten back to me by the time we hung up, but it was already 6:05, and I couldn't make the nice old librarian keep the place open any longer. I wrote an email updating her on everything I knew, and then I packed up my things, thanked the man, and was about to step out the door when something made me pause.

Maria hadn't just told me not to go looking up information online. She'd specifically said, *Don't go asking about the story in town.*

I realized, much too late, why she would have said this. Obviously, there were people around here who'd lived in town thirty years ago when Damien went missing. Some of them might've been at the party that night. Maybe some of them had even seen things they'd never told the police.

I stepped back into the library, letting the door fall shut behind me.

The librarian looked up from his book, smiling politely. "Did you need directions somewhere?"

He seemed nice enough. He had an old hippie vibe, the top of his head balding but the hair in back long and tied back in a ponytail. He wore a tie-dyed shirt with a logo that read Woodsock on it. Below was a picture of a sock, so I knew it wasn't a typo.

"Actually," I said, "I was wondering if I could ask you a question. Have you lived here long?"

"Since I was born. Same house and everything."

"So, you remember the Italian restaurant from the nineties, Polpette?"

The librarian thumped the cover of his book with his thumb, chewing on his lip like he was thinking something over. "Oh yeah. That was big news, back in the day. Man, but people loved that place. Best meatballs I ever tasted."

"Did you know the guy who owned it? Damien Capello?"

I thought I caught a flicker of wariness in the man's eyes, but it was gone too quick to say for sure.

"Nah, not me," he said. He stared at me for another second, like he was trying to decide something, then shrugged and added, "One of the other librarians used to work there, though. Waitress, if I remember right. She lives just down the street."

13

THEA

THE LIBRARIAN TOLD ME HIS NAME WAS FRANK, WROTE AN address down on a scrap of paper, and wished me luck. The woman who'd worked at Polpette lived on the same street as the library, a few blocks down.

I was making my way up the sidewalk to her house when my shoe connected with something, sending it skidding over the concrete. My gaze followed the object automatically. It was just a cigarette butt, and it wouldn't have drawn my attention normally except there wasn't just one lying on the sidewalk; there were half a dozen. And they were all a bright canary yellow.

Amy had been here.

I leaned over and picked up one of the butts. I had no idea how common these CBD cigarettes were. But I was only a ten-minute walk from Perk Up!, and Amy had said something about coming to town to talk to a source. Was this woman her source? If she'd been a waitress at Polpette, it made sense that Amy would want to talk to her. I stared at the house for a moment. Amy could still be inside now.

I hurried to the door and knocked. Footsteps, and then the door opened, a pale face appearing in the crack, intercepted by a chain lock.

The woman was probably around fifteen years older than me and small, with short black hair cut to her ears, cool in the way I always thought Gen-Xers seemed cool, a kind of Janeane Garofalo type, sardonic and unsmiling and world-weary. I was immediately intimidated.

"Can I help you?" Her voice was not much like Janeane Garofalo's, I was relieved to hear. It was much higher and less sure of itself.

"Yes," I said cautiously. Then, clearing my throat, I added, "I mean, I hope so." What to say? When I saw the yellow cigarette, I let myself hope that Amy would already be here. I even half expected to hear her voice from inside the house calling out, "It's okay. She's with me."

That didn't happen. The woman just waited, eyes narrowing, and I knew she was moments away from closing the door in my face.

I said, "I'm sorry to bother you. I got your address from the librarian, Frank. He told me you used to work at Polpette?"

The question seemed to put her on edge. She narrowed her eyes. "*Who* are you?"

"My name's Thea Woods. I had a few questions about the Capellos, if you don't mind." I hesitated a moment, hoping she might invite me in. She only lifted her eyebrows, waiting for an explanation. "Frank thought you might be willing to talk to me."

The woman turned her head away slightly and said, irritated, "Fucking *Frank*. I told him to stop sending people over here."

People? My heartbeat picked up a little. "Did he send someone else to talk to you? A woman named Amy Ryan?"

"If Amy Ryan was the woman sniffing around here a few days ago, then yeah, he did. And I'm going to tell you the same thing I told her, which is that I don't know anything about the Capellos and I wouldn't be stupid enough to tell you anything even if I did. Now, if you'll excuse me." The woman leaned away from the door like she was about to shut it.

"Wait," I rushed to say, stopping the door with my foot. "Amy hasn't been here for a few days?" The cigarette butts on the sidewalk didn't look days old. They looked fresh.

The woman's eyes flickered. I wondered if she was trying to decide whether to tell me to fuck off.

After a moment, she said, "She was here three days ago. I told her if she bothered me again, I'd call the police."

"What did she want to talk to you about?"

The woman popped an eyebrow, as if to say, *You really think I'm going to tell you that?*

"Right." I hovered on the porch for another second, trying to think of anything else I could say to get her to open up. My mind was a complete blank. It was clear that she had no interest in talking to me. "Okay, I'm sorry to bother you."

The woman was watching me carefully. After a beat of silence, she asked, "You aren't another social media person, are you?"

"No, I'm not."

She still didn't pull the door open any further, didn't invite me inside. But she swallowed, seeming to make some decision. "You want some friendly advice? Don't believe a thing Amy Ryan tells you." She met my eye, not a hint of humor in her expression. "That woman's full of shit."

"What do you mean?" I wanted to know.

But the woman only said, "She's a liar," and slammed her door in my face.

I stared at the door for a moment. I wanted to laugh or scream or both.

Amy was a liar. Maria was manipulative. And someone back at the farm was trying to keep me from leaving.

Who the hell was I supposed to trust?

....

I made it back to the BMW and collapsed inside. I felt deflated. Confused.

Why did that woman think Amy was so full of shit? What had Amy said to piss her off so much that she threatened to call the police?

I swore and rubbed my eyes with my palms. The library was closed now. The windows were all dark, and the only other car that had been parked on the street with mine—a silver Toyota minivan that I assumed had been Frank's—was gone. I got my laptop out anyway, praying I could still connect to the Wi-Fi.

I lucked out. The signal was weak, but it was there. I pulled up my email to double-check whether Cassandra had gotten back to me. But there was only one new message in my inbox, from my mom's bank.

The last time I gave my mom money, I'd changed the settings in her account so any alerts would come directly to me. This was the first time I'd gotten one. An oily feeling flooded my stomach before I even clicked the screen and read what it had to say.

Overdraft notice, it read.

"Fuck," I murmured, out loud. The staticky, white-noise sound of encroaching panic filled my head. Mom couldn't have overdrafted. I'd just transferred another thousand dollars into her account last week. Almost everything we had left.

Fingers shaking, I navigated to the bank website, keyed in my mom's username and password, held my breath while I waited for the page to load.

Negative forty-seven dollars.

I closed my eyes. I couldn't look at the computer screen. My head felt dizzy, soupy. I was having trouble breathing, so I shifted the laptop to the passenger seat, doubled over, and put my head between my knees. Tried to count to ten.

There was only one way my mom could've burned through a thousand dollars in a week.

Once I'd calmed down a little, I picked up my laptop again and pulled up her number on FaceTime, just like I had with Gloria. Only this time I hit the icon to voice call her. I didn't have it in me to look my mother in the eye right now.

I chewed my lip as I waited, trying to figure out what I would say when she answered, what words I could use in what order to magically get her to understand that she couldn't keep doing this, that she was going to ruin us both.

I didn't get the chance. The voice that answered wasn't my mother's. It was deeper, a slow southern drawl, familiar though I'd only heard it a handful of times. "Hello?"

Everything inside of me clenched. *This is your dad*, I thought, words that had been echoing in my head since I was sixteen. *Wild, huh?*

"Hello?" the voice asked again. I didn't say anything. I couldn't. I was too angry.

"Is someone there?" he asked, a touch amused now. "Thea? Honey, your name's coming up on the caller ID."

It was the amusement that did it. I pictured that man sitting in my mother's kitchen, sipping his damn Jim Beam, laughing at me. I wanted to scream. I took a breath.

I had to fix this.

"You need to leave," I said. My whole body was trembling, but I managed to keep my voice calm. "Leave now."

"Thea—"

"If you don't leave, I swear on my daughter, I will kill you."

I think he could hear from the tone of my voice that this wasn't some idle threat. There was a sharp intake of breath on the other end of the line. He said, "You don't mean that." But he didn't sound so sure.

"There are people I could find online," I said. I wasn't entirely sure if this was true, but in that moment it didn't matter. All that mattered was the conviction in my voice, the fact that I believed what I was saying. "I could pay some guy five hundred bucks to shoot you in the back of the head. It would be the best money I ever spent."

My dad was quiet for a long moment. I couldn't tell if he believed I was telling the truth. If he was scared.

"Leave," I said, again. And I clicked the button on the screen to end the call.

I knew my mom. Even with my threat, this wouldn't be the last time she let my dad back into her life, gave him everything she had—everything *I* had—in exchange for even the slightest possibility that he might stay. It didn't matter what I did, what I said. She always chose him.

I needed money. I needed that promotion. I *needed* this book to work.

The thought actually calmed me, some. It made things really clear. It didn't actually matter who was lying to me or manipulating me, as long as I could convince Maria to tell the story of what happened to her husband the night he disappeared. As long as the manuscript got to Cassandra in a week.

Dread inched up my throat. I gripped the steering wheel. I knew what I had to do, but it was a long moment before I could turn the car back on and start to drive.

When I got back to my room, I found a new chapter waiting for me.

THE SECRET INGREDIENT

CHAPTER SIX

There was no reason for me to go to the restaurant when the kids were young, but once they'd both started school, I found myself with something I hadn't had in years: time of my own.

It was a decadent thing. An unreal feeling of absolute freedom, made all the more precious because I knew it would only last a few hours. I felt like an alcoholic sneaking a drink when no one else was watching. I felt like I was doing something illicit.

Those first few days, I had no idea what to do with myself. I cleaned the house from top to bottom, even going so far as to dust the baseboards and the ceiling fans and each individual blind on our windows. I took long, meandering walks through town, going into every shop, buying things I didn't remotely need or even want. A candle that smelled like a fir tree. A tea towel with a picture of a cow on it.

Overpriced wooden spoons that warped and cracked as soon as I actually tried to cook anything with them.

I asked Damien about returning to the restaurant part-time. He always kissed me on the cheek and told me there was no need for that, as if it were a chore I was offering to shoulder for him. "You deserve a break. Don't worry about Polpette. I've got everything under control." And he'd call me his angel, tell me he was so impressed with how hard I worked, how much I'd sacrificed for our family. At the time, it had made me feel so seen, so taken care of, that I couldn't bring myself to tell him that I *wanted* to go back.

Then, my mother had a stroke, and it quickly became clear that she would no longer be able to care for herself. I moved her into the farmhouse, with Damien and me and the kids. Very quickly, my days were once again taken over by the act of caregiving. Making sure my mother took her meds and did her exercises. Cleaning up after her, cooking for her. Luckily, she had a more adventurous palate than my children did, and for the first time in years, I was able to flex my skills. I made roast spiced game hens with red cabbage, chicken with sage and onion confit, Tuscan short ribs.

Isabella was twelve and Enzo was ten when my mother passed away. I still remember watching her coffin being lowered into the ground, how utterly alone I felt despite the two children hovering beside me, Damien's arm tightly gripping my shoulder. My mother understood me in a way no one else in this world ever would again. And she was gone. It was devastating.

She'd left me her prized possession, a sky-blue Le Creuset Dutch oven that was the only wedding gift she'd saved after my father left, the sides browned from years of simmering sauce and grease splatter. And a stack of savings bonds she'd been holding on to since the '70s. Once cashed, those bonds would have been worth about $243,800. A fortune, in the early '90s. Today, they'd be worth much, much more. Millions.

For my Maria, the love of my life, she'd written, right into her will. *So that she may follow her dreams.*

My dreams. What were those, I wondered? Did I want a bigger home kitchen, so that I might cook the way I'd always hoped to? A trip to Italy, to eat gnocchi di patate and vitello tonnato in sidewalk cafés in Rome? I didn't know. I didn't want the bonds at the house—I was terrified of losing them—so I opened a safe-deposit box in town and kept them there. And then I went about the process of trying to remember what my dreams were.

I knew I missed being around food and people who loved food. I missed our restaurant, the energy of it. Polpette had been Damien's and my dream for so long. It had sustained us in those early hard days of marriage. Was it still my dream?

I thought of everything a quarter of a million dollars might do for our restaurant. We could update the appliances or think about expanding, maybe move into the space next door. Damien had talked about wanting a take-out window where we could sell sandwiches and coffee. The possibilities were endless. Maybe the restaurant was still my dream. Maybe this money was the way I was going to get back in. I realized I wouldn't know unless I went there.

Damien left early one morning a few months after my mother passed, claiming he needed to be at Polpette to go over the menu at the all-staff meeting. I'd wanted to go too, but I didn't tell him that. I thought I would surprise him. My plan was to show up at the meeting, and just before Damien adjourned, I'd raise my hand and tell him I wanted to use the money for Polpette.

I took time getting myself ready and curling my hair, squeezing into the one pair of jeans I had that still fit and a button-down shirt, the fabric strange against my skin, like I was wearing a costume. I put on mascara and high heels like I was meeting a lover, and then I went straight to the restaurant after dropping Issie and Enzo at school.

I was so excited I was practically buzzing. I was actually *humming* as I walked through the doors. I couldn't wait to tell him my plan, to see the look on his face.

But the restaurant was empty. When I used to work there, we'd set out coffee and pastries on all-staff meeting days. People would begin to gather in the front room twenty minutes to a half hour before the meeting started, talking and laughing and eating together like a true family.

There was no one in the front of the house that day, no food or coffee set out. I heard someone shuffling around in the kitchen, the sound of pots and pans rattling, doors closing. Otherwise, the place was empty.

I assumed I'd gotten the time wrong. Meetings had been held at noon back when I was in charge, but that had been years ago. Damien could have changed the time. Or maybe he'd been wrong about the day of the meeting when he told me about it that morning, had been too embarrassed or busy to come back home when he'd realized his mistake. I made my way to the back of the house, calling out for whoever was there so I wouldn't surprise them.

It was our general manager, Leon, a man in his mid-thirties who'd been doing night school for restaurant management back when I'd hired him. I loved Leon. He was a lighthearted guy, always smiling. He was doing inventory in the pantry when I reached the kitchen, banging things around like they had personally insulted his family. I'd had to yell to make myself heard over the din.

He'd seemed surprised to see me. His expression darkened and he said in an unpleasant tone, "Maria. Wow, it's been a while."

That was strange. Leon used to call me "Mama Maria" and had always greeted me with a hug, had readily agreed to work late and come in early whenever I'd asked. Before that day, I don't think I'd ever seen him without a smile on his face.

"Leon, it's so good to see you again," I'd said. "How are you doing? Is everything okay?"

He'd shrugged with one shoulder and gone back to the inventory, his back to me. "About as 'okay' as it can be, considering. Are you looking for Damien? Because I haven't seen him yet today."

That stung. Even if Damien had innocently mixed up the days, he'd still have needed to stop by the restaurant to confirm. My mind spun, trying to come up with an excuse to explain it away, but there wasn't one. My husband had lied to my face, had probably gone straight to his mistress's house. The hurt was like taking a bullet. I'd actually had to bring a hand to my chest to remind myself to breathe. Perhaps I should've been used to it, at that point. I wasn't. I never quite accepted that the love of my life would choose to be with someone else.

Leon had turned and was looking at me with undisguised curiosity. I couldn't have the staff gossiping about the state of my marriage, so I'd put on a fake smile and said, "Of course you haven't. I left him back at the house. I just missed this place. I wanted to see what you were all up to!"

Leon had cocked an eyebrow, clearly not fooled by my fake-cheery tone and my smile, which I'm sure was too tight, too thin. I'd cleared my throat, looked around for something to talk about to distract him.

There were freshly printed menus sitting in a pile on the island. I picked one up, idly looking over the offerings. It was an entirely new menu, but the dishes themselves were familiar. Every last one of them was mine.

I hadn't known Damien was going to use them; he hadn't told me. It was a shock, seeing them all written out like that. I swallowed the bitter taste that hit the back of my throat, tried to make myself feel proud. This was something, wasn't it? The work I'd been doing was making it out into the world, was going to be enjoyed by the very people I'd wanted to enjoy it. I was able to be home with my family and still balance a job, a passion. There were women who'd kill for that. But then I flicked my eyes down to the line at the bottom of the menu that read *Executive Chef: Damien Capello.*

Leon caught me studying the menu and turned, still holding a can of tomatoes. "They're good, right? We had a tasting the other day. People can't stop talking about that duck."

I nodded, distracted, studying the description Damien had added next to a duck recipe I'd created. Dill. Tomato sauce. Cream. I made a face. The dill was new. And he'd subbed out a tomato and cream sauce for the demi-glace.

"Is Cheryl cooking tonight?" I asked, looking up at Leon. Cheryl had been our sous-chef since we'd opened. "Tell her to try a few of the duck dishes with sage instead of dill, and with demi-glace and Vidalia onions?"

I used to do this all the time, subbing a few ingredients at the last minute, A/B testing recipes. It wasn't unusual. But Leon was studying me, a funny look on his face. He scratched the back of his head. "Uh, yeah, I would, but Cheryl doesn't work here anymore."

I'd blinked, taken aback. "What?"

"She quit. A few weeks ago, actually."

That didn't make sense. Cheryl had been with us since the beginning. She was almost as loyal to this place as Damien and I were. Yes, it had been a while, but I was sure she would have called me if she were planning to leave. *Damien* would have told me. How could I not know?

"I don't understand," I'd said to Leon, working hard to keep my voice steady. "What happened? Did she get another offer?"

That funny look on Leon's face again, a little V between his brows, like there was something I was missing. "No," he'd said slowly. "I mean, not that I know of."

"Then why would she leave?"

He'd shrugged with one shoulder. "I guess... Well, she has a kid, doesn't she? I think she said something about needing to take another job." And he'd turned back to the pantry shelf before adding, under his breath, "We can't all just wait around for you to start paying us again."

I remember feeling like I'd been hit. That was the exact feeling, like someone had sucker punched me straight to the gut. I couldn't breathe, couldn't get a single word out.

Damien wasn't paying our staff. *Why* wasn't Damien paying them?

I didn't want to let on to Leon that I had no idea what he was talking about, so I'd simply excused myself and gone to the office. I still had the key. For a split second before I slipped it into the lock, I worried that it wouldn't work, that Damien had locked me out of my own restaurant. But it turned easily.

I spent the next few hours going over our books, studying everything Damien had written, but I couldn't make sense of any of it. He seemed to have forgotten to mark down sums for days, sometimes weeks in a row. At that point, I got a sick feeling in the pit of my stomach. It was clear that we were in major trouble, that we'd probably been in trouble for a while. And Damien hadn't trusted me enough to tell me, had lied to my face whenever I'd asked him. How far would he go to cover this up, I'd wondered.

I found myself hurrying down the street to the bank where I'd gotten the safe-deposit box for my mother's bonds. Damien had opened the box with me. His name was on the account, right beside mine.

The banker looked confused when he sat down at the desk across from me. "Mrs. Capello," I remember him saying, lacing his fingers together. "What can I do for you today?"

I still didn't have a clear enough understanding of how bad things were. I could see that, after. I thought I was being paranoid, needing to check the box to see that my mother's bonds were still where I'd last left them.

"I need to get into my safe-deposit box," I'd told him, sliding my key across the desk.

I will never forget how that man looked at me. The pity on his face. He'd taken off his glasses and leaned forward as though preparing to tell me a dreadful secret, something he didn't want anyone else in the bank to overhear.

"Mrs. Capello," he'd said, "your husband emptied that box last week."

EMPTY SAFE-DEPOSIT-BOX DUCK

Commercially available duck has an amazing amount of fat that can be rendered and stored for a variety of purposes such as making duck confit at home, sautéing vegetables, or tossing with popcorn before a movie. In this preparation I use the fat to confit onions and sage, creating an amazingly haunting flavor with very few ingredients.

INGREDIENTS

2 mulard duck breasts
1 small Vidalia onion
6 to 10 garlic cloves
1 large sprig sage, picked
¼ cup chicken demi-glace, or 1 cup chicken broth
Kosher salt and black pepper to taste
Canola oil, as needed

STEPS

Serves 2

1. Season the duck on both sides with kosher salt. Thinly slice the onion and garlic; pick the sage leaves from the stems. Preheat your oven to 225°F.

2. Heat an oven-safe frying pan over medium heat and lay in the duck breasts, fat side down. Cook for about 20 minutes until most of the fat is rendered, leaving a crispy skin. If the skin appears to be darkening too quickly, reduce the heat slightly. Pour off the fat from the pan. You should have about ¾ cup. If there is much less, you can augment with more duck fat or a neutral oil such as canola. Place the duck in a covered container and refrigerate.

3. Add the onion, garlic, and sage to the pan with a big pinch of salt along with the reserved duck fat. Lower the heat to medium low and cook, stirring occasionally, until the onion is wilted. There should be enough fat in the pan to not quite cover the onion-garlic mixture.

4. Slide the pan into the oven and let the onions and garlic confit, about 45 minutes, stirring occasionally until deeply browned and very fragrant. Remove from the oven and strain the fat from the confit aromatics, then set aside.

5. When the confit is 15 minutes from completion, remove the duck from the fridge to temper and season all over with black pepper. Heat a frying pan over medium high and add in a drizzle of canola oil. Sear the duck on the skin side to re-crisp, then flip and cook on the flesh side, about 3 minutes for medium rare. Remove from the pan and tent with foil to rest.

6. Deglaze the pan with a few tablespoons water and add in the demi-glacé or chicken broth. Simmer rapidly, evaporating the liquid until a crust just forms on the bottom of the pan. Pour any remaining fat out of the pan and deglaze with 1 tablespoon water to form a jus, which should coat the back of a spoon.

7. Brush the duck with the jus and slice on the bias into ½-inch slices. Brush with more of the jus, pouring all that remains over the top, and top the slices with the confit aromatics. Serve hot.

NOTES FOR THE HOME COOK

- The duck fat that is strained from the confit aromatics will have incredible flavor. It can be strained and stored in the refrigerator for up to 1 month. Save it for roast vegetables or fried eggs.

14

THEA

I FINISHED READING ABOUT HOW MARIA FOUND OUT THAT Damien drained their accounts, my hand tired from jotting down so many notes:

Was this before or after she started burying her money in the yard? I wanted to know. If it was after, why didn't she bury the bonds? Why would she put Damien's name on the safe-deposit box if she was worried about his gambling?

I felt like there were parts of the story that were missing, but I thought I knew what was coming next: Damien had stolen Maria's mother's money. Now it was time for him to vanish.

I was desperate to know how he'd done it. It was like finally watching the series finale of a soap opera I'd started thirty years ago.

I was itching to get to the end.

....

The sun had just begun its descent beyond the distant hills when Maria's assistant knocked on my door. I'd been hoping she'd come with another chapter, but her arms were empty, and she told me she was there to let me know that dinner would be at seven o'clock in the dining room.

I didn't want to go to dinner. I wanted to eat in my room, keep working. I'd been here two full days already, and while Maria had steadily fed me pages, I hadn't seen anywhere near the length of a book. I'd have worked straight through the night if that had been an option.

Tomorrow was Monday. I still had to find a time and place to call Cassandra and the marketing and publicity departments, set a schedule for when I could get the manuscript to managing editorial, start figuring out a timeline for sending the book to the printer. And it wasn't just work I'd be missing. I wanted to wake up with my family in the morning, help get Ruthie to school. I wanted to fall asleep on the sofa while watching *The Sopranos*, Jacob stroking my hair. If we kept working at this pace, I'd be here for a week. Longer. I didn't know if I could take that. I wanted to go home.

I decided to talk to Maria about the schedule over dinner. I made my way to the dining room and politely greeted the family. Amy, I noticed, wasn't there. There was an empty chair at the end of the table where she'd been sitting.

"Where's Amy?" I asked.

There was a brief hesitation, the family's expressions carefully blank, and then Enzo said with a tight smile, "She had some work to catch up on." And before I could ask any follow-up questions, he started talking to Issie about some acting class he thought Ava might like, and I was left with the distinct feeling that he was intentionally trying to change the subject.

Around the table, voices mingled with the sound of clinking glasses and the scrape of silverware against dishes. I loaded a plate with cacio e pepe, panzanella, ricotta gnudi and filetto di pomodoro. But I paused before accepting a meatball when the tray was passed to me. I'd always found Maria's meatballs so appetizing, but just now there seemed to be something off about them. The surface of the meat glistened, slick with congealed grease and fat. Deep-red tomato sauce pooled in the corners of the tray. Reminding me of blood.

Amy hadn't taken any meat when she'd been at dinner last night, I remembered. She'd spooned sauce over vegetables, made some comment about how heavy all the food was.

Murder, I heard her say. *Cannibalism. Meatballs made of people.* My stomach twisted. I was being ridiculous, I knew that. But I waved the tray away regardless, my gaze drawn back to the empty chair beside Enzo. Did he mean she was working back in her room? Or was she still in town with her "source"?

By the time we were finishing up, I still hadn't managed to bring up the schedule with Maria. I was stalling, nervous. Then the plates were cleared, and Maria was handing out the same digestifs we'd had the night before. It seemed like the right time to push. Maria was being delightful, laughing with the rest of us, insisting I take more pasta. The sun had set and the dining room was intimate, candlelit, and the end of her story, the truth about what had happened that night with Damien, felt so close I could almost hear it shuffling in the shadows around us, creeping toward the table like a dog drawn to the smell of food.

But when I finally found the courage to ask about the rest of the manuscript, Maria just shook her head and covered her face with her palm.

"I'm sorry, Thea," she said, her voice cracking slightly. "I know you're getting impatient. It's understandable that you want this to go faster, it is. But there's a reason I need to do it like this. I've never been able to talk about that period of my life, not in interviews, not ever. I find it all incredibly difficult. It just reminds me of how bad things got."

She lowered her hand and gave me a look over the tips of her fingers. The emotion in her voice was real and raw, but the look was different.

It was...calculating.

I swallowed. I'd known she wouldn't want to be rushed. But something was nagging at me, urging me to push. "Of course. I understand," I said quickly. "Do you have any sense of how much longer you'd like me to stay?"

"Oh, don't worry about that, dear. We love having you here. It's not an imposition at all." Again, that look. What did it mean?

It occurred to me that Maria hadn't actually answered my question about how long she needed me to stay. She'd sidestepped it, turned it into a different question, one she actually wanted to answer. She did that a lot.

"Drink," Maria said, nodding to my digestif. Everyone else downed theirs quickly but I'd set mine aside, remembering how bitter it had been. "It will help with your digestion."

I smiled a little stiffly and brought the glass to my lips. The bitter herbal smell filled my nose. The liquid trailed down my throat, burning.

"I'll get you the next batch of pages tonight," Maria said. "Don't worry. You're nearly done."

Finished, I correctly silently, cringing as I choked down the digestif. Every editor had a few grammatical errors that bothered them, and this was one of mine.

The word *finished* meant you'd completed a task. The word *done* was correct only when you were referring to food. Technically, the phrase *You're nearly done* didn't mean I was almost finished.

It meant I'd been thoroughly cooked.

....

I stopped by Amy's room after dinner, but she didn't answer when I knocked.

"Amy?" I called through her door.

Nothing.

I knocked again but the door wasn't latched, and it creaked open below my hand, swinging inward to reveal an empty room.

Not just empty. Pristine. The bed was made, the curtains drawn. There were no bags, no clothes, nothing that might indicate another person had been staying here. Amy was gone.

A sharp, animal sense of unease filled my body. This felt wrong. I let my eyes move over the neatly made bed, the fresh vacuum marks on the rug. Amy hadn't done that. She'd been gone long enough that Maria had already had someone in to clean.

There was a sound further down the hall: footsteps, someone coming. Compulsively, I stepped into Amy's room and pulled the door shut behind me.

For a moment I just stood near the door, breathing hard, my heartbeat speeding. *What the hell was I doing?* That could have been Enzo or Maria, or Issie looking for a place to pump.

I waited, certain I was about to be discovered. But no one came.

Feeling a bit calmer, I turned toward the empty bedroom. The wrong feeling was stronger now that I was alone in here. Something was tugging at my brain. Amy had said something earlier, something that indicated she'd be staying for at least one more night. I closed my eyes. What was it?

It came to me after a few long moments: *Unless you're planning on following me into the woods tonight,* Amy had said when we'd spoken earlier. That's what was bugging me. As of this afternoon, she'd been planning to stay. Something must've changed when she went into town, something big enough that she'd come right back here and packed and left in a hurry.

My fingers itched. I wished I had my phone so I could text her.

Then, I thought *phone.*

I hurried over to the king-sized bed and lifted the same corner of the mattress I'd watched Amy lift just a few hours ago.

There was no reason her burner should've been there. Amy had texted me the number so I could get in touch after she went back to the city, which meant she'd been planning to keep it.

But when I shoved my hand under the mattress, my fingers enclosed hard plastic. I grasped the object, pulled it out.

Amy's phone was still here.

I turned to face the room, my heart thumping in my throat. If someone else had packed up Amy's things for her, they could have easily missed the phone. Only Amy—and I—knew where she'd hidden it.

That's what this wrong feeling was, I realized, bile rising in my throat. It didn't feel like Amy had left.

Or, at least it didn't feel like she'd left of her own will.

....

Back in my room I found a glass filled with the same murky, green sleeping draft Maria had given me the night before, along with a fresh batch of pages.

I considered the draft but didn't pick it up, remembering how groggy it'd made me this morning. And I could still feel the burn of the digestif in my chest. I couldn't stomach another mystery drink, even if it would help me sleep.

I sank onto my bed with a grunt and reached for the new chapter instead. I flipped through it.

Six pages. That was all.

I collapsed back into my pillows and began to read.

The Secret Ingredient

CHAPTER SEVEN

I don't know how I made it back home that day, how I picked my children up from school or fixed them dinner, how I smiled and hugged them. All I thought about was the bank, the pity in the teller's voice, the disbelief in his eyes.

Your husband emptied that box last week.

The way he'd said those words. It was like he was really saying, *But didn't you know? How could you not have known?*

I couldn't believe I had become this woman. The woman whose husband cheated on her, whose husband lied to her, *stole* from her. I felt like a character from a bad Lifetime movie, one I wouldn't even bother to watch all the way through to the end.

Two hundred and fifty thousand dollars. My mother's money.

My money.

According to the teller, Damien had taken it a week ago. And afterward he'd come home to me, crawled into bed beside me. He'd touched my back, my breasts. He'd kissed me on my neck, the spot below my ear that he knew I liked. And all the while, he'd been hiding this terrible secret.

I didn't cry, not in front of the kids, but I wasn't able to eat. Not a crumb. Every time I swallowed, I tasted bitterness. It was like a film coating the back of my throat. Disgust? Betrayal? It was a harsh, sour taste, like battery acid.

How could he? *My mother's money.*

At some point, the children went to bed and I went to the dining room and got the vodka from the freezer, pouring myself several fingers. And I waited.

Two hundred and fifty thousand dollars.

Gone.

....

Damien got back sometime around two in the morning, long after the restaurant had closed for the night. He smelled of bourbon and cigarette smoke and something else, something metallic. Pig's blood, maybe. He'd been in the slaughterhouse after work, stayed there for hours doing God knows what.

The odor followed him like a cartoon fog. I smelled it as soon as the door swung open, even though I was down the hall, still in the dining room nursing my vodka.

I went through the options as I listened to him clumsily kick off his boots, swearing under his breath when he stumbled, keys jangling drunkenly in his hand. Had he been at a casino before going to the slaughterhouse? A late-night poker game? And how many times had he come home reeking like this, hopped in the shower while I slept, scrubbed the evidence away before I was ever the wiser?

He was surprised when he found me sitting at the table. "Maria. God, I didn't think you'd still be up." Then, rubbing his bloodshot eyes, blinking hard, as though that might be enough to sober him up, he said, "What time is it?"

"Where were you?" I asked. There was no way he was going to tell me the truth, but I wanted to see him lie. I wanted to commit his tells to memory. I didn't even listen to whatever excuse he spewed out. I just watched the way he dragged a hand over his mouth to hide his lips as he spoke, how he shifted his eyes to the floor, those heavy brows rumpling. How had I never noticed this before? He was a forty-year-old man behaving like an eight-year-old boy, worried he was about to get in trouble.

His eyes caught on my glass when I took a drink, and at that moment, his whole body went still, the way a deer goes still when it sees a predator. When you've been married for a long time, you learn to predict the big fights before they come. It's like watching for a storm, noticing the change in air pressure, how the clouds build on the horizon, how the leaves on the trees turn over. You can smell it on the air, all ozone and dry grass.

I rarely drank. The vodka was a sign that something was badly wrong. Damien took a breath when he saw it and crossed his arms over his chest. I wanted to tell him his poker face was shit. If he'd gambled with my money, it was no wonder he'd lost it all. I could easily see his fear through all the machismo.

All I said was, "The bonds aren't in the safe-deposit box anymore. They're gone."

I don't know what I expected. Contrition? Apologies? Tears, maybe? But he'd only nodded, once: *And?*

I took another sip of vodka. "And Leon told me you've stopped paying our staff."

Damien closed his eyes. He hadn't been expecting that. He exhaled. It was dramatic, a man too tired of holding it all together himself. I could've smacked him. "We're having a minor setback, Maria. I'm going to get it all back."

"Get it all back? It's a quarter of a million dollars, Damien. Where could it possibly have gone?"

He wouldn't even look at me. "I have a plan. I need you to trust me."

God, I could have laughed in his face right then. *Trust me.* Like he'd taken apart our damn toilet and wanted me to let him figure out how to fix it instead of calling a plumber. I didn't think he understood just how bad this was. I didn't think he had the capacity to understand.

"Trust you," I repeated. "We could face charges for withholding wages, Damien. Someone could call the *police*."

He still wasn't looking at me. God, you'd think someone had drawn a pair of tits on the toe of his sock. "All I've been trying to do is provide for you, for the kids..."

"Don't you dare bring the *kids* into this. Where did the money go? Was it drugs?" My voice was low, dangerous. I drank a little more, and when I spoke again, the words cracked in half. "Gambling?"

Damien laughed, that kind of under-his-breath laugh that meant he thought I was being ridiculous. "You just don't get it, Maria," he said in a completely different tone of voice. He hadn't exactly been apologetic before, but now there wasn't a hint of shame in his words. You'd think he was pissed at me. "You *can't* understand. You've been home with the kids, taking it easy. You haven't seen how ugly it's gotten out there. Food costs are up seventy percent. Seventy percent! Labor costs are through the roof, and I just found out the plumbing in the restaurant is shot. I'm going to have to have it all replaced. Do you have any idea how much that costs?"

I hated the implication that I somehow wouldn't understand this. That I'd had it easy at home while he did the real work. "So, the restaurant isn't making money? That's what this is about?"

Another laugh. "The restaurant is hemorrhaging money. It's *eating* money. And the more successful we get, the worse it is. You say gambling like it's this terrible thing, but that's the only way we've been able to stay afloat for as long as we have. I was trying to *fix* this. I never wanted you to have to know."

So, it was gambling. I was right. "That was my mother's money," I said. I could barely breathe, I was so angry. I pictured Damien trading the money my mother left me, handing it over in exchange for poker chips, which he'd toss into the center of some table, acting like a hotshot. I imagined booze and cigars, men laughing, the sound of chips clicking together. It was all so sordid, so fucked up. I wanted to scream.

"I was trying to save our restaurant. I was trying to pay for *this*—" He made a sweeping motion, indicating the house: clothes and books scattered across the furniture and dishes drying in the drainer by the sink, balled-up socks on the floor and a tangle of sneakers by the front door. "How do you think we've managed all this time, Maria? Sports equipment and new shoes, field trips, Enzo's new braces, Issie's sleep-away camp… It all costs money—"

"I understand what things cost, Damien."

"*Do* you? Because I gotta say, Maria, I'm having a hard time believing that." He spit the words out so casually, like they were something he'd thought a million times before but never had the balls to say. It was like a slap, hearing that.

I remember staring at him, my mouth hanging open, so utterly confused and lost. I don't know when it happened, but at some point in the last twelve years, I'd changed. Or no, that wasn't exactly right. I hadn't changed, but the way Damien thought of me had. I was no longer the woman he loved, the woman he'd respected enough to want to marry, his business partner. I'd become something completely different. The dumb wife who couldn't possibly understand what he was going through. The woman holding him back, holding him down. The ball and chain. The thing every man fears hitching himself to, that every woman fears becoming. I'd sacrificed everything for him. And he resented me for it.

"That was a shitty thing to say, Damien," I said.

He didn't answer right away. He'd gone back to staring at his foot.

After a long moment, he inhaled and said, "When we first got together, I thought we'd agreed. The restaurant was going to be our baby. The *restaurant* was going to be our dream. All this other stuff—" Again, that sweeping motion, a dismissive gesture that seemed to include everything I'd spent the last decade building: our kids, our home, our life. "I never wanted…"

His voice trailed off, but it was too late. I knew where he was going. *I never wanted kids. I never wanted a family. I never wanted this.*

I'd never been quite as frightened as I was in that moment. I was certain he was about to say the thing I'd spent the last fifteen years fearing he would say to me. *I'm leaving.*

I didn't breathe. I braced myself.

But Damien only looked at me and said, "I never wanted it to be this hard. I don't think it's supposed to be this hard."

And then he went to bed, leaving all of it, the responsibility for everything that he'd done, at my feet like a pile of dirty laundry. Just another chore for me to take care of.

The Smothering Wife's Broccolini Smothered with Schmaltz and Pistachio

Schmaltz is rendered chicken fat that is used frequently in Jewish cuisine. It's a shame we don't see it more in the American kitchen, because chicken is so easy to source, and as a cooking fat it's hard to match. When I break down a chicken, I like to cut away any skin and fat I'm not using to render schmaltz for recipes like this, and as a bonus you get little crispy pieces called gribenes, which are kind of like chicken bacon.

Ingredients

2 bunches Broccolini
2 cloves garlic
1/4 cup pistachios
3 tablespoons schmaltz (see note)
Salt and black pepper to taste

Steps

Serves 4

1. Rinse and dry the Broccolini, then trim away the root ends and tough stems. Coarsely chop the pistachios and sliver the garlic.

2. Heat the schmaltz in a large cast-iron skillet over medium high and add the Broccolini in a single layer. Season with salt and pepper and cook for about 4 to 5 minutes on the first side, until well browned. Flip the Broccolini with tongs and season on the second side, then sprinkle the pistachios over it.

3. Reduce the heat to medium low and continue cooking, stirring frequently, about 5 to 8 minutes. When the Broccolini is browned all over and crisping, add in the garlic and toss together. Continue cooking and turning a minute longer until the garlic is just browning and has lost its raw smell. Serve hot.

- The best way to prepare this dish is when you have just made chicken legs and have the rendered fat remaining in the pan. To that you can add an additional 1 tablespoon schmaltz or olive oil and proceed as directed.
- Schmaltz can be made by slowly simmering cubed chicken skin and fat in water. Once the water has evaporated, add a half cup more to extend the cooking time until the skin pieces are reduced in size and starting to darken. For an extra treat, remove the bits of skin—now called gribenes—with a slotted spoon and crisp in a 350°F oven for 5 to 10 minutes, until golden brown. Sprinkle with fine salt and enjoy as a snack.

15

THEA

THE PIGS STARTED SCREAMING AGAIN THE NEXT MORNING, JUST before dawn.

I rolled over in bed, onto the scattered pages I'd fallen asleep rereading. I'd stayed up late, and then I'd woken up at three in the morning—desperate, exhausted—thought *Screw it*, and swallowed the draft Maria had left for me.

I regretted it now. I felt bone-tired, disoriented. A big part of me wanted to shove my face into my pillow and fall back asleep, give in to a few more minutes of oblivion.

But the screams persisted. High-pitched keening at frequent but irregular intervals. The space between them sometimes stretched for one minute, two, long enough to think maybe they'd stopped for good. And then another would cut through the dark outside my window.

It's probably a good thing, I told myself as I dragged my heavy body out of bed. I needed to get to work. I dug a pair of expensive earplugs out of my overnight bag and shoved them into my ears, trying to block out the sound. But even with silicone pressed against my eardrums, I could still hear them.

I was sure there was no way I'd be able to concentrate, that I was too groggy, that the screams would distract me. But I managed to find a rhythm—going through the notes I'd taken on my laptop and distilling them down to the most salient points: *How did you find out for sure that he'd gambled the money away? How did he go through $250,000 in just a week? Was there any more information about his mob ties? Were you ever officially investigated by the FBI?*

My biggest note was that we seemed to be nearing the end. She'd mentioned that her mother had died in 1996, which was the same year Damien had gone missing. There couldn't be much more to the story, could there? I thought for a second, mentally calculating how many pages I'd already read. Fifty? Tops? Not nearly enough for a full memoir, even if we added more recipes to fill it out.

It was Monday. I pictured my work inbox, imagined all the emails that had to be coming in now that the weekend was over. Marketing and publicity and sales and managing editorial would all want an update, all wonder when the manuscript would be ready. And I hadn't even read all of it yet.

At some point, I looked up and realized several hours had passed. Watery sunlight streamed through my bedroom window. I popped the earplugs out of my ears: the screaming had finally stopped. Groaning, I hauled my still-tired body out of my room and up to the landline in the kitchen. I needed to call Jacob.

The house had an eerie, otherworldly feeling to it. It felt like I was moving underwater, everything quiet and still. I wondered if Enzo had gone back down to the city, if Issie had some sort of job or responsibilities she'd be taking care of during the workweek, if Ava was in school.

Jacob didn't answer, which felt like a reprieve. At least I'd tried. I placed the phone back on the receiver, blinking slowly. My eyelids felt weighted down. I was in no state to hold a conversation, but at least he'd see the attempted call and know I wasn't ignoring him. That earned me another hour or two, at least, before he started pressuring me to come home, again.

Still, there was the problem of needing to get in touch with

Cassandra, find a way to read my email, make contact with the outside world. Everyone at Hanes knew I was out of office working on this top-secret project, but it was still a workday, and they would expect me to be online. I needed Wi-Fi. I considered driving to town. I'd left the keys to the Beemer in the lockbox in the garage, but I could probably get them back. I immediately dismissed the idea. I couldn't imagine getting behind the wheel of a car right now. I was too out of it. It didn't seem safe, especially not on these winding country roads. If I had my cell, I'd be able to use it as a Wi-Fi hot spot and Zoom Cassandra from my room. I didn't have it, obviously. But I had Amy's burner.

I pulled the phone out of my pocket. Examined it. It wasn't an iPhone, like mine, and it took me long minutes swiping through the settings screens before I figured out how to turn on the personal hot spot. But the service in the house wasn't good. I had a single bar, not nearly enough.

I sighed, squinting into the early morning, trying to urge my brain to work faster. Amy had taken all her calls outside. I'd assumed it was because she hadn't wanted to be overheard, but it might've also been because she'd found stronger reception elsewhere on the grounds.

I grabbed my jacket from my room and slipped out the back door. The air smelled like woods and cold and something else, something tangy and wrong.

Pigs' blood.

I gagged. Breathing through my mouth, I picked my way toward the trees, where Amy had taken her calls. Once I reached the tree line, I dug the phone out of my pocket and checked my service. My one line had disappeared. *Shit.*

I considered a moment, then decided to try the barn Maria had given me a tour of. I carefully pushed the door open. It was dark inside, seemingly empty.

"Hello?" I called. No answer. I tested the signal. Two bars. Better, but still not strong enough to use as a hot spot.

"C'mon," I murmured. I just needed a few minutes of service, enough to check my email, shoot an update to Cassandra. I walked slowly down the center aisle, watching the signal. Sawdust crunched beneath my boots. The air was heavy with the smell of manure and hay. Every now and then, one of the animals moved in its pen, a soft shuffle or grunt. It creeped me out, actually. In my heavy, groggy state, I couldn't process the movement quickly enough. My addled brain kept transforming the animals into monsters.

I was close to giving up and trudging back to the house when a shadowy mound moved in the corner of my eye: Ava.

The little girl was fast asleep in the center aisle, hair fanned around her, wearing that Little Mermaid nightgown again. I blinked at her, my brain slow. She was like a cursed child from a fairy tale, one of the twelve dancing princesses sneaking out of their beds each night to go on magical adventures. Her skin was so pale, it seemed to glow.

I stuck the phone in my pocket and knelt beside her, touched her arm. "Ava, sweetie?"

Her skin reminded me of Ruthie's. It was crazy soft, silk-soft, skin not yet damaged by the sun and time. Her hair was so fine that it clung to everything it touched, electric with static. She groaned and rubbed her eyes with her hands. "Mommy?"

"No, honey, it's not your mommy." I glanced around the dark barn, frowning. "Do you know where your mommy is?"

"She doesn't like when I come up to sleep with the animals," Ava murmured. And then she was out again, snoring softly, eyelids fluttering, lashes dark against those pale cheeks.

I gave up on my quest for Wi-Fi. I felt weird, lightheaded. I probably needed a nap. My eyes couldn't seem to focus. And I couldn't leave Ava here alone. I scooped her in my arms and she nestled her face into the crook of my neck, legs and arms winding around me. The weight was familiar. Something inside of me throbbed, and for a moment, I missed my daughter so much that I couldn't breathe.

"Let's get you back inside, okay?" I whispered. Ava didn't say anything but just held tighter. There was a piece of gauze taped inside the crook of her elbow, I noticed. Like she'd given blood. I stared at it for a moment, unnerved. She must've been to the doctor recently. I hadn't seen her or her mother leave, but they could've slipped out while I was napping.

I turned to carry her back to the house—

Wham.

The gate inches from my left arm shuddered violently, a hulking, dark shape slamming into it. The darkness turned the shape into something horrifying: a monster from that same fairy tale I'd conjured for Ava, coming to rip her from my arms. My heart jackknifed and I leaped backward, holding Ava close, colliding with another pen just behind me.

I waited. My breath was short and shallow. Ava didn't even open her eyes.

After a few seconds, the shadows in front of me moved, reflective eyes peering out from the darkness. I couldn't breathe. Every inch of my skin buzzed with fear. The shape detached itself from the darkness and moved toward the gate, grunting. The shadows transformed into skin and muscle.

It was a pig. She was very large, almost as big as a cow. Her eyes found me in the darkness and I caught her earthy animal scent. She gave a rumbling snort that I felt in my bones.

"It's okay," I murmured, patting Ava's hair, even though Ava hadn't stirred. I was dazed, keyed up from the rush of adrenaline that'd spiked my blood. I couldn't quite get my brain to accept that it was just a pig. My pulse kept jumping, assuming danger.

I watched her for another long moment and then, swaying slightly, I carried Ava to the back of the barn.

I'd been thinking the door at the back of the barn let outside, but it opened into another room, a large pen-like space with dirt floors. It was dark inside, so dark I could barely make out the walls around me, but even so, I knew I was in the slaughterhouse. It smelled even more strongly of blood.

I stood in place, waiting for my eyes to adjust. There were no windows, but I could see from the dim light streaming in through the door behind me that the dirt floor was slightly slanted toward the center of the room, like a drain. A chain hung from the ceiling above the lowest point, a hook dangling from the end of it.

My stomach turned over. The dirt was stained a darker color near the center, from all the blood. I lifted my boot, saw reddish-brown clinging to the sole. It was fresh.

I grimaced. That was enough. I turned back to the door I'd come through, my boot smacking into something hard and light on the ground. I hesitated, squinting.

A small leather notebook.

Shifting Ava so that I was holding her in one arm, I knelt to pick up the notebook. Even before I curled my fingers around it, everything inside of me went very still.

This was Amy Ryan's notebook. The same black notebook she'd pulled out when I confronted her about Damien.

No one sees this notebook but me, she'd said.

And yet she didn't have it on her now, wherever she was. She'd left it here. In the slaughterhouse.

I flipped the notebook open: half the pages had been torn from the spine. The rest were blank.

My whole body had gone very still. I could feel my heart beating where my thumb pressed into the notebook, that steady *bomp, bomp, bomp*. Had Amy been snooping around here? Looking for something to put in her book? If so, she might've dropped the notebook. And then...

Here, my brain went blank. If Amy had dropped her notebook, she would've picked it up again. She'd made it clear that it was important to her. Why just leave it where anyone might find it?

My eyes shifted from the notebook to the dirt floor near the center of the room, stained black with blood. My palms started to sweat. Ava's breath was hot and sticky against my neck. Her body seemed to weigh a thousand pounds. I felt like I was opening my eyes and seeing things clearly for the first time.

The only reason Amy would've left this notebook behind was if she *couldn't* come back for it.

I heard a shuffling sound. It must've started a few moments ago, but I didn't register what it was until right then. I jerked my head to the door on the far side of the slaughterhouse, the one that led outside.

Footsteps. Someone was coming.

A sour taste hit the back of my throat. *Adrenaline*, I realized. The same thing rabbits and deer taste when they realize a predator is nearby. My body telling me to run.

I slid the notebook in my pocket and carried Ava back through the door that led into the barn, pulling it nearly closed behind me. But I left a crack of space between the door and the frame and pressed my face right up to it and waited, holding my breath.

The door on the far side of the pen jerked open and a man walked in. It was still dark. Early morning sunlight streamed in through the door, but I couldn't make out much besides the silhouette of his body.

It had to be Enzo. The man was too short to be Hank, and he had Enzo's broad shoulders. But then he glanced behind him, sunlight hitting him full in the face for a fraction of a second, just long enough to catch silver threaded through wild, curly hair, deep lines etched into an aging face, a strong jaw, thick eyebrows, and blue, blue eyes.

Wolf's eyes, I thought. My breath caught, and I heard a sudden roaring in my ears, a sound like rushing water. Those eyes looked exactly like the photograph I'd seen in the article on *Delish*'s website, the one someone took to prove that Damien Capello was still alive. Every detail of this man's face looked just like that photograph.

The man stepped into the room and the door fell shut behind him with a soft *whoosh*, leaving us in darkness again. A shard of terror worked its way into my lungs.

It was Damien. It had to be.

The room was quiet, the kind of quiet that seemed to be made up of a half dozen small sounds: cicadas buzzing in the grass outside and Damien's boots shuffling across the dirt, Ava's slow, even breathing in my ear. My heart was beating so loudly I could feel it in the center of my forehead, a single vein pulsing like a metronome. I could no longer see Damien's face, but that didn't matter. The instant he'd been illuminated was burned into my brain.

I couldn't breathe. I couldn't move from behind the door where I was still crouching. If it'd been any brighter, I'm sure Damien would've noticed that the door on the opposite side of the room was still open. He would've spotted my eye peering out at him. As it was, it was much too dark. I didn't let myself blink as I watched the faint outline that was all I could make of his figure shuffling across the room.

It was so strange to watch him move, to know he was standing just a few feet away from me. My whole life, I'd only ever known Damien Capello as a photograph in an old news story, an anecdote in the introduction to one of Maria's recipes and, over the last few days, the villain of her memoir.

But now, here he was. In the flesh. Not a character but a whole person.

He moved slowly, carefully. He didn't lift his feet all the way when he walked but sort of shuffled them along the dirt, and he appeared to be muttering something to himself, his voice so low I couldn't make out his words.

My eyes were getting tired from going so long without blinking. I closed them for a few seconds to keep them from drying out, then squinted and pressed my face closer to the gap of space between the door and the frame. I could feel the wood leaving marks on my face. I wished it was just a little bit brighter so I could see what Damien was doing, so I could get a clearer look at his face.

Almost as soon as the thought entered my head, a light switched on.

My heart leaped and I flinched away from the door. But the light didn't move toward me. After a moment I leaned back toward the gap, holding my breath. Ava stirred in my arms but didn't wake.

It was the flashlight on a cell phone. Damien had it aimed away from him, so I still couldn't see his face, and he was moving the beam back and forth over the ground. Looking for something.

My mouth went suddenly dry. I slipped my hand into my pocket, felt the cool leather of Amy's notebook against my fingers. If this was what he was looking for, he was going to realize it wasn't there pretty quickly.

But Damien crossed to the opposite side of the slaughterhouse from where I'd found the notebook and dropped to his knees beside the far wall. Light glinted off something in his hand and I tensed, thinking he was holding a knife. But then he started to dig.

Not a knife; a shovel.

I was frowning, trying to work out what was going on when Ava released a soft groan in her sleep. Her breath tickled the hair at the nape of my neck, and I cringed, but Damien didn't lift his head. Whatever he was looking for held all of his attention.

Still, it would only be a matter of time before Ava woke up, before I was caught. I backed away from the door as silently as I could, letting it settle into the frame without a sound.

My thoughts were wild as I hurried back down the center aisle of the barn, Ava heavy in my arms. I was aware, dimly, that I'd just unearthed an answer to one of the biggest mysteries of my generation. Damien Capello was alive.

It was good news. Maria wasn't a killer. She hadn't murdered her husband and added him to her meatball recipe, no matter what the conspiracy theorists had been saying for the last thirty years. I was relieved.

I thought of my father as I walked back to the farmhouse. His voice on the other end of the phone line. *Thea, I know it's you.* The *Ren & Stimpy* playing cards I never had a chance to give him, that I still had in a shoebox in the back of my closet, for some reason. I thought of my mother's sobs reverberating through the walls of our small apartment. The soundtrack of my childhood. And I thought of Maria. The look of adoration she had on her face in photos of her and Damien. The way she'd described slowly drinking that glass of vodka as she realized how deep her husband's betrayal went.

I realized that some small, shameful part of me was disappointed she hadn't killed him after all.

....

Issie was waiting when I got back to the farmhouse. Ava slid out of my arms the second I stepped through the back door and went right to her mother, hanging her head as Issie lectured her about how she wasn't allowed to go visit the animals alone, thanking me for a second before the two of them disappeared down the hall.

Back in my room, I start to pace. My brain was going crazy, pinging around the inside of my skull like one of those little rubber balls Ruthie was always bringing home from birthday parties. My thoughts were moving too fast and in too many directions.

Damien was alive. He'd come back.

Why? He'd gone through so much trouble to disappear, had done God only knows what to stay gone for thirty years. What would bring him back here now, after all that time? What could possibly be that important?

I was deep in thought when I felt a change in the stillness around me, a flash of shadow across the light coming in from below my door, a groan of floorboards. Maybe I was still disoriented from the draft Maria had given me last night, still tired and out of it, but the noise touched something paranoid inside of me. I had the bone-deep feeling of being watched.

It was this house. This damn house.

I stopped moving and whipped around to face the door that led to the hall. There was nothing, not even a shadow at the crack between the bottom of the door and the floorboards. I forced my breathing to steady. My brain was playing tricks on me. No one was out there.

Almost as soon as the thought entered my head, a thin stack of paper shot below the door and into the center of my room.

The next chapter was here.

THE SECRET INGREDIENT

....

CHAPTER EIGHT

I woke the day after our fight expecting everything to look different. A sky full of clouds, the weather gray, maybe there'd be sleet. I expected every piece of fruit to be rotten, bread moldy, dust coating the surface of all my furniture. Maybe that sounds dramatic, but you must understand—it felt like my life as I had known it was over. Everything I'd trusted had been a lie. I wanted acknowledgment of that. I wanted the world to look like I felt.

But when I opened my eyes, roused by the sound of Issie's bare feet slapping down the hall, her voice calling out, asking me to make pancakes, I found the sky blue, cloudless, massive. There was golden sunlight pouring in through my window, goddamn *birds* chirping in the trees. I remember blinking into my pillow, listening to the sounds of cars rumbling down the street. It was just another normal day. Everything was different, but everything was the same.

I started making pancakes, yelled at Enzo to get out of bed when he hit snooze on his alarm the third time. Damien was already gone, left before dawn. I actually thought he was gone for good, that he'd finally left me. A part of me had even hoped for it the way you hope for something you've been dreading, if only to get it over with.

I'd steeled myself as I made my way down to the kitchen, preparing to go on hating him. But he'd only gone to the farmers' market for produce for that night's menu. He'd left me a note and made coffee before he'd gone out and had washed my favorite mug for me, placed it beside the pot. A small gesture, the sort of thing married people do for each other all the time to let the other person know they are thinking about them. It nearly brought me to tears.

Over those next few weeks, Damien would be home in the mornings when we woke up. He'd help Enzo find his soccer jersey, start the coffee, wash the dishes from the night before while I double-checked

Issie's geometry homework. He'd reach across the table while we ate breakfast, squeeze my hand. God, the feeling of his hand pressed against mine, his skin on my skin. It always felt like the first time he touched me, the first time I realized how in love with him I was. I don't think I could ever do that feeling justice, don't think I could adequately describe the way it was like fireworks exploding all along my fingers, my heart filling up with hope, with want. Even now, remembering, it brings me close to tears. Every night, I'd hear the door creak open at midnight, right after the restaurant closed, and I'd lie awake as Damien crept into the room and kissed me on the cheek. If he saw that I was awake, we made love quietly in the dark so we wouldn't wake the kids. People joke about how it isn't sexy to try to find time to be intimate when you have children, but I disagree. To this day, those nights with Damien were among the most romantic in my life.

Maybe he's coming back to us, I remembered thinking. Hoping. It was what I'd so desperately wanted, but it wasn't what was happening, not exactly. Damien was just going through the motions, doing the things he thought he should be doing. But he wasn't all there. Some vital part of him was missing. And the harder he tried, the longer he stayed, the more obvious it became.

A few weeks after I found out about our debt, Damien asked me about insurance. He'd never been interested in the details of our policies before. I'd been the one in charge of setting up meetings with the agent, filling out the forms, signing everything on the dotted line. Then suddenly, out of nowhere, he was asking about insurance on the restaurant, on the house, the cars. He wanted to know if we had life insurance and how much.

I hadn't wanted to answer. My throat had closed right up, like someone was pinching my windpipe between their fingers. I pictured my love in the dark of our restaurant after close, a match in his callused fingers, thinking that getting rid of our problems would be as easy as letting the fire eat them all away. I wondered if he would even bother leaving the barn, or if he'd let the flames consume him, too.

The thought terrified me. I started hiding money. I didn't trust the banks anymore, not after what happened with my mother's bonds, so I'd take the cash from the restaurant home at the end of the night and stow it in an old shoebox at the back of the closet or in an empty Eggo carton in the freezer, or put it in a Ziploc bag, dig a hole out in the barn, and bury it. It felt safer that way. At least then I knew where the money was. I could see it, if I wanted to.

Twice, people I didn't recognize showed up at the restaurant, a man and a woman dressed in drab clothing. Both times, Damien greeted them before I could and then ushered them to the back office without a word to me, closed the door so that all I could hear of their conversation was the muffled rise and fall of voices.

Were they mob? Detectives? Loan sharks? I demanded to know, but Damien was cagey, avoidant.

"I'm handling this," he'd promised me. "I know I fucked up, but it's all going to be okay. Trust me."

I tried. God, how I tried. There were things you had to let go of in a long marriage. We both knew that. But he would get this look on his face sometimes, when he thought I couldn't see him. It was a look of utter hopelessness. As though the life had already drained out of him.

It was Damien's idea to have the party. I didn't want to spend any more money than we absolutely had to in those days, but Damien wanted to do something for the staff to boost morale. He said it was a message that we were moving past the mistakes we'd made, a new beginning. It was so rare to see him excited about anything, and I found myself getting excited too. Maybe this could be our new beginning. Maybe we could start over. I found an old dress in the back of my closet, got it dry-cleaned, pulled Damien's suit out for him and insisted he try it on so we could make sure it still fit. I spoke with caterers daily, arranged for extra chairs and tables to be delivered, hired a band.

This is going to be fine, I told myself. *Better than fine. We've had a brief setback, but we're getting it under control. After this, we'll be stronger than ever.*

But sometimes I'd wake up in the middle of the night, suddenly remembering something I'd forgotten to do, a call I'd needed to return or a notice from one of the kids' schools that I'd ignored for too long, and I'd get out of bed and see a light outside in the slaughterhouse. I'd hike out to the barn and Damien would already be there. Fully dressed, boots knotted, jacket on. Not doing anything, just standing in the middle of the room, boots sinking into the bloodstained mud, a look on his face that I recognized from when I found mice caught in the glue traps we left around the barn. Wild, black terror. Once or twice, it even looked like he'd been crying.

Times like that, I'd feel like I was sinking. And I'd think to myself that my husband, the man I'd fallen in love with at first sight, the man I'd devoted my entire life to, that man was already gone. He'd left us a long time ago.

So you see, I didn't really have a choice in the end. I could have begged him to stay with us, of course. But it wouldn't have been the same. Some fundamental part of him was already gone.

I loved my husband more than anything. If you take anything away from this book, I want it to be that. Despite his faults, despite his sins, I loved him.

And when you love someone, you can't let them destroy themselves.

The day of our party, Damien left his suit jacket on the back of a chair in his home office after he'd finished trying it on. I'd grabbed it, thinking I would hang it up for him so it wouldn't lose its shape. After I put it on the hanger, I ran my hand over the fabric a few times to smooth out the wrinkles.

But something in the pocket shifted, a piece of paper. I didn't think anything of it until I pulled it out and saw my name written in Damien's handwriting and realized that it was a goodbye letter. Damien was finally leaving us. Leaving me.

I must've read that note a dozen times, a hundred times. But I wasn't mad, I was resigned. This was always going to happen. Our love story was always going to end like this. I thought of those mice in the glue traps in our barn. How once they'd realized they were trapped, they'd chew off their own legs in order to get free. I thought of Damien sitting alone in the slaughterhouse in the dark. Crying. Looking so lost.

At that moment, holding his note, I remember feeling a kind of release. I remembered thinking that it was all going to be okay. For the first time in years, I knew how to be a good wife. I knew what Damien wanted: not just to leave, but to disappear. To no longer be "Damien Capello." To start over completely.

And I could give him that. Damien had written me a three-page note explaining why he had to go. But without the second page, it read like a suicide letter. I could release the first and third page to the press, let the world believe he was dead. And Damien could have what he'd always wanted: an anonymous life somewhere warm. No more fame, no more family hanging around his neck like a noose. A fresh start.

I wouldn't let Damien chew off his own leg. I was stronger than that. If he wanted his freedom, then I owed it to him—as his wife, as the woman who loved him most in this world—to let him go.

Starting Over Stuffed Chicken Legs Wrapped in Prosciutto

For most home cooks, the idea of boning and stuffing a whole chicken is daunting, but a chicken leg is much more doable. If you're not an adept butcher, you will find that the first leg will take you a little while, but your speed will improve with each leg you debone. Alternatively, if you have a good butcher, you can ask them to do it for you.

INGREDIENTS

4 whole chicken legs
½ small vidalia onion
½ cup walnuts
3 sweet Italian sausages
3 large sprigs of sage
Olive oil as needed
1 large egg
½ cup Parmesan Reggiano
¼ cup breadcrumbs
4 thin slices of prosciutto
Salt and black pepper
Balsamic glaze

STEPS

Serves 4

1. First, debone each of the chicken legs: using a sharp paring knife or boning knife, cut along the bone of the drum and thigh and over the joint, and pull back the flesh to expose the bone. Cut all around the foot, detaching the tendons from the bone. Then, using the fingers of one hand, pull back the meat while using your knife with the other hand to scrape the meat away from the bone. Cut all around the joint, making sure to leave behind the tendon on the skin side. Finally, cut away the bundle of tendons at the foot end.

2. Preheat your oven to 400°F, convection. Cut the onion into fine

dice, and finely chop the walnuts. Remove the sausage from the casings. Pick the sage from one of the sprigs and finely mince.

3. To a frying pan add a drizzle of oil with the onions and a pinch of salt. Sweat over medium heat until translucent, then add the sausages, breaking up with a spoon. Continue cooking and breaking up the pieces until all is browning, about 10 minutes, then add in the walnuts. Continue cooking until well browned, about another 5 minutes, then add the sage and cook 1 minute longer. Remove the stuffing to a mixing bowl and let cool.

4. Beat the egg and add to the stuffing, along with the cheese, breadcrumbs, and a generous grating of black pepper.

5. Season the deboned chicken legs on both sides with salt and pepper, then assemble each: lay 1 slice prosciutto on your working surface, followed by a deboned leg, skin side down. Spread spoonfuls of the stuffing onto the flesh side, then roll up, starting with the small end, jelly-roll style. Truss securely with kitchen twine on both ends. Place the rolls on a wire rack set over a sheet pan and slide into the oven. Cook for 35 minutes until well browned. Remove from the oven and let stand for 10 minutes.

6. While the chicken is in the oven, pick the sage from the remaining sprigs and fry in olive oil over low heat until darkening. This should only take about 1 minute. Turn the sage leaves carefully with a fork, and remove with a slotted spoon to a dish, sprinkling immediately with salt.

7. Cut the kitchen twine and remove from the chicken, then slice crosswise using a serrated knife. Plate immediately, garnishing with the crispy sage leaves and balsamic glaze. Accompany this dish with preserved fruit flavors such as fig jam, mostarda, or dried cherries soaked in vinegar.

NOTES FOR THE HOME COOK

- Any leftover stuffing can be baked in a buttered ramekin for a crispy snack.

16

THEA

I DIDN'T CLOCK IT UNTIL I WAS HALFWAY THROUGH MY SECOND read of Maria's new pages, and then it sent a feeling like cold water shimmering down my spine.

It was this: *I'd take the cash from the restaurant home at the end of the night, stow it in an old shoebox at the back of the closet or in an empty Eggo carton in the freezer, or put it in a Ziploc bag, dig a hole out in the barn, and bury it.*

Maria told me she'd done this. I remembered sitting in her kitchen, nursing a coffee as she explained how she'd hidden money all over the farm, how she wasn't totally sure she'd dug it all up.

And I wasn't the only one there when she'd said it. Amy had been in the kitchen, too. Hovering, taking her time with her coffee. Listening to every word.

I'd wondered what would be so important that it would bring Damien back here, after he'd tried so hard to get away. I felt stupid now that I hadn't put it together immediately. It was the same thing that had brought my dad back again and again. *Money.* Damien was looking for the money Maria had hidden.

Suddenly, a phone beeped. After two days without my cell, the sound was so unexpected that I released a breathy shriek. It took me several long seconds to remember Amy's burner.

I pressed a hand to my chest, willing myself to calm down. Then, heart still hammering, I pulled the burner out of my pocket and swiped to pull up the new message:

Something happened. I need to see you. Twenty minutes.

A second later, another message appeared below it: a dropped pin.

I stared at the screen for a long time, trying to get my breath to steady. I felt like I was holding a live grenade. My face was numb, my hands cold.

I read the text again. *I need to see you.*

I couldn't meet this person. I knew that, somewhere in the back of my brain. I wasn't a risk-taker, I wasn't the kind of person who put themselves in unnecessary danger, and I had no idea who this was. They could be dangerous.

Something happened.

A tingle of anticipation shot up my spine. I felt like Pandora with her infamous box, Eve holding an apple. The answers were just on the other side of this phone, near enough to feel them brush against my arm as they drifted past, skittering in the corners of the room like mice, gone if I waited even a second too long.

I felt my thumbs moving on their own, keying words into the phone without consulting my brain about them first. Adrenaline burst inside me as I hit Send on my response.

I'll be there.

....

The air outside was cool, crisp. I shivered, hugging my arms around myself. The hair on my arms stood straight up, angry with me.

The pin the texter had sent was close enough to walk to, only a mile or so away from the house. I pulled the back door closed and cut across the field, listening to the soft crunch of fallen leaves, the occasional snap of a twig beneath my boots. Twisted tree roots sprawled across the ground. I had to be careful where I put my feet.

The grass grew high, past my knees, almost to my hips, forcing me to fight my way through. Trees loomed here and there, casting deep shadows. I had almost made it to the location on the map when I realized I knew exactly where I was going. It was the same place Amy had met whoever had texted her last time: the old, decrepit barn near the creek.

I stopped walking the moment I figured it out, anxiously digging into my thumb with my teeth.

The texter was Damien. It had to be Damien. I knew he was in contact with Amy. It was only the two of us in the kitchen with Maria when she mentioned the money, and I didn't think he'd found out about it some other way. The timing was too coincidental. I'd bet anything that Damien was the one Amy had been calling late at night, Damien was the one in the car I'd seen pull up to the barn.

I turned in place, peering back over my shoulder to where the farmhouse loomed in the distance. God, it looked perfect, fog creeping toward the windows, sun hanging in the distance, tinting everything gold. It was like an image from a design magazine, not real, not something you could ever reach out and touch. It'd break apart the second you tried, slip through your hands like smoke. A dream.

But I was starting to see it differently after three days here. It had a way of bending the air. I didn't know much about physics, but I knew that when objects got too big, they created their own gravity, distorted the world around them. That's what this felt like.

The barn the texter was leading me to was a perfect isolated location. And I was alone. Damien could do whatever he wanted to me and no one would know I'd even gone out there. The thought made my mouth go dry. I slipped my hand into my pocket, touching Amy's notebook with the tips of my fingers. I played back everything that had happened since I'd last seen her: her inexplicably clean room, the screams that had started at dawn. The blood soaking into the slaughterhouse floor.

My paranoia was working on me now, and without meaning to, I pictured Amy hanging from the ceiling of the slaughterhouse like a pig, strung up by her ankles over the dirt floor, eyes open, frozen in a look of complete and utter terror. Throat slit. Skin pale. Blood dripping down her chin, clinging to her nose before dropping to the ground below.

I squeezed my eyes shut, shoving the image away. It wasn't real. I was being paranoid, letting the horrible stories that had been circulating for the last three decades get the best of me. Damien was alive, which meant no one had been murdered here. Even the suicide note that wasn't really a suicide note made sense now. Maria had made it clear in her last chapter that she'd made peace with letting Damien leave. She was giving him the fresh start he'd always wanted.

I was so close to learning the whole truth. This wasn't just about the end of Maria's book, not anymore. This was about a thirty-year mystery. It was about answers to one of the biggest scandals of my time. I needed to know. I was desperate to know. I would do anything to know. If I turned back now, I never would. Could I live with that?

I felt my heart go still inside my chest. I barely breathed. I kept walking.

The barn was larger than it looked from a distance. At least two stories tall, with gray wooden walls, paint stripped clear away from years of being left to the elements, a flat roof, the windows little more than squares cut into the siding. One strong breeze could blow it over.

I pushed the front door open, releasing a long, low creak. My heart was beating like crazy. It was dark, the only light spilling in from the few windows scattered over the bare wooden walls. The ground was made soft with hay. In the air hung the long-forgotten scent of animals, of sweaty bodies and manure.

The car I'd seen Amy get into the other day was already parked inside. As I watched, the door creaked open and a woman who looked remarkably like Maria stepped out.

She was plump and short, older than me, with long hair nearly the same shade as Maria's, and like Maria's, it was threaded through with thick patches of gray. She had Maria's small, pointed face, though her nose was a little longer, her jaw a bit more angular. They could have been sisters. But there was something about this woman's eyes and the shape of her mouth that told me she'd been very, very beautiful when she was young. The kind of beautiful that turned heads.

I blinked, recognizing her. "Nina?"

She looked just like the photo on Hank's wall, only older. She wore an ankle-length skirt, stacks of bracelets around each wrist, and she had a cheap tote bag slung over one shoulder with some faded, bookish logo on the side—the type people in publishing tended to get for free.

Her eyes skittered around, anxious. "Who the hell are you? Where's Amy?"

"Amy's not here. She left."

Nina started backing toward the car, shaking her head. "No," she said, under her breath. "No, *shit.*"

"Wait—" I said before Nina could climb back into the car. "Don't leave. I'm a friend of Amy's. My name is Thea. I'm the one who got your text. I have Amy's phone."

Nina said nothing but kept her hand on the car door. Any moment she was going to climb inside and disappear. I needed to say something to get her to stay, offer her some sort of proof that I could be trusted. But I had nothing. Or, almost nothing.

On instinct, I pulled the notebook out of my pocket, held it up so she could see. Her eyes widened slightly, recognizing it.

"That was Amy's," she murmured.

"I found it this morning," I explained, looking back toward the car. There was no one else inside, just Nina. I frowned, confused. "Where's Damien? Isn't he with you?"

Nina threw me a look I couldn't read. The air around us sharpened to a knifepoint.

Very carefully, her eyes never leaving my face, she said, "Damien's dead."

Her voice was solid, certain, no room for argument.

"No," I said slowly. Damien was just here. I'd seen him. "No, that can't be right."

"I know he's dead," Nina said, cutting me off. "I was there when she killed him."

PART THREE JUST DESSERTS

17

MARIA

I'VE SPENT MOST OF MY MARRIAGE PLOTTING MY HUSBAND'S death. Anyone who'd planned a murder for that long was past the point of claiming crime of passion. When I stood before a jury—*if* I ever stood before a jury—momentary insanity would be off the table.

What I'd planned was not momentary. And it might have been the sanest thing I'd ever done in my life.

....

I sat at my desk in the basement, right outside the industrial freezer we kept locked at all times, smiling a little as I went over the notes Thea had scrawled into the margins of my last batch of pages. She seemed to have bought in to the love story I'd written. That was such a relief. I'd worked so hard to scrub my hatred of Damien from the pages. If I was being totally honest (and, at this point, why wouldn't I be honest?), I could no longer remember a time before I'd wanted to kill him. It was a bit like childbirth, how the memory of the pain seemed to disappear the moment you were no longer in it. I know I used to love him, but I hadn't for such a long time, so long that I could no longer remember what that love had felt like. All that remained was the anger, the hatred. The deep, nagging need to have him gone.

Not just from my life, but from *existence*.

That kind of anger didn't fade nearly as fast as the love did. I should know. I could feel it bubbling below my skin even now, thirty years later. A low simmer, so much cooler than it had been but still there, still boiling.

A sound like a thump came from behind the freezer door. I snapped my head up and waited, listening. It didn't come again. Besides, I had the door padlocked. Nothing was getting out of that freezer.

I put the pages of my memoir aside and picked up Thea's phone. Her background photograph was of her family: her husband, their beautiful daughter. The phone was password protected, but I'd hired a tech guy to break in. I keyed the new password in and the screen brightened, instantly unlocked.

I'd done my research on Thea Woods, executive editor at Hanes House Press. I knew her. *Really* knew her. By the time she'd walked into that conference room for our very first meeting, I had her biography memorized. A private detective I'd hired gave me the names of everyone in her family, all her friends. I knew how much money she had in her bank account and how much her daughter's day care tuition cost and exactly how much she would need to get her mother out of debt. I knew she was loyal and thoughtful, that she believed in things like justice.

It's hard to trick a person like that, someone smart and good. You can't buy them, even if they are desperate. You can't blackmail them.

I'd needed Thea to love me.

The memoir pages should've gotten her most of the way there. They were intended to create a version of my life she could relate to, the kind of woman she would *want* to help. Someone who reminded her of her own mother, perhaps. Or the mother she'd wished she had. The kind of woman who knew when to let a man go, who would choose her family over her shitty husband every time. Nurturing, maternal.

It was easy. Memoir Maria wasn't so unlike TV Show Maria, who was really just an extension of Cookbook Maria. *That* Maria was my masterpiece. I'd spent decades creating her, omitting the more offensive details of my life with Damien, shaving down the rougher edges of our story, breezing past anything that wouldn't land with the housewives in the middle of the country.

Not that I was dismissive of the housewives of Middle America. I *loved* the housewives. They'd watched my program for three decades. They bought every new cookbook I released and shopped my line of frozen foods and pasta sauces. The housewives were the reason I had the life I had today.

But people like that expected mothers to be perfect. They would accept nothing less. Fathers were allowed to be complex, flawed, *human*. Fathers could make mistakes. Not mothers. Not *me*.

And so I'd allowed them to think I was perfect, that Damien and I had been perfect together, that what happened was a tragedy, that I'd grieved and then gathered whatever strength I had left to move forward for my family.

But Thea was smarter than they were. She was going to learn the truth—or most of the truth—sooner or later. And when she did, I needed her to understand that my actions were justified. That I'd had no other choice in the matter.

I liked where I ended up. Memoir Maria was more like the real me than any other version of myself I'd ever put into the world. Which meant that Thea knew more about me than anyone. Even my own children. I wondered if she appreciated that, if she even realized.

I continued studying the photograph on Thea's phone. It had been taken outside in front of a waterfall. Her husband's beard and hair were streaked with gray, and he wore a baseball hat pulled low over his forehead. Her daughter was making a silly face, loose strawberry-blond curls blowing in the wind. I ran a finger over the line of the girl's cheek, smiling slightly.

Even after all of my preparation, this next part was going to be hard. When Thea found out what I'd kept from her, what I wanted her to do now.

Well. Any love she had for me was going to disappear.

18

THEA

I WAS THERE WHEN SHE KILLED HIM.

I'd already opened my mouth to keep arguing, but the word *she* stopped me. A cold feeling spread through me, wrapping around my bones.

"She?" I repeated.

Nina was backing toward the car, ready to drop this bomb and go. "I shouldn't have said that," she murmured. "I don't even know you. I have to…"

Her tone hadn't changed, but I felt something in the air, fear radiating off her. I suddenly remembered something I'd overheard Amy say the first time I'd heard her on the phone, that someone was "terrified of Maria." Had she been talking about Nina?

Nina wrestled the car door open, hands trembling too badly to work the latch.

"Wait." I pushed the door closed, blocked the way with my body. "You and Damien were having an affair, right?"

Nina was shaking her head, refusing to look at me. "I can't talk about this—"

"But you *were* talking about it with Amy. You must've decided you were okay with the story getting out. Were you and Damien planning to run away together? Was that why he abandoned his family?"

"You don't understand... Maria is *crazy*." Nina ran a shaky hand back through her hair, not looking at me. "You have no idea what she's capable of, what she'll do to..." She let her voice trail off, then started again. "Damien didn't abandon his family. He had to get away from *her*. Did you know she stole a bunch of money from him? His mom left him all these stocks when she died, but Maria took them and hid them, buried them out in the yard somewhere like a dog."

A jolt went through me, a tiny hum of electricity.

"No," I said, drawing out the word. "No, the stocks weren't his. They were Maria's. Damien stole them from *her*."

Nina gave me a look like I wasn't getting it. I opened my mouth to keep arguing with her, then closed it again. Because I didn't really know they were Maria's, did I? Everything I knew about what happened came from Maria's memoir, Maria's words.

I played the story back in my head, only this time I switched the names around. *Damien* had gone to the bank. Damien had discovered that his safe-deposit box was empty. And then he'd come home to his wife, calmly drinking vodka.

The bonds aren't in the safe-deposit box anymore. They're gone.

Something cold seeped through me, wrapping around my bones. That fit, too. There was no way of knowing which story was the real story, which woman to trust. Was Nina telling the truth now? Or had Maria been telling the truth in her memoir?

"You said she killed him," I said. "What happened? Why didn't he leave like you'd planned?"

Nina shoved me away from her car door, yanked it open. "No, I'm not doing this."

"Wait." I couldn't let her leave, not when I was so close to real answers. I searched my brain for anything I could give her to make her stay. "You want to talk to a journalist—"

"I never wanted to talk to anyone," Nina said, cutting me off. She climbed in her car. "Amy tracked me down and blackmailed me into talking to her."

"She *blackmailed* you?" Somewhere in the back of my head, I heard the click of two puzzle pieces slotting into place. "She threatened to tell Maria where you were, didn't she? That's why you agreed to talk? Because you were terrified that Maria would find you."

Nina's eyes snapped to mine. "That woman is a monster," she said in a hushed voice. "You have no idea what she'll do if she finds me."

She was still half in the car, hand on the door, seconds away from pulling it shut and speeding out of the barn, out of my life forever. I couldn't let that happen. I had to make her talk to me. I wanted her to stay so badly I could taste it.

I glanced at the car's license plate, a horrible idea forming in my head. A sick taste filled my mouth. *I can't do this... No.*

But it was the only thing I could think to do, the only way I could keep Nina from leaving.

"I might not know your address," I said, jerking my chin at her license plate, "but I bet Maria has some private detective on retainer who'd be able to track you down off that number alone."

"It's a rental," Nina said. But her jaw tightened.

"Rental companies have files. Names, credit card information." Even as I spoke, I could see how easy it would be to follow the trail back to where Nina had spent the last thirty years hiding. Maria had the kind of money that opened doors. People would fall all over themselves to give her whatever she asked for.

"You were going to run away with Damien," I pressed. "All you have to do is tell me why you didn't."

"You little bitch," Nina murmured, voice very quiet. "You have no idea what you're threatening me with."

I felt immediately guilty, but I wasn't about to back down. "Just tell me what I need to know and I won't say a word to her, I swear."

Nina wouldn't look at me. Instead, she stared at the wall of the barn, arms going tight around her chest.

"We were all set to leave that night," she said, after a long moment.

"Damien had a car hidden, clothes, money. We were going to meet here, actually"—she lifted one hand, motioning to the barn—"while Maria and the kids and everyone were distracted at the party, drive until we found a place we liked, start our new life there."

"What happened?"

"I found out Damien had been seeing someone else, a woman upstate." Nina blinked hard, the pain still there all these years later. "It was over with her, he'd ended it awhile before, but it still hurt." She stared at me for a long moment after she said it, waiting to see how I'd respond.

I had to work to keep the shock from my face. A *third* woman?

"So, you decided not to go with him?" I guessed.

But Nina shook her head. "Don't get me wrong, I thought about telling him to get lost, I really did. I was so mad. But in the end, I couldn't do it. I still loved him. So I came here, and I waited for him, just like we'd planned. Damien was the one who never showed. At first, I thought *he* was leaving *me*. And then—" Her voice cracked all of a sudden and she stopped talking, pressing her fingers to her mouth. "Sorry," she said, after a moment. "This is hard."

"Take your time."

"I was here in the barn, waiting for him, when all of a sudden I heard these voices outside. Yelling, angry voices. One of them was Maria. I heard her shout, 'You son of a bitch,' and then Damien said something back, something like 'You don't understand,' or 'You don't know what you're talking about.'"

I stayed quiet, listening. I could almost picture it: Damien and Maria standing in the woods, screaming at each other, while just a few dozen yards behind them, a party was in full swing.

"I figured she must've found out about us," Nina explained. "I even thought it might be a good thing, that Damien and I would be able to leave without all the secrecy, the hidden car, sneaking away in the middle of the party. But then I heard the gunshot—"

"Gunshot?" I interrupted, startled. "None of the reports said anything about a gunshot. And they didn't find any blood at the scene."

"We're too far from the farmhouse for anyone back there to have heard anything," Nina said. "That's why Damien had wanted to meet here, so we could start the car without anyone knowing. I don't know about the blood, though. I ran down to the edge of the creek to look for him after Maria went back up to the house, but his body was already gone. I figured he fell in the creek, that the current pulled him away."

"Why didn't you go to the police?"

"Don't you think I wanted to?" Nina snapped. "I thought about it the whole way back to the farm. I planned out who I would call and what I would say. But then I saw Hank walking back to the creek, carrying a pile of Damien's clothes, and I realized they already knew about us, both of them, and they'd cooked up some story to explain why Damien disappeared. I followed Hank, and I watched him dump the clothes at the edge of the water. He even arranged Damien's pants so it looked like he'd just stepped out of them. They'd *planned* all of it. For all I knew, they were going to kill me too."

"You still could've gone to the police."

Nina shook her head. "You really don't get it, do you? These people are *connected*. Maria has friends everywhere. I couldn't trust the police. I couldn't trust anyone. If I said the wrong thing to the wrong person…" Her voice trailed off, her eyes nervously skittering to the window like she was worried Maria herself might climb through. "I—I couldn't chance it. If they'd planned Damien's death that carefully, they'd have been able to come up with a reason I'd disappeared, too." Nina closed her eyes tight, a single tear leaking down her cheek. "So, I took the car and I drove. I didn't even tell anyone where I was going."

I chewed my lip, turning this story over in my head. It was convincing enough, and Nina was clearly terrified of something. But she was lying. Maybe not about everything, but definitely about the reason she didn't call the police. I could hear it in her voice. There was another reason she'd kept quiet for thirty years, another reason she was so terrified of Maria finding her now.

Nina swiped at the tear with her palm. "You should be scared, too. I don't know what you know about the Capellos or how you got mixed up with this family, but you're not safe here. You need to leave." She glanced at the window again and added, "As soon as possible."

"I'm not in any danger." But I felt a chill go down my neck, all the same.

"That's what Amy said. Celia warned her, but she didn't listen."

"Celia?"

"My friend," Nina explained. "You came by her place the other day? I heard you outside. I'm sure it was you."

I thought of the Janeane Garofalo–type woman whose door I'd knocked on. "She said she didn't see Amy that night."

"Yeah, well, she didn't exactly owe you the truth, did she? Amy was there. Halfway through our talk, she went outside to smoke and never came back. Left her bag behind and everything. She'd been hounding me about that interview for months. She never would have just walked away."

Nina swallowed and stared at the wall, tears shimmering in her eyes. "I think someone took him. That's why I texted. Because I was worried."

I stared at her. "You think someone took *him*?"

Her eyes snapped back to me. "I said 'someone took her.'"

But that wasn't what she'd said. I dropped a hand in my pocket, fingers curling around Amy's notebook. At some point, after leaving Nina's for her smoke break, Amy had gotten from Woodstock back to the farm. Or someone had *taken* her from Woodstock back to the farm.

"What do you think she did?" I asked. Nina stared at me for a long moment, and I felt a layer of sweat shimmer over my skin.

I thought of the meatballs Maria had served last night, the layer of fat glistening from the surface. The tomato sauce that had looked like blood.

"Listen, this was Amy's." Nina slid the tote bag off her shoulder and shoved it at me, causing me to stumble backward a few steps. "She had part of her book printed out. Read it, if you want any more answers. I'm out of here, either way." She stared at me for another moment, then said, "If you give Maria my license number, you're the one who's going to have to live with what she does to me."

I nodded, but I was already in the process of forgetting the numbers I'd read. I knew then that I wouldn't be the one to give her up.

....

Nina left before I could dig Amy's pages out of the tote bag. I heard the car's engine purr on as I found an old log to sit on, and then the car was pulling away.

There were around ten pages here, double-spaced. Amy had titled it *Damien*. I hesitated only a moment, front teeth digging into my lip, before scanning the first paragraph.

It was beautifully written. Amy was a confident writer, easily settling the reader into the story. It began with Damien's disappearance: *In the early '90s, the culinary world faced a shocking mystery when legendary chef Damien Capello vanished without a trace from his family's farm in Woodstock, New York.*

Amy went on to write about how the police had investigated and immediately determined that Maria couldn't have been involved with her husband's disappearance because of security footage taken at Woodstock Hospital, where she'd taken Enzo to the emergency room with a broken nose. It then flashed forward a few years to comment on Maria's rise to fame: *The narrative took an unexpected turn when Damien's wife, Maria Capello, emerged from the shadows of the tragedy to become a celebrated cookbook author and television personality. Today, she's a culinary world icon.*

I found myself breathing easier as I read. For the most part, this was the story I knew, a less polished version of the rags-to-riches tale Maria included at the beginning of all of her cookbooks. If Amy was planning a whole book, it would make sense for her to start like this. She was setting up the story the world was already familiar with, making sure we were all clear on the "facts." Then, at the end of the chapter or sample or whatever this was, she'd drop whatever bomb she had. A cliffhanger to keep us reading.

My guess was that she was going to include Nina's story, how Nina had planned to meet Damien in the barn, how they were going to run away together but he never showed. The sound of him and Maria arguing, the gunshot. I flipped to the last page, scanning the final few paragraphs.

"Shit," I murmured once I'd read.

Amy had dropped a bomb all right. But it had nothing to do with Nina.

Rumors of Damien's infidelity are widespread, but few know that Damien fathered a child outside of his marriage with Maria Capello, Amy had written. *The child's family worked hard to make sure they were never associated with the famous chef.*

Damien's child was sixteen years old the night his father went missing. And he attended the party the Capellos held at their farmhouse, a detail conveniently left out of every police report.

"I don't know what happened to Damien," Damien Capello's son, who has expressed a wish to remain anonymous, told me in a recent interview, revealing details he's never before shared with the public. "But I know he deserved what he got."

19

MARIA

I HAVE NEVER TRIED THERAPY, BUT I BELIEVE A THERAPIST would've told me my "murderous impulses" started with my own father.

He left. Naturally. Hardly a surprise—so many of them left. Mine left when my mother was six months pregnant, penniless, new to New York, far from her family, her friends. Once, when I was in my twenties and home for Christmas, my mother got drunk on too much spiked eggnog and admitted that my father had left her for a cute girl he'd met at their local bakery. I think that might have been what bothered her more than anything: she was betrayed by bread, which was one of the things she'd loved most in this world.

My father didn't leave behind a phone number or a forwarding address. He simply didn't come home one night. By the time my mother thought to wonder where he was, she realized that his toothbrush was gone, that he'd packed a bag of clothes and cleaned out most of the money from their joint account. But what really pissed her off was that he took the good toaster. For years, she refused to buy a new one, out of spite or because we couldn't afford it, I never knew. We toasted our bread by sticking it in the oven, on broil.

Every time I watched my bread slowly brown through the dirty glass of our oven, I'd remember that men were good for nothing. And if I ever forgot, even for a moment, if I had a crush, say, or a date, my mother was always quick to tell me. *Have fun, but know that he will only ever disappoint you. He'll cheat on you. He'll stop loving you.*

He'll leave.

Leaving. People didn't talk enough about what a privilege it was to have the option to leave. Women could and did leave their children, of course, but it wasn't the same. Women who left were monsters. They were unnatural. The cost was so much higher than it was for men, so high that most women would choose to destroy themselves rather than pay it.

Back when I used to attend church with my mother, Catholic service in Queens, lots of standing and sitting and crossing ourselves before eating stale crackers and watered-down grape juice, I always marveled at how priests would teach the story of Adam and Eve, how they'd try to get us to believe that women's punishment for original sin was pain.

What a laugh. Pain was never our curse. Our curse was that, no matter what happened, no matter if it destroyed us, if it killed our spirit, if it actually killed *us*, we would stay.

My mother planned my father's murder so carefully. I had always admired her for that. I was nine years old when she found him again. Pure luck. Or fate, if you believed in such things. We were in Manhattan to see the tree lighting, and there he was, walking down the street, distracted, checking his watch. She pointed him out to me, her finger trembling. *That's him. Your father.* I remember thinking I should have felt something when I saw him for the first time, some bond. But there was nothing. He was just some schlubby man in an oversized suit with too much belly and a bad comb-over. Nothing to me.

He didn't even notice when we fell in step behind him, or that we followed him to the high-rise office building where he worked, waited outside for him to be done for the day. My mother entertained me with a deck of cards she bought at a corner store, a slick, stiff, red deck that cracked whenever we shuffled them. She taught me to play solitaire and speed, crazy eights and go fish. And then it was after five, and he was leaving again. He didn't notice that we were still there, the sun dipping low to the horizon, the streets crowded with people hurrying for their trains. We followed him all the way home to the nice building with the doorman and the elevator.

My mother didn't take me with her again, but I know she continued following him. She left me with our neighbor, Gladys, who watched me sometimes when Mother had to work. She'd be gone for hours, and I only knew she was watching my father, tracking his movements, because she wrote it all down in the little spiral-bound notebook that she'd bought the same day she bought our cards. I found it tucked below her mattress when she was at work, pored over it like I was reading an illicit erotic novel: *12:15, lunch at the deli down the street. 9:00 p.m., a woman comes to his apartment, doesn't leave again until the next morning. 3:15, doctor's appointment in Midtown.*

She knew where he went, and when, and why. She knew when he'd be surrounded by people, and when he'd be alone. It took her months to gather all the information she needed, but my mother had always been a patient woman.

She waited. She bided her time.

We never talked about what she did. I only knew it was done when I saw a poster in the subway, my father's face staring out at me in black and white. *Local man, missing.*

You would think I felt something when I saw that poster, a stab of pain or sorrow for the father I had never known, perhaps. All I remembered feeling was satisfied.

Good, I thought. It had felt like justice, seeing that. He'd gotten what he deserved.

For years afterward, my mother told me men weren't to be trusted and I told myself that I would never be like her, that I would never allow myself to be hurt the way *she'd* been hurt. I didn't judge her for what she'd done to my father, but I never wanted to do what she'd had to do.

And then I met Damien.

Damien loved me. That was the real kicker. He *loved* me. And, more than that, he saw me. He knew who I was underneath it all. That night at La Villetta, he'd seen that I was a cook. He'd known without even having to ask, even though the idiot owner had insisted that I work as a hostess, hadn't believed I had any real talent because I was poor, because I was a woman, because I wasn't traditionally trained. But Damien had seen me. And when someone saw you like that, when they truly saw you, it was impossible not to fall.

And so I fell. I fell for Damien hard. I loved him so damn much that, for a while at least, I didn't see what he truly was.

That was my fault. I can accept the blame. I should've been smarter; I should've known better. But love could make fools of us all.

....

I found Damien's goodbye note exactly as I'd written: I was putting away his suit jacket the night before our party, and the note was tucked in his pocket. I hadn't responded the way Memoir Maria had, all that bullshit about understanding his need to be free and letting him go. No, I'd been shocked, then angry. I hadn't thought he would have the nerve. I *knew* he didn't have the money. He'd been planning on cashing out the savings bonds his mother had left for him when she died, but that wasn't an option any longer.

Yes, it had been *his* mother, *his* bonds. I altered that a bit for the memoir. Thea wouldn't have understood that I'd needed to take the bonds and hide them to keep Damien safe from himself, to keep him from leaving. I'd been so sure it would work.

And here he was, planning to leave anyway without them. It was humiliating that he would choose poverty over me, over our family. I couldn't let that happen.

....

I navigated away from the photograph on Thea's phone, called the familiar number. I'd tried getting in touch with Damien's son many times before this, but he'd long ago memorized all of my numbers and stopped answering. My letters and emails to him had, likewise, gone ignored. I had his address—a private detective I'd hired had gotten it for me. I could try showing up at his place. But I felt this would work better.

The phone rang once, twice. And then he said casually, "Hey."

My heart stuttered, just as it did every time I heard his voice. It was so familiar; that was the shocking thing. Almost as familiar to me as my own, as my children's. He sounded so much like Damien.

I wet my lips and said, "Hello, darling. Can I have a word?"

Silence on the other end of the line. I heard a change in his breathing as it grew shallow and ragged. I expected him to hang up on me, but first he said, "Maria…what the fuck?"

"I was hoping I could convince you to stop by the farm," I said. "There are some things we should discuss. All of us."

There was a beat of silence. And then the line went dead. I sighed and placed the phone on my desk. Of course, it was disappointing that I couldn't get him to talk things over with me like the civilized adults that we were. But that was okay. I was prepared to do this the hard way. I had no problem being patient. It wouldn't be long now.

I looked at the freezer door. There was another thump inside, followed by a sound like something being dragged over the floor. Then, nothing.

....

I stowed Thea's phone back in my desk drawer and made my way back upstairs, taking care to lock the basement door behind me. My mother taught me that the key to murdering a man was timing. You needed to watch, listen, pay attention to the details no one else noticed. If you did this, the right moment would make itself known to you. You just had to wait.

Thirty years ago, Damien's goodbye note had shot that all to hell. Damien was an asshole, but he wasn't an idiot. If he'd wanted to disappear, I had no doubt he'd disappear. Which put me in the incredibly difficult position of needing to plan his murder on the same day that I was hosting a party for all our friends, family, and colleagues.

It was incredibly inconvenient. I couldn't cancel; that would've been suspicious. When the police came (which they would, it was inevitable), people would say, *Oh, it was so odd. She was supposed to have a party but she canceled at the last minute,* and I would become an even more obvious suspect than I was already, on account of being the wife. No, I had to continue as if I didn't suspect a thing. That part was crucial.

And so I spent the rest of that morning with our catering team, making sure they understood exactly how to prepare the recipes we wanted served that night: braciole and meatballs in a red gravy, lasagna, agnolotti in broth. I spent hours discussing details like cooking temperature and times, making sure the recipes they were working off were up to date, inspecting ingredients. When I'd finished with them, I walked the furniture people through where to set up chairs and tables, I made sure the cleaners knew which rooms to focus on, I handled flower delivery and helped the DJ set up in the dining room. When the police interviewed them later, all anyone would have to say about me was that I was determined to throw a fantastic party.

But all the while, I was thinking. Plotting, you might say. Poison was out. In order to effectively use poison to kill a man, you needed to gather your ingredients far in advance so you didn't stick out in anyone's memory when the police started asking questions. I wasn't sure exactly when Damien was planning to disappear himself, but he'd already written his little note, so it would be soon. I couldn't risk it. That left me with few options to choose from. A knife or any other weapon that required me to get into a physical altercation with my husband wouldn't work. I was much smaller than him. I would easily be overpowered. We had a gun, a Colt 2000 that Damien kept locked in a safe in our closet. But it was loud. Someone would hear the shot.

I was still considering my options when I made my way up to our bedroom to start getting dressed. Damien was there, already in his suit and standing near the window that overlooked the woods, fumbling with his tie. I couldn't look at him without feeling a fresh shiver of rage, anger flooding my face like heat, so I went directly to our walk-in closet to find my dress for the evening. Our guests would be arriving soon.

Damien was still in the bedroom when I came back from getting dressed, facing that window, tying and untying that damn tie.

"Is something wrong?" I asked offhandedly. Damien had always been a melodramatic man. He had that power some people have, the ability to change the energy of the space around him according to his whims. Over the years, I'd become an expert at knowing his mood the second I walked into any room he was in. I could smell it in the air, like too-strong cologne. What a strange and horrifying gift, to infect everyone around you with your emotions.

That day Damien hadn't seemed to hear my question, didn't seem to register that I'd spoken at all. He didn't turn to me or even flinch at the sound of my voice. He just grunted and pulled his tie apart, started knotting it again.

This was when I became curious. "Dame," I'd said more urgently. He tilted his head toward me, his only indication that he'd heard me speak.

"Maria... Sorry, I didn't hear you come in." His voice was low, raspy. That was the moment, hearing his voice, that I started to get concerned. Damien was loud when he was feeling needy, all deep sighs and long, intentional glances to make sure I understood that I was hurting him with my mere presence. This version of Damien was new to me. He sounded scared. Damien was never scared.

I went to him, even though I only had a few minutes left to get myself ready before our guests would start arriving. Damien was still facing the window, so I turned him around by the shoulders. He put up no resistance. His face was haggard. Worn out. He looked... beaten. Not physically, but emotionally.

Tonight, I realized, staring at him. He was planning to leave me tonight. His appearance could only be because he was so stressed, so worried.

I knew it was going to happen, but I hadn't realized until that moment that it was going to happen so soon. It hit me like a slap, but I knew I was right.

There was no time for careful planning. I couldn't let him escape into his new life, with his new love, his fresh start, and leave me to clean up his messes. I had to act immediately.

I took his tie in my hands and knotted it myself. And then I left him alone with whatever demons were living inside his head. In the bathroom, I quickly applied my makeup and swept my hair into a loose chignon.

The gun, I remembered thinking. *I would have to use the gun.* It was the cleanest possibility, the easiest. I'd stage it to look like a suicide. Damien's own note would be the final, damning piece of evidence. I just had to figure out the right moment.

And I would need an alibi.

20

THEA

Damien Capello had another child. Damien had been sleeping with another woman, not Maria or Nina, but a *third* woman. And he'd fathered her child.

I rubbed my eyes, my head still spinning. That must've been who I'd seen in the slaughterhouse a few hours ago. Not Damien, but some adult son who looked just like him. I'd only seen his face for a second. And people could look older than they were, if they smoked or spent too much time in the sun. If Damien really was dead—and Nina seemed certain that he was—then it was the only explanation I could come up with.

I'd never heard anything about the possibility of Damien having another child. I hadn't read about it in any article on Maria, in any tabloid. How was Amy so sure that whoever this guy was, he was telling the truth? She had to have some sort of proof.

I slipped her pages back into her tote bag, noticing as I did that she had a stack of snapshots inside as well. Old ones, from what I could see. I started to pull one out—

Behind me: the clean snap of a foot coming down on a twig.

I jerked my head up, hand shaking so badly the photograph slipped right out of my fingers, settling back at the bottom of the tote. I looked around, scanning the shadows behind the trees, the bushes. I didn't see anyone, but that didn't mean anything. It would be so easy to hide out here.

I swallowed. I could feel my heart beating in my throat. My palms had gotten slick with sweat. I didn't have time to go through this stuff now. The only thing that mattered was getting the hell out of here. I could think about everything I'd learned later. When I was far, far away.

I stumbled to my feet, my knees shaking so badly I would've fallen if I hadn't braced myself against the side of the old barn. I doubled over, breathing hard.

Maria killed her husband, I thought. If I trusted what Nina told me, then Maria wasn't the kindly old woman she'd let me believe she was. She was a liar. A murderer.

I had to get far, far away from this place, as quickly as possible. I had to get Cassandra to drop the book. I had to forget everything I knew about Damien, about this twisted family.

Hands shaking, I pulled out Amy's burner and checked that I had service out here. I did, but the battery was already on red.

I closed my eyes. I had to think. I didn't know how much juice this phone had before it would die, and I had no idea if my rental car was drivable yet. I needed to call a cab company. But there wasn't enough battery left to look up the number.

Think, I told myself. I considered my options for another moment, then dialed Jacob. He was at his mom's place, only an hour away. He could either drive down and get me, or call me a cab.

His phone rang once, then went right to voicemail.

I frowned and tried again, but the same thing happened: phone rang once, then went straight to voicemail. Jacob was ignoring my call.

I swore under my breath. He wouldn't recognize the phone number to Amy's burner—that had to be why he wasn't answering.

I tried Gloria's landline next. It rang three times before, finally—

"Hello?"

"Gloria," I exhaled, my eyes closing in relief. "I'm so glad you answered."

"Thea? Is everything okay? You sound upset."

I forced myself to breathe as I carefully picked my way back through the woods to the house. "Listen, I really need to talk to Jacob. It's an emergency."

"Jacob?" Gloria sounded confused. "Honey, Jacob just—"

I paused, waiting for her to continue, but there was nothing. "Hello? Gloria?" I checked the burner's phone screen: black. Already dead. *Shit.*

Dread rose inside of me. Maria's farmhouse loomed in the distance. It couldn't be later than four or five o'clock in the afternoon, but there was already mist crawling across the ground, the darkness creeping in hours earlier than it should have. I stared, my breath shallow and raspy. I couldn't see anything beyond the dark farmhouse windows, but it didn't matter. I knew the whole family would be back there, napping in their rooms or getting ready for dinner. Or waiting for me.

I crossed the yard and stepped out of the grass and onto the back patio. The back door hung open, swaying slightly in the wind. Hinges creaked.

A chill moved up my neck. I hadn't left the door like that. I'd closed it behind me when I first came outside.

Hadn't I?

I looked around, checking back the way I'd come. There was no one out here with me. Nina was long gone by now.

I swallowed. I really didn't want to go back into that house.

I crept along the perimeter instead, making my way to the front doors. There wasn't a path through the high grass, and I found myself stumbling over stray twigs and rocks, my heart lodged in my throat. I kept thinking about Amy, picturing her hanging from the ceiling in the slaughterhouse. Neck slit, blood drained, like a pig.

I'm just being paranoid, I told myself. But what if I wasn't? What if that was exactly what happened?

Maybe my rental was drivable. Maybe Gavin had the tire fixed. I looked around, desperate to see his tall, gaunt frame silhouetted at the front door. But there was no sign of him. Instead, a large, green truck had parked directly in front of the house's double doors, the words HANK CASEY MEATS stenciled on the side.

Fear wormed its way through me. Nina had said Hank and Maria had planned Damien's murder together. It didn't seem like a coincidence that he was here now.

My heart pounded inside my chest, but there was no way I was getting out of here without going back into that house one last time. I made my way up the steps on trembling legs. The front door had been flung wide, like someone was going in and out regularly. The air inside smelled stale, musty.

I tried the garage first, but my Kia was no longer parked by the back wall. Gavin must still be fixing the tire. I considered the other cars. The BMW I'd driven earlier was here. Was it technically stealing if Enzo had told me I could borrow it?

I tried the lockbox where I'd left the keys but it wouldn't open: someone had locked it.

Nerves crept up my neck. "I just have to find a phone and call a cab," I whispered to myself.

Shadows crept closer to me as I made my way to the kitchen, wrapping around my ankles. Every creak of the floorboards echoed, making it seem like there was someone right behind me, following me. I looked over my shoulder twice but there was never anyone there. I forced myself to walk faster, legs trembling. When I finally reached the kitchen, I was sweating all over.

The kitchen was empty. *Thank God.*

I started toward the landline hanging from the wall—

Then a thud, right behind me. The sound of a door slamming open. My heart skipped a beat, and I spun around.

Hank Casey's massive frame took up the whole doorway, blocking the light. Even in the shadows, I could see that he was wearing a white apron stained with blood. He held a meat cleaver in one hand, gripping it so tightly his knuckles had turned white.

21

MARIA

THOSE DAMN MEATBALLS WERE THE FIRST INSULT. DAMIEN'S prized achievement, his "polpette." That was the first time my husband took credit for my genius.

Maybe I should've known then what he was. Maybe I should've run. But I was so young and we were so in love. And I was stupid. A woman in love is always so stupid.

Damien had found his grandmother's meatballs in the back of her fridge after her death. That part of the story was true. It was a rainy spring afternoon and we'd driven to her little ranch-style house in the suburbs of Boston. For hours, rain spit against her windows as we sorted through never-used china covered in tiny yellow flowers and scratched flatware, colanders that had holes rusted through them, repaired with fishing wire back when Damien's grandfather had still been alive. Damien's grandparents had grown up during the Depression, and nothing was ever thrown away, not if there was a chance it could be fixed. Most of his nonna's things were far, far past their prime. But we were desperate. We were weeks into our marriage, and every dime we had was going to the restaurant. We took it all.

Damien's uncle, Anthony, was going through Nonna's freezer, throwing out old food, when he found the Tupperware full of her meatballs. God, Damien was excited. I remember him grinning like a little kid, telling me and Anthony he was going to re-create the recipe, that we could use it at the restaurant.

Here's a secret I never even told Damien: I didn't like those meatballs. His nonna used far too much egg and not enough breadcrumbs. They were fatty, soggy. I imagine the only reason Damien loved them so much was nostalgia. He was remembering weekends eating at her house as a child, possibly the first time he'd ever really loved a meal. But the meatballs themselves were nothing special.

Nonetheless, Damien tried very hard to make his just like hers. Every Sunday, he'd prepare the gravy, and while it was cooking, he'd carefully portion out three different types of meat and measure out the breadcrumbs. He'd stir in eggs and roll the mixture into perfect little balls. Each and every time he vowed that *this* batch would be as good as the ones his nonna made. They were never even close.

This went on for weeks. Then months. I should have let him be. But it was torture, watching my new husband struggle to create something so mediocre, watching him fail again and again. And I knew how to fix it. I knew meat. I'd grown up on the cheapest cuts from the butcher shop where my mother had worked; I knew exactly what to do. So, I helped.

It was little adjustments at first. A slightly different percentage of veal to pork to beef, just to try it out. Then a recommendation to soak the breadcrumbs in milk, to add more to the mixture, cut the percentage of meat and egg in half. Little tweaks here and there until the entire recipe was mine.

The day he had his family over for dinner, he'd proudly placed the meatballs in the center of the table, told them all to dig in. They'd been so impressed, patting him on the back, telling him he was a genius, that these were even better than hers had been, that he was by far the superior chef. I kept waiting for him to correct them, to tell them that he hadn't actually come up with the recipe, that it was *mine*.

The fool never did. He simply smiled and accepted the credit as if it belonged to him.

It sounds like a small thing, a meatball recipe. I certainly thought so at the time. It was just *one* recipe, after all. And it meant so much more to him than it did to me. So I stayed silent while he told the story, and just like that, my recipe became his recipe.

I had no way of knowing what would happen next. I never realized that I would spend the next thirty years fielding interview questions on how it was possible that *I*, a mere housewife, the famous chef's widow, could possibly know how to cook. I listened to late-night talk-show hosts do monologues on how I must've discovered my husband's old recipes in a drawer somewhere, how *that* was the only possible explanation for my success. The idea that *I* stole recipes from him. Those were the rumors that got to me, even more than the stories of murder and cannibalism. To this day it makes me ill that there are still people who believe that I'm a hack, a fake, a grifter. Ironic, really.

Here's the truth: I never stole a recipe from Damien. Not a single one. It was just the opposite. I created every meal he prepared, every dish he became famous for. Every one of them was mine.

Maybe it sounds like an overreaction to kill a man because of a few recipes. But you have to understand, they were very, very good recipes.

After that, it was death by a thousand cuts. Damien always said the restaurant was his dream, and so it became my dream. I gave all of myself to it. I stuck with that damn money pit because he loved it, even when I could see that there were much better ways to make money. But Damien didn't want to franchise, didn't want to sell mass-produced versions of our food. He was a romantic that way. All he wanted was his chef's hat and his kitchen, to be photographed with famous patrons and written up in local magazines, to have fun with beautiful women on the side. It was so disappointing to realize his dreams were so mediocre, in the end.

For twelve years, I let my ambitions take a back seat to his. I handled his staff while he did the thing he loved to do most. I raised a goddamn family for him, a family *he* said he'd wanted, and I pretended I didn't know he was screwing around behind my back, even when I smelled her perfume on his coat, when his lies were so blatant, so childish that I swear he was hoping he'd get caught. For *twelve years.*

And after all that, after everything I'd sacrificed, he was still going to do the exact thing my mother had warned me he would do. He was going to leave.

....

I was in Ava's room, packing the last of her things, when I heard the sound of small, rapid footsteps racing toward me. Issie called, "Ava, bathroom."

Ava, whining: "But I don't have to *go.*"

"Please try. Remember, Nana said she'd give you a cookie if you didn't have any accidents today."

I smiled, suddenly desperately craving a moment with my granddaughter before they left on their trip. Her forever wriggling body, sticky hands pressed to my cheeks, pulling my face close to hers, soft voice in my ear whispering, *Nana, can I tell you a secret?* Yesterday, the secret she had for me was "Fishies don't fart." Darling Ava. I was going to miss her.

But Issie must've won the fight to get her daughter to use the bathroom because she appeared at the door to Ava's room alone.

"Hey," she said. Her voice had a wrung-out quality to it, and her sweater was on backward and inside out. It looked like she might've tried to rip the tag off but got distracted halfway through. It dangled from her collar by a single thread.

"Are you all packed?" I asked her.

Issie nodded and closed her eyes, pinching her nose with two fingers. Down the hall: the sound of a toilet flushing, the sink switching on.

Ava shouted, "Mommy! I need soap!"

"It's on the sink, lovie," I called back to her. There was a pause, then the sound of something small and plastic—a soap bottle, I assumed—clattering to the floor.

"I founded it!" Ava shouted.

"I'll go help her," I said, and I started out the door, but Issie put a hand on my arm, stopping me.

"I just heard from the doctor's office. They got the results of her blood work in," she said. "They want to do more tests before they can say anything for sure. But they don't think it'll be long now."

I closed my eyes and took a steadying breath through my nose. I couldn't be the one to fall apart here, as much as I wanted to. Not when my daughter needed me.

I opened my eyes again and forced myself to focus on the streak of sunlight across the wooden floorboards. Issie was leaning against the door, ankles crossed, the toe of one sneaker tapping the floor, anxious. She had always kept her sneakers unnaturally white, ever since she was a preteen. Didn't matter how old they were, how often she wore them. Issie took pride in making sure her shoes looked like they'd just come out of the box. It had been her high school superlative, actually. *Class of 2002: Isabella Capello, whitest sneakers.*

Today, there was mud crusted into the seams, the laces. She must've stepped in something.

"If this doesn't work…" Issie's voice trailed off, her eyes filling with tears. She wasn't looking at me and, God, her voice sounded tired. I wondered if she'd slept at all this week.

I took her hand and squeezed. "It will. Trust me, everything's taken care of. The plane is already waiting. We'll drive over together when this is finished."

Issie met my eyes. She was quiet for a long beat, and then she swallowed and reached for my hand, squeezed my fingers so tightly it hurt.

"Thank you, Mommy," she whispered.

"You know I'd do anything for my girls," I told her, leaning in to plant a kiss on her cheek. "Anything."

It wasn't supposed to happen like this. We were supposed to have more time. But you know what they say: if you want to make God laugh, tell him your plans.

My timeline might be a bit tighter, my plans a little messier. But a good chef has to be okay with a little mess.

I heard footsteps above us, voices in the kitchen. Thea was back.

I took a moment to brush the wrinkles from my slacks, to straighten my glasses. To Issie, I said, "Stay strong, my love. This will all be over very soon."

22

THEA

My entire body tensed as Hank walked past me, close enough that I caught a whiff of the smell coming off him: blood and a faint scent of wood chips from his shop. A moment later, I heard the snap of his knife hitting a cutting board.

I turned and saw a half-frozen animal spread across the butcher block table behind me. It'd been skinned, and frozen pink flesh and sinewy muscles remained, still attached to the bone. Whatever it had been, it was big. So big that Hank hadn't seemed able to fit the whole animal onto the table. Just parts of it.

A shiver went down my spine and I crossed my arms over my chest, unnerved.

What kind of animal was that?

Hank seemed to be cutting through a thigh piece. It was nearly as thick around as my own leg.

"Can I help you with something?" he asked.

I swallowed. My mouth felt suddenly dry. I nodded to the phone hanging from the wall. "I—I just need to use the phone."

"You might want to wait a minute. It's gonna get pretty loud in here."

He took a thick chunk of the animal and turned. Only now did I notice a large machine behind him, something stainless steel and vicious-looking. He hit a button and a whirring sound started as he began to feed the meat through the top of the machine.

A meat grinder. That thing was a meat grinder.

I lifted a hand to my throat, feeling faint.

The sound of the grinder was deafening, a metallic growl that drowned out all other noise in the room. I imagined crushed bones, the screams of some poor animal being slaughtered. And yet I couldn't tear my eyes away.

Thick, snakelike tubes of meat came out from one side of the grinder, spiraling onto the table below, reminding me of intestines. Hank fed more meat into the machine, his hands slick with blood. I could smell it in the air.

When I looked back up, I found him staring at me. "You don't have to watch if it bothers you."

"Right," I muttered. Then, clearing my throat, I said, "What kind of animal is that?"

"Cow," Hank growled, turning back to the meat grinder.

I had no idea whether he was telling the truth.

I headed for the phone, and I was halfway across the kitchen when the grinder jammed. There was a sickening crunching sound that made me jump, releasing a small *yelp*.

Behind me, Hank cursed. "Damn thing." I glanced over my shoulder as he dropped the rest of the meat back onto the cutting board with a sniff. He opened a door inside the contraption, frowned at the blood-slicked gears inside.

Trembling, I snatched the phone off the wall and lifted it to my ear, barely daring to breathe.

Nothing.

A trill went down my spine. My gaze snapped to the place where the phone should have connected to the wall. There was no cord. Someone had removed it.

I slowly placed the phone back on the receiver and turned around, trying to swallow the fear bubbling up in my throat. My heart was going too fast, and my palms were slick with sweat. Someone had *taken* the phone cord.

"No luck?" Hank asked, eyes fixing on my face.

Was it him? I stared for a moment, but I couldn't tell. His expression was carefully blank.

"Is there another landline somewhere else in the house?" I asked.

Hank shrugged, unconcerned. I could feel panic creeping in, the muscles in my jaw and shoulders tightening, every hair on my body standing straight up. I was trapped here. These people had intentionally trapped me here.

Stay calm, I told myself.

"Something got you spooked?" Hank's nostrils flared, slightly, as he said the words.

The breath went out of me. I caught it, swallowed. "I—I have to get home. I have a family emergency. Do you have a phone I could borrow?"

Hank shook his head. Lightning flashed outside the kitchen window, illuminating the dimly lit space. The clap of thunder that followed was so close and loud it made me jump.

I swallowed a scream and glanced outside, one hand clamping over my mouth. I hadn't even realized it'd started raining.

When I turned around again, Hank was blocking my path to the door, his huge frame impossible to get around. He had a cleaver in one hand, a monster of a knife, edge honed and sharp, metal dull from years of use. And there was a twist to his lips that hadn't been there a moment ago. Like he was biting back a smile.

I heard Amy's voice in the back of my head. *Murder, cannibalism, meatballs made of people.* Fear hit me like nausea. I swayed a little and had to brace a hand on the wall to steady myself.

What was he going to do with that knife?

"Started raining finally," Hank said unnecessarily. "About damn time. Sky looked like it was about to burst." He smacked the dull side of the blade against his open palm.

My neck prickled. I thought of how frightened Nina had been of this family, how she'd warned me to leave. I thought of all the people who'd mysteriously vanished after defying them. Enzo's friend from school. The editor Maria hadn't liked. The other butcher who'd tried to open a shop here in town. Damien.

I took a step toward the door, eyes never leaving the cleaver. Hank shifted in front of me, intentionally blocking my path. My chest clenched.

"What are you doing?" I asked.

"I'm afraid we're going to need you to stick around for a little while longer, Thea," Hank said. He really did sound apologetic. But that cleaver. I stared hard at the blade. This close, I could see that it was flecked with blood.

"Hank—" I started, but a voice interrupted me.

"Leaving us, Thea?"

I whirled around, my heart leaping in my throat. I hadn't heard Maria come up behind me.

She was holding a cutting board loaded with vegetables: long, green zucchinis and tomatoes the size of a child's head, onions, garlic. She crossed the kitchen. I flinched as she moved past me, but she only placed the cutting board on the kitchen counter.

"We were just about to prepare dinner," she said.

"Maria," I breathed. I shot another glance at Hank. He still hadn't moved away from the door. "I need to get my car. I really have to go."

Maria removed a butcher knife from a block on the counter and began slicing the onions and garlic. Her hands moved deftly across the board, the knife an extension of her fingers, blade slamming into the wood in measured increments, like a metronome.

Chop. Chop. Chop.

I flinched each time the knife made contact with wood, some muscle inside my body contracting inch by inch. Until I was wound so tight, I thought I might snap.

A glance outside. Rain fell in sheets, thundering against the roof and windows. Actual thunder rumbled in the distance. Lightning illuminated the sky in a brief burst, and I saw the stark silhouette of trees bending and swaying in the wind.

I pulled my attention back to the kitchen, watching Maria's small hands maneuver the sharp blade, unease creeping over me. I pictured that same knife wielded as a weapon, slicing through skin and muscle, coated in blood.

I tried again. "My husband called. I have a family thing. An emergency."

"Thea, honey, we both know that isn't true." Maria placed a saucepan on the stove and flipped on the burner. "I'm afraid I can't let you leave just yet."

"Why?" My voice sounded strange, jerky. I hugged my arms around myself. I thought of the blood soaking into the dirt of the slaughterhouse. The screams that started at dawn. Amy's abandoned notebook.

Maria gave me a small smile and turned to Hank. "I think you're making her nervous. Do you mind stepping outside?"

Hank's eyes flicked to me. "If she tries to run—"

"Then you'll be right outside the door, won't you?"

Hank nodded, once, and left the room. I flinched as he pulled the door shut behind him.

There was a hiss of gas, followed by the soft spark of fire. A blue and orange flame leaped to life below a burner, licking the blackened stainless steel. I wanted to cry. I wanted to scream. But who would hear me? Who would come?

"Maria," I tried again. My whole body was covered in cold, sickly sweat. "You can't keep me here if I don't want to stay."

"Oh, dear, it's not going to come to that," Maria said. "I just need you for a moment. That's all."

Why? I wanted to say. *What could you possibly need me for?*

But I was terrified that I already knew the answer. I glanced at Hank's meat grinder. I thought of the meatballs Maria had served for dinner last night, the slick of fat clinging to the surface.

Then Maria surprised me by saying, "I know Amy Ryan told you about her book."

It was so far from what I expected her to say that I turned to her, momentarily forgetting my fear. "What?"

"Oh, I know all about Ms. Ryan," Maria explained. "I know about her celebrity gossip account and the book she's writing. I've known ever since Enzo brought her home, in fact. Enzo didn't realize what she was doing with him, poor dear." Something in Maria's eyes darkened. "He's told me he doesn't want me interfering with his relationships anymore, and I've tried to respect his wishes. But I have thorough background checks run on everyone who gets involved with my children. Anything to protect my family."

I tried to swallow but my mouth was too dry. "Background checks?"

"Oh, yes. I doubt I would have trusted Ms. Ryan regardless. It was clear from the moment she walked into my house that she wanted something from us."

"Then why did you let her stay here?" I asked.

"I believe the saying is, 'Keep your enemies close'?" Maria said. She upended a bottle of olive oil over the rim of the pan. I watched golden liquid slosh inside, my chest tightening.

This was it. She was going to tell me what she'd done to Amy. What she was about to do to me. The air around us seemed to shimmer.

Maria picked up the cutting board and slid the onions and garlic into the pan with the blade of her knife, the sound of metal on wood like fingernails on cardboard, that rough, scratchy sound. "You've probably noticed by now how thin the walls in this house are," she said, "how easy it is to listen in on other people's conversations. Amy liked to talk to her sources late at night. She'd take the calls outside, but she didn't often move too far from the house. I could overhear her conversations as long as I left one of the upstairs windows cracked. After that, it was as simple as placing a few calls of my own to see how far along her project was, whether she could be persuaded to drop it."

Maria turned back to her vegetables and started chopping again. I waited for her to continue, but she didn't.

I couldn't take it anymore. I had to know. "What did you do to her?"

Maria considered me for a moment, eyebrow raised. "I followed her into town," she said, "found her on some side street on a smoke break."

The pile of CBD cigarettes I'd stumbled upon on the sidewalk flashed through my head. I could see it: Amy smoking, Maria pulling up to the curb in one of her sleek, fancy cars. Telling her to get in.

I took a breath. "And then?"

"And then I offered her some money—quite a bit of money, as a matter of fact—to drop the book and forget everything she thought she knew about my family. She refused; she seems to think she'll make more money after she publishes. So I drove her to the train station and made it clear it was in her best interest to leave."

I let her words hang in the air for a moment before saying, "That's all?"

"Honestly, dear, what were you expecting?" Maria studied me, head tilted. When I didn't respond right away, she chuckled. "Oh wait, let me guess. You thought I'd killed Amy, perhaps? That I had Hank chop up her body into little pieces so I could mix her in with my meatballs?" She pointed her knife at me, a few bits of onion still clinging to the blade. "This is exactly why I told you not to go looking me up online. Those ludicrous stories have a way of getting into your head."

The way she said it—*have a way of getting into your head*—like she completely understood why I'd come to that conclusion, like anyone would've thought the same thing: that was what got to me, even more than her actual explanation.

"But what about that boy Enzo went to school with?" I asked after a moment. "Amy said he just disappeared. And there was the butcher who was competing with Hank, that editor you didn't like... A lot of people have mysteriously disappeared when they've pissed you off."

Maria exhaled as though frustrated with me. "If you must know, we convinced that boy's parents it would be better if the two of them were split up; then we offered to pay for him to attend a much nicer school upstate. I imagine his classmates preferred the more exciting story, and as there wasn't any social media around to contradict them back in those days, it's persisted through the years. Now let's see... the butcher. I believe you're talking about Todd Sheridan? We bought him out. Last I'd heard he'd moved up to Vermont to be closer to his family. As for the editor, is it really that surprising for a young person to leave the publishing industry? I was under the impression it was rather common."

Maria let her hands fall open, knife dangling between her fingers. "Honestly, Thea, I thought you were smarter than this. Think about it logically: Don't you think someone would have noticed if I was murdering people left and right? It's a lot easier for a person in my position, with my resources, to just pay them off, no?"

"What about Amy's notebook?" I reached into my pocket and pulled it out. "If Amy just got into the car with you and let you drive her to the train station, then why was this in the slaughterhouse?"

Maria looked at the notebook but made no move to take it from me. She offered a thin smile. "Ah, yes. Amy left that behind in the car when I dropped her at the station. I gave it to Enzo to return to her, after I told him what she was up to. I assume that ripping it up like that was his little act of revenge. You can't exactly blame him, can you?"

My fingers closed loosely around the notebook. Something cold was spreading through my upper back like a salve.

Those ludicrous stories, Maria had said. Was that all it was? If I forgot about the stuff Amy had told me, the things Nina seemed to be afraid of, and all the crap I'd read online, what did I know, really?

Amy was gone. I'd imagined her swinging from the ceiling of the slaughterhouse, but I could picture her climbing into the car with Maria too, refusing the blackmail money, leaving that notebook behind in her hurry to get out. And it would've made sense that Maria already had her things all packed up. Amy wouldn't have been welcome back at the house once her lie was out in the open.

Amy had left things behind, but that also tracked if it had gone down like Maria said it had. The phone Amy had left was a burner, so it made sense she wouldn't go back for it. And she hadn't left her purse or wallet with Nina and Celia; she'd left some cheap tote bag that she'd probably gotten for free, along with a few pages of notes. Nothing she really needed. What else had convinced me that Maria and her family were murderers?

"The sleeping draft," I said. "And that weird digestif you gave me. I thought you were drugging me."

Maria had the decency to look apologetic. "Those were both simple home remedies, old-world medicines that have been passed down through my family. They're just herbs to help you sleep, to aid with digestion. I'm afraid they might be a bit strong if you aren't used to them."

"What about—" I started, then stopped. I couldn't tell her about Nina Casey. I'd promised her. But I had to know if what she'd told me was true.

"I spoke to Nina Casey," I said carefully. This, I reasoned, wasn't a betrayal. Maria had no reason to believe Nina had been here on her property.

I watched Maria's face for a reaction to her husband's mistress's name. She only smiled, angrily.

"Did you?" she said, teeth clenched.

"She's terrified of you," I continued. "She told me she saw you kill Damien."

I waited for Maria to deny it. She didn't. I lifted a shaking hand to my mouth. "Oh my God."

"I was completely honest with you in my memoir, Thea," Maria said, quietly. "I needed you to understand what kind of man Damien was. You, of all people—"

"But you weren't honest," I said, cutting her off. "If you were so honest, why didn't you mention that Damien had another son?"

Maria didn't even blink. But when she spoke again, her voice had a dangerous note to it. "Did Nina tell you that, too?"

There was something about the way she was looking at me, the shifting quality of her eyes. She was still holding something back, more secrets. I could feel them thickening the air between us, pressing against my skin like heat.

Everything she'd written had been shades of truth and lie, just accurate enough that I couldn't pin down exactly what she'd been omitting, only that it wasn't the whole story. I felt like I was playing a thirty-year-long game of telephone, that the shape of the story had been true, but all the details had been distorted and twisted through the years.

Maria's eyes moved to the tote bag dangling from my shoulder, a slight frown crossing her face. "Was that Amy's?"

I nodded. Maria didn't reach for the bag. Instead, she added several plump, juicy tomatoes to the pot, their skins bursting open the second they hit the hot metal. "Did you look inside?"

"Yes," I said, flinching with each small explosion. "There's just part of Amy's book and some photos, but I didn't get a chance to look at them."

Maria nodded. "This is convenient, actually. You mentioned Damien's other child. Did Nina tell you that he crashed our party the night Damien disappeared? He had a photograph with him—him as a little boy, with Damien. He'd wanted to prove to me that Damien was his father, you see. They didn't look a lot alike. They had similar eyes, but lots of people have blue eyes. The poor kid wasn't sure I'd believe him. Amy found it while she was poking around my things. I tried to get it back, but it wasn't with her stuff in her room." Maria pointed her knife at me. "Which means she had it in her bag."

I frowned, not understanding why she was telling me this.

"Could you check and see if it's still there?" Maria asked. "I'd like it back."

"If I do that, will you let me go home?" I asked.

Maria smiled. "Of course."

I opened the tote, carefully flipping through the thin pile of photographs until I found one of a younger Damien standing beside a little boy with sharp, angular features, dark hair falling in loose waves around his forehead.

My fingers went still. The edges of my eyesight were suddenly dark, fuzzy. I pulled the photograph all the way out of the tote and stared openly. For a long moment, I couldn't catch my breath.

I recognized that hair. I knew just how it would feel to run my hands through it, to brush it away from that forehead. And those eyes, I knew those eyes better than I knew my own. I saw them every day. My daughter had the same ones. Wolf's eyes, my mom called them.

Damien Capello's first son, the man who'd been there the night he was murdered—

He was my husband.

23

MARIA

Perhaps it was cruel to do it this way. Perhaps I should have been up front with her from the beginning, told her that it wasn't her I wanted; it was Jacob.

But it wouldn't have worked. Jacob has refused every request I've made of him ever since that night thirty years ago. He made it very clear that he didn't want to be part of my family, no matter how much I begged. If I went through Thea and he refused again, I would have lost the last piece of leverage I had left. I couldn't let it happen like that. Which meant I had to go about this differently.

I've frequently been told that my need for control makes me a hard woman to work with. I know what people whispered behind my back: *She's such a bitch, she's so difficult.* All those labels women are supposed to be so terrified of. And yet those labels became my armor. I watched as other women—my peers—had their own reputations dragged through the mud because of one offhand comment, one interview that went slightly off the rails, one bad photo shoot. These were talented women whose entire careers disappeared because of seemingly tiny mistakes. I couldn't afford mistakes. When you'd done the things I had done, control was the only thing that kept you protected.

I made it work in my favor. Thea didn't push too hard when I presented my bizarre requirements for our partnership, when I told her not to breathe a word about the project to anyone outside of Hanes House, when I took her phone and insisted she read the entire book here, where I could keep an eye on her, where I could be sure my story was hitting her exactly the way I needed it to. None of this would seem surprising, not coming from Maria Capello, the controlling bitch who stage managed every photo shoot, who had to look over every question before an interview, who demanded approval over when her books were published and how they were displayed. All this would seem normal, expected.

And yet, it was so necessary for what I needed. It allowed me to control every aspect of Thea's reading experience.

Thea was an editor. She understood the importance of a good story. All alone out here, in the middle of nowhere, without her phone, with my shoddy internet access, there would be no one to contradict the version of events I'd given her.

Perhaps most importantly, *Jacob* wouldn't be here to contradict the version of events I'd given her.

....

I'd been distracted thirty years ago when the party started, trying to figure out the rest of my plan. I knew I would need an accomplice. There were far too many factors for me to deal with on my own.

Hank was the obvious choice. Hank was family. And Damien and Nina had hurt him, too. I was certain he would want to see them punished as much as I did.

And so, while Damien finished getting dressed, I hurried down the stairs to find Hank. More partygoers were arriving every moment. I saw their cars pulling up outside when I reached the first floor, people in dresses and heels climbing out, the sounds of lilting laughter and conversation. They lifted their hands, waving to me, pulling me in for hugs and kisses on the cheek. I couldn't slip away right then, not without being obvious, so I scoured the party while making inane small talk. Hank, it seemed, was nowhere.

By the time I finally managed to step away, an hour had already passed and Damien still hadn't made an appearance. This was unusual. Damien was never happier than when he had all eyes on him, an audience semicircled around him, laughter following some inane joke I'd already heard him tell a dozen times and that I'd told him wasn't funny. Afterward, he would buzz for hours, that attention like a battery charge.

He'd never missed one of our parties before. Which meant something was happening without me.

I was worried, terrified I'd missed my chance, that Damien had already made his exit. I took the first opportunity I could to head back upstairs. Halfway to the second floor, I heard Nina's soft, slightly raspy voice.

Anger filled my stomach, my chest, my head. The nerve of her, going to my husband in *my* house. I wanted to kill her right then and there. But that wasn't part of the plan. And so I forced myself to breathe, to calm down. And then I followed the sound of Nina's voice down the hall.

My bedroom door was open a crack. I leaned in close and there they were: Damien standing with his back to the door, Nina perched on the edge of the bed (*my* bed!) cradling her head in her hands.

There's an energy between couples. Not a heat, not necessarily. It was more of a gravity, a weight. Damien and Nina hadn't been kissing, hadn't even been touching, but the way their bodies were angled toward each other, the way they were so aware of one another, it was almost worse than if I had found them in flagrante delicto.

I could tell, looking at them, that they weren't fucking. Or at least they weren't *just* fucking. They were in love. Damien wasn't just leaving me, though that would have been bad enough. He was leaving me *for* her. So they could be together.

In the bedroom, the floorboards creaked: Damien had begun to pace. He turned toward the door, and I shifted back into the shadows so he wouldn't see me.

"Probably looking for me outside," Nina was saying. "I don't think he saw me come up here."

"It doesn't matter anyway," Damien said. But he was worried. I could tell. Damien only paced when he was worried about something. "It doesn't change anything."

"You said we needed to act normally so no one will remember anything."

"We'll leave a little earlier than we'd originally planned. It's fine."

Nina lifted her face. It was teary, red. "You're sure?"

Damien leaned down, cupped Nina's chin in his hands. It had hurt to watch him touch her like that, just the tips of his fingers pressed to her skin, like she was too precious to hold any tighter. He'd touched me like that. A long time ago. He barely ever touched me anymore.

"The car's in the barn," he said. "Head over now and I'll slip out as soon as I can."

And then they were kissing, holding each other. I didn't need to hear anymore. I slipped back downstairs.

I found Hank in the kitchen and grabbed him by the arm. "Walk with me," I said under my breath, a smile frozen on my face so none of the pretty party people would be suspicious. "I have something to tell you."

Hank has always trusted me. He trailed behind me like a dog on a leash. I ushered him into the small powder room, when no one was watching. There, I told him about his cheating wife, my cheating husband. And then I outlined everything I had planned.

....

Perhaps it might seem strange that Hank would be so immediately willing to help me murder my husband. I see why it might confuse people. What they didn't understand—what no one outside of our family could possibly understand—was that we'd always had our own ways of taking care of each other. Of *protecting* each other.

Hank's parents had been happily married for twenty years, but his were the exception, not the rule. I've already told my mother's sad story. Her mother—Hank's and my grandmother—had a husband who liked to drink, who got violent when he had a few too many. Hank and I were children when we heard the story of how our Nonna Brigida mixed a little ethylene glycol in her husband's nightly cocktail. And she wasn't the only one. There was also Uncle Elio and Aunt Savia, and Great-Great-Great-Grandmother Adalasia. Every family has its secrets.

"All I need you to do is get his clothes and bring them to the creek," I told Hank that night. "He has another suit in our closet. It looks enough like the one he's wearing that no one should know the difference. I'll get the gun and handle everything else. Can I trust you?"

Hank had nodded and stepped out of the bathroom without a word.

I figured I'd handled as much as I could. Things hadn't gone perfectly, and I'd had to come up with a plan on the fly, but I thought my mother would have been proud of how I'd pulled it all together in the end. I just had to get to the safe and get the gun. Then I'd follow Damien out to the woods, stop him before he got to the barn, shoot him, and use the suit Hank brought to stage the scene like a suicide. Hank would back me up. And the note would provide the final bit of evidence. It already read like a suicide note, if I didn't include the second page. All I was doing was following the story Damien had already written. It wasn't a perfect plan, but it would do. I would make sure of it.

It's funny how you remember certain moments so clearly. Even now, thirty years after it happened, I remembered what came next as if I'd just lived it. I had turned back to the sink and switched on the faucet, splashed some cold water on my face to wake myself up. My eyes were squeezed shut, water dripping down my face as I reached for a hand towel, when someone started banging on the door.

Issie shouted, "Mom! Hurry, somebody's in a fight with Dad!"

My heart had leaped in my throat. I'd been so sure Hank would be able to handle the news of his wife's infidelity, that he would do as he was told. I grabbed the towel and mopped the water off my face, yanking the door open with my free hand. "Is it Hank?"

But Issie shook her head. "No, it's some other guy." She looked confused as she added, "He said he's Daddy's son."

Issie's eyes were saucer-wide. She was only twelve years old, and she still didn't always know how to respond when something strange was happening, when she was scared.

"Okay," I'd said, trying to sound calm, even as my thoughts were screaming at me. *A son. Damien had another son.* I hadn't known. I'd had no idea.

I put my hand on Issie's shoulder and gently guided her back to the party. "Where did you see them?"

"Living room," Issie muttered. "Dad's already out there talking to him. He sounded…" She blinked several times, fast, and said quietly, "Mad."

Damien was in the far corner of the living room by the time Issie and I made our way out. He was dressed, I saw, his suit perfectly pressed, tie neatly knotted at his neck. A man stood beside him. But no, he was not a man. He was lanky, thin, barely more than a boy. Late teens, at the absolute oldest. I did the math in my head when I saw him. If he really was Damien's son, he'd been fathered when we were together, likely back when we'd first married. It hurt, realizing that. Even after everything.

The boy was tall—several inches taller than Damien—with ruddy skin and dark, wiry hair. Unlike the rest of the guests, he didn't wear a suit or a tie but loose-fitting jeans and a flannel hanging open over a gray T-shirt. His eyes were narrowed, sizing Damien up.

I crossed the room toward them, my heart beating hard. There was time to fix this. I just had to act fast. Party guests mingled around the two of them, talking, eating, laughing. No one seemed aware that something was off, that the angry young man talking to my husband shouldn't have been there. I needed to get him out of here before they did. If anyone had noticed him, it would have stood out. People would mention it to the police, to reporters. As far as I could tell, no one knew Damien had another son. I needed to keep it that way. If it came out, it could be used against me. *Motive.*

Out of the corner of my eye, I saw Enzo peering around the corner, still in his pajamas, watching everything. The thought of him learning about a brother like this was excruciating. I needed to stop this.

I moved in beside my husband and his son, a fake smile plastered over my face. What I was about to do was cruel, but it was necessary.

"Who the hell are you?" I asked the boy through my teeth.

He rounded on me, his eyes cold and hard. He made no attempt to keep his anger in check, to keep his voice low. "I came to talk to my father."

I could tell he meant those words to hurt. *My father.* He'd correctly assumed Damien had never told me about him. And then, just to drive the point home, he'd pulled a photograph out of his pocket and flung it in my face.

It was him. Clearly it was him. He was young in the photograph, maybe ten years old. And the man standing behind him was Damien, younger, obviously, but with that same cocky smile, those same glinting eyes. I'd turned the photograph over, saw a label scrawled in some other woman's hand. *Jacob and his father, 1990.*

Enzo would have been four, Issie six. Those had been such hard years, the kids still so little, Damien spending all his time out of the house, working, giving interviews. And now, I realized, visiting a son I didn't even know he had.

It took all the strength I had to keep my face calm, to keep Jacob from being able to tell that his presence here, his existence, shook me down to my marrow.

"You need to leave," I said in a low voice. I needed him to leave for his sake as well as for mine. I put a hand on Jacob's arm, trying to steer him toward the hall. If I could get him to another room, I might still have managed to contain things. But he shoved my hand away.

"Not a chance," he'd snarled. "I came to talk to my dad."

A few of the guests standing nearest had stopped talking and turned toward us, curious about what was going on. I remember the muscles in my shoulders going tense, how it felt like I wouldn't be able to move or breathe without cracking in half. This wouldn't do. I *had* to get him out of here. It wasn't just about protecting myself anymore. If anyone saw him here, he could become a suspect in my husband's murder just as easily as I could. He was angry; he clearly had motive. I don't care what you think of me. I don't care if you think I'm a monster, but Jacob wasn't part of this. He just got caught up in his father's mess. I wouldn't do that to an innocent kid, my own children's brother. I had to contain this.

"Hallway," I'd said, still smiling at the two of them. "*Now.*"

I don't know what finally made Damien's son stomp out of that room and into the hall. Perhaps he was just used to following his own mother's instructions. Damien had a type. I had no doubt that whoever this woman was, she would be small and dark-haired, a younger version of me. In any case, I was finally able to convince the teen to move away from our guests, to step into the hall just outside the living room where we could speak in private. Well, mostly in private. As we rounded the corner, I saw Enzo's head disappear behind an open door. Still listening.

I grabbed my husband's arm with one hand and his son's with the other, pulling them close to me, keeping my voice low. "What is this about?"

"Doesn't she know?" Jacob demanded. "You didn't bother telling her you'd cut us off?"

I turned to Damien, frowning. *Cut them off?* That meant he'd been supporting them. Possibly for years. One more little lie between us.

Damien had swallowed, his voice obnoxiously patient, even now. "Listen…I didn't have a choice. Things are tight right now. But I'll make it right. I—"

"Don't bother with that," his son snarled. He'd sounded genuinely furious. "I know what your promises are worth."

"Jacob, I—"

Jacob had ripped his arm out of my hand and grabbed Damien's shirt, shoving him up against a wall—hard. The framed photographs hanging there trembled. One slipped from its nail and crashed to the floor, a hairline crack fracturing the glass.

The boy's face was inches from Damien's. He looked like he wanted to rip Damien's head off. He looked like he might try.

The next part happened quickly. A small voice called out, "Don't!" and then Enzo was barreling out of his room, launching himself at Jacob.

Jacob didn't see him. Or, if he did see him, he didn't seem to know exactly what he was seeing. He let go of Damien's shirt and Damien slumped against the wall. Then, Jacob turned toward the ten-year-old boy shooting toward him, a blur of messy brown hair and rumpled pajamas.

I saw the next part as though it happened in slow motion: Jacob turning too fast, one of his arms still swinging. It caught Enzo's face square in the nose with a sickening smack.

Blood appeared, neon red in the dark light of the hall. I remembered Enzo grasping for his face, his mouth open in a soundless howl. Jacob was backing away, horrified by what he'd just done, muttering under his breath, "I didn't see him, I didn't know…" while Damien merely stood against the wall, shocked and useless.

I pushed past them both, dropped to my knees. Enzo had both hands in front of his nose, and he was gasping, seconds away from howling in pain. I had to pull his bloody hands away so I could see his face more clearly.

His nose was crooked, broken.

"He needs to go to the emergency room," I said.

Jacob was beside me, crouched on the floor beside Enzo. "I didn't see him," he'd told me, desperate. "I swear, I didn't know he was there."

"I need to get him to the car," I'd said. At ten, Enzo was too big for me to carry, so all I could do was help him to his feet, slip his arm around my own shoulders. He was crying, scared. I'd started to turn to Damien, to tell him to bring the car around.

But Damien wasn't there. The hall was empty, the back door swinging open. He'd ducked away while Jacob and I were distracted.

He was gone.

24

THEA

I didn't remember sitting down, but I was sitting now.

I felt nauseous. I doubled over, hands gripping the sides of my chair. My head was hot and full, fuzzy black static crackling at the edges. I opened my mouth and then closed it again, gaping like a fish.

Jacob was Damien's son.

Maria was suddenly kneeling in front of me, her small, weathered hands on my knees, squeezing. She looked concerned, motherly.

"You need to exhale first," she said. "Breathe out, and then try breathing in."

I barely heard her, but my body must've registered what she'd said because air exploded from my lungs. I gasped and the black static pulled back, my eyesight cleared.

"No," I choked out, shaking my head. "No, it isn't true." *It can't be true. I need it not to be true.*

But even as I said the words, I thought of how the details all matched up: Jacob had never known his real father. He'd grown up with his mother and stepfather in Albany. His stepfather was a cop. I'd asked him about his real father a few times, but he only ever shrugged and said, "He took off when I was a kid."

And I, idiot that I was, never asked any follow-up questions. I'd also grown up with a deadbeat dad. I knew what it was like when people pried, how embarrassing it was to explain that you'd been thrown away, deemed unworthy of one of the most vital relationships a human being could have. I understood how deeply wounds like that hurt, how they never fully healed. I knew better than to go poking around someone else's pain.

But now…now I felt so, so stupid.

Maria opened her mouth, preparing to offer me something—an explanation or consolation. I never found out which. At that moment, the door behind us cracked open, hitting the wall with a smack.

Jacob stood just outside. Rain plastered his hair to his skull and left a wet sheen on his forehead. He looked pale, sickly.

"Thea." He glanced at Maria and his nostrils flared. He ignored her and took a step toward me instead. "Maria called me from your phone. She told me to come. I got here as quickly as I could—"

I nearly knocked over my chair in my desperation to stand. "Ruthie—"

"I left her with Mom. She's okay. Thea…" Jacob's voice was quiet, pleading. An apology. And I knew. I knew at that exact moment that he really was Damien's son. This wasn't a trick. Everything Maria had told me was true.

I lifted a hand to my mouth. "Oh my God…"

Jacob looked from me to Maria. His jaw tightened. "I told you to stay away from us."

"You're family," Maria said simply. "You can't just cut family out of your life. And you wouldn't answer my calls, my emails…"

I cut her off. "I can't believe this."

"I am *not* your family," Jacob spat. Turning to me, he said, "My father—my biological father—was never a part of my life. Not ever. When I was growing up, my mom used to say he might as well be dead. Stu Woods, the man you know, that's my real dad. He legally adopted me when my parents got married."

I said, "But you knew that Damien Capello was your biological

father. You've known this whole time, and you never said anything."
I thought of a million moments over the years, a million lies. When I
was pregnant, we met with a geneticist to go over our family histories
and Jacob said he didn't know who his biological father was, that there
was no way to trace that line.

A blaze of heat flashed across my skin. Embarrassment, not just
for that moment, but for all of them. For a million more that I wasn't
even thinking about now.

"I know." Jacob swallowed. "I thought about telling you so many
times."

"Why didn't you?" I could feel tears rising in my throat. "You *lied*
to me."

"It didn't feel like a lie to me. I didn't want it to be true. I never
wanted to be his son. Why do you think I ignored her for the last
thirty years?" Jacob motioned toward Maria. "I never wanted anything to do with her family."

I couldn't bring myself to look at his face. Instead, I stared at a spot
on the shoulder of his jacket, a light-brown smudge that I knew was
peanut butter, that was at the exact spot where Ruthie's mouth would
be when he held her on his hip.

It was strangely grounding, seeing that stain. We both had them all
over our clothes.

I couldn't breathe again. Maria's words went through my head. *You
need to exhale first.* I let out a breath, tried again. This time, it worked.

A dozen conflicting emotions fluttered through me. I wanted to
run across the room and fall into Jacob's arms. I wanted him to get me
the hell away from this place. I wanted him to hold me. I wanted to
slap him. I wanted to beat my fists against his chest.

But was what he'd done really so different from what I'd done?
He'd lied about his family, yes. Hadn't I done the same thing? I'd never
told him what was going on with my parents, what I'd done with our
money.

Exhale first. I felt my chest rise and fall, my breathing start to
steady. I could feel myself softening, wanting so badly to forgive him,

to forget all of this. He was still Jacob, my husband. He was still the father of my child. This didn't change that. What did it change?

"Why don't you want anything to do with them?" I asked. Jacob didn't answer right away. I looked from him to Maria. "It's about that night, isn't it? The night Damien vanished. What happened?"

Maria had been standing a few feet away from us this whole time, saying nothing, like she might be able to disappear into the walls of the kitchen if she stood still long enough. She glanced at Jacob, as though asking permission.

"Don't," he whispered. The blood seemed to have drained from his face. "Please."

The air in the room thickened. "Don't what?" I waited for Jacob to drag his gaze back to mine. I knew, knew down to my bones that there were still things he wasn't telling me. Still things he was trying to hide. "What is it?"

Jacob walked into the room and leaned against the wall. He looked like a man about to face a firing squad.

"Damien had stopped paying alimony a few months before the party," he explained. "Mom was going to let it go, but I—I just couldn't. We had nothing after he left. It was literally the least he could do for us. Albany's only an hour away from here, and I had to drive down here all the time to pick Mom up from the hospital. One of my friend's had heard Damien Capello was having this big fancy party, just a few months after he cut us off. It was too much. I snapped.

"So, after I picked my mom up from her shift at the hospital, I brought her here. I didn't want to be the one to talk to Damien. I thought she should do it. But she was so mad when she realized what I was doing. She wouldn't even get out of the car."

"Thank God she was there," Maria whispered. "I don't know what we would have done without her."

Jacob looked at Maria, and for a moment I thought he was going to snap at her. But he just nodded, a quick bob of his chin, and something passed between them, something I didn't quite understand.

I thought of the lie Jacob had told me at the beginning of our relationship about how his mom has seen Maria Capello at the hospital the night of Damien's disappearance. I'd assumed he was just trying to impress me, but now I saw it for what it was: a small lie, hiding an even bigger lie.

I let out a soft puff of air. Of course.

"The video footage of you in the emergency room," I said to Maria. "It was on the official police record. But it wasn't you, was it? It was Gloria."

Jacob's mom, Gloria, had looked so much like Maria. Same small frame and dark hair. Damien Capello really did have a type. And she'd been a nurse. She wouldn't have been able to resist helping a child in pain.

"The security video footage was blurry," Maria explained. "All it showed was a woman with dark hair. And this was before I was famous, before I'd had my picture taken in any of the papers. No one could tell it wasn't me."

"Mom had worked at that hospital for years," Jacob said. "The doctor on call in the ER knew her. He agreed to help the kid out, no questions asked. She paid for everything in cash and signed Maria's name to all the forms. She didn't want anything connecting us to their family."

"The cell phone tower showed that Maria called from a mile away," I said, putting it all together. "Because you never left the farm."

This was making more sense. But not enough. There was still something. I turned back to Jacob, frowning. "Did you stay behind, too?"

Jacob wouldn't look at me.

I started to say something, then stopped. I couldn't breathe. I felt like I was on the edge of understanding something, something important. "Jacob? Did you see her shoot your father?"

Jacob swallowed. In a low voice, he said, "Not exactly."

And, all at once, I got it. I knew why he'd refused to take Maria's calls and why he'd never told anyone he was Damien's son or that he was at the farm the night of the party.

No. The word repeated in my head like an echo, so loud that I almost didn't hear my husband say, "Maria didn't shoot Damien. I did."

I thought I'd been angry before. I was wrong. That feeling was nothing compared to this. This was white and hot and righteous. It filled every part of my body. I was blinded by it.

"It's not true," I said. "You wouldn't. You're not…" I stopped. I was too angry to keep talking.

"I was just a kid," Jacob explained. His eyes were wide, bloodshot. "I took my stepdad's gun with me when I went to see Damien. I thought it'd scare him. I never actually planned to use it. But then he tried to run away from me. That's what made me so angry, that he could make this mess and just leave us behind to deal with it, like he always did. It wasn't fair. I didn't mean to kill him. I just wanted him to stop running—"

"No. You couldn't." I covered my face with my hands. This was the man who scooped ladybugs off the floor with credit cards and carried them down four flights of stairs to set them free outside, who was so gentle when he applied Neosporin to Ruthie's scraped knees or tugged the knots from her hair.

I removed my hands and looked at him as if he were a stranger. A wiry middle-aged man with dark hair and a kind smile. If I were meeting him for the first time, bumping into him on the street or the playground, I wouldn't think he was a murderer.

I released a single laugh, a choked *ha!* It wasn't funny. It was so completely not funny. And yet I could feel more laughter rising in my throat. Wild, hysterical laughter that it took all my willpower to choke back down.

I'd married a murderer. I'd fathered a child with a murderer. I'd left my daughter with a murderer.

For the first time in my marriage, I thought about how much of a relief it would be to just leave. Pack up Ruthie and move back up to Albany. Find a cheap two-bedroom near town. It was proof of how fucked up things were that re-creating my miserable childhood didn't seem like such a bad idea.

I'd sunk to the floor without realizing it, and now I was huddled in a ball, arms wrapped around my knees. Jacob was still talking, I noticed. I heard his voice as if it were coming from a badly tuned radio. "Amy doesn't know I killed Damien. She just knows I'm his son. I only gave her that quote so she wouldn't publish my name. People saw me at the party that night but no one knew who I was, so the cops never came to question me. But if someone saw my photo and realized I was there, they could put two and two together. There's no statute of limitations on murder. I could still be charged. Even now, after all these years, I can't believe it was me. I can go whole weeks, sometimes, without thinking about it, and then I'll remember and—"

"Stop it!" I shouted at him. I couldn't take this; I couldn't listen to him talk about this.

I was going to have to go to the police, I realized. My thoughts were spinning. Would I have to turn him in? Would he try to run? Was he dangerous? I swallowed. We would need a lawyer. How much did lawyers cost? And what were we going to tell Ruthie?

That thought stopped me cold. We could never tell Ruthie. Not ever.

"I don't want to interrupt," Maria said after a minute. "But I see no reason why the details of what happened thirty years ago need to come to light at all."

I looked up at her, stunned. I'd forgotten she was there.

"What are you talking about?" Jacob said. "Amy—"

"I really don't think we have to worry about Amy," Maria said. "Her proposal relies on the quotes you and Nina provided. The only reason Nina agreed to give Amy a quote in the first place was out of fear that Amy would reveal her location to me. As it so happens, I was aware Nina was in town, and I had a message delivered to her friend's house earlier today, making it abundantly clear that I am more than capable of tracking her down again, and letting her know exactly what will happen if she speaks to another reporter. I don't think we have to worry about her. Once you pull your quote, Amy's proposal will be laughed out of every publishing house in New York."

Jacob looked confused. "If I pull my quote, Amy will reveal my identity."

"So?" Maria crossed her arms over her chest. "Damien died by suicide. We have his note to prove it. And your car was at the hospital. Who's to say that you weren't in the car? They have nothing on you, Jacob. Not a thing."

Jacob swallowed. "Why would you do this?"

"Because we're family, and family helps one another. Family is the most important thing there is."

I blinked, not understanding. "Family..." How could she possibly believe that? After everything she'd just put me through? "We're *not* your family."

Maria turned to me. "Thea, I can tell that you need more time to digest all of this. But it's important for us all to be on the same page here."

Rage flashed over me in a shiver. I blamed her, I realized. She'd known about all of this from the beginning. She'd been manipulating me this whole time.

"There is no *us*, Maria." The sound of my voice disappointed me. It was weak, pitiful. My eyes filled with tears, but I blinked them away. "Is this the only reason you brought me here? So you could use me to get to Jacob?"

"You've been trying to get to me for years," Jacob said, staring at Maria. "It's not just about getting me to pull the quote. I bet it kills you that you can't control me the way you control everything else."

"None of this is as cut-and-dried as you're making it sound," Maria said. "Jacob, you're part of my family whether you like it or not." She turned to me. "And you... I wanted to meet you as well, Thea."

"There are much easier ways to meet me than pretending you want me to edit your memoir." I stared at her, and something in her face softened. Was she sorry? Did she feel guilty for putting me through this? I couldn't tell.

She looked down at her hands, wiped her palms together like she was brushing off a coating of flour. "I wasn't pretending," she insisted.

"I read *Blue Body*, just like I told you I did, and I was completely blown away. You took this sprawling, heartbreaking story, and you helped the author find the universal truth at the center of it. Do you have any idea how difficult that is to do? I've been sitting on my own story for a very long time, but I had never found an editor I thought worthy of it. Not until you."

I glared at her. I didn't want her to compliment me. It made it so much harder to remember that she was still manipulating me, even now. "Then why do it like this? Why bring me here? Why cut me off from the internet and take my phone? Why dole out the book chapter by chapter?"

At least Maria had the decency to look apologetic. "That was selfish. I realize that. But I wanted to spend time with you. I wanted to get to know you, and for you to get to know me and my kids. That's what families do."

There was that word again. *Family.* "Stop saying that. We aren't a family. We're basically strangers."

"Your daughter shares the same DNA as my granddaughter," Maria said. "Your husband is my son's brother. If that doesn't make you family, then I don't know what does."

"Maybe I don't want to be your family," I said. I looked at Jacob. He was still leaning against the wall, body curled around himself. "I don't know what you expect me to do with any of this."

Jacob said nothing. Maria gave me a small smile, unfazed. She took a step closer and said, the sympathy evident in her voice, "I know a lot more about your situation that I initially let on, my dear. I'm aware, for instance, that Cassandra gave you an ultimatum. You were to get me to write about the night Damien died or else you would be fired, is that correct? As it happens, I'm perfectly happy to write a more palatable version of what happened that night."

I was appalled by what she was telling me. "But it's a *lie*."

"A lie that *benefits* you," Maria clarified. "You don't want your husband punished for something that happened thirty years ago. You don't want Ruthie growing up without her father."

She lifted her eyebrows, giving me space to speak. I had no idea what to say. Was what she was proposing even legal? Could I be arrested for doing what she suggested? I had some distant memory of true crime shows and trashy thrillers. I could be convicted of accessory to murder, or accessory after the fact. Interfering with an investigation. Something.

"And it's more than just protecting Jacob," Maria continued. "Publishing my memoir could completely change your career. In a few years, no one will even remember the Hughes mistake." She shrugged, and added, "Or…"

Her voice trailed off. I knew she was baiting me, that she wanted me to ask. I managed to hold off for a moment, but my curiosity got the better of me. "Or what?" I snapped.

"Or, you can leave." Maria shifted away from the door. "I know you think I'm trying to control you, but all I wanted was for you to hear me out. Now you have. If it really bothers you to publish something you know isn't true, then I can take this book to another editor. I assure you that another editor won't question the version of events I've written. If you want to leave, no one will stop you."

Out of the corner of my eye, I saw Jacob flinch, a flare of something like hurt crossing his face. He was still standing a few feet inside the kitchen, the door swinging open behind him. I studied him, looking for some clue to what was going on in his head. There was nothing. It took him a long moment to lift his eyes to mine.

"I don't expect you to just move past all this," he said, his voice miserable. "What I did. I know it's unforgivable. If you want to leave me, I won't fight you."

I swallowed. All at once, I felt mentally and physically exhausted. I couldn't move, couldn't think.

I pictured the apartment I'd grown up in. The lonely meals and gurgling toilet and sobs that shook the thin walls. I'd dreamed of so much more than that.

I heard Jacob take a breath. "But if you could forgive me, I would do whatever it takes to make it up to you. I would spend the rest of our lives making it up to you." He held out his hand.

I looked at his open palm and imagined placing my hand in his, letting him help me to my feet. I still felt so betrayed. But I wanted to forgive him. I knew that if I let him touch me, if I let him say even one more word, I would.

"I know this is all difficult to accept," Maria cut in. "But, Thea, you know just as well as Jacob and I do how damaging it can be to have a leech like Damien in your life, how desperate you can be to have him gone."

Everything inside of me clenched. I looked from Jacob to Maria. "What do you mean?"

"I know your father has drained your mother's savings account again and again, that you've spent every last dime you have trying to help her. I was hoping that reading my memoir would help you understand why I made the choices I made. You and I are the same, Thea."

My back teeth clenched together. "I am *nothing* like you."

Maria continued, undeterred. "I gave you those pages so you would know what kind of person Damien really was. He was like a disease eating away at the people I loved the most in this world. Sometimes the best thing you can do for your family is remove the disease. Wouldn't you agree?"

I already had my mouth open to argue, but I couldn't get a handle on my voice.

I hated it, but she was right. Everything she was describing, everything she'd been through, I knew exactly how it felt.

"I can help you, my dear," Maria said gently. "I can be persuasive when I want to be. I could make it so your father never bothers you or your mother again."

A want like hunger filled my body.

Tell her to shut up, I told myself. *Tell her I'd never accept anything from her, not after this, not ever.*

But I could already feel my anger cooling, the muscles in my chest unclenching one by one. And the word that came out of my lips wasn't no. It was "How?"

"I have resources. Money, if he can be paid off; lawyers if that doesn't work. You don't need to know the details. All you need to know is that I can make it so your father never contacts you or your mother again. You have my word."

I looked at Maria, studying the soft wrinkles on her face, the arty glasses, the gray streaked through her hair. Who was she, really? An anecdote at the beginning of a beloved recipe? A woman who knew how to make incredible gnocchi? A few pages of a memoir?

Everything she'd ever shown me had been manufactured with immense, calculating care. She couldn't just be doing this out of the goodness of her own heart. So, what was in this for her? Why would I trust her?

"I know I lied to you," Maria said. "But I only did it to protect my family. I would do anything to protect my family. As I'm sure you would."

I curled my fingers toward my palms, then released them. My mouth was dry. I looked at Jacob, then back to Maria. "So that's what we are to you? Family?"

The slightest smile crossed Maria's lips, gone a moment later. "If you'll have me," she said. "I know I'm not perfect, but there's no such thing as a perfect family, is there? There's only the one you have. You have to decide whether it's worth fighting for."

I pressed two fingers into the space between my eyebrows and closed my eyes. I couldn't stand to look at either of them anymore.

There was something else going on here. It tugged at the corners of my brain, dissolving like smoke the second I turned my full attention to it. Maria was manipulative. She was controlling. She wouldn't do all this out of the goodness of her own heart. There was something she still wasn't telling me. Something she wanted.

I thought of Ava perched at the kitchen counter, bare feet hooked to the bottom rung of a stool. *Mommy's making skull soup.* I thought of the way her face had looked covered in blood, her teeth slicked red. I thought of the sound the pigs made when they were slaughtered, that oddly human scream. The man out in the slaughterhouse, the one with Damien's eyes. If Damien had died thirty years ago, if Jacob was his long-lost son, then who was that man?

Maria wasn't telling me everything. She was still managing me, controlling me like a doll for her own reasons. This was about more than her husband's murder, her reputation, my family. There was something badly wrong in this house, something big and ugly. And Maria was desperate to keep that from getting out.

Somewhere deep within the house, a child started laughing. Ava. She sounded just like Ruthie, the sound of her voice so thin and high it almost didn't seem real. I felt that sound in my bones. In my heart.

I would do anything to protect my family, Maria had said. *As I'm sure you would.*

I searched for some certainty inside of myself, some moral compass to point me in the right direction. There was none.

I took a breath. My shoulders pulled back, my spine straightened.

Whatever ugliness Maria was hiding, maybe it was best that it stayed hidden.

★ *The Secret Ingredient,* Maria Capello. Hanes House Press, $31.99 (316p) ISBN 978-1-400-33387-5

In *The Secret Ingredient*, acclaimed cookbook author and television host Maria Capello presents a stunning navigation of the highs and lows of a relationship defined by brilliance and struggle, revealing the raw truths hidden behind the public persona of a celebrated couple. Maria's journey to culinary stardom was marked by determination and skill. Because she'd been raised in a modest household, her marriage to Damien Capello, a figure synonymous with culinary innovation, seemed like a fairy tale to the outside world. However, Maria discloses the intricate challenges they faced, offering an intimate glimpse into a life where love and hardship coexisted. Her candid recounting highlights how they navigated the pressures of fame, their own personal demons, and the relentless demands of the culinary world. In this memoir, Maria doesn't just reflect on her past; she advocates for embracing life's imperfections and finding beauty in the broken. Her story is a testament to the resilience of the human spirit, showcasing her belief in the transformative power of acceptance and the courage to build anew from shattered pieces. *The Secret Ingredient* will resonate with anyone who has faced the complexities of relationships and the pursuit of personal growth amid adversity. With *The Secret Ingredient*, Maria Capello cements her status not just as a culinary icon but as a powerful voice in literature.

25

THEA

SEVEN MONTHS LATER, I WAS IN THE BACK OF AN UBER, PULLING around the curved driveway at Maria's farmhouse. It was early evening and the sun was just starting to dip beyond the distant mountains. Everything was tinted rose gold.

The driver slowed to a stop directly in front of the oversized double doors. "Nice house."

"It is," I said and opened the door to climb out. "Thank you."

Voices reached out from the backyard, mingling with buzzing laughter and lighter sounds: cutlery scraping plates, glasses knocking together in cheers. A party. I only felt a little anxious as the Uber pulled away, once again leaving me at Maria's farm.

Last time I was here, I'd been desperate to get away. I was panicked, terrified. But things were different now. I had no reason to be afraid of what I might find, not after the deal I'd made. I was part of the family now. And Maria protected her family.

I hiked up my party dress and carefully picked my way around the side of the house to the crowd of guests spread out across the back patio. The night felt alive. It was crisp for November, but there were heat lamps scattered throughout the yard. Someone had strung golden twinkly lights from all the trees, and waiters in white tuxedos wove around the glittering crowd, drawn to the gleam like moths, holding trays filled with hors d'oeuvres and cocktails. The air smelled like roasting tomato sauce and slow-cooked meat. Garlic and onions sizzling in olive oil, salty pecorino, and earthy porcini mushrooms.

A live band played something old-fashioned on the patio. *It's a Barnum and Bailey world, just as phony...*

The atmosphere was electric, buzzing. I'd had my doubts about holding the launch party for Maria's memoir all the way up here instead of in the city, but I could happily admit that I'd been wrong. This was the party to be at tonight. Every time I turned, I saw another face I recognized. An incredibly good-looking A-list actor stood near the bar, sipping a cocktail. I'd heard he was in talks to play a young Damien in the film adaptation. Surrounding him were renowned chefs and television personalities, literary icons. All here to honor Maria.

I navigated the sea of people, neck craned as I looked for Cassandra. She'd driven here directly from her place upstate. She'd texted me twice on my ride from the train station.

Tell me you're almost here, one had said. Everyone wants to talk to Maria's brilliant editor.

Brilliant? I'd written back, barely able to bite back my smile. They aren't really saying that.

Her response was immediate: Are you kidding? You got her to write candidly about her marriage for the first time in thirty years. You're a legend.

Things had been different between us since Maria's book came out. Cassandra had dropped the cold shoulder, started inviting me into her office again, telling me about new projects. I could tell that she wanted to go back to the way things had been before, but I wasn't sure it was possible to go back. I was a different person now.

I saw her standing on the other side of the yard, surrounded by a swarm of glittering literati, the silver of her hair the only thing visible in the crowd.

"Thea!" she called, cupping her hand around her mouth so I could hear her over the din.

I was just starting toward her when the band stopped playing. I glanced toward the stage as Maria accepted a microphone from the lead singer. A low murmur of voices spread through the crowd, just as quickly going silent.

"Thank you," Maria said into the mic, her voice echoing over the yard. The golden twinkly lights had softened the lines on her face and created a halo around her head. She was wearing her costume, as I'd come to think of it: a blousy dress in a wild print, layers of beaded necklaces, dangling earrings. The silver streaked through her hair looked soft and lovely. She could be fifty years old, forty even.

"Good evening, my dear friends and family," she said. "I would like to extend a warm welcome to each and every one of you and thank you for joining me on this special night as we celebrate the release of my new book, *The Secret Ingredient*. Your love and support have meant the world to me, and I'm truly grateful to have you all here with me."

Maria lifted her glass. A smattering of applause broke out. She waited for it to die down before lifting the mic to her mouth again. "My late husband, Damien Capello, always said that a good recipe is like family: it's always hiding something. I don't believe this has to be true. I think both good food and good families are pretty simple. I believe in simple ingredients, in the freshest produce and meat from animals who've been allowed to roam freely and fed quality food. And I believe that you should know what goes into your food. No recipe should be a secret.

"To that end, instead of doing a reading from my new memoir, I would like to finally reveal the secret ingredient I include in all my recipes." Maria paused, looking over the guests with a smile. A hush had fallen over the crowd. Everyone was watching her, waiting.

Maria continued, "Those of you who've already read the book will know that my secret ingredient isn't all that special... It's powdered French onion soup mix." Maria held out her hands in an *oh well* gesture as the crowd erupted into laughter. She leaned close to the microphone and added, just loudly enough to be heard over the din. "Now you might understand why I've kept it a secret all these years. Buon appetito!"

....

As the night wore on, I allowed myself to be folded into Cassandra's crowd. It was a lovely night, as much my success as it was Maria's. Agents who'd never previously given me the time of day asked what I wanted to acquire, and editors several years my senior spoke to me like I was a peer, while publishers at rival houses slipped me business cards when they didn't think Cassandra was looking. I pocketed the cards. Maybe I'd consider making a move sooner rather than later. I would always love Hanes House. But it might be time for a change.

At some point, I caught a flash of brown from the corner of my eye, and when I turned, I saw Amy Ryan standing at the edge of the crowd, watching me. She lifted her hand in a half wave, but it took me a second too long to shoot her a nod and smile. Honestly, I was surprised she'd had the nerve to show her face around here at all.

Amy had tracked me down back in the city a few months ago, right after everything had happened, asked me to meet her for a drink. The only reason I'd agreed was to verify that everything had gone down the way Maria claimed it had. That image I'd had of Amy strung up in the slaughterhouse with her throat slit had been vivid. I wanted to know for sure that Maria had simply packed up her things and sent her home.

Amy told me that the story Maria had given me was more or less the truth, and then she'd begged me to get Jacob to go back on the record, to tell her what Maria had said to Nina to make her disappear. She'd been desperate, needy, unable to figure out how the book proposal that was going to change her life had disappeared like sand through her fingers. She'd even tried posting a few blind items on HushHush, but without Nina's and Jacob's quotes to back her up, the posts didn't gain much traction.

I'd been sympathetic, listened, and I'd even picked up the check at the end of the night. But I didn't feel particularly compelled to help her. Not after Hughes, and especially not after the way she'd blackmailed Jacob. Maybe that sounds cruel, but Amy was young, and she was hungry, and I had no doubt that she would pick herself up from this. She'd find another story, some other person's secrets to wave around for public consumption. As far as I was concerned, this setback might even be good for her. It was one thing to reveal the horrible secrets of people like Kincaid Hughes and Damien Capello. But she should think twice before going after regular people like me and Jacob and Nina.

"Thea," said a voice directly behind me. I turned and Maria was standing at the edge of the patio, holding two glasses of champagne. She held one out for me.

"Thank you," I said, reaching for the glass.

"No Jacob tonight?"

I shook my head. Jacob was home with Ruthie. We'd had a very long talk after the last time we were here, not just about his lies and mine but about so much more. My fear of ending up like my mother, my obsession with having the perfect family. I finally told him all the things I'd spent the last three years convincing myself I could never tell him. How I'd felt like I was drowning since we had Ruthie, how I didn't know how to balance it all. How I needed help.

And he'd surprised me by understanding. Completely. After my promotion went through, Jacob decided to take some time away from work to focus on our daughter and finally write his book. Instead of getting up early to run, he was getting up to pound out a few chapters before Ruthie woke up. And, in exchange, I was getting the time I needed to focus on work, on myself.

It wasn't perfect. But no family was.

I took a sip of my champagne. "He's home, watching Ruthie."

"I'm glad *you* came."

"You know I wouldn't have missed this."

Maria frowned as though trying to remember something. "I saw an announcement online a few months back... You were promoted, is that right? Editorial director?"

I smiled. Cassandra had put the promotion through right after Sarah stepped down, as promised. "That's right. Your book helped quite a bit with that."

"Nonsense," Maria said, shaking her head. "I don't believe that for a second. You got it because you deserve it." She lifted her glass of champagne. "Congratulations."

"Thank you," I said, blushing. "But I should be congratulating you."

The Secret Ingredient wouldn't be officially released until Tuesday, but it had already received glowing reviews in *Publishers Weekly*, *Kirkus Reviews*, the *New York Times*, gushing blurbs from Ina Garten and Martha Stewart and Joanna Gaines. It had been chosen for the celebrity book club of the moment, the film rights snapped up in a three-way auction, and the preorders were unbelievable. Cassandra privately told me the sales from this book alone would be enough to drag us out of the hole we'd dug for ourselves after everything that had happened with Kincaid Hughes. It was, by every account imaginable, a success.

But I knew none of that mattered to Maria. It wasn't why she'd done this.

I lifted my glass to my mouth, scanning the crowd until I saw Ava's small, dark head darting between neatly pressed suit pants and flowery dresses that were much too summery for the fall weather. The little girl was practically glowing. Her hair looked longer and thicker than it had been the last time I saw her, and her skin was darker, like she'd just gotten back from a tropical vacation, and flushed pink from dancing, and the deep purple circles beneath her eyes had all but disappeared. In place of the Little Mermaid nightgown, she wore a sparkly tutu and a T-shirt covered in rainbow sequins, bright-pink Doc Martens, a plastic tiara.

I smiled as I watched her follow a waiter holding a tray of pigs in blankets around, tugging on his pant legs every few seconds until he knelt down and allowed her to select one. I glanced at Maria. "How's Ava feeling?"

Maria had been smiling politely at me, but the corner of her mouth twitched at my question, the only sign she gave that what I'd said had surprised her.

Her voice was carefully measured as she said, "What do you mean?"

"She was sick the last time I was here." I made it clear that I didn't intend for this to be a question. "I couldn't figure out exactly what she had, though. Kidney failure, maybe?"

Maria opened her mouth, then closed it again, clearly shaken. She hadn't expected me to figure out the truth about Ava, I suppose. To be honest, I didn't at first, even though there'd been plenty of clues. The Band-Aid at the crook of Ava's elbow from a recent blood draw, and the slightly yellowish tint to her pale skin, the fact that she knew the word *urinalysis*. A kid her age would only know that word if she'd overheard it a lot—from doctors and nurses, from her own family.

Maria opened her mouth—probably to offer me some explanation that might or might not be a lie—but I shook my head, cutting her off. "Don't answer that. It doesn't matter. I'm just glad she got the help she needed." I smiled at her. "That's where she and Issie went, right? Some hospital down in Mexico or South America? Someplace that wouldn't ask a lot of questions?"

A few people broke off from the crowd at that moment and swarmed Maria for a little while, offering their congratulations to us both, going on about how incredible the book was, how much they enjoyed it, telling me I was a genius.

Once they'd gotten bored with us and started talking to one another about a new book out on submission, some celebrity YA fantasy novel, Maria leaned close to me and said quietly, still smiling, "What exactly do you think you know?"

I took a slow sip of my champagne, making her wait. I'd actually been looking forward to this moment. I was tired of playing this game with Maria, wondering if she knew what I knew and on and on and on. It was going to feel good to get it all out in the open.

"I know Damien's body couldn't have floated down that creek," I said. I spoke quickly, my mouth half-hidden behind my champagne flute. "Even at its deepest point it was far too shallow. He would have washed up somewhere. And Nina didn't want to go to the police the night she heard you shoot him. She told me it was because she was too scared, but that didn't make sense to me. What did she have to be scared of? You didn't even know she was there."

Maria wasn't looking at me. She was facing the surrounding crowd, smiling like the two of us were having the most interesting conversation. But I wasn't fooled. I was watching her eyes. She was scanning the people nearby, making sure no one got close enough to overhear anything I was saying.

"Nina always was kind of an idiot," she said through her teeth, smile never faltering.

"Jacob told me he followed you down to the creek and shot Damien. He saw Damien fall into the water, and he was so horrified by what he'd done that he ran back to the farmhouse. Right around that time, you went to get Hank so the two of you could stage the scene to look like a suicide."

"After you and Jacob left, I think Nina went down to the creek. She told me she was looking for Damien's body but she didn't find it, that it had already washed away." I shook my head. "That story doesn't hold together for me."

Maria laughed, a high tinkling sound, like I'd just told a joke. "You think *Nina* disposed of Damien's body? You didn't know her thirty years ago, dear. That woman couldn't have weighed more than a hundred and twenty pounds soaking wet. She wouldn't have been able to move a body if she'd wanted to."

"I don't think there was a body to move. Nina said she didn't go to the police because she was scared. I don't think that's why. I think Damien was still alive when you went to get Hank. I don't think the gun shot killed him. He wanted to disappear, but he couldn't have done that if they went to the cops. I think they took the opportunity to let the world believe he was dead. Nina helped him to the car and the two of them drove off together. I think you knew, or at least suspected, and for the last thirty years, you've let my husband believe he was a murderer while you tried to find Damien on your own. Only your private detectives never turned anything up, did they?"

Maria gave me a brief glance. "Interesting theory."

"You didn't call Amy out when you realized she was scamming Enzo," I continued. "You told me it was because you wanted to keep your enemies close. That's not true. You knew Amy had tracked down Nina, which meant she'd tracked down Damien. You used Amy to get to him. You got her to bring him here, in fact."

"There are a few plot holes in that story," Maria said. "Even if Damien was alive, why would he *ever* come back here? He spent an awful lot of time and money trying to get away."

"He came back to find the savings bonds," I said simply. "That $250,000 worth of bonds would be worth millions today. Your mother didn't leave them to you. That was a lie. It was Damien's mother, Damien's money. When you realized he was in love with Nina, you took them out of the bank and hid them on the farm so he couldn't leave."

Maria was no longer smiling. She was staring at me, her eyes dark. Calculating.

I turned toward her, staring right back. "You told Amy there was something buried in the slaughterhouse. That wasn't a slip, like I'd thought at the time. It was bait. You knew she would tell Nina, who would tell Damien. I'm betting there aren't many things that would've convinced Damien to come back here. But that would."

A waiter stopped beside us, holding out a silver platter filled with champagne flutes. Maria snatched one off the platter, put her empty down roughly enough that it nearly fell over. I waved him off. I was still working on my first.

Maria drank deep. Once she'd swallowed, she asked, her voice a touch colder than it had been, "Why would I want Damien to come back here?"

"You needed something from him." I glanced back at Ava. "If I had to guess, I'd say it was a kidney for your granddaughter."

The band had started playing again. We were both quiet for several long moments, watching Ava spin on the dance floor, her tulle skirt flaring out around her, sparkling as it caught the gold twinkly lights above.

"You weren't supposed to see any of that," Maria said in a quiet voice. "But she got so much sicker so fast."

I nodded, understanding. I'd wondered about that. For someone as disciplined as Maria, it seemed a bit sloppy to have Damien and Nina and Amy here the same weekend as me. But, if Ava was in the midst of kidney failure, Maria might not have had a choice.

"Have you told Jacob?" Maria asked.

"Not yet, but I will." I glanced at Maria and said, "But he's the only one I'll tell. It's like you said the last time I was here. Anything to protect our family."

"Too true, my dear." Maria smiled to herself, visibly relaxing. "We really should get the girls together sometime. It's important to keep family close."

I took another sip of my champagne. Maria was still watching me. "Is that all?"

I was quiet a moment, thinking. I'd been an English major back in college, and I'd been particularly interested in the literature of early modern Europe. I'd read Donne's "Love's Alchemy" and Shakespeare's *Othello* and Edmund Spenser's *The Faerie Queene*. There was a line in "Love's Alchemy" that I always remembered: "Hope not for mind in women, at their best, sweetness and wit, they'are but mummy, possess'd." Such a weird line. What the hell did *mummy, possessed* mean?

I'd looked into that line for my thesis, wound up writing about a disturbing practice known as corpse medicine. In other words, medical cannibalism. Strange as it might seem to us now, a long time ago people used to dig up human remains to use as medicine. This wasn't a niche thing, either. Priests, scientists, even royalty partook. They were convinced that eating human remains cured disease.

I thought of how I'd found Ava in the kitchen, seemingly sipping a plastic cup filled with blood. I thought of her tiny voice saying, "Mommy's making skull soup."

People used to drink human blood. They used to sprinkle bits of powdered skull into their soups. They even used the moss that grew over a skull. There was a special word for it, *usnea*. I'd seen that word scrawled on one of the dusty bottles locked away in Maria's basement.

Corpse medicine became less popular with the rise of modern medicine. But if you went to some of the darker corners of the internet, you could still find practitioners around today. They swore there were nutrients that you could only find in human flesh. Some even thought those nutrients could cure cancer and diabetes—and even reverse kidney failure.

My theory didn't answer all of my questions. For one thing, it was odd to take a kidney donation from a grandparent. And how had Maria convinced Damien to donate one in the first place? And why would Nina come here to the farm, if she was so terrified of Maria or Hank finding her?

Then again, a practitioner of corpse medicine might think that using one of the kidneys and eating the other would give you a better chance of survival than anything else. It was like Maria had written in her book: Her family believed in using *all* of the animal. By that logic, it was possible that Nina had been waiting for Damien, that she'd ventured onto the farm only when he didn't return home. That would explain her slip when we spoke. I know she said, "I think someone took *him*," not "I think someone took *her*."

I could tell Maria was trying to figure out what to say, if she should say anything. Before she could work it out, someone separated from the crowd, waving for her. "Maria," they called. "Can I borrow you for a moment?"

I felt my shoulders unclench, absurdly grateful for the reprieve. I turned to Maria. "Your adoring public awaits."

But Maria hesitated, still staring at me. She nodded to her friend, but before she stepped away to join her, she stopped beside me and said, her voice low, "Are we okay?"

I studied her. I had no idea how to begin to answer that question. This was a woman who'd manipulated and lied to me, who was probably still manipulating and lying to me. She was a killer, whether my theory about what really happened to Damien was correct or not.

And if my other theories were right, she might be something much, much worse than that.

A monster. A cannibal.

After a long moment, I said, "I tried making your meatballs after you released the secret ingredient. Sprinkled a little French onion soup mix over the top, just like you wrote."

Maria simply stared back at me, eyebrows raised, as though to ask: Where's the question?

"They were disgusting," I said, swallowing the rest of my champagne. "Way too salty. There's no way that is the real secret ingredient."

"I don't think the world's ready for the real secret quite yet," Maria said.

"Was anything you wrote about in that memoir true?" I knew the stocks had never been hers, that Damien had never run off with her money. It made me wonder about all the rest. The mob and the gambling, the restaurant being in debt, the FBI coming after Damien because he hadn't paid his taxes. Had any of it been real?

But Maria just smiled at me. "Thank you," she said, touching my arm. "For keeping my secrets. I won't forget it."

"I have my reasons," I said. "Which reminds me, have you heard anything from my father lately?"

Maria looked surprised. "Do you really want to know the answer to that?"

I considered a moment, then shook my head. I could live without knowing what happened to him. Maria had held up her side of our bargain. I'd gotten everything she'd promised me, everything I'd wanted. The promotion, the status, the money, the security. I'd finally found some balance, a way of living for myself as well as my family. I was happy.

And I hadn't seen or heard from my father in over seven months. As far as I knew, no one had. He'd simply disappeared.

Just like Damien.

26

MARIA

I left Thea at the party and made my way back inside, through the kitchen and down the stairs to the basement. It felt different down here than it had a few months ago. Empty, the light coming off the lamp on my desk all thin and weak, dust motes hanging in the air, the smell of something musty seeping up from the floors.

No thumps coming from inside the freezer tonight, no padlock on the door. There wasn't a need for one, not anymore. Everything inside the freezer was already dead.

The caterers were out of canapés and we'd stowed the extra trays back here. For reasons that should be obvious, only family was allowed in the basement. I pulled the freezer door open with a soft grunt, icy air wafting over me. A few new slabs of meat dangled from the ceiling. Unlabeled.

Ava had needed a new kidney. Thea had gotten that part right. She'd already rejected a donation from Issie, and neither Enzo nor I were a match. Time was running out and we were getting desperate. I'd arranged for Issie and Ava to fly down to a hospital in Mexico that I knew wouldn't ask a lot of questions. And I went about finding a donor.

Damien was so easy to lure back here. He'd come for the money, just like Thea had suspected. He never forgave me for stealing those bonds. Once I realized Amy was in touch with Nina, I slipped the info to Amy and even made a point of pulling Amy aside later, in private, and telling her to please not to tell anyone what she'd overheard me saying about burying money in the slaughterhouse. I heard her on her burner phone with Nina minutes later, blabbing everything. People are so predictable.

Hank had found Damien in the slaughterhouse and knocked him out, then dragged him down to the freezer, where we kept him until it was time to take him to the plane. Nina had come to the farm to look for him when he didn't return to the house where they'd been staying. I caught up with her before she managed to disappear again, and we bribed her with the bonds, told her if she disappeared without a word, she could keep the money. We wouldn't come looking for her again. She hadn't wanted to leave without Damien, but she'd agreed in the end. She had to understand that it was better than the alternative.

Damien had lived through one murder attempt thirty years ago, had disappeared into the night with Nina while I was back at the house, looking for Hank. By the time we'd made it back to the creek, every trace of him was gone. Even the blood had washed away.

"We still have to go through with staging the suicide," I'd told Hank. It had been our original plan. We already had Damien's clothes, the goodbye note.

Hank had frowned, confused, and though he hadn't asked the question out loud, I could already tell what he wanted to know: Why bother? Damien was already gone. With the note and without a body, everyone would assume he'd just run away.

I understood that, of course. But Damien shouldn't have been allowed to "just run away," not after what he'd put me through. It was unacceptable. And I was already thinking ahead, like my mother taught me. I remembered that day in Manhattan when we'd run into my father, how it'd felt like fate. There was a reason Damien had gotten away. But I knew that someday, somehow, I would find my husband again. For thirty years, I've been planning his murder. When I finally accomplished it, I needed the world to believe that he was already dead.

....

Killing our husbands has become something of a tradition in my family. But the real tradition, the thing that distinguished us—our secret—was what we did with their bodies.

The week my mother killed my father, she worked late, sometimes not returning home until two or three or even four in the morning, no matter that the butcher shop where she worked closed at six at the latest. I'd wake to the sound of our apartment door creaking open and closed, the hiss of our gas stove being lit.

She cooked every night that week, no matter how late it was when she got back. She made meat marinated in vinegar, herbs, spices, and dry wine, meat flattened by pressing it down with a weight while it fried in a pan, ground meat prepared outside over an open fire and served with plum sauce, sliced tomatoes, and pomegranate seeds.

And, my favorite, polpette. Italian meatballs slow-cooked with sausage in a thick tomato gravy.

My first lesson in murder was also my first lesson in cooking. Slow roasting meat on low heat keeps it from becoming too tough. It's easy to disguise a distinct flavor by soaking less traditional meat overnight in a solution of vinegar or salt.

And, of course, the most important lesson: no body, no crime.

That week, we destroyed the evidence of my father's murder one bite at a time. It was about hiding the body, of course, but it was also about so much more than that. My family always prided ourselves on using every last bit of the animals we'd butchered. Not just the meat itself, but *everything*. Blood was rich in nutrients. Bones were necessary for making broth, and they could be ground to a powder in a high-quality meat grinder, providing an excellent source of calcium. Any meat not used in cooking could be dehydrated and ground to a powder using any mortar and pestle. And I found that a sprinkle of powdered meat gave a dish depth and flavor.

Thea had been right about all of it. Or almost all of it. The timing hadn't been quite as tight as I'd led her to believe. I could have pushed Damien and Nina and Amy off by a few days, maybe even a whole week. But I didn't. I'd intentionally lured Damien to the farm the same weekend I knew Thea would be staying here.

I would do anything for my family. But you only make it as far as I have by keeping people very, very close. I need my family to be willing to do just as much for me as I do for them. I need them to be willing to lie for our family, to kill for us. That's why I lured Thea and Jacob here when I did. It wasn't just about the quote. I'd wanted them both to see exactly what happens to people who don't put our family first.

Maybe that seems a little controlling, but oh well. I've been called worse.

I made my way to the back of the freezer, past what was left of Damien, to the tray of polpette sitting on a shelf.

All night, guests had been telling me how incredible the meatballs were, how rich they tasted, unlike anything they'd ever eaten.

I've included the recipe in the back of my new book. You're welcome to try making them yourself.

But they won't taste the same.

My Dead Husband's Meatballs

1 handful parsley
3 to 5 cloves garlic
¾ cup breadcrumbs, plus more as needed
¼ cup milk (optional)
1½ pounds meat mixture
2 to 3 eggs lightly beaten, divided
¾ cup grated pecorino romano
1 scant teaspoon salt, plus more as needed
Black pepper to taste
¼ cup olive oil, plus more as needed
5 cups tomato sauce

STEPS

Serves 4 to 6

1. Finely mince the parsley and garlic, set aside. Soak the bread-crumbs in the milk, reserving more dry breadcrumbs for later. After 3 minutes, remove the breadcrumbs through a strainer and press the milk out with your hands. You may skip this step and use more egg if desired.

2. In a large bowl combine the meat mixture, soaked breadcrumbs, pecorino, garlic, parsley, and 2 eggs. Sprinkle over 1 scant tea-spoon salt and grate over black pepper to taste. Using your hands, combine the ingredients with a folding motion. Do not overmix! If the meat mixture feels wet and not sticky, sprinkle on a coating of dry breadcrumbs to take up some of the moisture, then fold to mix. Conversely, if the mix is too dry, add some or all of another egg. Mix lightly again and repeat until the mixture holds together and is sticky, not wet.

3. Test the salt levels by frying a little chunk in the pan and tasting for seasoning. The amount of salt you will need depends on how salty your cheese is and the volume of other ingredients, but

1 teaspoon of table salt per 1½ pounds is about right. If the salt level is low, sprinkle on a coating of salt and mix lightly again. Now shape the meatballs with your hands, smacking them back and forth in your palms and rolling in your hands to form balls. The resulting meatballs should be slightly larger than a golf ball, smaller than a tennis ball.

4. Choose a heavy-bottomed pan and pour in the olive oil. Heat over medium, then gently add as many meatballs as will fit without crowding the pan. Cook until browned on one side, then turn carefully with a spatula. There is a danger that they will stick to the bottom of the pan during this step, so be careful because they can break apart. If they are sticking, wait a minute and allow the pan to release them, or if they are too dark, use your spatula to separate from the pan. Continue turning until the meatballs are browned all over, then remove them from the pan and set aside. Repeat until all of the meatballs are browned.

5. Pour the fat off the pan, then deglaze with ½ cup water. Add the deglazing liquid to your tomato sauce, then heat the tomato sauce in a large stockpot until bubbling. Drop the meatballs into the sauce, adjust the heat to a slow simmer, and partially cover with a lid. Simmer for up to 1½ hours, stirring and skimming the fat from time to time. The meatballs are ready after 1 hour but will improve in tenderness if cooked longer. Keep hot until ready to serve, or refrigerate to reheat later.

NOTES FOR THE HOME COOK

- You need real breadcrumbs to create the perfect meatballs. Breadcrumbs are easy to make and last almost forever in the freezer. Whatever you do, do not use fake, preseasoned breadcrumbs.
- You'll want to add enough breadcrumbs, cheese, and egg to your mixture. Beginners tend to think that scaling up the meat is a good idea, but it produces a much drier meatball.

- Don't overmix your meatballs. Think of it like a burger: the meat should still be meat. To this point, do not mix using a blender.
- As for the choice of meat, well, I'll leave that up to you.

READ ON FOR A LOOK AT THE
INSPIRATION FOR FX'S
*AMERICAN HORROR STORY:
DELICATE* STARRING EMMA
ROBERTS AND KIM KARDASHIAN

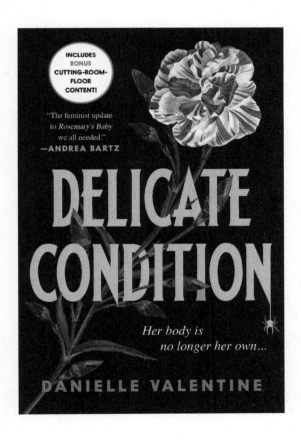

1

MY HUSBAND NEVER CALLED ME. I ALWAYS JOKED THAT THIS WAS because he didn't know how to use his phone, that he was the only tech bro in the world who still had an iPhone in the single digits. But, that morning, Dex called three times—at 6:55, 7:01, and 7:02—which was how I knew something was very wrong.

I'd been in the shower, water spray in my face, my ears, blocking the sound of the phone vibrating on the marble counter. After, I stood dripping on the tile, looking down at those three calls and thinking all the normal, horrible things you think when your husband calls you so many times in a row: that the tiny plane he'd been on this morning had crashed or was crashing, that he was dead, dying, that he'd called to say goodbye, but I'd missed him and I'd never hear his voice again. A part of me even thought maybe I deserved it, that things were going too well, that I was overdue for some trauma.

"Where the hell are you?" he snapped when I called him back at 7:04 a.m. His normally low, easygoing voice sounded irritated, which weirdly made me feel a flutter of relief. He wouldn't snap at me if he was dying.

"I'm getting dressed now. Why? What's wrong?" My abdomen was killing me. I folded the waistband of my yoga pants down while we talked, unable to avoid catching sight of the bruises from my injections. There were three of them, each as dark as a streak of mud, the width of a handprint on my softly bloated lower belly. As if there was something inside of me, some creature pressing its hands right up against the underside of my skin, trying to get out.

"You're still at home?" Dex asked. Definitely irritated. "You know you were supposed to be here an hour before the appointment, right?"

I felt a skip of paranoia but reminded myself that I'd planned this morning down to the last minute, the last second. I'd spoken with Cora, the receptionist at the Riverside fertility clinic, just yesterday morning and confirmed I'd gotten the time right. I'd set three alarms. The traffic wasn't bad, and my friend Georgia—the only person I knew who owned a car in the city—had just texted to let me know she was on her way over to pick me up. All I had to do was throw on some clothes and head out. I had plenty of time.

"It should take me less than an hour to get there. I'm walking out the door in fifteen minutes."

"The appointment *starts* at eight, Anna. You were supposed to be here ten minutes ago."

A cold gripping panic washed over me as I counted the hours back in my head, thinking *no, no, no.* "No…I wrote down the time I was supposed to be at the clinic in my calendar." I tried to remember the exact time Cora had told me when I called, but it was no use. The only way I'd been able to keep all the times and dates straight was by putting them in my online calendar. This appointment was the only thing on my schedule, other than Dex's flight from San Francisco. I'd double-checked it before I went to bed last night. *Triple* checked it. I'd written the reminder in all-caps. GET TO CLINIC BY 8 AM!!!

"You must've written it down wrong," Dex insisted.

"No," I said. "I'm sure I didn't."

"Obviously you did, since you were supposed to be here at *seven*. Jesus, Anna, we talked about…never mind. How soon can you get here?"

I didn't answer right away. I couldn't have made such an obvious mistake, such a *dumb* mistake. I'd been on the IVF roller coaster for a while. I knew better.

This morning was my egg retrieval surgery, arguably the most important appointment in the entire IVF cycle. Perfect timing was crucial, otherwise I risked losing my chance—which meant starting over at the beginning. Going back to weeks of birth control and two, then three injections every single day, to bruises the size of fists on my abdomen, my thighs, to daily visits to the clinic for blood work and ultrasounds.

I'd already been through that part twice. This third round had taken everything from me, every reserve of strength I had left. I needed it to work.

"I'm leaving now," I told Dex. He sighed, and I could tell he'd moved his mouth away from the phone, hoping I wouldn't hear his frustration. I pictured him waiting for me in the Riverside Clinic lobby, jet-lagged in the dark jeans and pressed white shirt he always wore to meet investors, his leather overnight bag at his feet. He'd had to fly all night to make it in time for the 8 a.m. appointment, and he never could sleep on planes. And he was supposed to give sperm today, so he couldn't take an Ambien or even have a glass of wine. He was probably exhausted.

"Anna—" he started, but I hung up before he could tell me it was hopeless, that I was already too late. I was going to figure this out.

You couldn't get anywhere quickly in New York City, especially not from Brooklyn Heights, where we lived. And the Riverside Clinic was all the way in the Upper West Side, at least a forty-five-minute drive by car, and that was only if there was no traffic. This might be one of those rare times when the subway was faster—only forty minutes if I could catch the express.

I had to waste precious seconds digging through my dresser for the only pair of jeans that still fit me, hesitating a beat before grabbing a real bra with an underwire. I was an actor. Until recently, I was best known for a role I did in my teens on a beloved culty television show called *Spellbound* that was canceled after only two seasons. Since then, I've mostly worked as a character actor, playing the quirky best friend through my twenties, then transitioning to the frumpy housewife in my thirties, but almost never the lead. People tended to recognize my face, but they often couldn't quite place whether it was from a film or their daughter's preschool pickup. If they did realize I was an actor, I was always "that girl from that show; you'd know her if you saw her."

That all changed earlier this year, when my most recent project, an art house film called *The Auteur*, exploded into mainstream success. I'd just gotten back from a months-long press tour promoting it, which meant more photos of my face in people's feeds, more clips and GIFs circulating on social media. It was surreal and amazing—but it meant no more walking around the city without putting on a real bra.

A few minutes later, I somehow managed to fight past the dogs to get outside and lock the door.

I was distracted. Distracted enough that, the first time I saw her, she barely made an impression. She was a shadow at the corner of my eye, and I'd glanced over at her, squinting against the sun, as I pulled the front door shut and jerked my key in the lock. There were always people around in New York City, crying in public and breaking up on crowded street corners and making out on subways. I doubt I'd have noticed her if it wasn't for the blue baseball cap pulled low over her forehead, the giant sunglasses hiding half her face. It looked like what the really famous actors wore when they were hoping not to be noticed. Not actors like me, but like Jennifer Lawrence or Siobhan Walsh, the ones who couldn't step out their doors without being accosted.

She'd been staring at something on the sidewalk, transfixed. But then she looked up and saw me and immediately turned around, head ducked, walking briskly away.

I saw what she'd been staring at as I ran down the sidewalk, right past the spot where she'd been standing. It was a bird's nest. Someone must've knocked it out of a tree because it had crashed to the sidewalk, bits of straw and sticks scattered everywhere, a single blue egg smashed open, spilling yolk and a half-formed embryo on the concrete.

I hurried away, stomach churning.

READING GROUP GUIDE

1. How does Thea's experience balancing a demanding career with raising a young child reveal the pressures of modern motherhood? How do these challenges intersect with her involvement in the mystery at the Capello estate?

2. Thea often finds it difficult to ask her husband, Jacob, to step up at home. How does this tension reflect broader struggles in their relationship? How might it contribute to her emotional vulnerability amid the unfolding mystery?

3. In what ways does Thea's internal conflict between professional ambition and new motherhood shape her character? How does this dual identity influence her decisions as the secrets of the Capello family emerge?

4. How do you interpret Maria Capello's character? Do you see her as a victim of circumstance, a cunning mastermind, or something in between?

5. How does the media circus surrounding Maria's past shape the narrative? In what ways do public perceptions and the family's silence influence our understanding of the events?

6. How does Thea's experience of stress and isolation—both as a new mother and as someone caught in the family's dark web—affect her decision-making? What impact does this have on her ability to navigate personal and external challenges?

7. How do societal expectations of working mothers influence Thea's journey? How do these expectations compound her personal struggles and affect her dynamic with Jacob throughout the narrative?

8. How does the upstate farm setting contribute to the tension and mystery? In what ways does the isolation mirror the decay and hidden rot in the family's past?

9. How does Thea's perspective as an outsider affect your reading of the story? What does her gradual discovery of the family's secrets reveal about trust and betrayal?

10. What commentary do you think the author is making by intertwining the art of cooking with female ambition? How do you reconcile Maria's glamorous public image with the murky ethical choices hinted at in the story?

11. How does Damien's disappearance affect the characters' present lives? Do you believe the past can ever be fully reconciled or understood through storytelling?

12. What do you make of Thea's final decision to play along with Maria's narrative? Do you believe she and her family are safe as part of the extended Capello clan, or should she be wary about

what the future may bring? If you were in Thea's position, what decision would you make?

13. In the final recipe of the book, the author tells home cooks to use a "meat mixture" rather than clarify exactly which meats should be used to make the meatballs. Why do you think she does this?

ACKNOWLEDGMENTS

Every book is a team effort, but *The Dead Husband Cookbook* especially would not exist without the brilliant, generous, and tireless people who stood behind it.

First, to my agent, Hillary Jacobson, who has been my guiding light through every version of this novel (and there were a few!). You saw something in this raw—no pun intended!—strange little book from that very first moment I pitched it over a glass of wine. You have been its fiercest advocate and its most honest critic, and I am endlessly grateful for your faith, your grit, and your heart. Thank you also to my audio agent, Jennifer Simpson, for fighting for the very best deal; to my foreign rights agent, Gabby Fetters, for all the work you've done to sell my books abroad; and to Lauren Denney for your truly thoughtful notes at a pivotal moment. Really, I'm not sure if there's a single person at CAA who doesn't deserve some form of thanks—I've never felt so supported by an agency before. *Thank you.*

Mary Altman—what can I even say? You have been the steady hand that helped shape this book into something I couldn't be prouder of. Your notes made it better, and your passion made it real. I am so grateful to be one of your authors.

To the incredible team at Sourcebooks—thank you so much for lifting this book up. To Cristina Arreola for…*everything*. I know you worry about emailing too much, but every time I see your name in my inbox, it's a joy. I am forever blown away by the hard work and dedication you've shown in getting word of my books out to the world. *Thank you.* To Beth Sochacki, for dreaming up unforgettable ways to share this book with readers, as well as Molly Waxman, Aubrey Clemans, and Kate Riley—thank you, thank you, thank you!

To the sales team who championed it with enthusiasm—I see how hard you work, and I'm so grateful. Thank you to Paula Amendolara, Raquel Latko, Sean Murray, Tracy Nelson, Valerie Pierce, Margaret Coffee, Courtney Payne and team, and many, many others. You've helped *The Dead Husband Cookbook* find its people, and I couldn't ask for more. To all my incredible production editors and copy editors, notably Jessica Thelander and Ellina Litmanovich: my eternal thanks for helping me sound smarter. Dominique, you've put together a truly special group of people over at Sourcebooks, and I am so happy to be one of your authors. Thank you, from the bottom of my heart, for everything.

To my UK agent, Lucy Morris, thank you for being such a steadfast advocate across the pond. I'm so lucky to have you in my corner! To Miranda Jewess and the entire team over at Viper, for truly on-point notes and for everything you've done to get my book the most incredible package and help it find its readers in the UK.

Thank you, thank you, thank you to my film team—Olivia Blaustein, Josie Freedman, and Matthew Doyle. Your early enthusiasm for this project has meant everything to me. I'm fully convinced I have the best film team there is. Thank you for everything.

I, of course, have to thank some early readers who helped make this book what it was. Thank you to Anne Heltzel, for that early convo over a glass of wine and to my incredible beta readers, Leah Konen and Andie Bartz, for your time, honesty, encouragement, and brilliant notes. Your thoughts helped shape this book into this final version and your early faith has meant everything to me!

And finally—as always—thank you to my incredible family. Ron, your recipes inspired this book, and it would not be the same without them. Thank you.

ABOUT THE AUTHOR

Danielle Valentine is the *New York Times* bestselling author of *Two Sides to Every Murder*, *How to Survive Your Murder*, and *Delicate Condition*, which was recently adapted into the twelfth season of *American Horror Story*, starring Emma Roberts and Kim Kardashian. Danielle lives in a haunted house outside of New York City with her husband, daughter, and familiars.